FENTON BRESLER

REPRIEVE
A Study of a System

With a Foreword by

Baron Chuter-Ede of Epsom, P.C., C.H.

*"I felt choked as I walked across to the hospital.
It's a strange feeling, you never forget it,
when you're told you're not going to die."*
A reprieved murderer

GEORGE G. HARRAP & CO. LTD
LONDON · TORONTO · WELLINGTON · SYDNEY

First published in Great Britain 1965
by GEORGE G. HARRAP & CO. LTD
182 High Holborn, London, W.C.1

Composed in Caledonia type and printed by
C. Tinling & Co. Ltd., Liverpool, London and Prescot
Made in Great Britain

FOREWORD

In this book Mr Fenton Bresler deals with the use of the power possessed by successive Home Secretaries to recommend the Crown to reprieve a person convicted of murder and sentenced to death. As it seems certain that no more sentences of death for murder will be carried out, this is an examination of the ways in which the severity of the law was modified. The subject is carefully studied and can be accepted as a scholarly and well-informed analysis of the exercise of a civilizing restraint on the survival of a harsh aspect of the law.

Chuter-Ede
13th May, 1965.

PREFACE

The date was December 14th, 1964. A young man stood in the dock of the Old Bailey, in London. The judge donned the black cap and began to speak the words of the death sentence.

Many a man has broken down and wept at this moment. But twenty-six-year-old Ronald John Cooper, a croupier brought back from the Bahamas to stand trial for the capital murder of an elderly company director, smiled. Afterwards, as he went down to the cells, he waved cheerily to his weeping parents.

For Cooper knew that he would not die.

He knew that the following week Parliament was to debate a Bill to abolish the death penalty for murder, and that it had been 'leaked' to the Press that the Home Secretary would reprieve every convicted capital murderer until the issue was decided.

And so it turned out. Cooper was reprieved, and to the time of writing every subsequent capital murderer sentenced to death has been reprieved.

Very soon the Royal Assent will be given to some such measure as the present Murder (Abolition of Death Penalty) Bill—with or without a five-year suspension clause instead of outright abolition—and a thousand years of British history will come to an end. Technically, capital punishment will be retained for arson in the royal dockyards and piracy at sea and for treason. But for all practical purposes hanging in this country, for civil offences, has already ceased—most probably never to return.

How did it start? What was its history? How did it work? And when a person was sentenced to die, how was it decided that he yet might live?

This book is an attempt to answer all these questions. Though appearing in the past tense, it is not a quick pot-boiler hurriedly rushed into press within months of the impending end of hanging. I started my researches in the summer of 1961; the first chapters were written in the spring of 1963. I have been a long time a-writing.

Many books and scores of pamphlets have been written about capital punishment—most of them partisan, and many inaccurate.

I am not concerned with the question of whether it was right to hang murderers. There have been enough polemics. I have endeavoured to unfold the story of capital punishment in this country as honestly and as impartially as I can and, for the first time, to tell the history of the reprieve system, an aspect of the machinery of government that has never yet been separately studied.

For over a century the decision to reprieve was that of the Home Secretary, a politician who need have had no special knowledge of the law or of life, a man like any other. The judges worked in open court with full publicity. The Home Office worked in secret, in the seclusion of the Home Office. There was no publicity. No-one knew the reasons for his decisions: they were almost never made public.

Even the prisoner did not know why he was hanged or saved. Until forty-eight hours before the time scheduled for his execution he would not even know which was to be his fate: not until that moment when the prison governor entered his cell, and the warders on watch jumped smartly to attention.

I have attempted to lift the veil on years of secrecy; at first generally, and then, in Part III, through a study of individual cases where I have been able to unearth facts that have not before been published.

It would have been impossible to write this book without the active co-operation and help of a wide range of people who have been kind enough to see me or correspond with me. I am not always at liberty to disclose my sources or attribute particular remarks to individual persons, but everything that follows is factual. When I write that So-and-so says something I mean that he has said it to me.

I must, therefore, express my sincere gratitude to the following persons whom I am able to name as having helped me:

Lord Goddard, former Lord Chief Justice of England; Lord Chuter-Ede, the late Lord Morrison of Lambeth and Lord Tenby, former Home Secretaries; Sir Charles Cunningham, Permanent Under-Secretary of State at the Home Office; the late Sir Alexander Maxwell and the late Sir Frank Newsam, former Permanent Under-Secretaries of State at the Home Office; Lord Gardiner; Sir Malcolm Hilbery, formerly Mr Justice Hilbery; Mr Henry Elam, Deputy Chairman of the Greater London Sessions (Inner London); Mr J. H. Walker and Mr J. W. Holt, formerly of the Prison Commission; the Earl of Harewood; Sydney Silverman, M.P.; Sir Thomas Moore; Edward Gardner, Q.C., M.P.; Sir John Langford-Holt, M.P.; Lord

Bridgeman; Sir Maurice Bridgeman and the Hon. Geoffrey Bridgeman, sons of a former Home Secretary; Mr Hugh J. Klare, Secretary of the Howard League for Penal Reform; Mr Frank Dawtry, Secretary of the National Association of Probation Officers; Canon Smyth, former senior prison chaplain; the Rev. W. J. Jenner; the late P. Kynaston Metcalfe, former Under-Sheriff of the County of London; the late General Sir George Giffard; Professor Desmond Curran; Dr W. Spencer Paterson; Dr Felix Brown; Professor Francis Camps; Dr Donald Teare; Mr Michael John Davies; Mr Donald Chessworth; Mrs Judith Rose, J.P.; Mrs Elizabeth Howard; Mr Robert Hancock; Mr Lucien Fior; Mr Douglas Gibson; Mr J. H. H. Gaute; Mr William Scales; Mr Leon Simmons; the late J. D. Casswell, Q.C.; and the following solicitors of men who have been sentenced to death: Messrs. Simon Burns, N. H. Brown, Sidney Rutter, Christopher Arrow, Ellis Lincoln, Philip Stephens, Ambrose Appelbe, T. V. Edwards, John Bickford, Victor Mishcon, F. Morris Williams, and Anthony Hayes.

Without their help this book could not have been written.

Furthermore, I have to express my gratitude and acknowledgments to the following publishing companies and individuals for their kind permission to use or substantially reproduce copyright material:

The Bodley Head Ltd. for permission to quote extracts from *Cornish of the Yard*; Constable and Co. Ltd for permission to quote extracts from *Life of Sir William Harcourt*, by A. G. Gardiner; Eyre and Spottiswoode (Publishers) Ltd, for permission to quote from Volume 1 of *English Historical Documents* edited by Dorothy Whitelock; Her Majesty's Stationery Office for permission to quote from Hansard and from the Report and Minutes of Evidence of the Royal (Gowers) Commission on Capital Punishment, 1949-53; William Hodge & Co. Ltd for permission to quote from their series *Notable British Trials*; the Hutchinson Publishing Group for permission to quote from the *Memoirs* of J. R. Clynes; John Murray (Publishers) Ltd for permission to quote from *Sir Robert Peel: Early Life from his Papers* edited by Charles Stuart Parker; Odhams Books Ltd for permission to quote from *Famous Criminal Cases*, Volumes 6 and 7, by Rupert Furneaux; Penguin Books Ltd for permission to quote from *Hanged by the Neck* by Arthur Koestler and C. H. Rolph; Sweet and Maxwell Ltd for permission to reproduce extracts from their Crime Documentaries *Michael John Davies* and *Podola* by Rupert Furneaux, and from Volume 45 of their *Criminal Appeal Reports*; and the Times Publishing Co. Ltd for permission to quote extensively from *The Times* newspaper. Also: Dr Michael Ashby for permission to quote from a memorandum on

Guenther Fritz Podola; the Chief Constable of the Cornwall County Constabulary for supplying and permitting to be published a photograph of the Giffards' cliff-top home at Porthpean; Mr Rupert Furneaux for permission to quote from his *Famous Criminal Cases* series and from his Crime Documentaries *Michael John Davies* and *Podola*; and Mr William Scales for his permission to reproduce a drawing made of him by Victor John Terry.

Finally, I owe a special debt of gratitude to Lord Chuter-Ede for the honour he has done me by writing the Foreword.

F. B.

CONTENTS

12   *Contents*

Illustrations

14   *Illustrations*

Timothy John Evans arriving at Paddington with Police
  Escort   *page* 209
John Reginald Halliday Christie   209
Christie's Tobacco Tin containing Clumps of Female
  Pubic Hair   209

A Recorder's Report being received by the King and his 'Hanging Cabinet'.

'Half-hanged' John Smith being cut down from Tyburn Tree.

PUNISHMENT, ENGLAND.

Capital Punishment.

RULES DATED JUNE 5, 1902, MADE BY THE SECRETARY OF STATE FOR THE HOME DEPARTMENT, PURSUANT TO THE PROVISIONS OF THE CAPITAL PUNISHMENT AMENDMENT ACT, 1868,* FOR REGULATING THE EXECUTION OF CAPITAL SENTENCES.

1902. No. 444.

1. For the sake of uniformity, it is recommended that executions should take place in the week following the third Sunday after the day on which sentence is passed, on any week day but Monday, and at 8 a.m.

2. The mode of execution, and the ceremonial attending it to be the same as heretofore in use.

3. A public notice, under the hands of the sheriff and the Governor of the prison, of the date and hour appointed for the execution to be posted on the prison gate not less than twelve hours before the execution, and to remain until the inquest has been held.

4. The bell of the prison, or, if arrangements can be made for that purpose, the bell of the parish or other neighbouring church, to be tolled for 15 minutes after the execution.

5. The person or persons engaged to carry out the execution should be required to report themselves at the prison not later than 4 o'clock on the afternoon preceding the execution, and to remain in the prison from the time of their arrival until they have completed the execution, and until permission is given them to leave.

Chas. T. Ritchie,
One of His Majesty's Principal
Secretaries of State.

Whitehall,
    5th June, 1902.

---

* 31 & 32 Vict. c. 24.

The Statutory Rules governing Executions. This is the photostat referred to in the text by the author which, although white on black in the original, appears reversed in this reproduction.

PART ONE
History

CHAPTER ONE

Mercy: the Birth of a Concept
(450 B.C. – A.D. 1066)

In the earliest years of our history there was no law, no civilization, no State. But there was capital punishment. Four hundred and fifty years before Christ the Ancient Britons were drowning offenders in quagmires. We do not know how they were tried or what their offences were: the silence of history is inscrutable.

One thing appears tolerably certain: there was no single executioner carrying out the dictates of society. No judge pronounced sentence of death.

Four hundred years later, when Caesar's legionaries landed on the shores of England the men they found were still barbarians, according to Tacitus, the Roman historian. The Roman Conquest brought law, stability, and peace to the greater portion of our island. For over three hundred years something like a modern State, with all the apparatus of organized central power, existed in England. Then in about A.D. 400 the Roman army was withdrawn, and chaos came again.

Already the first bands of Saxon pirates from West Germany had plundered the East Coast, and now hordes of Angles, Saxons, and Jutes came in ever-increasing force. Law was a frippery, mercy an unpractised concept.

The chain of small kingdoms established by the invaders brought little order or quietude to the harassed countryside. Britain in the fifth and sixth centuries was a fearsome jungle of warring tribes and kingdoms: life was "nasty, brutish, and short".

There were still no written laws, or at least none that has survived. We know that capital punishment existed, but it was not the modern form, where the State metes out death to those who have offended against its edicts. The State was weak and did not meddle in such affairs as justice. There was no concept of 'crime', even the notion of guilt had faded into vague mists with the virtual departure of Christianity with the Roman colonizers. Society could be concerned only with the most heinous wrongdoing, that which imperilled society itself.

A person accused of treason, cowardice in battle, or offences against the pagan beliefs of the time would be taken before a court of his neighbours and confronted by his accuser. If he could not make satisfactory answer the presiding elder would sentence him. The penalty would not be death—that would presuppose a legal apparatus powerful enough to enforce the court's decree—but outlawry. In Professor Maitland's telling phrase: "Outlawry was the capital punishment of a rude age." For the effect of being outlawed was almost certain death.

It was the right and duty of every man to pursue the outlaw, to ravage his land, to burn his house, to hunt him down like a wild beast, and slay him. For he was, like the wild wolf which then dwelt in the forests, an enemy of society. Centuries later the official decree of outlawry was still: *Caput gerat lupinum*—"Let him be treated as the head of a wolf."

Nor, in the earliest days, was there any hope of a reprieve. If the local court sentenced a man to outlawry there was no central power near enough or strong enough to alter its decree.

Society took little interest in offences other than treason, cowardice, or profanity. If a man was killed or injured it was left to his family to wreak their own personal vengeance. The blood-feud of modern Sicily was the commonplace of Anglo-Saxon England.

No state that wished to grow stronger could long tolerate such chaos. By the end of the eighth century the low black ships of a new wave of invaders—the Danes—were appearing off the East coast. The young Saxon kingdoms could not afford the appalling wastage of manpower caused by these ruinous family feuds.

The Saxon kings' remedy was simple: they would have been at home in our materialistic society, for they realized the value of money. Nearly a thousand years before Sir Robert Walpole discovered that every man has his price they thwarted the urge to family vengeance by putting a price ticket on every man in the kingdom.

From the King himself down to the poorest peasant scratching out a living on an under-tilled farm every freeman had his value in money laid down by the law. It was his "wergild"—his "worth-money". Women as such had no wergild, nor did slaves. A slave's worth was simply his *manbot*—his value as a chattel to his owner. This was not just a dry exercise in accountancy. The kings decreed that if a person was killed the crime could be atoned for by paying his wergild to his relatives or his *manbot* to his owner. The logic was clear: why kill the slayer and his family if, instead, you could line your pockets? The profit motive appears early in our history.

B

Until the ninth century it was left to the individual citizen to choose whether his revenge should be homicidal or financial, and the offender's hope of mercy lay in the whim of his victim's kindred. But about A.D. 890 Alfred the Great decreed that the blood-feud was lawful only if wergild or *manbot* was first demanded and refused. The effect of this was twofold: first it meant that fewer people were slain, but second it meant that the rich could kill with impunity. As long as a man could afford to pay his victim's price he could exterminate his enemies at will.

Indeed, Alfred's law led to widespread abuse, and after less than fifty years it was amended. In about A.D. 945 King Edmund ordered that killers were to have twelve months in which to pay their victims' price. Murder was no longer to be a rich man's liberty: it was available on hire-purchase. At the same time Edmund limited the scope of the blood-feud by decreeing that his family, as well as the killer, could be slain only if the relatives had harboured him: "The illegal and manifold conflicts which take place among us distress me and all of us greatly," he said. By the end of the Anglo-Saxon era, as more crimes came within the sole jurisdiction of the increasingly powerful King, blood-feuds had almost completely ceased.

Murder was not the most frequent crime of early times or even considered the most wicked. The first reference to capital punishment in an extant law appears in the *Laws of King Wihtred of Kent* in A.D. 695, and the offender's crime is theft. "If anyone kill a man who is in the act of thieving," declared Wihtred, "he is to lie without wergild"—in other words, anyone catching a thief in the act could kill him at once without worrying about the dead man's 'price'. Offences against property ("then as now" may say the cynic) were considered more sinful than offences against life or limb. The first reference to hanging as a form of capital punishment appears in the laws of Ine, King of the West Saxons from 688 to 726 and again the offence is nothing to do with the preservation of human life. Said Ine: "If a penally enslaved Englishman runs away, he is to be hanged and nothing paid to his master."

The death penalty, in whatever form, appears but seldom in Anglo-Saxon laws. Criminals were hit in their money-bags, not in their person. Not only human beings, but almost every human act had its price, and in the most amazing detail.

The earliest written laws that survive—those of King Ethelbert of Kent, decreed in about 602—contain a detailed list of the various ways of causing grievous bodily harm to someone, each with its own appropriate money-compensation—or *bot*, as it was called. "For loss of each of the four front teeth, six shillings; for each of the teeth which stand next to them, four shillings; then for each tooth which stands next to them, three shillings; and beyond that, one shilling for each tooth," it reads—right down to the *bot* for loss of the finger-nails or toes.

This was the firm basis of later Anglo-Saxon criminal law. Modern historians are divided as to what happened if a man could not pay his *bot*. Either way it was unpleasant. Professor Maitland says that he went into slavery or was outlawed; a more recent expert, Professor Plucknett, claims that his life was forfeit and in the gift of the injured party. The King did not enter into it, except to demand his *wite*—a kind of fine payable to him in addition to the injured man's *bot*. Royal mercy had no place in the strict tariff of Anglo-Saxon crime.

But in the seventh and eighth centuries the royal power increased, and with it came primitive, early notions of royal mercy.

The same Laws of King Wihtred that permitted a thief caught in the act to be summarily killed also said that "If anyone captures a freeman with the stolen goods on him, the king is to choose one of three things; he is either to be killed or sold across the sea or redeemed with his wergild." Two centuries later Alfred the Great expressly decreed that if anyone drew his weapon in the King's hall it was for the King to decide whether he lived or died. And in the written laws of most later kings the monarch increasingly claimed the right to decide the form of punishment for certain specified serious crimes.

After Alfred had beaten back the first wave of Danish invaders and Edward the Elder had become the first King of all England, in about A.D. 900, the central power of the monarch grew apace. From being merely the nation's leader he became the lord of all men, almost the lord of all land. As Christianity after its second coming with Saint Augustine took a firmer grip upon the minds and hearts of men a new, holy sanctity was added to the person of the King. In the later codes of Anglo-Saxon law he appears as head and representative of the State, the defender of the Church, the protector of the oppressed, the Viceregent of Christ.

Such a monarch was no longer content to leave the suppression of disorder entirely to the caprice of his subjects. In about 940 King Edmund declared that forcible entry into people's homes in breach of his royal protection was henceforth to be *botleas*—incapable of being compensated. He went further: an offender was to forfeit all his possessions "and it is to be for the king to decide whether he may preserve his life." The words in themselves contain the exultation of supreme authority.

By the first quarter of the eleventh century the King was strong enough to declare that only he had power to quash a decree of outlawry. The number of *botleas* offences now included housebreaking, arson, obvious theft, open (as distinct from secret) killing, and betrayal of a lord. The King claimed sole jurisdiction to deal with these more serious crimes (which, it will be seen, still did not include 'secret killing' or murder), and he alone could choose the form of punishment. Hanging was already the most usual method of execution, but the King could also select burning, drowning, stoning, or casting from rocks. If he wished to preserve the prisoner's life he could substitute maiming or mutilation or even mere banishment or forefeiture of chattels. There was no certainty: the captured criminal did not know his fate until the King pronounced it.

But the King, though exalted by the early English Christians as a semi-divine figure, was also bidden by his new religion to be merciful. "We are urged by love for mankind to intervene on behalf of criminals", Saint Augustine had written. And his teachings had a profound effect upon the later kings.

In 1023 King Canute laid down the general principles that he said would guide him in sentencing offenders. It is an amazing document. Translated from the Old English of the manuscript now in the British Museum it reads like a modern Home Office memorandum crossed with a sermon:

"If anyone eagerly wishes to turn from wrongdoing back to right behaviour, one is to be merciful to him very readily, as best one can, for the fear of God.

"And let us always help quickest those who need it most . . .

"The weak man must always be judged and prescribed for more leniently than the strong, for the love of God.

"For we know full well that the feeble cannot bear a burden like the strong, nor the sick man like the sound.

"And therefore we must moderate and distinguish reasonably between age and youth, wealth and poverty, freedom and slavery, health and sickness . . .

"Also in many a deed, when a man acts under compulsion, he is then the more entitled to clemency in that he did what he did out of necessity.

"And if anyone acts unintentionally, he is not entirely like one who does it intentionally."

But nations are not governed by noble aspirations alone, and in early times the voice of moderation was often also the voice of weakness. The lasting achievement of King Edward the Confessor, who succeeded Canute, was to conceive and endow Westminster Abbey, but within ten months of his death the long-boats of William of Normandy were beaching on the shingle of Pevensey Bay.

CHAPTER TWO

The King becomes All-powerful

(1066–1509)

THE Frenchman who was crowned King of England on Christmas Day 1066 is one of the enigmas of history. In war he was ruthless, brutal, and without scruple. In peace he spurned the spilling of blood. William the Conqueror was the first English abolitionist. One of his first deeds as King was to decree: "I forbid that any person be killed or hanged for any cause."

It may seem fantastic, but for nearly forty years a millenium ago England was an abolitionist country. The gallows were unused, criminals unhung.

There was a dark side to William's generosity. Polite professors commenting upon his laws primly state that the punishment he substituted for hanging was mutilation. But if one studies the Latin text of the statute one sees that William was not so coy. "Let their eyes be torn out and their testicles cut off," he declared.

Legal historians usually say that most mutilated prisoners died from their injuries: the effect was much the same as that of hanging. But Dr Donald Teare, the Home Office pathologist, tells me that this is not necessarily so. The greatest danger to health would come from the victim's liability to infection, and we know too little about the prevalence of germs and bacteria in mid-eleventh century England to predict how severe a danger this was. The mere shock of the physical assault would probably not have been enough to kill, nor would the loss of blood.

William Rufus was content to follow his father's abolitionist track. He was not motivated by any high-flown views: he simply had other things to think about. His life centred on two joys— pederasty and hunting. The first was not yet a concern of the law, the second moved him to create the only capital offence of his reign: capturing a royal deer in the forests.

Henry I, the Conqueror's second son to succeed him on the throne, was more the stuff of which his father was made. Stern, hard-working, and able, he was determined to remedy the laxity and lawlessness that had pervaded the country during the rule of his degenerate brother.

Crime had become expensive, and criminals simply did not have the money to pay the plethora of compensations and fines into which the Anglo-Saxon system had by now deteriorated. Prisons were still almost a rarity. What could the King do to restore law and order?

Henry was not long in doubt. He brought back capital punishment, and with greater ferocity than the country had probably ever known.

On one day in 1124 forty-four thieves were hanged at the same time in Leicestershire. With dramatic suddenness crime ceased to be a matter of money. Treason, burglary, arson, robbery, theft, and now even homicide were made punishable by death. Occasionally the King relented and allowed a man to be maimed instead of killed. But, in the main, the gallows at last came into their own as the embodiment of the most dread sentence the law can pronounce.

Henry was not a cruel man, delighting in brutality for its own sake. At his Coronation he deliberately swore the old Saxon form of Oath, unused by his father and brother, in which he undertook to ensure "equity and mercy in all judgments". It was not his fault that this Oath could seldom be honoured.

The overwhelming need to re-establish order was not the only curb on royal mercy. The form of trial then almost solely used in the criminal courts left little scope for subsequent intervention by any man, even a king. For the real judge in our courts at this time was no human, but God himself. An alleged offender was left to *judicium Dei*, the "judgment of God", and once the Almighty had spoken it was not for any mortal to gainsay the verdict.

There were no courtrooms, jury, witnesses, or counsel. The prisoner and his accuser met face-to-face in some holy place, in front of the assembled freemen of the district. A priest asked the man to confess his crime, and if he refused he was "put to the ordeal". How the accused person fared in the "ordeal" was regarded as a divine indication of his innocence or guilt.

For a layman, the ordeal could take three forms; sometimes one was enough, sometimes he had to undergo all three. There was the Ordeal by Cold Water: bound hand and foot, the accused was thrown into a pool with a rope tied round his middle; if he sank he was adjudged innocent, and pulled out, if he floated he was guilty, for the pure water (blessed by the priest) would not receive the guilty. There was the Ordeal by Fire: the accused was made to grasp a heated bar of iron and hold it while he walked nine paces; then his hand was bound up, and if, three days later, it had not festered he was held to be as free of blame as his hand was free from blemish. There was the Ordeal by Hot Water: the accused was made to plunge his hand into a bowl of boiling water and take out a stone; afterwards it was bound up, and if, three days later, the skin was clear he too had "come clean from the ordeal". And, reserved solely for clerics, there was the Ordeal by the Coarsened Morsel: the accused clergyman had to swallow a piece of bread containing a feather, and if he choked he was adjudged guilty.

There were no half-way houses in such procedures: a man was either wholly innocent or wholly guilty. If all-merciful God had adjudged a person's guilt only the strongest king would dare to question the judgment. Such a man was Henry II, grandson of Henry I, who succeeded to the throne after the short, turbulent reign of Stephen.

This gifted and cultivated Frenchman—ruler of both France and England—reshaped our nation's law.

For the first time he instituted a centralized system of royal justice, with royal judges riding out into the countryside to rid the gaols of their prisoners and in the King's name decide their guilt or innocence. No longer was a man to be accused merely by whomsoever it pleased to accuse him. Although there may have been one or two earlier, tentative efforts it was in 1166 that Henry set up the jury of presentment (not to be confused with the later trial jury) consisting of twelve reputable men from every district, who were to bring up before the judges persons they suspected of crime. A system of civil justice also began to appear: if anyone was injured he could now not only demand punishment in the criminal courts, but also in a civil court. And the amount of damages was assessed by the judge: there was no more pre-fixed *bot*.

Henry even dared to tamper with the semi-holy ordeals. Trained in the best European learning of his day, he condemned their primitive barbarism, and was suspicious of the opportunities they gave for collusion between criminals and corrupt clerics. Even he could not abolish the ordeals completely, but he declared that henceforth a man cleared by the ordeal should not go free. If of bad repute he must within eight days leave the country, or else anyone might kill him. If Henry paid such little heed to "the Judgment of God" when the judgment was one of innocence there seems no reason to suppose that he was any the more respectful to a verdict of guilty. A condemned man's fate was in his hands: the King once again wielded personally the sceptre of mercy.

But the Church, angry at Henry's assault upon the ordeals (the officiating clergy earned substantial fees), retaliated by forcing him to concede a form of built-in reprieve for priests convicted of crime. William the Conqueror had permitted the Church to set up its own courts for clerics accused of temporal offences, and although Henry tried to keep these courts separate from secular justice the universal horror at the murder of Archbishop Becket compelled him to hand over jurisdiction over clerics in all kinds of cases (save treason) to the Church Courts. Thus was born benefit of clergy, an institution which was to survive for nearly seven centuries.

A cleric convicted of crime in the Royal Courts could escape his punishment by "pleading his clergy". The judge then had to deliver him to his local bishop, before whom he merely "purged his sin". In time not only clerics were able to contract out of royal justice: by the late fourteenth century all who could read could claim the privilege. All they need do was prove their literacy by reading, on their knees, the first verse of Psalm 51:

"Have mercy upon me O God, according to Thy loving kindness:

"According to the multitude of Thy tender mercies, blot out my transgressions."

In later years it was not even necessary to read the verse: an illiterate prisoner could learn it by heart, and, as he knelt in chains, hold the Bible open at the right place (found for him—at a price —by the gaoler) and pretend to read.

Until the time of the Tudors, at the end of the fifteenth century, benefit of clergy operated as a kind of automatic reprieve for convicted literates. Then, in 1490, the first Tudor king, Henry VII, enacted that every person convicted of "a clergyable felony" should be branded on the thumb, and if anyone claimed the privilege twice (which the brand would show) it should be denied unless he was indeed a cleric.

Henry VIII decreed that certain crimes should thenceforth be "unclergyable", and Elizabeth I substituted a year's imprisonment for purgation before the bishop. By the eighteenth century the privilege had become almost a dead letter, available only for certain minor offences—and then often leading to seven years' transportation. Parliament finally abolished it in 1827.

But to return to the chronological narrative: trial by ordeal ceased soon after November 1215, when the Fourth Lateran Council under Innocent III, perhaps the greatest of all the medieval popes, forbade the clergy any longer to participate in the rituals. The result was literally a hiatus in the administration of

English justice. The gaols were filled with accused criminals, but the judges had no means of trying them. Once "the judgment of God" was removed they were at a loss to find a less illustrious process. King John died, and his nine-year-old son, Henry III, succeeded. There was no strong directive from the centre. The judges had to cope with the problem as best they could. For a time they tried to carry on with the old ordeals. But without the presence of a cleric the ceremonies were meaningless. Lawyers were at a loss. For two to three years the administration of criminal justice was almost at a standstill. The position became so acute that in 1219 the young King's regent commanded the judges, as an emergencey measure, to clear the gaols as best they could without a trial—a total confession of failure.

Then someone had the idea—and to this day we do not know who he was—of using the jurors of presentment, who attended court to present the suspected criminals, as the tribunal to decide the further question of their guilt or innocence. So was born trial by jury—the greatest English gift to the jurisprudence of the world and, like the invention of the wheel, without a named inventor.

At first the process was far from popular. The prisoner could hardly be blamed for not wanting to be tried by the very men who had brought him before the court. There was still no question of anyone's giving evidence: the jury was supposed to bring in its verdict simply on the basis of its own knowledge of local events. Many a man refused to plead his innocence before so tainted a tribunal, and had to be forcibly coerced into submission by the judicially approved practice of piling heavy weights on him, until he either agreed to stand his trial or died.

Perhaps because the jury so directly took the place of the semi-divine ordeal, its verdict came to be regarded by judges as possessing almost a hallowed validity. Even today it possesses something of the same sacrosanct quality, so that the House of Lords has in the nineteen-sixties refused to go behind a jury's verdict and inquire what happened in the jury-room, even though positive malpractices were alleged.

Jury trial may now be commonly dubbed the cornerstone of our liberties, but originally it was all too often a vehicle for the obtaining of convictions. In treason and felony the accused could not even have counsel. Later, when witnesses could be heard for the King, the accused could not have them, and when eventually he was allowed them they could not be sworn to tell the truth—unlike witnesses for the prosecution. The subject's only protection lay in the King's power of pardon or the jury's sympathy.

But juries were not likely to be over-helpful: it was not until 1679 that the judges laid down that jurors could return whatever verdict they liked without fear of punishment. In the later Middle Ages the King alone had the effective power of mercy.

The limits of pardon were wide. There was little law about it, for all depended on the King's grace. As late as the fourteen-seventies English kings used sometimes to try cases themselves in court, and they were by no means always merciful. In 1285 Edward I personally sentenced the Mayor of Exeter and a city gatekeeper to be hanged for having failed to close the city's northern gate in time to prevent a priest's murderer escaping.

But in one important respect the royal right of pardon moulded and developed the law. It was the means whereby the defence of accident and self-defence entered into English jurisprudence.

In medieval times lawyers saw things only in black and white. If one man killed another it was murder. The fact that it was an accident or in defence of life or property was immaterial. As Henry I said, "Who sins unwittingly shall knowingly make amends."

In the late thirteenth century this was realized to be unjust and the King began granting his pardon whenever it was proved that the crime had been committed accidentally or in self-defence. "Thomas", a judge of Edward I's time said to one prisoner: "These good folk (the jurors) testify upon their oath to all that you have said. Therefore by way of judgment we say that what you did was done in self-defence; but we cannot deliver you from your imprisonment without the special consent of our lord the King. Therefore, we will report your condition to the King's Court and will procure for you his special grace." The King later duly pardoned Thomas and granted him "our firm peace".

Some kings were blamed for being too merciful. In 1309 Edward II's House of Commons told him: "Felons escape punishment by too easily procuring charters of pardon." In 1329 his son, Edward III, had to agree that charters of pardon would not be granted except where he could do it consistently with his oath. And over a hundred years later Henry VI's Council was again complaining that the King had been giving too many pardons.

The quality of mercy was not entirely unstrained. Fees were paid for pardons, and some medieval rulers also claimed forefeiture of the pardoned offender's goods. Mercy was a commercial proposition to impoverished monarchs.

CHAPTER THREE

From the Tudors to the Hanoverians

(1509–1782)

THE modern history of the reprieve system starts, like so much of England's story, with the reign of Henry VIII.

When Henry ascended the throne in 1509 the King was not the only person granting pardons. In England itself he was the sole authority, but in the Marches—the wild border areas between England and the old Principality of Wales—it was the individual Marcher lords who dispensed such mercy as there was in those anarchic regions. The lords were powerful brigands, each supreme in his own semi-kingdom, maintained by the might of his own sword. No earlier English king had been strong enough to subdue them, but they were to meet their match in the Welshman's son who defied the power of Rome.

By 1535 the first part of the Reformation had been accomplished. Katherine of Aragon had been divorced, the Pope's authority in England abolished, and Henry declared by Act of Parliament the "Supreme Head of the Church of England". Now he determined to show that his supremacy applied to all secular matters as well as temporal.

With the help of the same subservient Parliament that had enacted the Reformation Henry abolished both the Welsh Principality and the Marcher lordships, incorporating them into England. The area was divided into twelve counties on the English pattern, and English law made to run: it was a straightforward piece of annexation.

As part of this plan Parliament passed in the spring of 1536 an Act which is still on the Statute Book, and is still the law of England. It runs as follows:

"No personne or personnes of what estate or degree so ever they be of shall have any power or auctorities to pardon or remitte any tresons murders manslaughters or any kyndes of felonnyes . . . but that the Kings Highnesse his heires and successours Kinges of this realme shall have the hole and sole power and auctorities thereof united and knytte to the imperiall crowne of this realme."

Henry alone was to be the fount of mercy in his realm.

Today it is common form to refer to the reprieve system as "the Royal Prerogative of Mercy". But, despite the eminence of the lawyers and constitutional experts who habitually use this term, it is, strictly speaking, inaccurate. A 'royal prerogative' is an instance of royal power enjoyed by the Queen purely because she *is* Queen, and not conferred on her by Parliament. It is something which she possesses simply by virtue of being Queen. Yet here is a statute where Parliament has expressly bestowed the power of dispensing mercy on the Sovereign! Admittedly this particular Parliament was but a tool of the King—Henry VIII once told them, "I'll have my Bill or I'll have some of your heads!"—but constitutionalists cannot have it both ways. The Queen's power to pardon criminals is not a prerogative: it has been vested in her by Parliament.

So much for pedantry. Whatever the exact juristic nature of his mercy-giving power Henry did not put it to extensive use. According to one estimate 72,000 people were executed in the thirty-six years of his reign, and he was the only English king to permit Sunday executions and make boiling to death a legal form of execution.

He had a bizarre sense of humour. The first person whom he ordered to be cooked to death was, perhaps appropriately, a cook —one Richard Roose, who had poisoned two of his master's guests with a compound of hemlock and other fatal herbs. A huge cauldron slung from a strong iron tripod was set up over some logs in London's Smithfield, and before a large crowd the condemned man was boiled alive like a lobster. The process took two hours.

Elizabeth I was hardly more lenient than her father: in her reign there were over eight hundred executions a year. Nor were the early Stuart kings over merciful. Yet it is in Stuart times that one finds the first attempt by an English jurist to put the practice of royal mercy on some kind of sound theoretical basis.

The jurist was Sir Edward Coke, writing in retirement after James I had dismissed him as Chief Justice for continually defying the Crown. In his *Institutes*, Coke laid down the first great judicial curb on the royal pardoning power. He claimed that the royal pardon was no answer to a civil claim for damages or a criminal charge brought by a private prosecutor: the pardon applied only to public offences prosecuted in the Crown's name. Perhaps this now seems only of academic interest, but in Coke's days many criminal charges, including murder, were brought by private prosecutors. The ex-Chief Justice's aim was to prevent the private subject's just cause being baulked by a capricous royal pardon.

Coke went farther, and maintained that the King could not commute a sentence of hanging or burning to the milder sentence of beheading. He claimed that the royal prerogative only entitled the Sovereign to quash the death penalty altogether, not to vary one form of death for another. This hit in particular at the royal habit of making hanging, drawing, and quartering easier for noblemen, by saying that they should only be beheaded.

Hanging, drawing, and quartering had been invented especially for the benefit—if that be the right word—of one William Maurice, a pirate, as far back as 1241. It soon became the common form of punishing traitors, and remained the penalty for high treason in England until as late as 1870: surprisingly it remained technically possible in Scotland until 1950.

The 'drawing' part of the sentence originally referred to dragging the condemned man along the ground to his place of execution, tied to the tail of a horse. Later this was considered too unkind—possibly to the horse—and the victim was strapped instead to a sledge, on which he was drawn to the gallows. On arrival his fate was grim: he was half-hanged, cut down alive, his entrails taken out and burnt before him, and final oblivion reached only with beheading. Thereafter the body was cut into quarters and exhibited, together with the head, in some public place *pour décourager les autres*. It is easy to understand why noblemen preferred a straightforward beheading.

After Coke came Parliament as a challenger to the royal power of mercy.

By the sixteen-seventies the House of Commons was still far from being the undisputed centre of national power. But it was feeling its way towards it, and only thirty years after Charles I had lost his head it was quite happy to remind his devious son Charles II of the new realities of political life. It did so in the case of Lord Danby.

In the winter of 1678 Parliament had passed an Act to raise supplies to join Holland in her longstanding war with France. Yet five days later Charles II instructed his Chief Minister Thomas Osborne, Earl of Danby, to write secretly to the English Minister at Versailles offering neutrality at a price of 6,000,000 livres—most, if not all, of which would go into Charles's own coffers. Danby, who although unscrupulous was not a fool, was chary of writing the letter, and insisted on Charles's adding a postscript in his own handwriting: "This letter is writ by my order, C.R."

Danby must have been clairvoyant. Somehow the secret got out, and the irate Commons impeached him. He was ordered to be taken into custody. But before he went he obtained from the King a secret pardon discharging him of all the offences of which he was accused.

When called upon to answer to the impeachment the astute Earl promptly pleaded his pardon as a complete defence, anticipating Adolf Eichmann's "superior orders" plea by about two hundred and fifty years. The Commons appointed a committee to consider the matter, and on May 5th, 1679, the whole House solemnly resolved: "That the pardon pleaded by the Earl of Danby is illegal and void, and ought not to be allowed in bar of impeachment of the commons of England."

Even so, Danby's head stayed on his shoulders. Charles II prorogued Parliament, and the impeachment fell to the ground. But Parliament triumphed in the end. Twenty-two years later Charles's nephew, William III, gave his assent to the Act of Settlement enacting, "No pardon . . . be pleadable to an impeachment by the Commons in parliament."

William III could hardly refuse the Commons' demands: he owed his throne to Parliament. The 'Bloodless Revolution' of 1688 not only brought this dour, allegedly homosexual Dutchman and his wife Mary to the throne, it enabled Parliament to provide this country with the nearest she has to a written constitution. And it is significant of the essential rôle that mercy must play in the administration of justice that Parliament at one of the high-water marks of its progress towards supreme power incorporated in the 1688 Bill of Rights a section expressly declaring: "That it is the right of the subject to petition the King". The same Parliament also decreed that the oath sworn by every Sovereign at his Coronation should henceforth always include the ancient words, "Will you to your power cause Law and Justice, in Mercy, to be exercised in all your judgments?" with the express answer, "I will."

Neither William and Mary nor Mary's sister Anne were often called upon to honour this Oath. The need did not arise. When Anne died in 1714 the total number of capital offences was only thirty-two, and the nation, still recovering from the upheaval of the Revolution and preoccupied with foreign wars, was comparatively law-abiding. A moderate prosperity was over the country. Dutch methods had resulted in the land being drained and new crops being cultivated. Learning, literature, agriculture, trade, flourished together in moderation. Life had the quality of a Haydn symphony.

But with the accession of George I in 1714 the music changed its beat. The eighteenth century witnessed two armed rebellions against the King, epoch-making wars of empire and conquest, the shattering of English country life with the enclosure of the poor countryman's common lands by the wealthy landowners, and the complete break-up of the pattern of the nation's existence caused by the Industrial Revolution. And this turmoil was reflected in the law.

By the time Blackstone wrote his *Commentaries on the Laws of England,* in 1769, the number of capital offences had increased from 32 to 160; by 1819 they had risen to 220. At the end of the century all felonies except petty larceny and mayhem (maiming) were punishable with death, and Edmund Burke had declared that he could obtain the consent of the House of Commons to any Bill imposing the death penalty. Mackenzie, the historian, has written:

"If a man injured Westminster Bridge, he was hanged. If he appeared disguised on a public road, he was hanged. If he cut down young trees; if he shot rabbits; if he stole property valued at five shillings; if he stole anything at all from a bleach field; if he wrote threatening letters to extort money; if he returned prematurely from transportation; for any of these offences he was immediately hanged."

The eighteenth was a century in which mercy was needed.

It is fashionable among certain writers to represent the judges of the eighteenth century as being, almost to a man, complete and unremitted blackguards. Arthur Koestler and C. H. Rolph in their book *Hanged by the Neck,* ask: "What, then, was the cause, and which were the forces that kept the madness going and resisted all attempts to stop it, all measures of reform, until the mid-nineteenth century?" And they reply: "The answer is as simple as it is shocking: the Judges of England."

This is—largely—nonsense. It disregards one crucial fact—that between 1756 and 1808 the proportion of reprieves went up from one-third to seven-eighths of all those sentenced to death. What relevance has this to the alleged villainy of the judges? Simply that throughout this time they were largely exercising the Royal Prerogative of Mercy!

The very word 'reprieve' shows the importance of the judiciary's rôle. It derives from the French verb *reprendre,* "to take back", and was brought into the English language in the late sixteenth century to describe the process of judicial pardoning which had begun even then. Already the practice had started of the judge donning the black cap and pronouncing sentence of death, then immediately 'taking it back' and telling the condemned man that the sentence would not be carried out until the King had considered it. If the judge then backed up the reprieve with a personal recommendation to mercy, as often happened, the prisoner was almost always saved—on condition that he entered the army or navy, though later transportation was usually the alternative.

When Parliament passed an Act "for better preventing the horrid Crime of Murder", in 1752, this 'taking back' power of the judges became even more important. For the Act provided that all persons convicted of murder should be executed within forty-eight hours unless the execution day fell on a Sunday, when it was to be postponed till Monday. With communications so slow and hazardous, the two-day interval between sentence and execution—instead of the former two weeks or so—meant that unless a judge felt disposed to reprieve an offender there was no hope for him. He would be hanged, and his body hanging in chains on the gibbet, before the Sovereign even knew of his conviction. Indeed, judicial reprieve was so firmly established by the mid-eighteenth century that the 1752 Act expressly provided: "In case there shall appear reasonable cause, it shall be lawful for the Judge to stay the Execution of the Sentence at his Discretion". If he did so, the Act further entitled him to allow the prisoner more than the bread and water which was the sole diet permitted by the Act for murderers condemned straight away to execution.

In effect, the judges on assize were given a completely free hand. There was no Court of Criminal Appeal. There was no national Press vigilant to report proceedings in even the most remote courts. It was entirely up to the individual judge whether he left a prisoner to hang or gave him a further chance of life. He could not be censured if he failed to do so; he was unlikely to be praised if he did do so.

It would be stupid to claim that the judges of the eighteenth century were all models of sympathy and paragons of compassion. They lived in a time when different standards of human behaviour from ours applied, when women who murdered their husbands were still burned to death, and when public temper was such that if, as happened in the case of Dr Henesy in London in 1758, a crowd awaiting a public execution was cheated by a last-minute reprieve it was liable to riot and destroy most of the scaffold. Nor was it the judges who made the new repressive laws: practically all the new capital offences were created almost without debate by a completely passive Parliament. "The true hangman", Sir William Meredith told the House of Commons in 1777, "is the Member of Parliament; he who frames the bloody law is answerable for the blood which is shed under it".

c

The case of William York at Bury Assizes in the summer of 1748 gives a pretty fair impression of how the reprieve system worked in the middle of the eighteenth century. It was a pathetic story. Ten-year-old William was a parish child charged with killing a five-year-old girl, who was also a child of the parish, and with whom he lived under the care of a Lancashire parishioner. At first the boy denied his guilt, but later he broke down and confessed that he had killed the little girl, because she had fouled their bed. "The Devil put me upon committing the deed," he said.

Chief Justice Willes, who tried the case, had no option. He had to sentence the lad to death, but he immediately reprieved him so that he could seek the views of his fellow judges in London. Their verdict was unanimous against a commutation of the sentence. "He is certainly a proper subject for capital punishment and ought to suffer," they said. "Though the taking away of the life of a boy of ten years' old may savour of cruelty, yet as the example of this boy's punishment may be a means of deterring other children from the like offences and as the sparing of this boy, merely on account of his age, will probably have a quite contrary tendency, in justice to the public the law ought to take its course."

This ruling is barbaric. Nowadays it is inconceivable that such a charge would be brought, let alone prosecuted to conviction and sentence. And most writers upon the operation of eighteenth-century criminal justice are content to leave William York's case at this stage, with the enormity of the judiciary manifest for all to see in the record of their own words.

But this is not a complete picture. Firstly, it would still today be possible for William York to be convicted of murder if he had already displayed "a mischievous discretion" though, being under eighteen, he could not be sentenced to death. Secondly, it is only right to remember that in the eighteenth century childhood was not the indulgent period that it now is. The serious-faced and adultly clothed children that stare solemnly out at us from the paintings of the period are enough to show that. Chief Justice Willes was himself an Oxford undergraduate at fourteen, and at the age of ten would have probably achieved a degree of maturity unknown to most modern children. Thirdly, William York did not hang.

According to Sir Michael Foster, himself a distinguished judge, writing in 1762 two or three of the assembled judges "out of great tenderness and caution" added a rider to the joint opinion, advising Willes to send another reprieve in case it might appear on further inquiry that the boy had been instigated by another. Willes took this advice and granted several further reprieves, but eventually he decided to let the boy die, since all inquiries only confirmed that he had committed the murder alone and unprompted. Then the King stepped in. At George II's personal command William York was granted a formal pardon on condition that he forthwith enlisted in the Royal Navy.

It would be foolish to overstate the case. William York's judges were cruel men, and it is true that as late as 1831 a judge at Maidstone Assizes refused to reprieve fourteen-year-old John Bird, who was hanged for murdering a young playmate. But the holders of judicial office were not all monsters incarnate. They may not have been ahead of their age, but according to their own lights some at least tried to temper justice with mercy.

Records preserved at the Home Office show the diligent way in which many of the judges carried out their duties. Frequently a judge would not merely reprieve a prisoner and refer him to the King; he would also either recommend mercy, and suggest alternative punishment (usually fourteen years' transportation) or else state positively that he thought the death sentence should be carried out. In both cases he would give his reasons.

One judge would recommend mercy because a burglar "was young and his master and others gave him a good character". Another would recommend death for a labourer caught stealing from a dockyard, because he had "no extenuating plea of necessity. It is of more consequence, by way of example (the end of punishment), that one man in good circumstances should suffer than twenty miserable wretches."

These judicial reports were not considered by the King sitting alone at his desk. Special meetings of the Privy Council were called, and the King asked each Privy Councillor his view in turn before announcing his own decision. Usually about fifteen to twenty people were present, but the ultimate decision was undoubtedly the personal act of the King. There was no delegation of responsibility to any particular Minister or Privy Councillor: the King's mercy was meted out by the King alone.

As Blackstone put it in his own ponderous way: "The granting of pardon is the most amiable prerogative of the Crown . . . and it is that act of his government which is the most personal and most entirely his own."

In one case, for instance, all the Councillors but one had spoken and given their verdict—no reprieve, for a London street robber. But George III noticed that the Lord Chancellor, Lord Eldon, who lived in the very square where the offence had been committed, had remained silent. "I observe," he said, "that Lord Eldon has not yet spoken. What says he?" Eldon replied that he agreed it had been the custom to hang for street robberies, and indeed it was a very bad crime, but he thought a distinction should be made between cases where violence was used and where it was not. Here there had been no violence. Therefore, the man should be saved.

"Well, well!" laughed the King. "Since the learned judge who lives in Bedford Square does not think there is any great harm in street robberies there, the poor fellow shall not be hanged." And he was not.

The rôle of the Sovereign in his 'Hanging' Cabinet, as it was called (to distinguish it from the 'Efficient' Cabinet presided over by the Prime Minister), was so essential to the country's legal administration that in London they had to approve every single capital sentence except those for murder.

At the end of every monthly session at the Old Bailey there was the ceremony known as 'the Recorder's Report'. The Recorder of London would attend before the Council with a list of the past session's capital offenders, other than murderers, and ask the King for his decision in each individual case. Because of the nearness of the King's Court and the knowledge that there would be this inevitable call over at the end of the month, judges at the Old Bailey used to reprieve criminals far less than their brethren on assize in the country. In murder cases they were still the sole barrier between the condemned man and the scaffold, but for every other offence they were usually content to sentence the prisoner to death and leave it to the King and his 'Hanging Cabinet' to decide his ultimate fate.

The hearing of the Recorder's Report used to take on an average about two or three hours, though sometimes the Report—which usually contained about twenty cases—was dispatched in under an hour. "I was exceedingly shocked", once wrote Lord Eldon:

"the first time I attended to hear the Recorder's report at the careless manner in which, as it appeared to me, it was conducted. We were called upon to decide on sentences, affecting no less than the lives of men, and yet there was nothing laid before us to enable us to judge whether there had been or had not been any extenuating circumstances."

He resolved never to attend another report without having read and considered the whole of the evidence—and in consequence "I saved the lives of several individuals."

In the country the judges exercised their reprieving power on a clearly defined basis. Blackstone (himself a judge) tells us that judicial reprieves were assignable into two specific categories. Typically, both had a Latin tag: reprieves were either *ex arbitrio judicis* or *ex necessitate legis*.

The first—"by wish of the judge"—applied where he was dissatisfied with the verdict, the evidence was suspicious, or where, although the prisoner's guilt was not in doubt, he wished to recommend mercy.

The second category—"by necessity of the law"—was more rigid, applying in certain specified circumstances where the judge had no option. The most common instances were insanity, self-defence, accidental death, or where a woman prisoner pleaded her pregnancy.

In the eighteenth century a condemned woman's pregnancy did not mean that she would not hang, simply that she would have to wait until after she was delivered of her child. However, the mere fact of expectant motherhood was not in itself sufficient to effect this temporary respite: the woman had to be—in the opinion of twelve married women, who examined her at the court's invitation —'Quick with child'. If there was movement the unborn infant had 'quickened', and was deemed to be alive; if not, the woman was hanged immediately.

Not for nothing do lawyers have the reputation for hair-splitting. Blackstone stipulated that if a woman reprieved once because of her pregnancy were again found pregnant when brought eventually to execution, she must still die—for "she shall not by her own incontinence evade the course of justice". An earlier judge, Sir Matthew Hale, had been even harsher: he maintained that the woman's gaoler should also be punished for "not looking better to her". The logic is impeccable.

The sexes have always been the same. One of the few recorded instances of a Sovereign's mind changing about a condemned person's fate occurred when a woman was on the throne.

The prisoner was a Yorkshire ex-guardsman named John Smith. And on the morning of Christmas Eve 1705 he stood on the hangman's cart, beneath Tyburn Tree, about to pay with his life for two recent forays as a housebreaker. He had been told that all attempts to obtain a reprieve had failed. Quietly he muttered his prayers, then let the hangman place the noose round his neck and tie the rope's free end to the beam above. As the crowd watched fascinatedly, the executioner pulled a white cap over his head, gave the horse standing in the cart's shafts a stinging crack of the whip, and jumped back out of its way. The horse moved sharply. There was a hush from the throng, and Smith lay dangling in space.

For fifteen minutes he hung, suspended in the cold, December air. Then someone cried, "A reprieve! A reprieve!" and an official messenger pushed his way towards the scaffold brandishing a warrant. Queen Anne had relented: Smith's sentence was quashed on condition that he rejoined the Army.

The prisoner was cut down, and, according to one report, "soon recovered". Understandably they asked him what it was like to be hanged. Here is his answer:

"When I was turned off, I was sensible for some time of very great pain, occasioned by the weight of my body, and felt my spirits in a strange commotion violently pressing upwards. Having forced their way to my head, I, as it were, saw a great blaze of glaring light which seemed to go out at my eyes with a flash. Then I lost all sense of pain."

Smith was not very grateful to his rescuers:

"After I was cut down and began to come to myself (he said) the blood and spirits, forcing themselves into their former channels, put me to such intolerable pain that I could have wished those hanged who had cut me down!"

Nowadays such an incident would be impossible. Modern hanging breaks the neck immediately, and death comes "in an instant", to quote ex-hangman Albert Pierrepoint. But in the eighteenth century—and, indeed, till quite late in the nineteenth—legal hanging was really death by slow strangulation. Hence the practice of letting the criminal hang for half an hour on the rope, a tradition preserved until recently in the hour which a condemned person's body used to hang upon the noose before the executioner was allowed to cut it down. Hence the fact that Smith could survive a quarter of an hour swinging on Tyburn. He became known as 'Half-hanged Smith', and his achievement is unique: he is the only man to have been successfully reprieved *after* the death sentence had been carried out.

Where does the Home Secretary come into all this? So far we have seen the King reprieving condemned persons, the judges doing it, even the Marcher lords. But what of the Home Secretary? When and how did he appear on the scene?

CHAPTER FOUR

The Home Office appears
(1782–1830)

THE Home Office was born because an eighteenth century politician named Charles James Fox, on his first ministerial appointment, was more interested in foreign affairs than home affairs. This may sound a strange reason for the creation of one of the most important and powerful Departments of State, but it is quite in keeping with the way in which the British Constitution has evolved.

For close on two hundred years there had been two Secretaries of State—one for the Northern Department, in charge of all business relating to the Northern Powers of Europe, and one for the Southern Department, who looked after France and the Southern Countries. The Colonies went to the senior of the two Secretaries: home affairs were handled by whichever of the two agreed to fit it in with his other, more interesting duties. Both Secretaries were really far more concerned with the fascinating dynamics of foreign affairs.

And it is difficult to blame them. For the main task of the Secretary dealing with domestic matters was simply to act as the official head of the King's secretarial bureau.

The very word *secretarius* originally meant someone admitted to the secrets of another, and, although the holder of the office had occasionally been able to wield immense power—as, for example, Thomas Cromwell in the reign of Henry VIII—he was really not much more than the King's personal private secretary.

Such a post did not appeal to Fox. Nor did he feel disposed to share the control of foreign affairs with his fellow-Secretary of State, the Earl of Shelburne, a scheming individual, of whom Horace Walpole once said that he was as fond of insincerity as if he had invented it himself. The King was weak. The collapse of Britain's fortunes in the War of American Independence and the fall of Lord North's Ministry of the 'King's Friends' had put an end to George III's experiment in personal government. So Fox was able to insist on the functions of the two Secretaries of State

being defined anew. Henceforth one Secretary was to deal with all
foreign affairs, and the other was to concern himself solely with
home affairs and the Colonies. Shelburne was assigned the latter
post.

The actual birthday of the Home Office is March 27th, 1782.
For on that day Fox sent a circular to all the foreign envoys in
London informing them of the change in departmental structure
and asking them in future to address their letters only to him.
It is typical of our Humpty-Dumpty system that the birth certificate of the Home Office should be the announcement of the creation of the Foreign Office.

Yet the Home Office was from the start the senior of the two
Departments of State. Shelburne took precedence, as a peer, over
Fox, and the same superior status attached immediately to their
respective offices. Certainly the work of 'the King's Secretary'
did not suddenly increase in importance because a new label was
put on his door.

Commissioners investigating the cost of running the principal
public offices three years after the Home Office was formed found
that its total staff, including the Secretary of State himself,
amounted to only seventeen people, ten of them clerks and one
'the necessary woman', eighteenth-century counterpart of the
modern charwoman. Nor was this puny force kept over busy. "The
clerks", said the Commissioners, "though not always employed,
are in daily attendance . . . If their number were reduced to eight,
Your Majesty's service might not suffer."

In fact, the Home Office existed for forty years before the Home
Secretary acquired anything like his modern, constitutional position as sole adviser to the Sovereign on the exercise of the Royal
Prerogative of Mercy, let alone an adviser whose advice must always be followed.

The domestic Secretary of State of the pre-Shelburne era had
already been a little involved in reprieves, because the judges'
reports came in from the country to the King via his office, which
had also usually been the channel through which the King's subsequent orders went out. But basically both before and after 1782
the domestic Secretary of State was merely one of the Privy
Councillors sitting round the Council table at the 'Hanging' Cabinet.

Even in the early nineteenth century the Home Secretary's advice was given no greater weight than that of any other Councillor.
Lord Eldon, speaking of his long period of office as Lord Chancellor, told the House of Lords in 1832, "For twenty years I have
been the individual who advised His Majesty as to the imposition

of the punishment of death". Even allowing for this octogenarian's notorious capacity for self-exaggeration it is clear that, of the nineteen or twenty men sitting round the table, if anyone was given precedence it was not the Home Secretary. Indeed, until an Act of 1827 the direct intervention of the Lord Chancellor was obligatory whenever a reprieve was granted, since a pardon had to be a document passed under the Great Seal of which he was the sole keeper.

Nowadays if for some reason the Home Secretary is not available his duty with regard to reprieves is undertaken on his behalf by one of the other Secretaries of State. In strict law all Secretaries of State are interchangeable, and although it has not happened in recent years Lord Templewood has written that (as Sir Samuel Hoare) he occasionally performed the Home Secretary's reprieving function in the nineteen-thirties, when he was Secretary of State for Air, and, later, when Secretary of State of India. Yet when, in February 1815, an urgent meeting had to be held on the eve of her proposed execution to decide whether to reprieve Elizabeth Fenning, a young cook convicted of attempting to murder her employer's family with poisoned dumplings, the decision was taken not by the Foreign Secretary or the Secretary of State for War (the only other Secretaryships of State then existing), but by a committee of Lord Chancellor Lord Eldon, the Recorder of London, and John Beckett, the Permanent Under Secretary at the Home Office. They decided against a respite, and she was hanged.

Nor was this lack of authority due to instability at the head of the Home Office: one man, Lord Sidmouth, was Home Secretary from 1812 to 1822. A slight, oval-faced man, with ice-cool eyes, he was content to be merely one of the voices round the Sovereign's table. If George IV, as Prince Regent or later as King, was minded to be merciful Sidmouth was content. If not he was also content: possibly more so.

In 1820 an accomplished lawyer such as Joseph Chitty junior could write a whole book on *The Law of the Prerogatives of the Crown* without even once mentioning the Home Secretary.

It took a man of really outstanding ability to make the post of Home Secretary one of the most powerful in the whole hierarchy of government. He had to be someone strong enough to stand up to the King yet pliable enough not to lose the confidence of Parliament or the support of his political party. On a morning in January 1822 George IV placed the seals of office into the hands of just such a man—Robert Peel.

Peel had jumped at the chance of being appointed to the Home Office. He had previously held several posts of Cabinet rank, but

for the last three and a half years he had been out of office and
champing at his inactivity. The messenger who arrived at his
country home bearing the Prime Minister, Lord Liverpool's, offer
of the Home Ministry left the very same day with his delighted
acceptance.

A large part of Peel's fame justly rests upon his achievements in
his eight years as Home Secretary. A brilliant reformer, he cut
cleanly through centuries of accumulated legal dross: benefit of
clergy was finally abolished, the jury system codified in one
statute instead of dozens, the criminal law extensively rewritten
and brought up to date, the Metropolitan Police Force inaugu-
rated. But above all, the horrifying number of capital offences
was cut to such a prodigious extent that by 1834 the City of
London had to discharge one of its two salaried executioners as
redundant.

All this is common knowledge. But too little recognition is given
in our history books to Peel's other work at the Home Office—his
contribution to the evolution of the modern concept of constitutional monarchy. When Peel took over the Department the King
decided for himself whether or not he would extend mercy to convicted criminals. By the time that Peel finally resigned he had
established that the King reprieved only upon the advice of his
Home Secretary.

George IV is known to most of us simply as the roué with the
carrot-coloured wig, who married Mrs Fitzherbert, and locked his
official 'wife', Queen Caroline, out of his Coronation. But deep
down in his indolent, sensual, indulgent personality was a strong
vein of kindliness and sentiment: he was continually wanting to
reprieve people.

Four months after Peel's appointment George was already writing to the new Home Secretary from his meringue-domed Royal
Pavilion at Brighton "desiring that Mr Peel will be so good as to
make every possible inquiry into the case of the boy Henry Newbury, aged thirteen, and to commute his sentence from transportation, in consideration of his youth, to confinement in the House of
Correction." Peel complied with the request. But the following
month came the first real clash between Sovereign and Minister.

The Recorder's Report for May 1822 had contained eight capital sentences for burglary, and at the meeting of the Council
these had all been confirmed. Later the King had a change of
heart, and wrote to Peel requesting that one of the sentences might
be commuted: Peel obeyed. But on the night before the remaining executions were due to take place Peel received a further
letter from the King reprieving by name one of the condemned,

a man of good family, and directing the Minister to select two others for mercy.

This was too much. On his own authority Peel postponed all the executions for forty-eight hours, and summoned a Cabinet to consider the issue. Afterwards he wrote to the King: "It is the unanimous opinion of your Majesty's confidential servants who met at the Cabinet this day, that the law ought to be permitted to take its course on Friday next." Faced with this united front George was forced to give way. But it was not a complete defeat: as a concession the Cabinet approved one more reprieve—though, possibly to show their independence, they did not choose the man expressly earmarked by the King!

A year later Peel felt strong enough to rebut the royal dictates without appealing to the Cabinet for its formal support. And he won the day.

George had been persuaded by his current mistress, Lady Conyngham, to write to his Minister on behalf of a young man named Mills, who was under sentence of death for uttering forged notes. Peel had already decided that no reprieve was possible, because a few weeks before, the death sentence had been commuted in a similar case, and experienced forgers were already using that instance of royal clemency to induce young men to pass notes for them. Peel stood firm and refused to obey his royal master, confiding to Henry Hobhouse, his Permanent Under-Secretary, that if the King persisted he would send a respite and resign his office. But the King did not persist, and the Duke of Wellington promised Peel that he would undertake to dissuade Lady Conyngham from any further interference in judicial administration.

Henceforth there were several such incidents—the King, warm-hearted and a prey to various more-or-less interested parties, seeking to exercise his power of dispensing mercy as he pleased, the Minister attempting to temper the royal caprice with considerations of overall policy and continuity of administration.

The King was driven into petty, stupid ways of venting his displeasure. In July 1825 George suddenly brought forward the next meeting of the 'Hanging' Cabinet from August 8th to August 2nd, simply to annoy Peel. "It will put Mr Peel to some inconvenience", he wrote to a friend, "which I hope may tend towards its being a useful lesson to him for the future."

But 'the lesson' was not learned. On the contrary Peel's power— and, in consequence, that of the office which he held—increased.

It is true that throughout his tenure of office the Recorder's Report continued to be delivered as before at monthly meetings of the Council, which also continued to receive reports from the assize judges in the country, but in the eighteen-twenties the Council ceased to be the court of last resort. Even if the Council had decided against a reprieve there was now a new tribunal to whom one last, desperate appeal could be made. It was not the King: it was not the Lord Chancellor: it was not the Prime Minister: it was the Home Secretary.

Of sixty-two persons ordered for execution by the Council between May 1827 and April 1830 seven were subsequently reprieved by the Secretary of State.

Alfred H. Dymond, a prominent abolitionist of the middle years of the nineteenth century, relates a good instance of how this early jurisdiction of the Home Secretary worked in the late eighteen-twenties. A young man of good country family had been a constant source of anxiety to his relatives because of his dishonesty. Determined to teach him a lesson, his aunt put £5 into a drawer to which he had access, assuming that he would not be able to resist the temptation.

In fact, he took the money. She complained to the authorities, and he was duly arrested, tried, and found guilty. Everyone expected that the judge would deliver a stern lecture to the now thoroughly penitent young man, and then sentence him to some nominal penalty. He did not: he sentenced him to death.

Yet no-one believed that he would hang. To be taught a lesson by your family is one thing; to be executed—and over £5—is another. But the 'Hanging Cabinet' did not vary the judge's sentence: it really looked as if the prisoner would die.

Finally, on the eve of the day appointed for execution, workmen began to erect the scaffold. The Sheriff had a worried consultation with the Mayor, and they decided to ride at once to London and visit Peel at the Home Office. "It must be an oversight," said the Sheriff, and took it upon himself to postpone the execution.

Arrived at Whitehall, the two men, tired and exhausted by their journey, hastened to the Home Office. Peel was not there, but they saw his next-in-command, the Under-Secretary. He listened politely to all they had to say, and then said calmly: "There is no mistake at all in the matter, gentlemen. The evidence has been fully considered, the judge holds to the opinion that this is a case for capital punishment, the Secretary of State agrees with the judge, and you must bear the responsibility of having ventured to interfere with the course of the law!" But they managed to make him change his mind. By the time they left the building they were carrying a free pardon.

Thereafter the young man became a model citizen, and every

year, on the eve of his proposed execution, he dined at the Mayor's table wearing a shroud.

Apart from the human interest of this story it has a further significance in that the Under-Secretary, Henry Hobhouse, appears to have acted without consulting either his superior or his Sovereign. He was the most senior person available at the Home Office, and that seems to have sufficed.

Sir Robert Peel was not a particularly merciful Home Secretary. He was more concerned that the criminal law as a whole should be made more consistent than that mercy should be shown in individual cases.

Indeed, juries were often more merciful than the Home Secretary. Ever since Blackstone's time jurors had themselves been operating what one can only call a wild kind of mercy, a sort of unofficial reprieve system of their own. Appalled by the large number of capital offences and the frequent lack of proportion between the punishment and the crime, juries had developed an increasing tendency not to convict in cases where they thought mercy should be extended. Blackstone himself remarked: "The mercy of juries will often make them strain a point, and bring in larceny to be under the value of twelve pence when it is really of much greater value." He called it "a kind of pious perjury".

By Peel's time this process had waxed apace. A jury would often assess the amount taken from a shop at 4*s*. 10*d*. so as to avoid the capital penalty which fell on a theft of 5*s*. In one case where a woman had actually confessed to stealing £5 from a dwelling-house the jury solemnly brought in a verdict that the amount was 39*s*. because theft of 40*s*. or over from a dwelling-house was capital. And when Peel, in 1827, passed an Act through Parliament raising the capital limit from 40*s*. to £5—in order to decrease the number of thieves liable to be hanged—juries promptly went one better and raised their verdicts to £4 19*s*. 0*d*.

Peel was a powerful Home Secretary, but the nation's jurors probably saved more condemned persons' lives than he did. He "piqued himself on his firmness", alleged Edward Gibbon Wakefield, a contemporary abolitionist. Even so he was a stern believer in the equality of all before the law. Politically conservative, and opposed to the enfranchisement of the emergent middle classes, he brooked no class distinctions in the application of the law. His last joust with George IV was over just such an issue.

A member of the Irish gentry named Peter Comyn had been ejected from a tenancy in County Clare by his landlord. Hot-headed and stupid, Comyn forged documents to secure a legal injunction against him. Then he burnt down the man's house, and gave sworn evidence against three innocent men accused of the crime—at that date still capital. Luckily the truth was discovered, and Comyn himself convicted of the triple offences of perjury, forgery, and arson. He was sentenced to death.

His relatives immediately appealed to fellow-Irishman Lord Conygham, the complaisant husband of George IV's mistress, to prevail upon his wife to intercede with the King on his behalf. The first that Peel knew of their efforts was a letter from the Duke of Northumberland, the Lord Lieutenant of Ireland, enclosing a remarkable document he had just received from the King at Windsor:

"My dear Duke, [wrote the King] Having received a petition from the respectable inhabitants of the county of Clare in favour of Petery Comyn . . . and there being some favourable circumstances in his case, I am desirous of exercising the best prerogative of the Crown, that of mercy, in saving his life, leaving to your Grace the commutation of punishment you may think fit."

It was signed simply "Your sincere friend, GEORGE R."

The arrogant simplicity of the document astounded Peel. The language was almost exactly the same as that of the first letter he had received from his Sovereign at the start of his Ministry directing a reprieve in the case of Henry Newbury. Had the King learnt nothing in eight years? In considerable anger Peel wrote immediately to his Prime Minister, the Duke of Wellington, expressing his "great surprise" at the letter, saying that he had already rejected many requests for mercy addressed to him from proper quarters and that this latest demonstration by the King was "quite intolerable". He enclosed a copy of a letter to the King that he had that morning dictated. It is a fine example of the delicate art of putting one's Sovereign politely but firmly in his place.

Peel began by telling the King that he had had the honour of receiving the Duke of Northumberland's letter informing him of His Majesty's commands, but

"I feel it to be my painful duty humbly and respectfully to submit to your Majesty that, had your Majesty been pleased to consult me on this occasion, one which I consider of deep interest to the administration of the law in Ireland, I could not have advised your Majesty to command the remission of the capital sentence."

He quoted and endorsed the Duke's view that if these excesses were to be "pardoned in a gentleman, merely as such, we shall in vain attempt to restrain the vindictive passions of the more humble tenantry", and stated that he would, "with your Majesty's gracious permission", forbear from making any further communication to him on the subject until he should again have heard from the Duke of Northumberland, who had meanwhile ordered a respite of the execution in order to enable the matter to be considered further.

Upon receipt of Peel's letter and its enclosure Wellington hastened to Windsor and sought an audience of the King. By now George was slowly dying: dropsy was wreaking its effect upon his body, and in an atmosphere of pain, drugs, and acute physical prostration he no longer had the strength or desire to indulge in sustained opposition to his Ministers' wishes:

"I have just returned from Windsor [Wellington wrote to Peel that evening]. The King is very unwell. I did not talk to him about business of any kind. I understand, however, that he is quite prepared to receive and act in conformity with any suggestion that may be made to him respecting the affair of Mr Comyn."

And so it turned out. Peel wrote a further letter stating that under the circumstances he considered it to be his "painful but imperative duty humbly to tender my advice to your Majesty that the law should be permitted to take its course". George was too weak to acknowledge the letter himself. The following night his personal secretary wrote to Peel that he was "honoured with the commands of the King to send you his Majesty's kind regards and to acquaint you that his Majesty desires that the law should take its course with respect to Comyn by the execution of the capital sentence." The words have the sad, defeated air of a dying man sending another to his death.

The King did not long outlive Peter Comyn: in the early hours of Saturday June 26th, 1830, he died quietly and without pain. But his was the final garland: in the General Election caused by the dissolution of Parliament after his death the Tory Government was returned with a much weakened majority. After three precarious months in office the Ministry was defeated on a vote in the House of Commons, and resigned. Seven months after his royal adversary's demise Peel ceased to be Home Secretary.

CHAPTER FIVE

Brief Return of Royal Power

(1830–1837)

THE immediate effect of Peel's resignation was to put the clock back eight years. He was succeeded by Lord Melbourne, a politician distinguished neither by his intelligence nor his industry, who, if he had not been fortunate enough seven years later to provide a father-figure for an eighteen-year-old Queen would have merited only a footnote on the pages of history.

In contrast to the supine Melbourne the new King—William IV, "Sailor Billy"—was an outspoken, forthright character, who may not have taken much interest in many things, but once he did was determined to see that he got his own way. From the start William took a great personal interest in the exercise of his Royal Prerogative of Mercy. His strong interest, coupled with the comparative weakness of Melbourne and his immediate successors at the Home Office, led to an Indian summer of the royal pardoning power.

The King's impact was so pronounced that after four years the *Morning Herald*, an abolitionist newspaper, joyously acclaimed: "No Sovereign ever sat on the throne of this country who was more disposed to 'administer justice in mercy' according to the terms of his Coronation Oath." For two and a half years, from April 1833 to November 1835, there was not a single hanging in London or Middlesex; the Council, presided over by the King, reprieved every capital offender in over twenty-five consecutive Recorder's Reports.

Even in point of strict constitutional form the Home Secretary's status diminished during William's reign. In November 1835 the *Morning Herald*, though continuing to eulogize the King for his merciful disposition, conceded that technically he could extend mercy only in accordance with advice, but it specified the source of such advice as "his responsible Ministers"—in the plural. For convenience the Home Secretary still remained the sole channel of requesting the King to display mercy, but he seems to have lost his pre-eminent position. In practice the King was more of a free agent than he had been for many years, especially in London. In country areas the assize judges were left much to their own devices, as in pre-Peel days.

Probably because communications between different parts of the country were still so slow and precarious, Peel himself had in the first year of his office piloted through Parliament a Bill which gave assize judges more streamlined powers to administer the reprieve system themselves. Instead of the country judge ceremonially sentencing a prisoner to death, and then telling him that he could not die at once, but his case would be considered by the King in Council, the judge was empowered to order that sentence of death be recorded—without actually pronouncing it—and to tell the prisoner straight away that he was recommending a reprieve.

The Act conferred an unfettered discretion to do justice as the judge considered right, and has not wholly been repealed even today. In the unlikely event of anyone's being convicted of piracy on the high seas or arson in the royal dockyards (both of which offences are still capital) the Act still applies, and the judge can himself reprieve the offender—even in the nineteen-sixties.

Sometimes, in the eighteen-thirties, the prisoner did not realize what was happening.

A man called Fleming Coward, when convicted of attempting to murder his brother, lived up to his name and burst into tears, imploring the judge to be merciful. Baron Platt wasted no time on explanations. He simply said, "Let sentence of death be recorded." The result was an even bigger howl from the prisoner, and only when Platt shouted, "You'll not be executed! You'll not be hanged!" did Coward quieten down. With typical human perversity he then said, "I should much prefer that, my Lord, to a long sentence!"

Assize judges were not restricted merely to recording formal sentence of death. They could also decide the alternative sentence—and at once impose it. It was entirely up to them. To one man convicted of a particularly brutal attempted murder Baron Martin said: "I shall pass upon you a sentence I have never passed before, and which, in my opinion, will be a greater punishment than the momentary pain of sudden death; for you will live like a slave labouring for others, and have no reward for your labours. That sentence is that you be kept in penal servitude for life." The words have a cold, steely impact on the printed page: it is not difficult to imagine their effect upon a small, crowded court, with candles guttering low at the end of a day-long hearing.

The harsh Act of 1752 still persisted: all persons convicted of murder, whether in London or in the country, were hanged within

D

forty-eight hours of being sentenced unless the judge granted a
reprieve or they were given one day's respite by a Sunday inter-
vening. By the eighteen-thirties most judges thought this was
too short a time for a person to make his peace with his Maker,
and they contrived, if the number of days allotted to the assize
permitted, to fix murder trials for a Friday so that the prisoner
would at least have one extra day of life. This was common form.

But apart from the religious aspect there was a powerful practical objection to the shortness of the interval between sentence
and execution. Undoubtedly many people went to their death
who, if only more time could have been provided for checking
their story, would have had their innocence vindicated.

Sir Fitzroy Kelly, himself a judge, used to tell the story of a
Suffolk farm worker called Edward Poole Chalker, who, in March
1835, was convicted on a Friday evening at Bury St Edmunds
of murdering a gamekeeper, and was duly hanged on the following Monday, still protesting his innocence—only for an English
soldier lying on his deathbed in India seven years later to confess
that he had been the real killer.

There were several such cases. For instance, on another March
day in 1835 'Daniel Savage', a wandering Irishman, was sentenced
to be hanged at Waterford Assizes on the next day but one for
the murder, ten years earlier, of his wife Peggy. 'Savage' had
been positively identified by only one witness, all the others having
either said that the prisoner was not the wanted man or that
they were unsure.

After sentence the prisoner's beard was shaved to facilitate the
hangman's task, and clean-shaven he was allowed 'his' sister as a
final visitor. She took one look and said, "Him? My brother? He's
nothing like him!" But there was no time to check the matter and
at 1 p.m. on the following day 'Daniel Savage' was hanged.

Only later was it discovered that Miss Savage was perfectly right.
The prisoner had, in truth been an inoffensive, somewhat weak-
minded man called Edmund Pine, who had not even known the
murdered woman. Daniel O'Connell made an angry speech about
it in the House of Commons, but the only response from the
Government benches was an admission by Lord Plunket that "some
mistake as to identity" had been made—"though happily such a
mistake is not one of ordinary occurrence".

Lord Plunket sounded sanguine, but, nevertheless the era of
swift hanging was nearly at an end. The following year Parliament
removed the forty-eight-hour limit on murderers' executions.

The new Act increased overnight a convicted murderer's chance
of getting a reprieve. At last his advisers or sympathizers would

have time to canvass support to save his life: no longer were they wholly dependent, outside London, on the inclination of the judge.

A year later William IV died, and the young Victoria ascended the throne. Once again the change in monarch had a profound effect upon the reprieve system: only this time the effect was to be permanent, and one that has lasted to the present day.

CHAPTER SIX

The Home Office again

(1837–1861)

THE English Sovereign ceased to be the practical head of the nation's Government, because German-speaking George I could not effectively preside over his English-speaking Cabinet. Similarly the Sovereign ceased to have any practical voice in dispensing mercy to the nation's criminals because eighteen-year-old Queen Victoria was both too young and of the wrong sex to preside over the 'Hanging' Cabinet.

"It would have been indecent and practically impossible to discuss with a woman the details of many crimes then capital," wrote Sir James Fitzjames Stephen in the eighteen-eighties.

Result—a Bill which changed radically the whole reprieve system was rushed through Parliament. Within twenty-eight days of William IV's death the Central Criminal Court Act, 1837, had been read three times in each House and received the Royal Assent: Hansard contains not one word spoken by any Member of Parliament or peer on the enactment. No-one appears to have attached importance to it. No-one appears to have realized that the Constitution of England was being altered in a vital respect. The number of prisoners waiting to know whether they were to live or die was mounting daily, and a practical solution had to be found quickly to the problem of clearing the nation's condemned cells.

The answer was, at least in theory: leave it to the judges. Parliament, at the invitation of Home Secretary Lord John Russell, who introduced the Bill, put the clock back over fifty years. The Recorder's Report was abolished: Old Bailey judges were given the same power to reprieve condemned prisoners as their brethren on assize had been in effect enjoying for centuries. The Home Office was not even mentioned in the Act: none of the legislators seems to have considered that any reprieving power was being given to the Home Secretary. The judges were to be the arbiters of life or death: the eighteenth century had come again—only more so.

The Act did not itself refer at all to the Queen or the 'Hanging' Cabinet. Such directness would have been quite at variance with the English zigzag attitude to constitutional development. But it followed as a natural result of the disappearance of the Recorder's Report and the Old Bailey judges' being empowered to record sentence of death that the 'Hanging' Cabinet need no longer meet. And from the date of William IV's death it was never convened again.

This, in turn, had further consequential effects. It meant that the Queen never met with her Councillors to consider the reports and recommendations for reprieve that continued to come in from the judges in the country. The Home Secretary remained the channel whereby such recommendations and reports were submitted to the Sovereign, but it was no longer a question of the monarch announcing her personal decision before her Councillors, arrayed at a formal meeting of the Council. Obviously the young girl was likely to lean heavily upon the advice proffered her by the one Cabinet Minister with whom she came into contact with regard to such cases. And that is exactly what happened.

Furthermore the Sovereign no longer had to sign death-warrants. Until 1837 the monarch had still himself signed the warrant condemning to death any person whose fate had been referred to him by an assize judge or the Recorder of London. This ghoulish act of administration was now removed from the roster of the Queen's duties: the 1837 Act specified that the judgment of the Court should be sufficient warrant for the condemned prisoner's execution.

In later life this was to be one of the few diminutions in royal authority of which the redoubtable Queen approved. Through some quirk it was forgotten to change the law for the Isle of Man as well and for over forty years the oversight remained unnoticed. Then, in the summer of 1872, a murder was committed on the island—it appears to have been the first in Victoria's long reign—and the Queen found herself having to perform the unpleasant duty of signing the warrant for someone's execution. A man had killed his father. "I have had to sign this warrant for the first, and I hope, last time in my life," Victoria confided to her journal. She protested to her Ministers, and in the same year, the law was changed.

At first sight it would seem that the events of 1837 were in no way designed to increase the influence of the Home Secretary or even bring it back to what it had been in Peel's heyday. Indeed, as we have seen, the 1837 Act expressly conferred far-reaching and novel powers upon the judges. But that was not how things worked out in practice.

During the ensuing years the Home Secretary became more and more the effective source of criminal mercy.

Alfred H. Dymond, writing in 1865 about his many efforts to obtain reprieves over the preceding twenty-five years, makes it clear that the Home Secretary had by then acquired a great deal of power, and that a criminal's chance of escaping the gallows depended very much on which particular politician happened to be in charge of the Home Office at the time.

Lord Palmerston, "that most genial and good-natured of ministers", had a method of dealing with such cases that was "generally prompt and decisive"—though he acted perhaps too stringently on the rule that intoxication was no excuse for crime. Spencer Walpole "always exhibited a most earnest desire to act both justly and humanely". Sir James Graham was "the most merciless of Home Secretaries", and aptly dubbed by *Punch* "Justice in Granite". Sir George Grey was far too prone to "weak-minded subjection" to the trial judge.

Yet, despite the personal predilections of individual Home Secretaries, some early basic principles of the exercise of the Royal Prerogative of Mercy were being hammered out.

In 1843 Sir James Graham refused to reprieve Allan Mair, an eighty-four-year-old Scotsman awaiting execution at Stirling for the murder of his wife. In the result Mair died amid appalling scenes. "Oh dinna hurt me, dinna hurt me!" he cried when the hangman pinioned his arms. "I'm auld—I'll make nae resistance!" He was hanged sitting down. Yet less than a decade later Home Secretary Spencer Walpole refused to countenance the hanging of an eighty-three-year-old poisoner, and so established a precedent that was followed within two years by Lord Palmerston and was ever after Home Office policy: a man could be too old to hang.

In 1849, during Sir George Grey's tenure of office, it was established once and for all that a pregnant woman should be reprieved permanently and not merely respited until the termination of her pregnancy. By one of the traditional paradoxes of history Charlotte Harris, whose case established this ruling, was one of the least sympathetic of killers. Finding herself pregnant by another man, she had poisoned her husband's tea, and on the very day that (after her devoted nursing) he was buried she married her lover. At first respited only until after the birth of her child, Mrs Harris was saved by a massive petition signed by some 40,000 women. The principle was thus established, although Parliament did not proclaim it a rule of law that pregnant women should not be hanged until an Act of 1931. For nearly a hundred years the Home Office was more merciful than Parliament.

The year 1849 also saw another principle of mercy established: that no woman should be hanged for the murder of her child if under the age of one. Again the Home Office was in advance of Parliament. It was not until 1922 that the Infanticide Act was passed, making the offence of a mother who kills her newborn child no longer murder but manslaughter.

By the mid-eighteen-fifties two other basic principles of the modern reprieve system seem to have evolved. The case of John Murdock shows that youth alone was already not sufficient to save a man from the gallows, and that a jury's recommendation to mercy was not conclusive: as in the nineteen-sixties, both youth and recommendation were merely circumstances that a Home Secretary took into account.

Murdock was an eighteen-year-old thief who escaped from Hastings gaol, and in a struggle unwittingly killed an elderly gaoler. Captured soon afterwards, he wept when told of the old man's death. The jury at Lewes Assizes added a very strong recommendation to mercy on the ground that he had not intended to kill. But when orders were received for the scaffold to be erected and the hangman to be engaged it became apparent that he was not going to be reprieved. A juror then wrote to the Home Secretary, Sir George Grey:

"Although we returned a verdict of 'Guilty', it was my impression that the extreme sentence of the law would never be enforced. I hear with dismay and sorrow that the execution is appointed for Tuesday next . . . Surely, sir, this is a case where the clemency of the Crown may be permitted to step in and save a fellow creature from a shameful death?"

Grey did not reprieve. But he did something that no modern Home Secretary would do. He instructed his Under-Secretary, Horatio Waddington, to write to the juror and explain his reasons. The letter provides an interesting insight into the reasoning of the Home Office in early Victorian times.

"To have reprieved Murdock [wrote Waddington], would have been to lay down the principle that the penalty of murder should not be inflicted in a case in which the destruction of life is not in itself the sole or even the principal object in contemplation, but where the violence is resorted to, without regard to the consequences, as a means of accomplishing some other unlawful end, such as robbery, rape or escape from prison . . . Cases of this kind, moreover, cannot be considered apart from the bearing they must have on others of a similar nature."

As Judge Buller once told a prisoner: "You are not to be hanged for stealing a horse, but that horses may not be stolen."

The strange thing to understand is why the Home Secretary should by the eighteen-fifties have acquired such an ascendancy over the judges that a definite policy was both discernible and necessary.

The explanation appears to be that "you cannot teach an old dog new tricks". For centuries the judges at the Old Bailey had sentenced nearly every capital prisoner, except murderers, to death, and then left it to the King in Council to decide the person's ultimate fate. By nature conservative and disliking change, they simply went on doing the same thing: only now there was no longer the 'Hanging' Cabinet to decide the ultimate destiny, but a girl Queen acting upon the advice of her responsible Minister. Much the same seems to have been happening with the assize judges in the country. The old practice continued—they occasionally reprieved themselves—but for the most part they recommended mercy to the Sovereign. Those recommendations had to go somewhere. They no longer went to the 'Hanging' Cabinet but to the young Queen, who acted on the Home Secretary's 'advice'. The same applied to reports from assize judges who merely respited condemned prisoners for "the Royal pleasure to be taken", without going so far as positively to recommend mercy. In all these cases the only voice that whispered in the Queen's ear was that of the Home Secretary.

The yardstick of this quiet waning of the judicial reprieving power is the unprotesting silence amid which, in 1861, Parliament —almost as an afterthought—formally abolished it. "This is the way the world ends, This is the way the world ends", wrote T. S. Eliot, "Not with a bang but a whimper."

In 1861 Sir George Cornewall Lewis, during his last months as Home Secretary, presented to Parliament the result of several years' diligent work by Parliamentary Counsel, the backroom lawyers who draft Government Bills. It was the last great batch of nineteenth-century legislation designed to reform the Criminal Law. It removed the death penalty from all offences but four— murder, treason, piracy at sea, and arson in the royal dockyards; it repealed scores of redundant Acts, and tidied the law up to such an extent that much of it has remained untouched to the present day. Sir George told the Commons: "I hope that every possible effort will be made to carry these Bills, for the amendment of the Criminal Law, through the House with as little delay as possible."

The House responded nobly to the call. The Offences against the Persons Bill, the Larceny Bill, the Malicious Injury to Property Bill, the Coinage Offences Bill, the Accessories and Abettors Bill, and the Criminal Statutes Repeal Bill all went through their

Committee stage between 12 noon and 6 p.m. on June 11th, 1861.

The judges' reprieving power was abolished by one short sentence in Section 1 of the Criminal Statutes Repeal Bill, and by naming the 1837 Central Criminal Court Act as one of the 106 repealed statutes in the Bill's voluminous Schedule. Not one single word was spoken in debate by any Member of Parliament or Peer of the Realm as this enactment passed through both Houses of Parliament. Bearing in mind the high number of politicians who were then, as now, barristers, this is either a remarkable tribute by the Bar to the exemplary worth of the Home Office or a typical example of politicians' lack of interest in vital but non-political legislation.

Later, protests were to be made. Alfred Dymond in 1865 dubbed the abolition "an accidental error in an otherwise substantially good and useful reform", and hoped it would soon be rectified. In the following year Sir George Grey, Cornewall Lewis's successor, told the 1866 Royal Commission on Capital Punishment that he thought it had been a mistake. This view was shared by another Home Secretary, Spencer Walpole, and by the judges who gave evidence before the Royal Commission. Indeed, the Commissioners agreed, and recommended in their Report that the judiciary should have restored to them their right of reprieve.

But the die had been cast, the mould set: the Home Secretary alone was to have the power of life or death over persons condemned to execution. The 1861 legislation may have been only a slip. No-one may ever have intended such immense power to be placed in the hands of one man—as Baron Martin said to the Royal Commission, "I think it is a very unfair thing for the Secretary of State to have perpetually put upon him the remission of the punishment of death, nine-tenths of the community do not understand it at all." But in accordance with the traditions of our Constitution such considerations were to prove absolutely irrelevant. The law was not changed: the Home Secretary's position is technically the same now for the three remaining capital offences as that which Parliament enacted in the hot, dusty summer of 1861.

CHAPTER SEVEN

The Home Secretary as Master

(1861–1900)

MUDDLING through is a characteristic of the incompetent and the English. The Home Secretary may have become dispenser of the Crown's mercy largely through chance. But that did not prevent an efficient and reasonably smooth-working system coming into effect.

In 1866 Spencer Walpole, who had been three times Home Secretary, gave this description of Home Office methods to the Royal Commission on Capital Punishment:

"The practice may be stated very shortly . . . to examine the memorial [what we would now call the prisoner's petition], to consult the Judge who had tried the case; to have a report from the Judge of the evidence; to lay before the Judge any new facts or any facts which had been brought under the notice of the Secretary of State and to request from the Judge a report as to his opinion upon that new evidence or upon the matter. Upon all these materials being brought before the Secretary of State he was then in a position, not in the least degree to re-hear the case, but simply to advise the Crown whether there were any circumstances which would justify the exercise of mercy."

Respect was obviously still shown to the views of the trial judge, but even at this early stage his opinion was not regarded so decisive. Although the Home Office "always followed the recommendation of the Judge as respects a mitigation of the sentence" Walpole told the Commissioners that he had himself once run counter to the judge's opinion when it had been against a reprieve. And Sir George Grey, also three times Home Secretary, confessed that he had not always bothered to consult the trial judge.

As for the rôle played by the Permanent Under-Secretary of State, the head of the permanent staff of the Home Office, and its senior civil servants, Walpole said:

"Mr Waddington invariably went through the papers separately from myself. Then I invariably went through them separately from him. I never decided one of those cases without writing down on a slip of paper all the reasons which induced me to arrive at my conclusions. Having done so, I conferred with Mr Waddington and talked the matter over with him in every single instance."

"The determination of these cases imposes a very painful duty on the Secretary of State," Sir George Grey told the Royal Commission, "but the duty must be imposed upon somebody, and if a person assumes that office he must assume it with all its duties and with all its responsibilities. Painful as it is, he cannot shrink from it."

Quickly a working regimen was improvised: as early as 1865 Alfred Dymond was able to refer to the Home Office's "usual stereotyped letter 'regretting the Home Secretary could see no reason to interfere with the course of the law'". But it took some time for the latter-day policy of secrecy to evolve.

In this century, the Home Secretary never usually gave the reasons for his decision—neither to an individual nor to Parliament. The matter was not even debatable in Parliament until after the prisoner had been executed or a reprieve granted. It was a power exercised in secrecy and shadowed in obscurity. There are arguments both for and against this, but it is an historical fact that initially this embargo on publicity was not strictly enforced.

On at least two occasions in the eighteen-fifties and sixties two different Home Secretaries divulged the reasons behind their decisions—once where it had been against a reprieve and once where it had been for it.

The first incident is related by Dymond. He tells how in the winter of 1852-53 he tried to get a reprieve for a burglar called Levi Harwood, who, with three other men, broke into Frimley Parsonage, in Surrey, and attempted to raid the bedroom of the parson and his wife. The Rev. G. W. Hollest was a brave man, and made a show of resistance. One of the ruffians shot him dead, and at their trial one of the accused turned Queen's Evidence with the result that largely thanks to his testimony, Harwood and another defendant were convicted of murder. It was popularly believed that the turncoat had, in fact, been the man who fired the fatal shot, and it seemed to many people wrong that the actual killer should get away scot-free, while his two companions, who were not involved in the shooting, were hanged. So Dymond headed a deputation to the Home Office.

Spencer Walpole, the Home Secretary, not only received the deputation—nowadays they would almost certainly have been entertained by a senior civil servant—but explained to them in

detail why he could not interfere with the normal course of the
law. He explained that, for his part, there was a distinction to
be drawn between persons such as these men, who went to commit a crime armed with lethal weapons, and others who, in a panic,
to avoid arrest or make sure of their escape, pick up the nearest
thing to hand and kill someone with it. "If", said Walpole, "one
of these men had seized the poker and dealt a fatal blow, I
might then be disposed to interfere. But here is the obvious preparation to commit murder, if that be necessary, for the accom-
plishment of their purpose." Dymond confessed that the distinction seemed "very fair", and the two men were duly hanged.

The second incident occurred in the summer of 1861, and
shows the Home Secretary, if one is brought up on a diet solely of
abolitionist "histories", in the unusual rôle of defending against the
angered gentry his decision to reprieve a poacher who had shot
and killed a policeman.

There was no doubt as to the man's guilt. Returning from a
successful night's forage, Thomas Richardson walked straight into
P.C. M'Brian. "What have you there?" asked the constable, and
received as reply a shot from one of the barrels of Richardson's
gun. Terrified, the poacher dropped his weapon—the other barrel
still loaded—and ran. It took the policeman two weeks to die,
and when he did Richardson was charged with his murder. The
local landowners regarded it as very salutary when the judge at
Lincoln Winter Assizes sentenced the poacher to death.

Then came news of his reprieve: instead of hanging he was to
serve the newfangled sentence of penal servitude for life; penal
servitude being introduced round about this time, as transportation, owing to the colonists' increasing objections, had ceased
to be a practical alternative. Private overtures seem to have been
made to the trial judge to ask why he had been party to such a decision. His answer was quite simple: he had never been asked.

The result: Banks Stanhope, a Lincolnshire M.P., rose in the
House of Commons on June 20th, 1861, and asked the Home
Secretary whether it was true that Richardson had been reprieved
without consulting the judge, and, furthermore, whether it was also
true that the Chief Constable of the County had warned the Minister of the dangers of his decision and of the probability of future
attacks on the police. Obviously there had been considerable dis-
approval in certain quarters in Lincolnshire.

The reply of Sir George Cornewall Lewis, then Home Secretary,
is interesting. He said that it was much to be deprecated that his
decision should be made the subject of discussion in the House.
But that did not stop him giving his reasons: "It was clear that it

was not a case of premeditation, and it was doubtful whether the person who fired the gun intended the fatal effects." His allusion to the judge was both curt and significant: "There was no dispute as to the facts of the case and, therefore, no necessity for any reference to the judge."

For over twenty years the Home Office maintained this ambivalent attitude to public knowledge of their affairs. They did not like disclosing what went on, but sometimes a chink in the curtains would appear.

Then occurred the case which Mr R. A. (now Lord) Butler told the Commons in February 1961 was the first he had been able to trace in which a Home Secretary was asked to give information to Parliament before a reprieve had been granted or the death sentence carried out. He refused—and thereby established a precedent. The case concerned a man named Israel Lipski.

Lipski was a young foreigner living in a sordid lodging-house in the East End of London. A slight, cowed little man, with a straggly moustache and unshaven chin, he was a refugee from the Polish pogroms—poor, struggling, and lonely. One morning he was found in a girl's bedroom. But he was still lonely. She was dead, and he lay unconscious: strange noises came from his throat and an acrid smell from both their mouths.

The explanation was bizarre—acid had been poured down their throats. Lipski survived, but the girl had suffocated herself in her paroxysms.

Lipski's story was that he had been passing by the girl's room— they lived in the same house—and had heard cries for help. He had rushed in and found two men assaulting her. One of them struck him to the floor and held him there while the other poured acid down his throat. Coughing and spluttering on the ground, he then saw them pour acid down the girl's throat and make off with her few pounds' savings, which they found in a box under her bed.

It sounded wildly improbable, but it also seemed incredible that anyone would swallow acid to bolster up a shaky defence, even on a charge of murder. After Lipski had been convicted and sentenced to death at the Old Bailey on July 30th, 1887, a great public outcry for a reprieve swelled. The London newspapers took up the story. Appeals were made for anyone who might have seen the true murderers to come forward. The condemned man's solicitor delivered a fully detailed petition to the Home Office. Rumours were so frenzied that the trial judge, Mr Justice Stephen, had to issue a formal denial to the Press that he was anything but in complete agreement with the Home Secretary in his attitude to the case.

What was that attitude? Henry Mathews was not the greatest

Home Secretary of all time. Two years later his handling of the
Mrs Maybrick Case was to ensure him a certain historical notoriety, and he now displayed to the full his capacity for weakness
and vacillation. Two days after it was announced that he would
not advise the Queen to interfere with the due course of law and
on the eve of the proposed execution he relented and granted
Lipski a week's respite. "The convict must clearly understand that
unless these inquiries put a new aspect upon the case, the sentence will be carried into effect," he wrote to the governor of Newgate Prison.

It was on the afternoon of August 12th, 1887, the day that
Mathews first said there would be no reprieve—but before the
official announcement—that Cunningham Graham, an indefatigable parliamentary questioner, rose in his place in the House of
Commons and asked the Home Secretary: "Whether representations have been made to him concerning the case of Israel
Lipski, now lying under sentence of death; and whether he could
hold out any hope of a reprieve."

Mathew's answer probably seemed at the time yet another exercise in ministerial stone-walling. Yet over the years it became
near-sanctified as the Home Secretary's Declaration of Independence of parliamentary interference. It deserves to be quoted in
full:

"I must begin by saying [stated Mathews] that I think it highly
inexpedient and injurious to the administration of justice that
the circumstances of a criminal case, on which the exercise of
the Prerogative of Mercy depends, should be made the subject
of discussion in this House. The case of Israel Lipski has been
for some days under my earnest consideration, and the advice
I tender to Her Majesty will be made known in due time in the
normal manner."

No subsequent Home Secretary ever retreated from this position,
though it was not until 1920 that it received the formal support of
a ruling by the Speaker of the House of Commons.

As for Lipski, the excitement mounted as the days of his one
week's extra life were flicked from the calendar. It was reported in
the Press that his solicitor had collected the exhibits in the case
from the Home Office and was subjecting them to further scientific
study, and that various new witnesses had come forward. But on the
afternoon of Saturday, August 20th, 1887, after a long, anxious
conference at the Home Office, which was attended, among
others, by Mr Justice Stephen, it was announced that no further
respites would be granted: Lipski would be executed the following Monday.

No-one knew why the decision was taken. No-one knew what were the 'inquiries' Mathews had mentioned in his letter a week earlier informing the Prison Governor of the respite. The drums began to roll for Mathews. As Sir Edward Troup says, "A storm of protest was raised which would almost certainly have driven him from office."

What saved the Home Secretary? The fact that on Sunday, August 21st, Lipski confessed!

In answer to the entreaties of a rabbi he broke down and made this statement. "I, Israel Lipski, before I appear before God in judgment desire to speak the whole truth concerning the crime of which I am accused. I will not die with a lie on my lips. I will not let others suffer, even on suspicion, for my sin. I alone was guilty of the murder of Muriel Angello." He had entered her room to see if there was anything he could steal. He thought she was out. But she was still asleep, stirred, woke—and he panicked. He hit her, and she fell back unconscious. He had bought some acid only that morning to kill himself. On an impulse he poured some down the girl's throat, and then the rest down his own. He had wanted to die.

At eight o'clock on the morning of Monday, August 22nd, after considerable, avoidable delay, his wish was granted.

Just over a week later Rabbi Singer, in a letter to *The Times* provided an intriguing epilogue to the story. He revealed that on Sunday, August 14th, when Lipski thought he was going to die the following day he promised to tell him "the whole truth", provided he withheld it till after his death. The rabbi agreed, called for pen, ink, and paper—and then the respite arrived. "No", said Lipski; he refused to carry on with his confession. It was only one week later, when he knew there was no hope of survival, that he broke silence.

Mathew's successor at the Home Office was a doughty, bearded Liberal politician called Sir William Harcourt, whom Lord Chuter-Ede, himself an ex-Home Secretary of considerable distinction, has described to me as "the greatest Home Secretary this country has ever had".

Writing in 1886 to Queen Victoria (with whom he had had some minor disagreements), Harcourt set out the three main principles which he said guided him in advising her on the exercise of her Royal Prerogative of Mercy.

The first was *compassion*. He illustrated this by the story of a girl who had killed her own baby and "was very young; her seducer had gone abroad; her mother had turned her out of doors; she loved her child and except for the bread and water that she ate and drank gave all her money for her."

The second was *a possibility of an unjust conviction*:

"Only a few weeks ago on the careful study of the case of two
men sentenced to death Sir William, on a careful consideration,
conceived that there was so much doubt about the case that
he respited the prisoners for a week in order to enable an
inquiry to be held. The result of the inquiry was to prove the
innocence of one of the prisoners on the confession of the
other man sentenced with him. Your Majesty will sympathize in
the feeling of relief which Sir William felt in having been the
means of rescuing an innocent man from a terrible and un-
deserved fate."

The third governing principle was that *mercy should be shown
where there was no intention to kill.* Two years earlier he had discussed at great length with the judges a Bill to classify murders
on the basis of intentional (capital) and unintentional (non-capital): "But on mature consideration Sir William found that there
was so much difficulty in obtaining an accurate definition . . .
that he thought it more prudent to abandon the attempt and
leave the principle to be applied by the Secretary of State in each
particular case, as it now is."

Harcourt concluded that "he endeavours to act so that all the
world should feel that no man is spared who ought to be hanged,
and no man is hanged who ought to have been spared."

This man was the one great politician at the Home Office whose
influence bridged the gap between the nineteenth and twentieth
centuries. It persisted until the effective end of hanging.

In April 1907 Mr Secretary Herbert Gladstone repeated to the
House of Commons words first uttered by Harcourt in Parliament
in the mid-eighteen-eighties:

"The exercise of the Prerogative of Mercy does not depend on
principles of strict law or justice, still less does it depend on
sentiment in any way. It is a question of policy and judgment
in each case, and in my opinion a capital execution which in its
circumstances creates horror and compassion for the culprit
rather than a sense of indignation at his crime in a great evil."

In 1949 Sir Frank Newsam, then Permanent Under-Secretary of
State at the Home Office, told the Royal Commission on Capital
Punishment that the Home Office still stood by this statement,
and in August 1961 Sir Charles Cunningham, the present Permanent Under-Secretary, told me in his room at the Home Office that
it yet applied in the nineteen-sixties.

But principles and statements are but words. How were they
applied in practice in the twentieth century?

CHAPTER EIGHT

The Home Office in the Twentieth Century

(1900–1957)

To look at, there is nothing twentieth-century about the Home Office. Admittedly at the time of writing it is housed in the group of buildings known as the 'New Public Offices', which flank one side of Whitehall, from Parliament Square to the Cenotaph. But 'New' is a relative term. The buildings were designed by the Victorian architect Sir George Gilbert Scott: they were erected in the eighteen-seventies, and at the moment are threatened with demolition.

The Home Office is a staunchly Victorian edifice, little changed by time. Harcourt could still find his way easily to the Home Secretary's large, lofty room on the first floor, overlooking a somewhat dank, secluded inner courtyard. When Sir Charles Cunningham showed me over it I almost felt he should have been wearing mutton-chop whiskers and stove-pipe trousers rather than a well-cut, modern suit.

The architectural Victorianism of the building is reflected in the image that many people have of the persons who work inside it.

"The intense conservatism of the Home Office has trapped nearly every would-be reforming Home Secretary," comments Anthony Sampson in his *Anatomy of Britain Today*. The Department has acquired an aura of being a power unto itself, a true stronghold of the Establishment, holding out as long as it can against every change. "From its early days the Home Office has been a fashionable department and a powerful one," writes Civil Service historian G. A. Campbell. "When in 1870 recruitment by open competition to posts in the Civil Service became general, the Home Secretary of the time succeeded in excluding the Home Office from the new arrangements and for many years its administrative staff continued to be recruited by nomination and to be paid on a scale higher than that in most other public offices."

The official language of the Department is not of this century. If a Permanent Under-Secretary wished to announce the refusal

E

of a reprieve he used a basic formula which was already existing in the mid-eighteen-sixties—namely, "the Home Secretary regrets that he can see no reason to interfere with the course of the law." If he wanted a doctor to examine a condemned prisoner he wrote telling him that the Secretary of State "would be grateful" if he would be "good enough" to undertake the inquiry. Even the Department's statutory rules governing executions are almost Victorian museum-pieces: dated June 5th, 1902, they were last printed so long ago that in 1963 no fresh copies were available at HM Stationery Office, and I had to pay an extra shilling to obtain an official photostat of one of the few surviving originals. They are not even accurate any more: they stipulate that the prison bell shall be tolled for fifteen minutes after an execution—a practice which was discontinued in the nineteen-twenties.

Aloof, hidebound, ultra-conservative, the Department does not have a very lovable *persona*. But the officials have only themselves to blame. Their public utterances nearly always seem designed to preserve the impression of undisturbed continuity. Nothing changes. Policy is immutable. The true principles of conduct were worked out long ago: all we need do now is follow precedent. In the magisterial words of Sir John Anderson, one of the most powerful of modern Permanent Under-Secretaries: "The accumulated wisdom of a long succession of Home Secretaries is not something to be lightly disregarded."

In 1949, after an abortive parliamentary attempt to suspend capital punishment, and the appointment of a Royal Commission (the 'Gowers Commission') to consider the future of the penalty, the Department had a unique opportunity to present its record to the public. But the senior officials who gave evidence before Sir Ernest Gowers and his colleagues were determined to maintain this façade of timelessness and changelessness. They claimed that over the first fifty years of this century the proportion of reprieves had "tended to remain constant over the whole period." Yet this simply was not true. As the Commission duly reported on the basis of the officials' own statistics, there had been an "increase in the percentage of commutations", which "may possibly reflect some change in the practice of the Home Office". Furthermore, the Commissioners added, "there had been an increased tendency to leniency on the part of the Home Office."

Few abolitionists would have agreed with this assessment. "The Home Secretary is only responsible to God; but he has certain responsibilities towards the Police Force he represents; and to his political party and to his future career," wrote Arthur Koestler in his *Reflections on Hanging* in 1956. Yet on the other side of the

fence the very same Department was being attacked by the viru-
lently pro-hangers: "The trouble is that the Home Office jumped
at every chance to let a man off," a retired judge has said to me
of his years on the Bench in the nineteen-forties and fifties. The
result of the Home Office refusal to reveal the reasons for any
individual reprieve decision—"they are regarded as confidential
and never disclosed," said the Gowers Commission—was that
the public was starved of information on which they could make
an objective assessment. "What did you think of this abuse from
both sides?" I once asked a retired, senior Home Office official:
he just shrugged his shoulders.

The shrug may have shown commendable stoicism. But it was typical of an attitude which forced the public to reply on the Department's own apparent estimate of itself, its own consciously pro-
jected image—stolid, unmoved, and unmovable.

In fact, this was an increasingly false picture. Perhaps in the first
two or three decades of the century the Home Office was far from
forward-looking. But from about 1930 onward the crust began to
break, and the Department ceased increasingly to be as dead,
as hidebound, as remote as its own advocates would have had us
believe. Inside the gloomy offices of their Victorian morgue—to
use Anthony Sampson's striking phrase—the permanent officials
and the changing politicians changed substantially both the manner and the spirit in which they considered capital cases. By the
nineteen-fifties the old lady may still have worn a crinoline, but
underneath she sported a modern petticoat.

In truth, this gradual change of costume began as far back as
1907. Up till then the Home Secretary, although ostensibly only
exercising the Prerogative of Mercy, in practice did considerably
more. He not only decided whether mercy should stay the law's
hand, but whether it had landed on the right person in the first
place. Although a man could take a piffling debt to appeal in a
civil case, there was no criminal appeal court: in the great majority of cases the Home Secretary was the only person who could
decide whether a criminal judge or jury had erred.

The result was that the Home Secretary became, in effect, a
court of appeal. Condemned prisoners not only pleaded with him
for mercy, they asked him to say that they were innocent. If a
judge had misdirected a jury, or evidence had been wrongly admitted, or fresh facts had come to light, or some impropriety
had occurred during the trial, there was no-one to turn to—except
the Home Secretary.

Without any of the ordinary powers of a court of law the Department had reluctantly to do the work of a court of law. And it did not always do it very well.

In the notorious case of Adolf Beck in the early nineteen-hundreds the Home Office failed, despite sixteen petitions by the hapless Beck—twice convicted of theft and petty fraud—to follow up a clue which would have proved his complete innocence. The consequent furore, fanned by the Oscar Slater case in Scotland, eventually forced Parliament to set up a criminal appeal court, which Sir William Harcourt had been advocating as far back as 1878. Later Sir Edward Troup, newly appointed Permanent Under-Secretary at the Home Office commented, "Happily, by the passing of the Criminal Appeal Act, the Home Secretary was once for all relieved of a responsibility which ought not to have belonged to him."

Much of the criticism to which the Home Office has since been subjected overlooks the vital significance of the establishment of this court. As Troup himself wrote in 1925: "The decision whether a convicted person is guilty or innocent no longer rests with the Home Secretary." The Department has continued to pay lip-service to the theory that the Home Secretary always reprieves if there is a "scintilla of doubt" as to guilt, and we will discuss later how effectively it has done so; but if words mean anything at all Parliament in the 1907 Act was clearly telling the Home Office: "Compassion for the guilty is your proper concern. Whether they *are* guilty is a matter for the courts." With the appointment of a competent appeal court it ceased to be the Home Secretary's task to detect judicial error.

As Henry Brooke, when Home Secretary, told a meeting of magistrates as recently as October 1963: "It is not the Home Secretary's function to re-try cases. It is not his function to act as if he were a court of appeal. It is not his function to consider whether a court reached the right decision on the facts before it.

"In these matters the Home Secretary is not some sort of umpire. He is much more like a long-stop. The essence of the Prerogative is that it provides a means of considering matters which the courts have not been able, or free, to consider."

There also occurred in 1907 the case of Horace George Rayner, which, like the setting up of the Court of Criminal Appeal, has had a considerable, though almost unknown, effect on the modern reprieve system. It was the last time that a monarch forcibly objected to a reprieve decision taken by the Home Secretary.

Rayner's story was like something out of the Victorian melodrama *East Lynne*. A sallow-faced young man, he strode into

Whiteley's department store, in London, on January 24th, 1907, and demanded to see William Whiteley, the proprietor.

He claimed to be the bearded tradesman's illegitimate son, pleading with him for money, because he was out of work and his wife was pregnant. But Whiteley, a canting hypocrite of a man, who combined Bible-readings with a shrewd commercial instinct and a penchant for womanizing, brusquely told him that the Salvation Army existed for such purposes.

"Then you are a dead man, Mr Whiteley!" cried Rayner, and shot him dead. He then turned his gun on himself and fired again.

He meant to die, but his hand was too shaky. Two months later, his right eye shot away, he stumbled into the dock at the Old Bailey. He was obviously still in great pain, and as he told his sordid tale of Whiteley's 'friendship' with his mother, a former shopgirl, many in court felt sorry for him. Besides, he was such a good-looking young man.

He swore that the killing was unintentional: he had only brought the gun to threaten suicide if his 'father' rejected him. But he lost all control—"my head was in a state of blankness"—and he could not even remember firing the fatal shot. Unfortunately for him, a note was found in his jacket-pocket which read: "William Whiteley is my father. He has brought upon himself and me a double fatality by reason of his own refusal of a request perfectly reasonable. R.I.P." The killing could only have been premeditated. Prosecuting counsel did not even bother to cross-examine: the youth's guilt was obvious.

A desperate defence of temporary insanity was raised by defence counsel, but there was little medical evidence to support it. The jury took exactly ten minutes to find the prisoner guilty. They did not recommend mercy, and Lord Alverstone, the Lord Chief Justice told him that he could not expect any. "I cannot hold out to you the slightest hope that the sentence of the law will not be carried into effect," he said.

But his Lordship was not reckoning with the power of the Press. Ever since Whiteley's death the newspapers had been full of revelations about his liaisons with his employees and ex-employees. No-one will ever know for sure whether Horace Rayner really was his son, but it was beyond doubt—and plastered all over the journals—that his mother had been Whiteley's mistress. The more the public realized what a canting humbug Whiteley had been the greater grew the sympathy for his murderer.

By the Saturday after his conviction 179,000 people had signed a highly publicized petition for his reprieve. It was a fantastic number: Rayner's solicitor had suspended all other work and opened special offices to cope with the crowds. The following Monday he was due to present the petition personally at the Home Office.

Then, on Sunday, came the startling announcement: "In view of all the circumstances" the Home Secretary had advised the King to respite the sentence with a view to commuting it to penal servitude for life. The solicitor was bewildered: "Such prompt action comes as somewhat of a surprise," he admitted to a *Times* reporter. Obviously he had attached greater weight to Lord Alverstone's views than the Home Secretary had done.

At this stage the King stepped in. He too was amazed at the development—but horrified. He did not deny that he had to confirm the decision, and no inkling of his distaste leaked out to the general public. But he dictated this private protest to Herbert Gladstone, then Home Secretary:

"The King has signed the Pardon which as a Constitutional Sovereign, he is bound to do, but H.M. would prefer not to express any opinion on the reasons which have led to its adoption . . . The murder of Mr Whiteley appeared to be a very cold-blooded one, incident on a failure to obtain blackmail, and this circumstance seems to have been somewhat lost sight of in the agitation which has taken place. The King is entirely averse to any form of punishment which errs on the side of severity, but he feels that as long as capital punishment is laid down as the penalty for murder, the commutation of that punishment should be based on legal or moral grounds, and that the tendency nowadays to regard a criminal as a martyr, and to raise an agitation on sentimental grounds in order to put pressure on the Home Secretary, is one which may eventually prove very inconvenient, if concessions are too readily made."

Gladstone replied courteously, but he remained firm in his decision. Edward was not satisfied. On April 17th, nineteen days after the reprieve had been announced, he still felt sufficiently angered to dictate a second letter to the errant Minister:

"The King fully realizes that the grave responsibility that rests with you as Home Secretary must be a matter of the greatest difficulty, but in this case His Majesty cannot help feeling that you have been actuated by sentiment. The King entirely concurs with the views expressed by the Lord Chief Justice and considers he puts the case very forcibly from the legal point of view. [Obviously Alverstone had urged upon Gladstone in privacy the same view as he had proclaimed in court.] His Majesty does not attach much importance to the letters and petitions in favour of the prisoner. They are usually the outcome of agitations organized by the halfpenny press, which invariably takes the part of the criminal. The point to be considered is the effect that such a reprieve will have generally, and this the King fears will not be for the best.

"As however the matter has already been decided, His Majesty has no wish to re-open the question, but desires me once more to thank you for having so fully replied to the observation he made on the subject."

And that was the end of it. But the incident had three epilogues, none lacking in irony.

First, Horace Rayner did not want to be reprieved. "Thank God, for my poor wife's sake," he told the prison governor. "So far as I am personally concerned, I would have preferred to get the whole business over and done with instead of having to endure years of misery behind iron bars." Six months later he tried to commit suicide by opening an artery in his wrist, and the following year he was given a spell of solitary confinement for setting fire to his prison bedding. Eventually he served twelve years in gaol.

Second, it was in answer to a question in the House of Commons about why he reprieved Rayner that Gladstone—at the very moment that he was still struggling privately with the King—made his classic, much-quoted pronouncement about its being "neither desirable nor possible to lay down hard and fast rules as to the exercise of the Prerogative of Mercy, etc."

Third, and perhaps most ironic of all, Gladstone's biographer later wrote: "Towards the end of his life Gladstone was prepared to admit that the King might possibly have been right."

Nevertheless, the lesson was learned at the Palace. Edward VII never again interfered in such matters, and his son George V, throughout his long reign from 1910 to 1936, was careful to preserve the strict constitutional proprieties. J. R. Clynes's guarded comment on his dealings with the King during his two years as Home Secretary, from 1929 to 1931, reveals George V as playing no very positive part in questions of reprieve: "He considered his prerogative of royal clemency in murder cases as something of much more responsibility and importance than a mere casual signature on whatever dotted line was indicated by his advisers."

Similarly, George VI appears never to have 'intervened' in any real sense of the word. Lord Chuter-Ede, who was Home Secretary for six years during his reign, has told me that he never had any difficulty with the King, and that there was never any dispute between them on any question relating to the Prerogative of Mercy. The late Lord Morrison of Lambeth, also one of his ex-Home-Secretaries, has written that twice George VI raised capital sentences with him in audience—"but he accepted the proposition that his ministers had the last word."

As for the present Queen, "she was never brought into it," said an informed source. "She was never consulted in advance. If no reprieve was decided on, the papers did not even go to her."

Before a prisoner was told he was reprieved, the Queen would normally be informed and her formal consent obtained: after all, it was her prerogative that was being exercised. But information and formal consent were not the same as consultation. Appeals for clemency sent to Buckingham Palace were remitted as a matter of course to the Home Office. Thus, the Sovereign was effectively removed from the controversy that inevitably surrounded the application of the death penalty: as Lord Chuter-Ede comments, "No-one says that George VI hanged Timothy John Evans—they say I did!"

For over twenty years after the setting up of the Court of Criminal Appeal and Rayner's Case nothing very much happened to alter the steady, routine running of the reprieve system. Admittedly the immediate result of the new appeal court was that the percentage of reprieves dropped. But this was only to be expected: because of the existence of the new court, the Home Secretary no longer had to reprieve prisoners whose trials had been unsatisfactory or whose guilt had been inadequately proved.

The tenor of the Department in these two decades was captured by Asquith when he said to Sir John Simon upon his appointment as Home Secretary, in May 1915: "Your main job is to prevent second-class rows from becoming first-class rows."

There were various, minor developments. In 1908 Parliament abolished the death sentence for youths under sixteen (later raised to a minimum age of eighteen); from 1907 to 1922—some sixteen years—no woman was hanged, every female murderer being reprieved; in 1922 mothers who killed their newborn children were taken out of the category of murderers altogether by an Act which created the new offence of infanticide, but anyway such women had not in practice been hanged for nearly a century; in 1922 also the principle of not hanging a madman was reaffirmed in the case of Ronald True. But, in the main, the Home Office just plodded on along its well-worn path.

Even the coming of the first abolitionist Home Secretary, J. R. Clynes, in the Labour Government of 1929 did not substantially affect the quiet humdrum of the Department's routine. Clynes, an ex-mill-worker, who never quite recovered from his sense of wonder at being one of His Majesty's principal Secretaries of State, was only too anxious to prove his 'sense of responsibility' by tampering as little as possible with the tradition of the Home Office.

But with the advent of the nineteen-thirties a new mood began to be felt within the Department. Outwardly, as ever, nothing changed. Indeed, in 1930 a parliamentary committee's recommendation that the death penalty should be suspended for a trial period of five years was effectively defeated by the Conservative Members of the committee refusing to sign the report and the National Government's subsequent failure to bring in any amending legislation. Ostensibly the law continued as before.

Yet statistics reveal that in the nineteen-thirties the percentage of reprieves went up from 38.9 in the previous ten years to the remarkably high figure of 53.3. By the end of the decade more murderers were being reprieved than hanged. And even throughout the Second World War and immediate post-war years, when violence was at a premium and the number of murders increased, the proportion of reprieves continued at roughly the same level. So that by 1949 nearly half (48.5 per cent) of all murderers were being reprieved. "I think too many people are being reprieved," Lord Goddard, then Lord Chief Justice, told the Gowers Commission in the early nineteen-fifties. "I think the tendency has been of recent years to reprieve much more freely than used to be the case."

How had this come about? How was it possible, particularly in the light of the Home Office's assertion to the same Commission that there was a uniform "practice followed by successive Home Secretaries?" How could the unchanging change?

The answer comes from an unexpected, though uniquely authoritative, source: the late Sir Alexander Maxwell, a Cornishman with a Scottish name, who was from 1932 to 1938 Deputy Under-Secretary of State at the Home Office, and from 1938 to 1948 Permanent Under-Secretary of State. Shortly before his death in 1964 Sir Alexander told me: "The principles on which the Prerogative of Mercy is now exercised are the same as in the early part of the century. But the application has changed. With the greater preponderance of abolitionist views it has become more lenient."

Viewed objectively—and without saying whether it is a good or a bad thing—it is obvious that the twentieth century is the Century of Abolition. Whether or not capital punishment continues to exist when this book is published it is clearly on the run. The basic trend of the last thirty years has been against hanging. In the same way as Edward VII (when Prince of Wales) was not entirely jesting when he told bewildered dinner guests at a Guildhall banquet in 1895, "We're all Socialists now!" so one could say with considerable justification "We're all abolitionists now!" *Complete* abolitionists may perhaps still be limited in number, but we are all abolitionists to a certain extent: Lord Goddard, pilloried by the militants as an arch-reactionary, told the Gower Commission that there were cases where killers had been reprieved "and it would have been better if they had not been sentenced to death."

Home Secretaries and Home Office officials do not work in a vacuum: the air on the north side of Whitehall is not rarified. They breathe in the spirit of the times, as we all do. And they are affected by it.

The more strident abolitionists seem to think that the Department is peopled to a man with personal representatives of the Devil, determined to send the maximum number of victims to the gallows: "But surely if you're right, the Home Office crowd must be the most heartless, cynical group of people!" I have said to a most eminent and vociferous abolitionist. He smiled, shrugged his shoulders, and replied: "Don't quote me!"

The truth is that several Home Secretaries in recent years have been abolitionists. Apart from J. R. Clynes, Sir Samuel Hoare (1937-39) and Lord Chuter-Ede (1945-51), one of the most able of modern Home Secretaries, made no secret of the fact that they were opposed in principle to capital punishment. And Lord Tenby (1954-57), one of the most controversial of modern Home Secretaries, who refused to save Ruth Ellis, the last Englishwoman to be hanged, has told me: "I'd rather have reprieved everyone if I could, but I had to administer the Law of England."

Furthermore, the people who actually administered the system were themselves often abolitionists or inclined, on balance, to favour that view. "Personally I don't believe in capital punishment," said Professor Desmond Curran, a psychiatrist who since 1938 has carried out more than sixty medical inquiries for the Home Office into the mental health of condemned murderers. "Basically I'm an abolitionist, which may seem odd," said Dr Donald Teare, who has probably carried out as many post-mortems on murderers' victims and executed murderers as any other living pathologist. And perhaps most surprising of all: "I never could see the point of hanging. I couldn't see what good it did," the late Sir Alexander Maxwell told me.

Of course, not everyone at the Home Office during the last few decades has been so minded. At a pretty shrewd guess one could say that the overwhelming majority of politicians and civil servants who have worked in the Department during this century have been in favour of capital punishment as the ultimate deterrent to murder and the only suitable penalty for so heinous a crime. But this does *not* mean that they have failed to contribute to the humanizing of the reprieve system over recent years.

For instance, consider the case of the late Sir Frank Newsam. Succeeding Sir Alexander Maxwell as Permanent Under-Secretary of State in 1948, he held that office for nine turbulent years, right through the many storms and vicissitudes that eventually culminated in the Homicide Act of 1957 and the restriction of capital punishment to only six grades of murder. It is no secret that Newsam was a retentionist, believing firmly in the efficacy of the death penalty. Indeed, he was personally most unpopular with abolitionists: gruff and sharp-tempered by nature, he was generally considered an inhuman and unpleasant man, veering too much on the side of harshness and reaction.

Yet I can reveal that it was Newsam who was responsible for possibly the most important—and progressive—change in Home Office internal practice since the end of the Second World War.

Until Newsam took over as head of the permanent staff of the Department murderers who might be mentally abnormal were treated strictly in accordance with the antiquated basis of the Criminal Lunatics Act of 1884. In other words, if it was thought that a condemned prisoner was insane the Home Secretary appointed an inquiry of two or more doctors—in practice, usually three—to inquire into his sanity. If they then certified that the prisoner was insane he was reprieved and sent to Broadmoor.

Lord Chuter-Ede, when appointed Home Secretary in 1945, had partly improved this procedure by ending the practice of appointing the same doctors always to carry out the inquiry. Instead he set up a panel of psychiatrists of varying experience and qualifications, whose different members would be called upon in turn to advise on the different cases, thus ensuring greater flexibility. Even so, the system remained unsatisfactory for the reason that it did not go far enough.

It applied only to cases of full insanity, and this was inadequate. Only a minority of murderers are certifiably insane, but, as the Home Office Research Unit has reported, "The majority of murderers are mentally disturbed in some way." This means that throughout the first half of this century persons were being hanged who might well have been reprieved on medical grounds if only the doctors had been able to examine their mental condition. Newsam—the so-called ogre—thought this wrong, and directed that in future if there were any grounds for suspecting any kind of mental abnormality, even though it might not amount to insanity, a medical inquiry should still be held 'informally' and outside the provisions of the Act. In such a case it was unlikely that the doctors would certify insanity, but they would be free to state whether there were any medical reasons for recommending the Home Secretary to grant a reprieve. The Home Secretary retained a discretion whether or not to accept such a recommendation, but a psychiatrist who has sat on many such inquiries assures me that he does not know of a single case where a Minister has failed to follow the doctors' lead. As Sir Samuel Hoare (later Lord Templewood) has written of the old-type statutory inquiries: "Upon the issue of mental responsibility, I had no other course than to accept the medical opinion that was available to me."

Newsam's broadening of the scope of these medical inquiries undoubtedly led to the reprieve of persons who would otherwise have been hanged.

In April 1948 the House of Commons, on a free vote, passed a clause, introduced by Mr Sydney Silverman, M.P., into the Government's Criminal Justice Bill then going through the House, suspending the death penalty for an experimental five-year period. Lord Chuter-Ede, then Home Secretary (who had spoken against the clause in the debate), thereupon immediately announced that he would automatically reprieve all prisoners sentenced to death in the courts, until the future of the clause was finally resolved. At the time Lord Goddard criticized this action as amounting, he said, to an abuse of the Executive's dispensing powers that William III had expressly renounced in the Bill of Rights. However, the Home Secretary remained undeterred by this somewhat academic attack, and continued to reprieve automatically every convicted murderer, including Donald Thomas, who had shot dead a policeman on duty and would otherwise certainly have been hanged, until eventually the House of Lords crystallized the issue by rejecting the clause and defeating all attempts at a compromise measure.

However, one result of the agitation was the Government's appointment of the Gowers Commission to inquire into the question: "Whether capital punishment for murder should be limited or modified and, if so, to what extent and by what means."

The Commission held 63 meetings, heard evidence from a total of 215 witnesses in this country and abroad, and took four years to bring out, in September 1953, a monumental report, which is still a standard work of reference.

In this document the Commission recommended several changes in Home Office and prison practice which would profoundly affect the reprieve system.

So far as the prisoner himself was concerned, the Commission recommended brighter furniture in the condemned cell, brighter lighting, improved facilities for exercise, wireless-sets and the provision of a greater variety of games. They also recommended the cessation of the practice whereby (if not reprieved) the prisoner's body hung on the rope for an hour after execution: it should be removed as soon as the prison medical officer certified that life was extinct, they said. It is typical of the Home Office and the Prison Commissioners (now merged with their parent office as the Prison Department) that neither made public whether or not these eminently humane recommendations were implemented. In fact, "they have all been accepted and acted upon," Mr J. W. Holt, one-time Director of Prison Administration, has told me.

Even more important, and in keeping with the trend to attach greater significance to the mental condition of the accused, the Commission recommended that there should be a fundamental change in the medical handling of all persons charged with murder.

At the date of the Report every prisoner on a murder charge was medically examined as soon as he arrived in prison pending his trial. He was detained in the prison hospital and kept under continuous observation by a hospital officer, who reported regularly on his behaviour. The prison doctor also saw him every day and compiled a case-history. And (at least since 1949) if the prisoner consented he was subjected to an electro-encelphalographic (EEG) examination to see if there was any evidence of epilepsy or other functional disorder of the brain.

Furthermore, any outside doctor nominated by the defence was given full facilities to examine the prisoner and advise his lawyers accordingly.

In due course the prison doctor submitted a detailed report on the prisoner's mental and physical state to the Director of Public Prosecutions, and a copy was also given to the defence and the Court.

It seems pretty comprehensive, but, in fact, the system was woefully inadequate. The prison doctor was the *only* doctor appointed by the State to inquire into the prisoner's medical condition on behalf of the prosecution, and most prison doctors at that time had no qualifications whatsoever in psychiatry: some were not even full-time members of the prison medical service. One would have thought that if the State wished to have a truly reliable report on a prisoner's mental condition an experienced, full-time psychiatrist would at least have been one of the people to examine him.

This was the view of the Gowers Commission, and they recommended that every future prisoner charged with murder in England and Wales should be specially examined as to his state of mind on behalf of the prosecution by two doctors, of whom at least one should be a psychiatrist of standing, who was not a member of the prison medical service, and the other usually an experienced member of that service.

As was perhaps only to be expected, neither the Home Office nor the Prison Commissioners ever made any formal, public announcement of whether this vital recommendation was accepted. But it was. The information slipped out seven years later, almost in passing, in the course of a Home Office written reply to a routine parliamentary question, in December 1960. It is not possible to give the exact date when the change was made, but it was probably decided sometime in the mid-nineteen-fifties.

At first sight this may not seem an important development: in fact, it transformed the whole application of the reprieve system. Now everyone in authority in a case knew from the start whether there existed any possible question of mental abnormality such as might affect the jury's verdict or if the prisoner was convicted justify a reprieve. Inevitably this new pre-trial psychiatric examination reduced the scope of the old post-trial Home Office medical inquiry: if the earlier examination revealed no likelihood of mental abnormality it was highly improbable that a post-trial examination would be ordered.

Where mental factors were the only possible basis for a reprieve it sometimes became possible to assess whether a reprieve would be forthcoming before ever a prisoner stood trial. If the pre-trial State psychiatrist and prison doctor gave the accused a clean bill of health one could know before he was even convicted that he would probably be hanged if convicted.

Yet this startling innovation came about almost secretly, with hardly a public word from the Home Office. The Civil Service, far more than the modern Royal Navy, is the Silent Service of the twentieth century.

In 1957 occurred an innovation which was far from secret, and which occasioned many a public word—the passing of the Homicide Act.

Ever since the short-lived success of the 'Silverman Clause', in 1948, the abolitionists had been waiting watchfully for the opportunity to strike again. Two unpopular refusals of a reprieve —in the cases of Derek Bentley in 1953 and Ruth Ellis in 1954— coupled with the enigma of the Evans-Christie affair (all three of which I discuss later in detail) gave them their cue. In November 1955 Mr Silverman returned to the attack: with the backing of nine other M.P.'s from all three parties he introduced the Death Penalty (Abolition) Bill. Again he won over the House of Commons: in February 1956, on a free vote, the Commons resolved, "That this House believes that the death penalty no longer accords with the needs or the true interests of a civilized society."

The Home Secretary, Major Gwilym Lloyd George (now Lord Tenby), did not thereupon—as Lord Chuter-Ede had done in a similar situation in 1948—incur Lord Goddard's wrath by publicly announcing that all murderers would automatically be reprieved until the issue was decided. He said nothing, but in effect did exactly the same. He reprieved everyone throughout the ensuing thirteen months of parliamentary debate. The House of Commons passed Mr Silverman's Bill; the Lords rejected it; the Government brought in their own Homicide Bill containing compromise proposals to cut back capital punishment to only six categories of murder; this Bill was passed—and throughout the judges were solemnly sentencing murderers to death and the Home Secretary just as solemnly reprieving them all in turn. Not that he escaped Lord Goddard's censure: "The judges are feeling a sense of the greatest embarrassment," he complained to the Lords.

However, in March 1957 the Homicide Bill received the Royal Assent. Mere murder ceased to be a hanging offence. The new crime of 'Capital murder' was born. The death penalty—and the reprieve system—started on the last phase of its history.

CHAPTER NINE

The Homicide Act to the End

(1957–1965)

ONE would have expected the Homicide Act to have had a profound effect upon the exercise of the Prerogative of Mercy.

For a start the question of reprieve no longer arose in the majority of murder cases. Most murderers were henceforth no longer sentenced to death. Their penalty was life imprisonment. The decision of one man was no longer necessary to save them from the gallows.

Even when a person was condemned to death for capital murder and the question of reprieve did arise it was unlikely that the Home Secretary would have such a free rein as before. Prior to the Act the names of all kinds of persons convicted of all shades of murder found their way on to the calendar of impending executions kept on the Home Secretary's desk. But the effect of the Homicide Act was to retain capital punishment only for "those forms of murder for which the death penalty is not only particularly necessary but is also believed to be a particularly effective deterrent", to quote R. A. Butler, a subsequent Home Secretary.

It followed that capital murders were considered the most heinous forms of murder and capital murderers the most heinous kinds of murderer. Medical considerations apart, they were unlikely to be fit subjects for mercy.

And this applied even though this confused and confusing enactment left out of the category of capital murder two of the most infamous grades of killers—the child-murderer and the poisoner. Nevertheless, the six grades of capital murder, if they possessed any underlying logic at all, appeared to be aimed at the kind of person who was the least likely to be reprieved if convicted—the professional killer, or the professional criminal who might be tempted to kill.

These were the six grades: murders in the course or furtherance of theft, murders by shooting or causing an explosion, murders in the course of resisting arrest or escaping from custody, murders of policemen or those assisting them in the course of their duty, murders of prison officers in similar circumstances, and murders where the same person had killed more than once and been convicted on separate occasions. It was a roster of the most anti-social forms of killing. Only in the rarest case could compassion be felt for an offender.

Indeed, the Government gave what many people considered a public pledge that under the new Act there would be few, if any, reprieves. It occurred on February 21st, 1957, during the debate in the House of Lords on the Second Reading of the Homicide Bill. Said Lord Goddard: "It seems to me that there is one virtue in this Bill. I cannot believe that if it is passed and there are murders which are declared by the Bill to be capital murders the law will not be allowed to take its course. If the law is not to take its course, then in Heaven's name let us abolish the whole thing altogether."

The perplexed Lord Chief Justice got a categoric answer from the Government Front Bench. "I have made inquiries, and I am able to make the following statement," said Lord Salisbury, then Leader of the House and Lord President of the Council. "So far as the future is concerned, there is no doubt at all that once this Bill becomes an Act no difficulties of the sort envisaged by the noble and learned Lord can arise; and this is the determination of the Government."

These words were not forgotten. "We have no doubt that the small number of reprieves these days stems from this firm assurance," Hugh J. Klare, Secretary of the Howard League for Penal Reform, told me seven years later. And an ex-prison governor, perhaps a little out of touch with current events, even went so far as to say to me: "They don't reprieve any more these days, do they?"

The Government's 'pledge' and the greater perfidy of capital murders were not the only factors which might have been expected to cut down the proportion of reprieves. The Homicide Act limited the scope of the Home Secretary's powers in another way as well—in the section dealing with the possible 'diminished responsibility of persons charged with capital murder.

In the pre-Act days the question of a killer's diminished mental responsibility for his crime was essentially a matter for the Home Secretary, acting upon the advice of the doctors who carried out the post-trial medical inquiry in the condemned cell. If medical considerations were to affect a man's fate it was really the doctors who decided: certainly, if they recommended a reprieve on medical grounds the Home Secretary invariably accepted the recommendation. And this had been so for many years.

F

The late Lord Samuel was Home Secretary as long ago as 1916. Yet when talking about his years in office he once said: "I do not know of a case in which a Home Secretary has gone contrary to the report of his doctors." It is difficult to see how a lay Minister could possibly have done otherwise. One does not employ a doctor, only to make one's own diagnosis.

The Homicide Act fundamentally changed this aspect of the law. In Section 2 it specified:

"Where a person kills another, he shall not be convicted of murder if he was suffering from such abnormality of mind (whether arising from a condition of arrested or retarded development of mind or any inherent causes or induced by disease or injury) as substantially impaired his mental responsibility for his acts and omissions in doing or being a party to the killing."

In such circumstances his crime was reduced from either murder or capital murder, with their mandatory sentences of life imprisonment or death, to manslaughter, where the judge had a complete discretion to pass whichever sentence he liked, from a period of probation to life imprisonment.

In simple language Section 2 meant that if mental factors were involved in a case a prisoner faced with a capital charge could choose whether to make the arbiter of his life or death the Home Secretary or a jury. Instead of secret debate between three Home Office doctors writing out their report to a single Minister of the Crown a prisoner could choose open debate between Crown doctors and his own doctors carried out in court amid the bright glare of a public hearing, and with twelve fellow-citizens as the final judges.

It was, for instance, not Henry Brooke the Home Secretary, who decided that Harvey Leo Holford should not die in March 1963 for the killing of his wife Christine, after she had driven him to despair with her boastings about adultery committed on holiday in the South of France with a wealthy business man. It was the jury at Sussex Assizes which accepted his plea of diminished responsibility, and thus reduced his crime from capital murder to manslaughter, for which the judge sentenced him to three years in gaol (of which eventually he served only two.)

In suitable cases, where a person was sentenced to death and his mental condition was suspect, the Home Secretary still appointed three doctors to carry out a medical inquiry prior to execution. And this continued, even if a jury had failed to accept a diminished responsibility plea, as for instance with Victor John Terry, the young London gunman who in 1961 claimed that he was a reincarnation of 'Legs' Diamond, a notorious American gangster of the nineteen-thirties, and whose story I discuss in some detail later.

In 1959 Parliament gave the Home Secretary greater freedom to institute such inquiries: which was perhaps a little paradoxical when one reflects that only two years earlier the same Parliament's Homicide Act had rendered them largely redundant. Still, the Mental Health Act of 1959 repealed the seventy-five-year-old Criminal Lunatics Act and, with it, abolished the distinction between 'statutory' mental inquiries for the possibly insane and 'informal' medical inquiries for the merely abnormal. In their place Parliament provided—nothing! In not one of the 154 sections and 8 schedules of the 1959 Act did the politicians insert one word about inquiries into the mental or medical condition of condemned capital murderers. It was a supreme example of legislation by default.

The result was a vacuum. The Home Secretary continued to appoint such inquiries, but without any statutory authority whatsoever. It was the sort of situation that the English normally call 'Irish'.

Despite the 'diminished responsibility' section of the Homicide Act, and despite the fact that Parliament had chosen to ignore their existence, Home Office mental inquiries still continued to play an important rôle in the administration of the reprieve system. Vital questions of mental abnormality could not entirely be left to the whim of defendants choosing whether to raise the defence of diminished responsibility or the caprice of juries attempting to assess the rival theories of contending courtroom doctors.

The Home Secretary had to retain a residual power to reprieve on medical grounds.

Thus it was possible for a man to raise the defence of diminished responsibility at his trial, parade his medical evidence, have it rejected by the jury, and yet be reprieved. It happened in 1959 in the case of David Lancelot Di Duca.

This twenty-one-year-old naval steward got drunk one night. It was calculated that he must have consumed the equivalent of a pint of neat spirit. In that condition he broke into the flat of a Portsmouth antique dealer, who was reputed to keep large sums of money hidden about the place. The dealer put up a fight, and Di Duca beat him to death with a heavy wash-basin. He then made off with about £44. At his trial he pleaded that the dealer had struck first, and that, in any event, he was so drunk as to be suffering from 'diminished responsibility'. The jury threw out both defences, and Di Duca was sentenced to death.

"In our judgment there was no evidence of abnormality of mind", said Lord Chief Justice Lord Parker when dismissing the appeal. Yet within two weeks Di Duca's reprieve was announced. A possible reason is that the Home Office doctors disagreed with both the Crown doctors and the Lord Chief Justice, and advised the Home Secretary that Di Duca's responsibility for his crime had, in fact, been diminished by the alcohol he had consumed.

It has also happened that a prisoner for whom the defence of diminished responsibility could fairly be put forward has deliberately refused to let his counsel do so. In such a case only the Home Secretary—and his doctors—could save the man from the price of his own folly.

This happened in November 1961 when John Christopher Mc-Menemy, a twenty-four-year-old Liverpool labourer, was convicted of murdering his nineteen-year-old girl friend for the £3 in her handbag. His guilt had been obvious from the start of the trial, but he refused to let his counsel put forward the only valid defence—diminished responsibility. He withstood the plea of both his father and his lawyers.

But, "Depend upon it . . . when a man knows he is to be hanged in a fortnight, it concentrates his mind wonderfully," said Dr Johnson. And so it proved with McMenemy.

After nine days in the condemned cell he changed his mind and told his solicitor that he wanted the medical evidence called. But it was too late. It was a foregone conclusion that the Court of Criminal Appeal, hamstrung by legal precedent, would throw out any request for leave to call fresh evidence, since all the evidence had been available at the trial. Yet Mr Justice Ashworth clearly indicated the court's view as to what should happen to Mc-Menemy when he dismissed the appeal: "Any misgiving which the Court might have felt is completely set at rest by the fact that the applicant's mental responsibility will be carefully investigated in other quarters."

The Home Office took the hint: seven days later McMenemy was reprieved.

In all forty-eight persons were sentenced to death for capital murder during the seven and a half years that the Homicide Act was effective—from March 1957 to December 1964, when Sydney Silverman introduced his final Abolition Bill into the House of Commons. Of that number only twenty-nine were executed. Despite the Government's so-called 'pledge' to Lord Goddard in the Homicide Bill debate, nineteen capital murderers—including one woman—were reprieved. Despite the greater perfidy of post-1957 capital murderers over pre-1957 ordinary murderers, just under 40 per cent of all persons sentenced to death were saved from execution by the Home Secretary. The drop from the pre-1957 level of reprieves was only 5 per cent.

The allegedly hidebound, ultra-conservative Home Office had had to administer a rigid and arbitrary law of homicide. Yet it still had succeeded in tempering rigour with compassion.

Then, on August 13th, 1964, Gwynne Owen Evans and Peter Anthony Allen, two young Lancashire Dairymen in their early twenties, were hanged in separate prisons for murdering in the course of theft a middle-aged van-driver. And the hangman had performed his last task on English soil in time of peace.

PART TWO

What Actually Happened

So much for history. Writing now it is possible to look back on the last, recent years of capital punishment and try to discern if there was a pattern.

What were the mechanics of the system? What actually happened? How did the Home Secretary decide whether a murderer lived or died? And what happened to the prisoner after the decision was taken?

Apart from the guarded evidence of senior Home Office officials to the Gowers Commission some fifteen years ago there has not been an official, authoritative answer to these problems. The public never really knew what was done in their name.

The next four chapters, therefore, set out "what actually happened". The Home Office have co-operated in giving me certain information: Sir Charles Cunningham, the Permanent Under-Secretary, saw me at the start of my inquiries, some four years ago, and has been most helpful.

But this is far from being an official account of the system that now has gone.

One has to glean the truth from stray items in old newspapers, close-printed columns in Hansard, slightly indiscreet paragraphs in published memoirs and biographies, and from talking to the few people who themselves had first-hand information and, subject to the Official Secrets Acts, were prepared to discuss their work.

CHAPTER TEN

Before the Decision

It took less time to sentence a man to death for capital murder than to send him to prison for three months for petty theft. When a prisoner was convicted of a lesser offence than murder or capital murder the judge could not immediately pass sentence. First he had to hear evidence from the police as to the man's character and antecedents, then he had to listen to any witness that the defendant wished to call, and finally he had to endure a speech in mitigation by defending counsel.

All these matters were necessary because the judge had a discretion. He could be swayed to pass any sentence below the maximum provided by law. But when it came to a capital conviction the judge had no option. He had to pronounce the sentence of death.

In post-war years, this was done directly, without any prior homily by the judge, as used to be the wont. In March 1963 Mr Justice Roskill brought back a rare memory of the nineteen-twenties, and judges such as Mr Justice Avory when he told an armed thug called George Frederick Thatcher, convicted of killing an innocent lorry-driver in the course of a raid on a Mitcham dairy depot: "You shot this man brutally and without pity and for that crime the law prescribes but one sentence, that you too shall die!" In fact, Thatcher was not hanged. On appeal, his conviction was reduced to non-capital murder, and a sentence of life imprisonment imposed.

Since 1957 the sentence of death was itself short and quickly uttered. Accepting a recommendation of the Gowers Commission, the Homicide Act adopted the simple formula: "The sentence of the Court upon you is, that you suffer death in the manner authorized by law." It took only a few seconds to say, even allowing for the customary benediction, "And may the Lord have mercy on your soul."

No sooner had the court chaplain—usually the parish priest of the county squire who was High Sheriff of the County for the year—intoned "Amen" than the prisoner was hustled out of the dock and down to the cells below.

Few murderers are on record as to what it felt like to be sentenced to death. But a man who was condemned to die for the murder of an elderly stranger in a drunken brawl outside a public house has told me in simple words just what it was like: "I thought my heart had stopped. My legs went, and they had to help me down the stairs. I think no-one should be sentenced to death if they know they are not going to hang him." This man, who was recommended to mercy because of what the jury called his 'low mentality', continued: "I was sentenced on March 3rd, 1948, and released on February 23rd, 1959—you always remember dates like that!"

A man stood his trial and heard his fate clad in his own clothes. But once sentenced to death, he did not wear them again until the day of his execution. Back at the prison he was examined by the prison doctor, stripped, searched in case he had hidden something with which he might kill himself, and his clothing replaced by the special garb of a prisoner under sentence of death. In happier circumstances it might have been called 'casual wear'. The shirt had no tie, he wore soft slippers instead of shoes or boots, and his jacket had tapes instead of buttons. For Prison Rules provided: "Every article shall be taken from him which the Governor deems is dangerous or inexpedient to leave in his possession"— ties, laces, and buttons came within this category.

On his return from court the prisoner saw for the first time the condemned cell. That was where his change of clothes took place, that was where, apart from the twice daily exercise period and a Sunday visit to chapel, he spent the next few weeks until either reprieve or death ended his sojourn.

It was larger than an ordinary prison cell. Usually it was two, sometimes three, cells knocked into one—"A spacious apartment", L. W. Merrow Smith, a retired prison officer, has called it. It contained a bed, three chairs, two tables, a wireless—but no clock. It was a suite complete within itself. Leading out of the cell was a separate lavatory and bathroom; on one side was a visiting-room, and on the other, its intercommunicating door sometimes (but not always) covered by a screen or wardrobe, was the execution-room.

When the prison doctor and the reception officer had gone the prisoner was left alone with the first of the two 'death-watch' prison officers, who would now guard him night and day. Only one officer used to 'sit' in the condemned cell, until in 1889 a child-murderer named Spicer nearly killed his solitary guard: thereafter safety was found in numbers.

As the prisoner blinked around at his new quarters so the

judge who had sentenced him sat down to write a formal letter
to the Home Secretary. It was terse and to the point:
   "Sir,

Regina v. A—— B——

   I have the honour to inform you that A—— B—— was tried
before me for the capital murder of C—— D——. The jury
returned a verdict of guilty and I passed sentence of death.

Yours faithfully"

   That afternoon too the Governor wrote to the Under-Sheriff of
the county informing him. "I have received A—— B—— into
custody under sentence of death."

   The following morning, upon receiving the Governor's letter,
the Under-Sheriff would put into motion the procedure of execution. Hanging was not the task of any official of the Government
or prison service. It was the direct executive act of the Sheriff
(acting through his deputy, the Under-Sheriff, a local solicitor in
private practice). This official was not a servant of the Government, but of the Crown. Since Saxon days the Sheriff has been the
personal representative of the monarch in the county: no Government Department can command him. The prison governor merely
informed him that a man had been sentenced to death: he did
not order him to set in train the execution. The Sheriff did that
of his own volition.

   Usually he fixed the date almost immediately, on the very same
day that he received the prison governor's letter. In 1902 Charles
Ritchie, when Home Secretary, recommended that executions took
place at 8 A.M. on any weekday but Monday, in the week following the third Sunday after sentence had been passed. Though
the normal time of execution in the nineteen-sixties was 9 A.M.,
the three-week limit was still invariably applied.

   A panel of prison chaplains told the Gowers Commission that,
"without being excessively long", they thought this interval was
roughly right. It allowed time to deal with any further developments in the case, and for the prisoner to set his worldly affairs
in order and prepare himself spiritually for death. But not everyone agreed with it. "I thought three weeks was too long. It imposed
too great a strain on the man," an ex-prison governor has told
me. "I've always understood that there were two reasons for fixing
the three weeks' period. First it gave the man time to make his
peace with his Maker. I thought this was nonsense. His Maker
would be well able to receive him without any notice. Second it
allowed time for any new evidence to come to light and the
Home Office to make their inquiries relating to a reprieve—well,
two weeks would have sufficed for that! In my view a man should

have spent no more than a fortnight in the condemned cell once he'd been sentened or his appeal dismissed."

These words were echoed by a prison officer who 'sat' with many condemned men and attended three executions. "The worst time was the waiting," he told me. "The trial was an ordeal, but many of them went through it in a sort of trance. The end also was not so terrifying—by then they were sick to death of the whole thing; they just wanted to get it over with. They just couldn't have cared less. But the middle—the waiting time—that was terrible. It was too long."

Such considerations did not, however, affect the under-Sheriff. After fixing the date of execution—usually the first Tuesday after the third Sunday from the day of sentence—he notified the Home Office, the prison governor, the trial judge, and the executioner, whom he selected from a panel of hangmen supplied by the prison authorities.

On hearing from the Under-Sheriff the prison governor at once told the condemned man of the proposed execution date. If a prisoner did not appeal it was possible for him to be dead within twenty-one days of his sentence : in one case a naval petty officer, who refused all his solicitor's entreaties to appeal, was hanged within eighteen days of being sentenced to death.

But 98 per cent. of all convicted capital murderers appealed, and once formal notice of appeal was lodged, the date of execution was automatically cancelled. But that still did not give him very much extra time, for the 1907 Criminal Appeal Act stated that a capital appeal should be "heard and determined with as much expedition as practicable".

The case of Oswald Augustus Grey, a twenty-year-old penniless Jamaican baker, convicted in the autumn of 1962 of shooting a Birmingham shopkeeper, offered a typical example of the time-schedule in operation. Grey was sentenced to death on October 12th, 1962; on October 16th his solicitor announced that he was appealing; on October 29th, the Court of Criminal Appeal dismissed his appeal; on Saturday, November 17th, the Home Office announced that there was no reprieve; on Tuesday, November 20th, he was hanged. His total stay in the condemned cell—thirty-nine days.

Hamlet complained of "the law's delays". If he were a convicted capital murderer he would not have been so querulous.

In many cases a capital-murder appeal was a mere formality. The man's lawyers often knew that they stood little chance of success. Up till the mid-nineteen-fifties it was common for defence

lawyers to wrack their memory of the proceedings, scour the transcript of the trial, and try to find some possible argument for
the Court of Criminal Appeal. Time thus wasted could seem well
spent to a client languishing under sentence of death. But in May
1955 Mr Justice (now Sir Malcolm) Hilbery, then Senior Queen's
Bench Judge, effectively put an end to the practice.

He was presiding over the Court of Criminal appeal, hearing an appeal by an eighteen-year-old Cypriot, Michael Demetris
Xinaris, against his conviction of stabbing to death a middle-
aged Londoner outside an Islington café. Nine grounds of appeal
had been alleged, and leading defence counsel addressed the
Court for over five hours. Yet the judges dismissed the appeal
without even calling on prosecuting counsel to reply. In the course
of his judgment Mr Justice Hilbery remarked: "Too often grounds
are framed, in order to give an appeal the appearance of substance, which, on examination, are found to be worthless." He
slated the notice of appeal as "frivolous, and a compilation which
reflects no credit" upon the counsel who had drafted it.

Since this judicial rebuke it became increasingly rare, perhaps understandably, for defence counsel to argue unarguable
cases. They simply told the three appeal judges that they had
carefully considered the appeal, but could not advance any argument in its support. "How on earth can a man do such a thing?" a
hot-headed young barrister once asked me, but it was undoubtedly
the proper course for defence counsel, devoid of ammunition, to
take. It was done in the case of Grey, and in the far more controversial case of George Riley in January 1961.

Why then bother with what was so often a farce? I suppose one
answer is that defence lawyers wanted to do everything they could
to assist their client. If you had two strings to your bow, appeal and
reprieve, it was foolhardy not to pluck both. Indeed, in the early
nineteen-sixties one convicted capital murderer succeeded on appeal
on the basis of a defence that was never put forward at his trial.

In July 1961 George Anthony Porritt claimed—on his trial at the
Old Bailey—that his shooting of his stepfather was an accident.
They were both being attacked by thugs in a gang-fight in Peckham,
London, and he fired to defend the older man from two assailants
who had grabbed him and were holding a knife to his throat.
Unfortunately, the bullet hit the wrong man.

The jury convicted. But the Court of Criminal Appeal said that,
although no-one had suggested it at the time, the judge ought to
have asked the jury to consider an alternative defence of provocation. They therefore quashed the capital-murder conviction, and
substituted a ten-year prison term for manslaughter.

Yet this was a highly unusual case, and defence lawyers could hardly rely on its recurring. Undoubtedly one of the reasons why so many prisoners sentenced to death appealed was because of the generally held belief among lawyers that the Home Office wanted them to. In fact, the Home office attitude was that a prisoner should not rely upon the exercise of the Prerogative of Mercy in deciding whether or not to make an appeal—"It would obviously create an impossible situation if a prisoner who would otherwise have appealed did not do so because of his belief that the Prerogative of Mercy would be exercised—and then found that it was not!" explained Sir Charles Cunningham.

The Home Office never formally expressed a wish that prisoners sentenced to death should appeal. Nevertheless, it perhaps came to much the same thing in the end. I know of two cases where defence counsel were given to understand that a reprieve would not be considered by the Home Secretary until the condemned man's conviction had first been tested in the Court of Criminal Appeal.

The late J. D. Casswell, Q.C., who defended more than forty persons charged with murder, told me that once, knowing that the trial judge had written to the Home Secretary agreeing with the jury's recommendation to mercy, he himself wrote to the Home Office telling them that he was holding up lodging an appeal to give the Home Secretary time to make a decision. But back came the reply: "Carry on with the appeal!"

So engrained was this popular belief among lawyers that when, in 1959, the Home Secretary himself referred the case of Guenther Fritz Podola to the Court of Criminal Appeal many observers commented that the only reason for the reference was that Podola had himself decided not to appeal, and that the Home Secretary was—more or less—doing so for him. In fact, this was not so. The reference was not influenced by Podola's own failure to appeal.

Even so, only once in the final years before the successful Second Reading of the Murder (Abolition of Death Penalty) Bill, in December 1964, was a capital murderer reprieved without appealing—in the 1958 case of Arthur John Bosworth.

While breaking into a factory in London's Kentish Town twenty-year-old Bosworth and a seventeen-year-old accomplice were surprised by the caretaker, who was then beaten to death with a wooden mallet. Both youths were charged with capital murder (during the course or furtherance of theft). Bosworth's accomplice was acquitted, but he was sentenced to death, the jury having rejected his plea of self-defence.

Bosworth's solicitor, Victor J. Lissack, thereupon proceeded ably to drive a coach and pair through the normal reprieve procedure. "I consulted with counsel," he says, "and we were all agreed that there was absolutely no chance of an appeal succeeding. So I simply told Bosworth that the thing to do was for me to write to the Home Secretary putting before him all the reasons why he ought to recommend a reprieve." And that is what Mr Lissack did.

He had quite a good case to argue: the jury had strongly recommended mercy, there was no evidence of premeditation, and there were certain other factors.

Lissack's letter was written on May 6th, 1958. It was briefly acknowledged, and he heard no more until May 17th, when he received a letter from Sir Charles Cunningham telling him that the Secretary of State had "advised Her Majesty to respite the capital sentence and that the sentence has been commuted to one of imprisonment for life." And that was that: it was almost mercy on the slot-machine basis.

According to some sources the hearing of a condemned man's appeal was the watershed of his time in the condemned cell. In the words of an ex-prison governor of over twenty years' experience: "When they first came into the condemned cell after sentence they were distressed, shocked, and a bit troublesome. That continued up to the appeal. But once the appeal was dismissed, they somehow managed to get a grip on themselves. They realized that—reprieve apart—there was now no hope. And that seemed to enable them to come to terms with their plight. Thereafter a condemned man seemed to be able to find a form of strength within himself."

Often the man himself heard the result pronounced by the presiding judge. Technically most capital-murder appeals were only applications for leave to appeal, and no prisoner had the right to be present upon the hearing of a mere application. But for many years it was the Court's practice to treat every application for leave in a capital case as if it were the appeal itself, and the prisoner was accordingly entitled to be there. Surprisingly not everyone availed themselves of this opportunity of getting out of the condemned cell and making the journey to the Strand.

In any event, a few days later the prison governor would tell the prisoner of the new execution date, which now only the rare chance of a further appeal to the House of Lords or a reprieve could alter.

The Under-Sheriff in fixing the new date would follow the same pattern as before—the first weekday other than a Monday after three clear Sundays. Apart from telling the prison governor, he would also communicate the date to the Home Office, the executioner, and, as a matter of courtesy, to the trial judge. If he had not done it before he now asked the governor for details of the prisoner's height and weight—necessary information for the hangman.

The brake was now taken from beneath the wheels of the apparatus of death. It began slowly to trundle downhill. At the Home Office confidential police and other reports were collated, documents prepared, evidence sifted. If there was to be a medical inquiry letters went out to three doctors asking them to take part. The trial judge and, sometimes, the judge who presided over the appeal court might be invited to visit the Home Secretary. The official gathering of all relevant information got under way, irrespective of what the prisoner was doing.

But what *was* he doing? How was he faring?

He found little difference in his daily routine. Within about a week to ten days the three doctors would arrive and question him about himself, and then, the following day, return and ask some more questions; but that would be about the only change in his daily routine.

As before, the prison governor came to see him once a day—"almost the only duty he would never ask his deputy to do"—says a former governor. As before, the prison medical officer visited him twice daily, the prison chaplain—if the prisoner wished to see him—once, twice, even three times a day. His solicitor too continued to have easy access, though always in the presence of his warders.

The interminable games of dominoes and draughts went on, the newspapers, with details of his case blacked out, continued to come in, and magazines and books. His food would be rather better than the average prisoner's, coming from the prison hospital and liable to be improved at the discretion of the prison medical officer. In fact, eating was one of the few delights permitted in the condemned cell. "The average condemned prisoner gained up to two stones in weight and normally ate and slept well," says Professor Desmond Curran, and it is on record that Thomas Henry Allaway, hanged in the early nineteen-twenties for a brutal sex murder, was ten pounds heavier when he mounted the scaffold than when he entered prison. Perhaps it was a form of what the psychiatrists call 'grief fat'—taking solace in food, a type of consolation not unknown outside the condemned cell.

The prisoner was permitted visitors at any time of the day,

though never more than three at once, and always with the warders present. Physical contact was impossible. A glass panel with a
wire-mesh base separated him from his guests. He could refuse
to see people he did not want, and visitors were let in only if
their names appeared on a list approved by both the prison authorities and the prisoner. Sometimes he wished to spare a parent
the ordeal of a visit, sometimes he did not want to see a wife or a
friend whom he thought had let him down: always his wishes were
respected.

In one rare case in Scotland, in October 1958, a condemned
man was even allowed to marry. The girl was the mother of his
eight-month-old daughter, and, as it said on her application for
a special marriage-licence, there was 'reasonable excuse' for the
parties' failure to take the necessary steps to secure normal pro-
clamation of their marriage banns, in that the would-be groom
was due to be hanged. It must have been a strange scene inside
the prison: a condemned man placing a wedding ring on his
bride's finger while in the background stood the prison chaplain,
who had conducted the ceremony, the prison governor, and four
warders. Luckily there was a happy ending: the twenty-three-
year-old prisoner, convicted of murdering an elderly night watch-
man, was reprieved.

A careful note was taken of how a man reacted during those
vital days following his appeal, when, with varying degrees of
speed, he began to realize that death was becoming an ever
closer reality. Accounts differ as to the mental effect upon condemned men of this post-appeal period. An experienced prison
chaplain has told me, "They lived on hope. Firstly the hope of
their appeal being successful. Then they waited for the reprieve,
and it was only in the last few days, if the reprieve was not
granted; that they began to face up to what was ahead. It was
in those last days that you got a wonderful chance to help." Ex-
prison governor Major Ben Grew does not agree:

"On my first visit to a prisoner in the condemned cell (he has
written) I had expected to find him bowed down with despair, a
pitiful figure, perhaps, with whom conversation would be most
difficult, if not impossible. Instead I usually found him in good
heart and playing a game of cards with the two officers 'on
watch'. Most condemned men—and I met many of them—
appeared to accept the situation with commendable stoicism
and retained that air of calmness until the end."

Ex-prison officer L. W. Merrow Smith has written of a Negro
prisoner who carried 'commendable stoicism' so far that he spent
most of his waking hours jiving. On the other hand many people

Above: Scene outside Shrewsbury Prison on the morning of George Riley's execution.

Photo: "Sun" Newspapers

Inset: George Riley. *Photo: Associated Press, Ltd.*

Below: Scene outside Wandsworth Prison when Notice of Execution of Derek Bentley was placed on the gate. *Photo: Associated Press, Ltd.*

Inset: Derek Bentley. *Photo: United Press International (U.K.), Ltd.*

Mrs Florence Maybrick.

Photo: Mirrorpic

Sir Charles Russell, Q.C. (later Lord Russell of Killowen).

Photo: "Radio Times" Hulton Picture Library

James Maybrick, (a little-known photograph).

Photo: "Radio Times" Hulton Picture Library

took the view expressed by Sir Ernest Gowers that "during the time the prisoner is waiting to hear the Home Secretary's decision he suffers conscious and acute mental distress." Perhaps the true answer lay in what a prison officer once said to the Gower Commission: "It depends on the make-up of the prisoner."

The prison officers who 'sat' with the man were supposed to record his reactions in the Occurrence Book, a daily log designed to record any incident or remark which reflected the prisoner's frame of mind, particularly if it related to his crime. "We were supposed to put everything in," one officer tells me, "but I can assure you very few of us did. We only put something in if we thought it would help the man, not do him down."

A very close relationship developed between the prisoner and the six officers of the 'death watch' who sat with him in pairs in eight-hour shifts. "We were often the only friends he had," says the officer. "The man talks to you, you know, and you really get to know him. In fact, if a prisoner was to complain about any of the officers he would be changed—and rightly so. We were with him all the time, when he had his bath, when he ate, when he slept. Even when he went to the lavatory we kept the door open."

A lurid account of life in the condemned cell that appeared in a popular magazine over the signature of an ex-'trusty' prisoner described how the officers "constantly awaken the condemned man during the night so that they can be sure he stays alive for the final settlement." "That's plain ridiculous!" says the officer. "If we acted like that how do you explain the fact that every prisoner would always be ready to help a prison officer caught smoking while on duty? The prisoner was allowed to smoke twenty cigarettes a day, but we were not supposed to—at least, while on duty. But, of course, we did, and you should see the pantomime that went on when we got a visitor! One officer quickly dips his cigarette and pops it in his pocket, the other slings his at the prisoner—who smartly puts it in his own mouth and starts to puff at it, even if he wasn't a smoker! You wouldn't have got that sort of attitude if you were enemies with the man."

Nor was the keeping of the Occurrence Book a meaningless chore. Every day the governor looked at it on his routine visit, and if it disclosed anything which could affect a possible reprieve it was his duty to report it to the Prison Department at the Home Office, who then passed it on to the Permanent Under-Secretary.

As the days were flicked from the calendar so the tempo quickened. Precious few, if any, prisoners languished in the condemned cell without someone taking up the cudgels on their behalf. Usually

G

it was the condemned man's solicitor, sometimes a social worker or an industrious (or ambitious) M.P. or the prisoner's relatives.

From whichever source, the Home Office within a short time of an appeal's being dismissed usually used to receive representations for a reprieve. It was customary to call them 'petitions'. But often they were simply letters putting forward reasons why a reprieve should be granted. They were not drafted according to any particular form, and the medieval-sounding word 'petition' had no real relevance. As one solicitor said to me: "I did not know what the form was, so I just wrote a suitable letter!"

In the rare instance where there was a formal 'petition' the prisoner had to sign it. But where the solicitor merely wrote on his behalf only the lawyer needed to sign—which gave rise to the question, Was a solicitor entitled to ask for a reprieve when his client had deliberately told him not to?

There was no easy answer in academic, legal ethics. But in practice the problem seldom, if ever, occurred—not because every prisoner jumped at the chance of trying to get a reprieve, but simply because solicitors were generally able to persuade the occasionally reluctant client into letting them do their best for him, often on the basis that the prisoner owed it to his family to try and stay alive. "I talked him into the petition," is actually the phrase used to me by one emotionally involved solicitor.

If he was dealing with an illiterate or semi-illiterate client a solicitor's task was less delicate. He had more freedom of action. Mrs Charlotte Bryant, convicted in the nineteen-thirties of poisoning her husband, Dorset cowman Frederick Bryant, could neither read nor write, and her solicitor, Mr Christopher T. Arrow, who made strenuous though unsuccessful efforts for a reprieve told me: "I am sure that at no time did she ask me to obtain a reprieve for her and I do not think the matter was discussed with her."

In fact, it was possible for a man to be reprieved even though he had never asked for it. Sir Frank Newsam has written in his official book on the Home Office: "Before the law is allowed to take its irrevocable course, it is the long established practice for the Home Secretary to review every case whether or not he receives any representations on the man's behalf." I myself know of a case in the mid-nineteen-fifties where a man was reprieved who had pleaded guilty, made no efforts at all to ask for mercy, and literally wanted to die. Admittedly, the facts were exceptional: after killing his ex-fiancée he had thrown himself under a train in an attempt at suicide, and lost both his legs. It would have been impossible to hang him without a prison warder holding him up on either side.

Sometimes if the case had attracted a great deal of attention in the newspapers petitions in the proper sense of the word, long documents bearing hundreds, sometimes thousands, of signatures, arrived at the Home Office. But no public petition since the First World War brought about a reprieve which would not anyway have been forthcoming. As long ago as November 1924 Sir William Joynson-Hicks, when Home Secretary, said, "I am not prepared to allow my decision to be diverted one hair's breadth just because eight or eighty thousand people choose to present a petition." And in the early years of the Second World War Sir John Anderson refused to reprieve two IRA men convicted of bomb outrages in Coventry, despite much popular pressure from both sides of the Irish Sea. "I was not prepared to proclaim the helplessness of the law," he later said.

Even the dedicated opponents of capital punishment who automatically took up every case did not pin much faith on petitions. They preferred to write privately to the Home Secretary though, as Lord Gardiner once ruefully confessed to me when he was still at the Bar, "I'm pretty sure that my letters—though always courteously acknowledged—go right into the waste-paper basket. The Home Office are so experienced that they are likely already to have taken into account every relevant factor. The odd letter is, therefore, not likely to have much effect."

Nevertheless, there is evidence for saying that the Home Office kept a wary, unofficial ear to the ground.

According to one informant the police were usually asked to make discreet inquiries in the neighbourhood where the crime was committed to ascertain if local public opinion would be affronted by a reprieve. The Home Secretary was obviously not bound by the result of such an inquiry, but it seems to have been something that he took into account.

In 1936 the Bar Council formally ruled that it was contrary to professional etiquette for a barrister engaged in a capital case to take part in a public campaign for a reprieve. As the late J. D. Casswell, Q.C. told me, "I never signed a petition in all my forty years at the Bar. I didn't think one should." But it was never considered professionally improper for defence counsel to exert himself behind the scenes. In at least two recent instances the solicitor's letter to the Home Secretary asking for a reprieve was, in fact, drafted by counsel, one of whom now sits on the High Court Bench.

This was, of course, a matter of personal temperament. Some defending barristers maintained their interest in their client long

after their professional involvement ceased. Mr Casswell, for instance, habitually used to write from time to time to the Home
Office asking for a date to be fixed for the early release of a
client who had been reprieved and was serving an indeterminate
term of 'life imprisonment'. Others took a more conventional
view of their responsibilities, and said—as a one-time defence
counsel, now a judge, has said to me—"Well, as you know, it's
nothing to do with us once the Court of Criminal Appeal have upheld the conviction. That's really more the solicitor's side of it."

In one case in the early nineteen-sixties defence counsel wrote
a long letter to the Home Secretary submitting detailed arguments for a reprieve, and was promptly telephoned by the Home
Office and asked to come and see Sir Charles Cunningham, the
Permanent Under-Secretary. He went, and was most sympathetic-
ally received.

It was, in fact, the practice of the Home Office to see any reputable person asking for a reprieve who thought that a personal
interview might help. The practice was to see anyone—including
a relative—who asked to be seen, to listen to what he had to say;
but not to comment on the merits of the case. "I was treated with
great politeness," a social worker told me of such a visit. "There
was much opening and closing of doors and offering of cigarettes . . . They said they would be only too willing to pass anything
which was relevant on to the Secretary of State. The atmosphere
was coldly friendly." Lord Stonham has paid tribute in the House
of Lords to the way in which one such interview was conducted
when, as an M.P., he took up the case on behalf of a constituent:
"Naturally, Sir Charles could express no opinion, but I want to
say most gratefully and warmly that he gave me all of his time
that was necessary and all the help that I needed, even volunteer-
ing, because time was so short, to make copies of notes and documents." In fact, the man was reprieved.

The Home Secretary himself rarely saw anyone who wished to
make representations about a capital case—on the ground that
he ought not to be subjected to the pressure of personal and
possibly emotional appeals. This rule was rarely broken, and
usually only in the case of ambassadors—when dealing with a
foreign national—bishops, and, at a lower level, fellow-politicians.
He never saw the parents or any relative or friend of the convicted man, and resolutely refused to see any of the lawyers. "I
once had defending counsel come to see me at the Home Office,"
a retired senior civil servant told me. "He was in tears, imploring
me to arrange an appointment for him with the Home Secretary
so that he could plead for mercy for his client. I refused to do

so, and told him it would be imposing an intolerable strain on the Secretary of State to subject him to a personal interview of that nature. Later I met the same counsel on a social occasion, and he admitted to me that he thought I had acted correctly. Furthermore, that he now thought his client was rightly hanged!"

If there was to be a medical inquiry the doctors were by now going about their task. Armed with a transcript of the trial, confidential police reports and medical representations on both sides, they spent two days at the prison. On the first day they interviewed everyone who had had any contact with the prisoner, from the governor down to the orderly who attended him in hospital before the trial. They would ask all the same basic question: "Have you seen anything to make you think he is not in his right mind?" Then, at about four o'clock in the afternoon, they saw the prisoner, and questioned him about his crime and life.

"What the man said *after* he had been questioned could sometimes more affect his fate than what he said while being questioned," says a retired governor. "There's many a man who's hanged himself on what he said to the warders after the doctors had seen him." They wrote it all down in the Occurrence Book; and it was the first thing that the doctors looked at when they returned the following day. "If they found he'd said something like, 'Well, I've pulled the wool over *their* eyes!' or 'I told those silly sods a right story'—he'd had it. And I've known it happen!" Whatever was written in the Book, the doctors would again see the prisoner. Then, on leaving the condemned cell, they would have a final discussion between themselves and at once, in prison, sit down and write their report—a report which stated whether or not medical reasons existed for recommending the Home Secretary to recommend a reprieve.

What did the doctors look for? Professor Desmond Curran says: "I do not think it is possible to state in so many words what would justify a Board to recommend that there were medical reasons for a man being reprieved. In practice, I seldom found any real disagreement." A clue is, however, perhaps to be found in the incorporation of 'diminished responsibility' in the Homicide Act, reducing capital murder and murder to manslaughter when the prisoner was suffering from

"such abnormality of mind (whether arising from a condition of arrested or retarded development of mind or any inherent causes or induced by disease or injury) as substantially impaired his mental responsibility for his acts and omissions in doing or being a party to the killing."

The Gower Commission recommended that this doctrine, developed over the last century by Scottish judges, should not be brought into the law of England. Yet when the Home Office were concocting the Homicide Act they selected it as an essential ingredient of the new English law of murder. Why? A possible reason is that it coincided with the basis on which Home Office doctors over the last two decades had been deciding whether or not to recommend a reprieve. Such an explanation would make sense of why there was imported into a supposedly compromise measure what would at first sight appear to be an alien doctrine and the last thing to be found in a Bill designed to reconcile two bitterly opposed points of view. The section was in the Act because it made no difference: it merely proclaimed as law what had hitherto been the practice.

A psychiatrist who has himself taken part in these inquiries tells me that this assessment is "not far off the mark." And there is perhaps a further clue in the evidence of Canon Smith, then Senior Prison Chaplain, before the Gowers Commission, when the Canon, talking about the one-time statutory medical inquiries, said: "Many of us have attended these inquiries. We have been amazed at the results . . . I have never seen a man executed who has been suffering from mental disease or abnormality."

But doctors were not the only experts consulted by the Home Office. Sometimes a pathologist was called in. In one case in the nineteen-fifties a person had been convicted where undeniably the body had been disposed of in circumstances of great suspicion. A pathologist had given evidence for the Crown that the cause of death was consistent with murder, but a query still persisted in the minds of those in the Home Office as to whether, bearing in mind the state of the body, this had really been proved beyond a reasonable doubt. With the knowledge and consent of the Crown pathologist another pathologist, who had done much work for the Crown in the past, was called in. He examined the evidence, and in an interview at the Home Office at which the Home Secretary, the Permanent Under-Secretary, and the Crown expert were present reported that there was too much doubt on which to hang someone. He could not say with certainty what was the real cause of death. The result—a reprieve.

Of course, such a case was highly exceptional. Normally the quiet routine of amassing the evidence for and against a reprieve went on without such dramatic interventions. Eventually all the reports and representations were in, and then someone in the Department sat down to write a summary of the facts and a Departmental recommendation to the Home Secretary. The late Sir Alexander Maxwell told me that in his day it was the Deputy Permanent Under-Secretary who first prepared the memorandum and then submitted it to the Permanent Under-Secretary, who if he agreed with the recommendation countersigned it, and if not overwrote his own view. The memorandum then went to the Home Office. Often in Sir Alexander's time the Under-Secretary and his deputy would discuss the case before the memorandum was drawn up so that there would be no disharmony in the recommendation. In recent years this would appear to have been the standing rule: seldom, if ever, was the Home Secretary presented with anything other than a single recommendation. A recommendation which only he could convert into a decision.

CHAPTER ELEVEN

The Decision

"CONSIDERING whether to recommend the commutation of the capital sentence is certainly the most onerous and painful of the duties of my office," said R. A. Butler (now Baron Butler of Saffron Walden) when he was Home Secretary. And few will find this strange.

A man led a perfectly ordinary politician's life. He endured the tedium of constituency meetings, the frustrations of inter-party struggles for power, the slow corrosion of the soul that is for many an inescapable feature of British political life—and then, for his reward, he found himself set up as the final judge on whether some wretched person should live or die. No wonder William Clive Bridgeman, Home Secretary for fifteen months in the early nineteen-twenties, said: "If you ask me what I would like as Home Secretary I should say that anyone in the world had better have the job than me!"

Different men reacted to it in different ways. I asked the late Lord Morrison of Lambeth what it was like. "Before I went to the Home Office in 1940, I had heard stories of Home Secretaries striding up and down the room and taking three days over it," he told me. "Of course, one must carefully weigh up all the relevant considerations, but I alway took the view that if you'd come to a decision there was no sense in getting into a state about it. I don't say I did it quickly: sometimes I said 'Give me twenty-four hours'—and then pronounced my decision. But a good many of the cases are very clear: and if you're clear about it and your obligations under the law, there's no point in undue delay."

On the other hand the late J. R. Clynes, also a Socialist Home Secretary, did occasionally 'get into a state about it'.

He was a publicly confessed abolitionist when he took office, and this made his task all the more difficult. One night he had an hallucination.

It was a couple of days before a man called Podmore was due to be hanged. The murder had been brutal, but it had taken the police over a year to arrest Podmore, and the evidence was finely balanced. Nevertheless, the jury convicted, the Court of Criminal

Appeal upheld the conviction, and Clynes decided against a reprieve.

Then came a newspaper report that fresh evidence was forthcoming. Clynes cut short his Easter holiday and returned to London. He spent all day at the Home Office, but nothing arrived.

Tired and worried, he returned alone to his deserted suburban house, and sat up late, reading.

Suddenly, "just at midnight", he relates in his *Memoirs*, "there came a knock on my door, hollow-sounding, as if made by a stick or a bony hand. I opened the door and there, standing a few yards away was a dim figure, coarsely bearded, looking as like an apparition from the grave as anyone would care to imagine."

"I have come to speak to you about the hammer used in the Podmore case," said a gentle voice.

But the Home Secretary knew his protocol: "I, as gently, replied that it would be improper for me to discuss such a matter in private, but that I would do so at the Home Office next morning, according to the requirements of my position."

"I-cannot-come-then," replied the visitor.

Clynes closed the door, and next day gave special instructions at the Home Office for any caller on the Podmore case to be brought straight up. But no-one arrived, and Podmore was hanged. "It was something like a true ghost story," commented Clynes a little sadly.

Other politicians did not take the job so much to heart. Sir John Anderson was Permanent Under-Secretary at the Home Office for ten years and Home Secretary for a year, but this particular aspect of his duties impinged so little upon his life that his gifted and experienced biographer, Sir John Wheeler-Bennett, does not mention it at all, except to quote one short extract from a speech, in the 430 pages of his official biography. Sir William Joynson-Hicks, whose nickname 'Jix' and notoriously tall collars made him a cartoonist's delight, held office for five years in the second half of the nineteen-twenties, and almost certainly hastened his death by the gruelling work he put in at the Home Office at a time of constant political unrest. But in a memorandum he dismissed the non-political chore of dispensing mercy as "perhaps one of the most trying and painful tasks which can fall to the lot of any Minister". One can almost hear the langour in the voice as the busy dandy dictates the minute.

Outward appearances can sometimes be deceptive. Few people will be surprised to learn that Sir Samuel Hoare (1937-39) often used to take days over his decisions. It is well known that during his two years of office this confirmed abolitionist reprieved 60

per cent. of all persons sentenced to death, as against the average
for the thirties of 47 per cent. But if one was asked to guess how
long Sir John Simon took over the job one would be tempted to
say, "Thirty seconds flat!" He had that look about him: cold and
calm and clear. In fact, the late Sir Alexander Maxwell says that
this apparently austere man, former Attorney General, twice Home
Secretary, and for five years Lord Chancellor, "used to have difficulty in making up his mind, and once reprieved a woman on the
ground that if he had defended her he would have got her off!"

A man's attitude to this task is irrespective of party politics.
This is how Lord Chuter-Ede, Home Secretary in the Labour
Goverment of 1945-51, described to me the nature of his duties,
and how he carried them out:

"No extraneous principles affect a Home Secretary's mind . . .
The Home Secretary has to administer the law as he finds it.
He has to do it on his own inner conscience. When Attlee
appointed me, he said: 'You cannot ask for advice from your
colleagues. They are not bound to support you in your decision' . . . I was told by the head officials that my great advantage was that I always reached a decision quickly . . . There is a
certain tradition about the office. In the old days if I had a
borderline case, six cases as analogous as possible would be
presented to me on one side and six cases on the other, and
my attention would be directed to the salient points."

This differs little in spirit from what Lord Tenby, one of Lord
Chuter-Ede's Conservative successors, has also told me:

"It's a difficult question to answer if I have any regrets. I
gave the most terrific consideration to every case. It's a terrible
responsibility . . . I would have liked to reprieve everyone but
I had to administer the law of England . . ."

One other thing seems clear: the Home Secretary's family had
nothing to do with it. Often when it was publicly known that a
reprieve was being considered letters of abuse descended upon
the Minister and his family, particularly his wife. But, "My father
never discussed his cases in the family", says the present Lord
Bridgeman, William Clive Bridgeman's eldest son, "though I know
that each one distressed him greatly." Comments Lord Tenby:
"Sometimes when I was worrying about a case I would mention it
to my wife, but I would never ask her opinion, and she would
never volunteer it."

All this, of course, looks at the position from the point of view
of the Home Secretary himself. Like most self-portraits, they are
painted not without a certain sympathy. Some outsiders feel that a
few warts have been left out.

"It's impossible to tell what goes on," a barrister who has defended several murderers told me that in the last years of capital punishment, "you just don't know what affects the Home Secretary's mind." "It seemed hit and miss," comments an ex-prison chaplain. "You couldn't put a farthing on it. Half the time you'd say to yourself, 'This one will go'—and he'd be reprieved: half the time you'd say to yourself, "He's sure to be reprieved'—and he'd be hanged!'" says a former prison governor of considerable experience.

One might have expected so dedicated an abolitionist as Sydney Silverman, M.P., to say: "It was the arbitrary decision of one man taken in private." But it was perhaps a little surprising for the late P. Kynaston Metcalfe to say to me in the summer of 1962, towards the end of his fifty-two years as Under-Sheriff of the County of London, during which time he had been responsible for over four hundred executions: "I just don't know the basis on which reprieves are granted. There probably are no set rules. If there is a definite policy I would like to know what it is . . . I think it's all a matter of the individual Home Secretary's personal attitude." One might have expected the judges to be more attuned to the ministerial wavelength. Yet one judge wrote to me: "If you want my ideas on how and why—i.e. the principles on which reprieves are given in capital cases—I can only say I have not the least idea and often wished I knew."

Were there any rules? Only 2 per cent. of all convicted capital murderers had their convictions quashed in the Court of Criminal Appeal. Did the fate of the other 98 per cent. depend upon the personal caprice of the current Home Secretary or his advisers; or was there a canon by which they worked?

The Home Office always denied that it was capricious. "There is a clear distinction between the type of case where a reprieve is granted and where it is not," Sir John Anderson once said. "It is not a knife-edge. It is a somewhat blurred line. But it is a recognizable line and the vast majority of cases are quite clearly above the line or quite clearly below it." The late Sir Alexander Maxwell told me much the same thing: "There are summarized filed reports of precedents to which one can refer. But it is seldom done. One has a 'feel' of the tradition—like a barrister with reports of decided cases."

Home Secretaries themselves in their public utterances were of little help. They invariably hid behind a smokescreen of vagueness; as, for instance, R. A. Butler in a debate in the House of Commons in 1961: "The Home Secretary takes into account all available information, including information which cannot be made public, and has regard to all the relevant considerations and circumstances." But what was relevant? Lord Butler did not say.

This vagueness persisted to the end.

When eighteen-year-old Peter Anthony Dunford was reprieved, in January 1965, for his part in a stabbing at Wakefield gaol there was one predominant reason in most people's minds: because the House of Commons had two weeks earlier passed the second reading of Sydney Silverman's Abolition Bill. No other compelling grounds existed for extending mercy to this brutal young killer, who at the time of the stabbing was already serving a life sentence for an earlier murder. Even so, the Home Secretary, Sir Frank Soskice, hedged. "I had a full report and studied the case very carefully," he said. The Silverman Bill was merely "a weighty consideration", he told a *Sunday Times* reporter.

In 1950 the Home Office was compelled to show some of its hand by the setting up of the Gowers Commission. In a detailed memorandum presented to the Commission they repeated the classic proposition "the grounds on which reprieves are granted do not admit of exhaustive categorisation," but went on, none the less, to set down three categories of murder where reprieves were a 'foregone conclusion', and, apart from the question of insanity or other mental abnormality, they also set out ten further categories which "are recognized as needing specially close scrutiny to see whether there are such extenuating circumstances as would justify reprieve."

The three categories of certain reprieve—'mercy killers', survivors of genuine suicide pacts, and mothers who kill their young children—ceased to exist with the passing of the Homicide Act. But for the rest the catalogue remained: "There has been no change in our practice so far as I am aware," Sir Charles Cunningham told me.

The list contained much the sort of material one would have expected—unpremeditated murders—provoked murders—murders with no intent to kill, especially in a quarrel—murders committed while drunk—murders committed by more than one person with differing degrees of responsibility—youth, though not enough in itself, 'is always taken into account'—'there is a natural reluctance to hang a woman'—rare cases where 'it has been found right to commute . . . in deference to a widely spread or strong local expression of public opinion'—very rare cases where the physical condition of the prisoner has made it impossible to hang him 'expeditiously and humanely.'

It is easy to criticize this catalogue of mercy. It was not exhaustive: it did not, for instance, include old age, though no-one over seventy has been hanged in England since 1927, and even in the Yemen the successful military insurgents in the 1962 Revolution did not carry out the death sentence on Ali Ahmad Ibrahim, former Royalist Army Chief of Staff, because he was eighty-five. Also, of course, the list said nothing of the circumstances in which a convicted person would *not* be reprieved.

But the most serious criticism is that the list was mere window-dressing, that in private the Home Office did not comply with the rules it had laid down in public. "It's a lottery," a cynical solicitor once complained to me. Arthur Koestler and C. H. Rolph were more explicit: in a detailed analysis of the 123 murderers hanged between January 1949 and February 1961 they calculated that nearly a quarter were cases "where the presence of extenuating circumstances could hardly be denied." Why then were they not saved?

Was there duplicity in Whitehall?

The Home Office have not made it easy to give a definite answer. Their refusal to reveal officially the reasons for any individual decision means that one can only surmise and conjecture, or indulge in amateur detective work, as I have done for the later chapters of this book.

It is, in fact, not difficult to find examples where the popular known facts appear to bring a case within one of the categories of mercy, but the killer was nevertheless hanged.

In December 1953, for instance, a twenty-four-year-old furnace-man named Francis Wilkinson was executed for murdering his landlady's five-year-old daughter. He had battered the child to death, then attempted to assault the body sexually. Two psychiatrists gave evidence that he was a psychopath, and his mother claimed that as a young child he had found a newborn baby torn in half in a dustbin. It is difficult to believe such a man could not have been suffering from some form of mental illness or diminished responsibility. Michael John Davies, a young Londoner himself awaiting execution in another condemned cell in the same prison, saw Wilkinson a few days before he died, and his description is both terse and expressive, though not couched in psychiatric jargon: "He had wide, staring eyes. He was a nut!"

Neither Davies nor I are experts on mental illness. Bearing in mind the evidence at the trial, a medical inquiry must have been held in Wilkinson's case, and one can only assume that the doctors saw no reason to recommend a reprieve on medical grounds.

The truth is that the law of reprieve was like the law of cruelty in divorce cases. Defining the circumstances in which a reprieve would be granted was like defining the circumstances in which a judge would hold that a married person had been 'cruel': it cannot be done. It is impossible to crystallize into one trenchant sentence or paragraph what is and what is not cruelty in all cases or what would or would not have led to a reprieve in all cases. Each case turns on its own specific facts. Only a mad genius like William Blake can hold infinity in the palm of his hand.

Sir John Anderson stated the situation prosaically but accurately when he once told a parliamentary committee: "It is the cumulative effect of a variety of considerations that is ultimately decisive rather than some particular aspect."

Take the case of a youthful murderer. The Home Office are on record that youth, over the minimum age of eighteen, was a factor. But this did not stop several teenagers being hanged. Why? Because there were other considerations that rightly or wrongly outweighed the culprit's youth—such as the extreme violence of his crime, as with Henry Jacoby, or its cold brutality, as with 'Flossie' Forsyth—two eighteen-year-old murderers whose cases I discuss in later chapters.

Sometimes there was such an upsurge of horror at the enormity of the crime that it was difficult for reason to prevail. One may pride oneself on one's toughness, but the photographs of what Neville George Clevely Heath did to Doreen Marshall, his second victim, turn the stomach. "I don't think Heath stood a chance of a reprieve—his crime was just too awful!" says Mr Henry Elam, now a judge at London Sessions, but in 1946 junior prosecuting counsel at this sexual sadist's trial.

"There was as near to consistency as you could get," Lord Chuter-Ede has told me. "There could not be apparent logic, because all the facts were not apparent," says a retired senior Home Office official.

Sometimes it was all a matter of interpretation: Rex Harvey Jones, a twenty-two year-old miner from the Rhondda Valley, was hanged, despite his jury's strong recommendation to mercy. He had strangled his girl friend after drinking seven pints of beer and making love to her. He had not been in trouble before, and he was under the influence of drink—both relevant factors in considering a reprieve. In 1961 Koestler and Rolph wrote that this was one of the many cases which made nonsense of Home Office pretensions to consistency. They may be right. Or the truth may simply be that seven pints of beer were not enough to make a lusty young Welshman lose control of himself or to excuse murder.

And while one is attacking the catalogue of mercy it is perhaps only fair to bear in mind the very many cases where it quite obviously was complied with.

Lord Chuter-Ede has told me of one such case in his own experience. The list specified "murders committed under provocation which, though insufficient to reduce the crime to manslaughter, may be a strongly mitigating circumstance." Says Lord Chuter-Ede: "John Simon had laid down—as Lord Chancellor in *Rex* v. *Holmes*—that words could not provoke. Despite this, I had a case where a man and woman, who were living in low conditions in the North, had gone to a public house, where they had a quarrel. The woman shouted at him, 'The trouble with you is that you can't use a woman when you've got one. You're impotent!' He hit her, and she never regained consciousness. There are some words in some circumstances that are a provocation that cannot be ignored. I reprieved that man, and I am sure I was right to do so."

Lord Chuter-Ede was in advance of the law. It was not until the Homicide Act that Lord Simon's dictum in *Rex* v. *Holmes* was overruled. Thereafter words could legally amount to provocation. But even in the more tolerant climate of the nineteen-sixties it was still possible to find a court throwing out a provocation plea— and the Home Secretary yet reprieving.

It happened in November 1963 in the case of Edgar Valentine Black.

Some two years before, Mrs Black had had an affair with another man. It did not last long, and Black, although suspicious, could not prove it. Yet it preyed on his mind; eventually he left his family, bought a shotgun—for which he duly took out a licence —travelled to Cardiff, and shot the man dead on his own doorstep. Mr Justice Glyn-Jones ruled that there was no evidence of legal provocation to go to the jury, and the Lord Chief Justice, Lord Parker, said on appeal that it was a clear case where a conviction was inevitable. Even so, Henry Brooke, the Home Secretary, reprieved—to be met by the comment of the murdered man's widow: "Black should have hung. He killed my husband in cold blood."

In theory the Home Office attitude to the hanging of women remained to the end the same as in its memorandum to the Gowers Commission fifteen years earlier: 'There have been occasions on which the Home Secretary of the day has expressly had regard to the prisoner's sex in deciding to recommend commutation.'

In fact, Ruth Ellis was the last woman to be hanged in July 1955. Three years later Mrs Mary Wilson, the notorious 'Widow of Windy Nook', was convicted of the double poisoning of her second and third husbands, and, according to a Press report, the police were convinced that she had also killed her first husband and a lodger. She was clearly an evil woman: before the Homicide Act poisoners were nearly always executed, and almost certainly Mrs Wilson would have been hanged. Yet she was reprieved.

It is possible that her age—she was sixty-six—was a factor. But in 1954 fifty-three-year-old Mrs Stylou Christophi had been hanged for the murder of her daughter-in-law, despite her jury's recommendation to mercy. It is more likely that Mrs Wilson was reprieved primarily because she was a woman: because, possibly among other reasons, Lord Butler, then Home Secretary, could not bring himself to order her execution, complete with the ritual donning of rubber knickers.

Whatever the prisoner's sex the death sentence was not carried out if his or her physical condition made it impossible to perform "in a seemly manner, or some scandalous thing may happen", to quote Sir Frank Newsam to the Gowers Commission. In the fifteen years prior to 1950 five murderers were reprieved for this reason, and there were at least two subsequent cases.

It seemed to be almost a matter of luck whether a murderer was physically capable of being executed.

In April 1948 William John Gray was reprieved although he had pleaded guilty to shooting his wife. After he killed her he turned the gun on himself, but survived—with two inches of jawbone shot away. And this saved him. He could not be hanged: the noose would have slipped over his head.

But another murderer in Kent slit his own throat, also with the intention of killing himself. He was nursed back to life in the prison hospital, sentenced to death, and hanged. His injury did not make the execution 'undesirable'. As an eye-witness at such an execution has told me: "A cut throat has no effect except that it makes a mess."

As recently as February 1964 a man may again have been saved because he could not 'decently' be hanged.

Christopher Simcox had already committed one murder when he shot dead his sister-in-law in the autumn of 1963. In 1948 he had killed his first wife, but had been reprieved automatically by Lord Chuter-Ede while Parliament was debating the suspension of capital punishment clause in the 1948 Criminal Justice Bill. Ten years later he was released from prison, remarried, then shot his new wife and killed her sister.

tre:

Sir Henry Curtis Bennett, K.C. (her counsel).

Photo: Mirrorpic

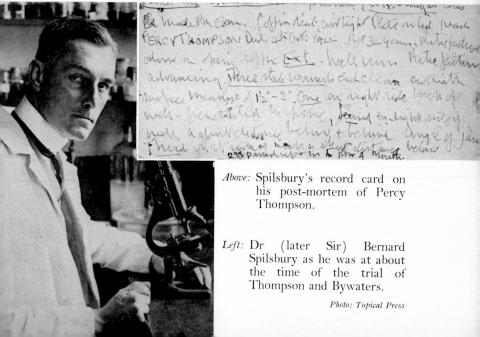

Above: Spilsbury's record card on his post-mortem of Percy Thompson.

Left: Dr (later Sir) Bernard Spilsbury as he was at about the time of the trial of Thompson and Bywaters.

Photo: Topical Press

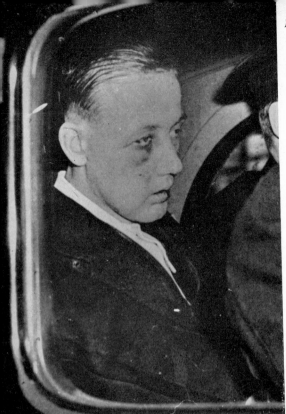

John Thomas Straffen on his way to Reading Magistrates' Court to answer to the charge of murdering Linda Bowyer after his escape from Broadmoor.

Photo: Keystone Press Agency, Ltd.

Horfield Prison (where Straffen is still detained) on the morning of 17th December 1963 when Russell Pascoe—see page 128— was executed.

Photo: Mirrorpic

The new wife told a reporter that all her family were "disgusted" by the reprieve. But Henry Brooke, the Home Secretary, had no option. Simcox, like Gray, had turned his gun on himself after the shootings and could not walk because of his injuries. According to some reports he would have had to be wheeled to the scaffold in a wheel-chair, and Mr Brooke, a much criticized Home Secretary, took the only human course in refusing to permit it.

Strangely enough the Home Office did not include in its catalogue of mercy cases where the jury recommended it. Sir Frank Newsam merely told the Gowers Commission: "The Home Secretary always attaches weight to a recommendation to mercy by a jury, and he would be very reluctant to disregard such a recommendation, *if it is concurred by the judge.*" The italics are mine, for the italicized words were indeed the sting in the tail. "The recommendation to mercy is a frill," confided Sir John Anderson to the Commission in an unguarded moment. And the truth is that jury recommendations weighed far less with the Home Secretary than the public, and jurors, supposed.

"The fact that juries sometimes add a recommendation to mercy to their verdict of guilty of murder does not necessarily imply that clemency is justified or acceptable," Sir Norwood East once wrote magisterially. The Home Office theory was that a recommendation in itself meant very little: it could merely be the price of unanimity forced upon eleven jurors by a doubtful or abolitionist twelfth. Unofficially the court authorities tried to prevent this by arranging that no known abolitionist was empannelled on a capital jury. But this was still England: most abolitionists held their views in private, and no court official could be sure.

The official scepticism towards juries' recommendations was reflected in the available statistics. In the first half of the twentieth century reprieves were granted in only 68 per cent. of the cases where mercy had been recommended. But where the judge agreed with the jury a reprieve was refused in only six English cases in fifty years. It seems as if the Home Office treated jurors like children, and said, in effect: "No, we won't listen to you unless a responsible adult—the judge—agrees with you."

Apart from the insult that this afforded the intelligence of the nation's jurors there was yet a further blemish. This was secret justice. For the judge never revealed in open court whether or not he sided with the recommendation. There was not even any uniform practice as to how he, privately, communicated his views to the Home Secretary.

One retired judge tells me that if he agreed with the recom-

H

mendation he would say so at once when formally reporting the jury's verdict to the Home Secretary: if he did not agree he would add nothing, and merely state flatly that the jury recommended mercy. Another judge says that his practice was normally not to say anything either way, but wait until he was asked. It takes all kinds of judges to make a judiciary.

Certainly where there was a recommendation to mercy the Home Secretary would want to see the judge, unless the recommendation was accepted by the judge and the case was absolutely clear-cut, such as a 'mercy-killing' before the Homicide Act. In all normal cases the judge would be invited to the Home Office, and the Home Secretary, probably with the Permanent Under-Secretary also present, would want to know what the judge's views were. What sort of jury did he think it was? Did they seem intelligent? Did they appear to be following the case? etc. As Lord Morrison explained: "I often saw the trial judge in such cases. They were always very helpful. They did not try, and I did not invite them to give me, a decided opinion as to what I should do.

"They would help with the background. Usually they were very good in this way: only once did a judge tell me that it was my job to evaluate the case. With this exception, they would give me their opinion of what they thought of the accused and the witnesses, and then leave the rest to me."

In a parliamentary speech Lord Chuter-Ede has given a good instance of the rôle a judge can play.

As Home Secretary he once disregarded a jury's recommendation to mercy, and a juror wrote to him complaining that he had let him down. The juror had stood out for a long time against a verdict of guilty, until the foreman said, "We have been here a long time and you are the only person standing out. If we make a strong recommendation of mercy, will you fall into line? . . . You can rest assured that the Home Secretary will grant a reprieve."

One of the reasons why Lord Chuter-Ede did not reprieve was that he asked the trial judge what grounds existed on the evidence for strongly recommending mercy, and the judge replied: "I haven't the remotest idea!"

CHAPTER TWELVE

Who really made the Decision?

No feature of the British constitutional scene was more strictly preserved than the tradition that the Home Secretary was alone responsible for recommending the exercise of the Royal Prerogative of Mercy. Home Secretaries and their civil servants never tired of maintaining that it was a personal decision.

Even in their private conversation civil servants furthered this image. They had a sort of built-in reflex for referring to "the Home Secretary's decision" or "the Secretary of State's responsibility". The late Sir Ernley Blackwell was one of the most powerful civil servants of the century: for twenty years he was Legal Assistant Under-Secretary at the Home Office, with special jurisdiction in murder and other criminal cases. The post no longer exists, and since his time few civil servants have wielded such immense power within the Department. Yet Sir Malcolm Hilbery, a retired judge, recalls that Blackwell would never, even in the most casual conversation, express a personal opinion on a case, "and would always talk in terms of the Home Secretary taking a particular point of view."

It was all most impressive. But the British have a genius for floodlighting the façade of power while all is darkness behind. What was the reality?

Within the thick walls of Sir Gilbert Scott's edifice in Whitehall where did the true source of power lie? Was it in the Home Secretary's lofty, spacious chamber or in the slightly less capacious quarters of his Permanent Under-Secretary?

Or was it outside Whitehall altogether? In Buckingham Palace perhaps, or Downing Street, or in the panelled consulting rooms of Harley Street, or in the dignified calm of a High Court judge's private room?

Who *really* made the decision?

It is amazing in a modern, constitutional monarchy how many people believed that the Queen herself had the power of decision.

Frequently when a prisoner lay under sentence of death relatives or friends sent urgently worded telegrams to Buckingham Palace, imploring the Queen not to permit the execution. Even some lawyers, anxious to do all they could for their clients, tried it in one last, desperate attempt to avert execution. In the case of George Riley in February 1961 the condemned man's solicitor, Mr Anthony Hayes, of Shrewsbury, took this desperate course. Its result left him disillusioned. "I don't care what the Bill of Rights says. It's so much bunkum that every citizen has the right to petition the Queen," he says.

Riley, a twenty-one-year-old butcher's boy, was due to be hanged for the capital murder of an elderly neighbour. Two days before the execution Mr Hayes received the official notification that there would be no reprieve, and that evening he sat down with Riley's junior counsel and hammered out on his dining-room table a petition to the Queen. There had already been the ordinary one to the Home Secretary, which had been rejected: this was Riley's last chance. "We were fighting against the clock," says Mr Hayes. "But we were just able to get it done in time. My wife typed it out neatly. We jumped into my car, and managed to get to Shrewsbury station in time to catch the night mail-train before it pulled out—in fact, we'd phoned, and they had waited for us."

Mr Hayes need not have bothered. At 10.45 the next morning the Queen's Private Secretary wired this telegram from Buckingham Palace: "In accordance with Constitutional Practice your petition has been forwarded immediately to the Secretary of State for the Home Department." Later that day came a telephone call from the Home Office: there was no change in the Home Secretary's decision. Mr Hayes is rather bitter: "What can you expect?" he asks. "If the Queen is bound to pass on a petition to the same man who had already dealt with an earlier petition—and rejected it! The man in the street is not getting the effective application of the Royal Prerogative to which he is entitled."

In fact, the Sovereign last played an independent, though ineffectual, part in the administration of the machinery of royal mercy in 1907, with Edward VII's abortive protest at the reprieve of Horace George Rayner.

Wherever else the true seat of decision may have been it was not at Buckingham Palace. And in a constitutional monarchy perhaps that was only right.

The man whom most people thought made the actual decision, other than the Home Secretary, was the Permanent Under-Secretary, the head of the Civil Service within the Department.

For many years his salary was greater than the Minister's—

£7,500 a year against his titular chief's £5,000—though since April 1st, 1965, the ratio has been changed with the Minister having a slight head, at £8,500, against the Permanent Under-Secretary's £8,200.

The Permanent Under-Secretary was always knighted: the Minister might or might not be, and most often was not. He held office for an average of just under eleven and a half years: the average span of a Home Secretary was about three years. In a department where great stock is placed upon tradition and regard for precedent it is not surprising that the Permanent Under-Secretary should have come to be regarded as personifying the spirit of the department rather than the transient politician who found himself at the Home Office for a few brief years *en route* to other things.

The calibre of the men was likely to be different. The Permanent Under-Secretary had reached the top of his tree: he was a man who had reached the summit of his profession. As Lord Butler once said about higher civil servants: "They have very silky minds, they've Rolls-Royce minds." In comparison only seven of the sixty-one Home Secretaries since the creation of the Department in 1782 have gone on to hold the highest political office of all, the Premiership; while one Home Secretary has been an ex-Prime Minister on the down-grade. The other fifty-three office-holders have ranged from men of outstanding ability to incompetent mediocrities. No fool has ever been Permanent Under-Secretary.

As Anthony Sampson has written, "The two heads of each department—the Minister and the permanent secretary—are from two different worlds, and their relationship is the vital joint in Whitehall." There is a story of one Labour Minister who, when suddenly asked his opinion in Cabinet, fumbled with his papers and read out slowly: "The Minister is advised to say . . ." Home Secretaries were no less likely than other Ministers to fall under this kind of spell.

When Sir William Joynson-Hicks became Home Secretary, in November 1924, he paid a visit to his Permanent Under-Secretary on the morning of assuming office. With his usual ebullience he burst into Sir John Anderson's room, rubbing his hands. "Well, Anderson," he said, "isn't this splendid? I hope you're glad to see me!" Standing with his feet in the fireplace and his back to the grate, Anderson pulled his glasses down upon the bridge of his nose and, staring over them, replied: "I have been brought up in a profession which has taught me that it is wrong to give expression to emotions either of pleasure or sorrow on occasions

such as this." His huge St Bernard of a face was absolutely ex-
pressionless.

It would be idle to pretend that men like Anderson did not
exert considerable power at the Home Office. "Joynson-Hicks was
an awful fool," says a man who knew them both very well. "But
Anderson knew how to manage him. He was a remarkable man of
outstanding ability who exerted immense authority, though he always spoke softly and used the language of moderation. Another
bad Home Secretary was Gilmour, who was inclined to be erratic,
though again his Permanent Under-Secretary, Russell Scott, was
usually able to control him."

"I have never known a weak Permanent Under-Secretary," commented the late Sir Alexander Maxwell.

As we have seen, when it came to deciding on a reprieve the
Home Secretary was faced with a departmental recommendation
hammered out between the senior civil servants and placed in
front of him by this daunting personage, the Permanent Under-
Secretary, who assumed full responsibility for it. What happened
then is a matter for conjecture. But a surprisingly good account
of what probably occurred comes from a completely unexpected
source—a man who has spent ninety-two days in the condemned
cell before being himself reprieved.

This is Michael John Davies, convicted in October 1953 of the
stabbing on Clapham Common of a seventeen-year-old boy, talking to me in the summer of 1962:

"I don't for one minute think that the Home Secretary sits
there with all these sheaves of paper and thinks Oh, well, I
think we can let that one off, or I don't think that chap warrants
a reprieve.

"I think he has a committee, maybe two or three of his secretaries, Under-Secretaries, they read through it; they put down
a list of all the things one way or the other. And I think it's then
more or less decided. I don't think he reads miles and miles of
papers. I think he just reads what they draw up, and then he
decides. But they already have almost told him what to do.
And I think he just sort of finishes up the rest. He probably
agrees with them most of the time—but I suppose he could go
the other way if he thinks to the contrary."

What were the chances of a Home Secretary's 'going the other
way'? Sir Alexander Maxwell comments. "I should have had
a great feeling of guilt if any Minister of mine took a decision
which I thought was wrong—and I never had occasion to experience that feeling!"

In the end it all came down to a question of the relationship between the individual Home Secretary and his Permanent Under-Secretary. I asked three ex-Home Secretaries whether they always followed their Permanent Under-Secretary's recommendation. Here are their answers:

Lord Morrison: "Overriding the recommendation was, for me, a two-way traffic. The Civil Service is very fair: if they can find any extenuating circumstances, they will tell you. Sometimes—not often—I would override the Department's recommendation for mercy, if I thought the facts did not warrant it. Though I more often overrode them when they advised against a reprieve."

Lord Chuter-Ede: "I would never, of course, overrule a recommendation to be merciful. Once the Department considered it right that mercy should be extended, I was not going to be astute to decide to the contrary. But I have sometimes overruled the recommendation when it has gone the other way."

Lord Tenby: "If the Home Office recommended a reprieve I would not dream of going against them. Of course not. But I have done so once to the contrary, when the recommendation was against a reprieve. It was a young guardsman and I asked, if I recommended a reprieve, did the doctors think he would make a good citizen; and I was told, 'Yes', so I recommended a reprieve. I've also changed my mind and gone back on a previous decision not to recommend a reprieve because of new facts that came to my notice."

Ministers and their permanent heads of department, neither then nor now, were supermen, all of the same standard. They were human beings of varying temperament and intelligence. Their relationship, the one with the other, varied as do all relationships between any two people. It seems clear that the permanent head of the Home Office wielded considerable power, and a weak Home Secretary might well have been a rubber stamp. But—as any Town Clerk who has had to handle successive Mayors will know—it was all a matter of the individual who happened to be in office at any given moment.

It was sometimes said that when cases of outstanding importance occurred, with possible international repercussions, the decision was taken not by the Home Secretary, but by the whole Cabinet. This certainly occurred during the First World War when the Cabinet as a whole decided that Sir Roger Casement should die. But there is no other authenticated instance, at least in modern times.

The reprieve decision was one time when the Cabinet's collective responsibility for Ministers' individual acts did not hold true. As Lord Attlee told Lord Chuter-Ede when he assumed office, "You cannot ask for advice from your colleagues. They are not bound to support you in your decision."

It even happened that a Prime Minister expressly disapproved of a particular decision, but still did not interfere. Towards the end of the Second World War a twenty-two-year-old American serviceman, stationed in this country, and a British girl, who was only just over eighteen, were convicted of murdering a London taxi-driver, whose cab they hired in order to rob him. Karl Gustav Hulten, the American, shot the driver, and the girl, Elizabeth Maud Jones, rifled his pockets before the two of them bundled his body into a ditch.

There was very little to be said for the girl, except her extreme youth, and it was on that basis alone that Herbert (later Lord) Morrison reprieved her. The American was left to die, much to the dismay of the American ambassador, who visited Lord Morrison at the Home Office and spent an hour trying to persuade him to save the man as well. Morrison refused, and Hulten was hanged. Only then did Sir Winston Churchill tell Morrison that he thought he was wrong to have reprieved the girl.

As for the Home Office doctors, Sir Malcolm (formerly Mr Justice) Hilbery once told me: "We're in the hands of the alienists or—as they're called nowadays—the psychiatrists . . . If they say there's a medical reason for not hanging a murderer he's not hanged!"

I am sure that this was true. The Home Secretary has never been a psychiatrist, and if reputable psychiatrists told him that there were medical reasons for reprieving a man because of his mental condition, why should he not have accepted that recommendation?

But Sir Malcolm Hilbery, and those who thought like him, did not so much attack the fact that Home Secretaries accepted their doctors' positive recommendations to reprieve. That was an inevitable consequence of having a Minister unqualified in medical matters making a decision on medical grounds. What really perturbed Sir Malcolm, and those for whom he spoke, was the increased tendency since the end of the Second World War to consult psychiatrists in the first place. The judicial antipathy to psychiatry is a well-known phenomenon of our time.

Some psychiatrists are indeed quacks; just as some judges are prejudiced and lacking in humanity. But Freud is not a dirty word: nor even Jung nor Adler. Modern psychiatry, properly applied by men of integrity, was and is our main source of knowledge about the workings of the human mind. Only with such knowledge can we assess a person's responsibility for his actions. And only when he knew the extent of a person's responsibility could the Home Secretary, on our behalf, decide whether that person should pay the ultimate penalty for his crime. When we study individual cases which we will do later in this book we will see that what is sometimes disquieting is, not that psychiatrists were consulted, but that they too had no monopoly on truth. They too may have made mistakes, mistakes that influenced the Home Secretary and may have defeated the ends of both justice and mercy.

Finally there were the judges; what rôle did they play in deciding on a reprieve?

As we have seen, they were sometimes asked to visit the Home Secretary to help him on some question of factual information about the trial. And if the jury recommended mercy the Home Secretary always wanted to know whether the judge concurred: if so, a reprieve was almost certain.

But over and above this basic mimimum the extent of a judge's contribution to the final decision depended on his individual temperament.

"I never gave my views unless I was asked", a retired judge of great distinction and long experience has told me. "I always did my best to keep clear of involvement in questions of reprieve. I believe implicitly in the division between the judiciary and the executive. The finding of guilt is a judicial act: the carrying out of the sentence is an act of the executive. It was not my concern."

Although some of the newer judges were probably abolitionists this had nothing to do with whether they would try and influence the Home Secretary to grant a reprieve. Like others caught up in the administration of the law, abolitionist judges had to apply the criminal law as they found it. Lord Donovan when he was a High Court judge presided over many capital trials with complete objectivity, although when he was a Labour M.P., in 1948, he voted against the death penalty in the House of Commons.

Yet traditionally the judiciary were hostile to reprieves. Lord Parker, the Lord Chief Justice, was stating the conventional view when he said in the summer of 1960: "Either the verdict of the court should be strongly supported or the death sentence should be abolished."

Even so, if a judge, abolitionist or not, set his heart upon it he could undoubtedly exert considerable pressure upon the Home

Secretary. Sir Malcolm Hilbery—who, incidentally, was far from being an abolitionist—says that in his experience judges more usually asked to see the Home Secretary than the other way round. And he told me this story:

"I had a case once at the Old Bailey when I summed up for manslaughter because I thought that the puny little man in the dock simply was not physically capable of having banged the dead woman's face against a wash-basin so that all her bones were smashed in—as was the medical evidence. I thought he had killed her all right: but in a quarrel when he had pushed her and her head had struck the wash-basin. He did not mean to kill her—but the jury still convicted of murder. I made it my business to see the Home Secretary, because I was determined that if I could do anything about it—and I knew I could —that man should not be hanged. And he wasn't!"

But judges did not always triumph. As far back as 1907 Herbert Gladstone, when Home Secretary, was prepared to make a public fool of the Lord Chief Justice, Lord Alverstone, and reprieve Horace Rayner though Alverstone had told him in court that he could not hope to be saved. "I have never been able to fathom the reason," commented Alverstone sadly in his memoirs.

At the start of this chapter I asked the question: "Who really made the decision?"

I think the answer was twofold. Where the reason for a reprieve was medical it rested largely with the doctors. It is just possible that a Home Secretary might have reprieved for medical reasons even though the doctors had not recommended it: he might have had some pet medical theory of his own. But it is inconceivable that where the doctors in effect recommended mercy the recommendation would have been ignored. To that extent we were—to use the words of Sir Malcolm Hilbery—"in the hands of the alienists".

Where medical considerations were not involved, the decision was generally the Home Secretary's alone. He may have been advised, he may have been cajoled, he may even have been high-pressured. But in the ultimate a reasonably strong-willed Home Secretary made up his own mind.

CHAPTER THIRTEEN

After the Decision

THE Home Secretary sat back in his chair and lit a cigarette. One way or the other the decision was made: the weight was lifted from his shoulders.

Now the Civil Service took over.

If the decision had been to recommend mercy two formal documents would be required: a respite and a conditional pardon. The respite was a document signed by the Home Secretary, and respiting the prisoner "until the Queen's Pleasure is known." Though bearing only the Home Secretary's signature it was issued by "The Queen's Commands", and had the immediate effect of suspending the prisoner from sentence of death.

The conditional pardon was a royal warrant, signed by the Sovereign and countersigned by the Home Secretary, which formally pardoned the murderer on condition that he served a term of life imprisonment.

In the modern practice no prisoner was told he was reprieved until the official submission to the Queen for her consent to the conditional pardon was received back, duly initialed, at the Home Office from the Palace. "Normally, no respite is forwarded to the sheriff or the prison governor until the Queen's consent has been obtained," Sir Charles Cunningham told me. "After all, it is Her Majesty's Prerogative that is being exercised."

Sir Charles would then send the respite and a letter announcing the conditional pardon to two different officers, though both would be dispatched the same day by different means. The respite would be addressed to the High Sheriff, and, being the more urgent, was sent by hand to the Governor for immediate communication to the High Sheriff and the prisoner. The letter was sent by ordinary post to the Governor and would arrive the next day.

At this stage also the Permanent Under-Secretary would write to the prisoner's solicitor, if he had made representations about the case, and to anyone else who had made such representations, informing them of the conditional pardon. He would also write to the trial judge and to the judge who had delivered the judgment of the Court of Criminal Appeal in the case, notifying them of the decision and enclosing a copy of the medical inquiry if one had been held. The Press would now be told.

There was no fixed time-limit for the Home Secretary's decision although a negative recommendation was usually made as late as possible. Furthermore with a negative recommendation the normal practice was not to tell the prisoner nor make it public, until forty-eight hours before the time of execution. This was sometimes criticized as heartless and keeping the prisoner in unnecessary suspense. But Sir Charles Cunningham defended it on the grounds of humanity: "It seems to us kinder to let the prisoner go on hoping until the last possible moment," he said. Forty-eight hours was about the minimum period that the Sheriff needed to organize final arrangements for the execution, and it also allowed the prisoner time to prepare himself spiritually for a death that was now inevitable.

The prisoner heard his fate from the prison governor. Some so-called experts have written that the man was taken up to the governor's office and told there. This was not so. Immediately he received the respite the governor would visit the prisoner in the condemned cell and tell him the news there.

How he did it would depend upon the personal temperament of the individual governor. "If a man was reprieved I always used to go straight to see him," an ex-governor has told me. "And I'd say, 'I've got good news for you. It's all right. The Home Secretary has reprieved you!' I'd then tell him that the rest was up to him. He would get life imprisonment, and how long he stayed in prison would depend on how good a prisoner he was. You had to say this, because they always wanted to know what would happen to them: you couldn't just tell them, 'You have been respited until the Queen's Pleasure is known', with the man standing there in front of you!" Other governors, particularly of the old school, were not so humanitarian or soft, if one prefers to call it that. They simply read the prisoner the Under-Secretary's letter and left it to the prison officers to explain what it meant. Whether they did it this way because they were tough or because they were weak a psychiatrist would be more qualified than I to say.

As for the prisoner, here is a reprieved murderer's account of such an interview. He had been in the condemned cell for two months, and this is how he described it to me fifteen years later as we sat talking quietly in my car, parked in a peaceful country lane near his present home:

"The first I knew was when the prison governor came in and said 'Stand up, Brown'. [This is not the man's real name.] He went on to tell me that the Secretary of State had directed him to tell me that I had been reprieved and that I was to be detained during the King's Pleasure. Then they took me to the prison hospital, and I think the doctor put something in my cocoa, because I went straight to sleep and woke up the next morning.

I felt choked as I walked across to the hospital. It's a strange feeling: you never forget it when you're told that you're not going to die. I thought all the prisoners were looking at me because I'd come out of the condemned cell."

Technically a reprieve could take effect only with the prisoner's consent. Sir Edward Troup has commented drily that this consent might be either expressed or implied. In practice it was always taken for granted.

"It is a nice question", wrote the late Professor Maitland in his classic study of constitutional history, "whether a condemned offender pardoned on condition of his going into prison, might not insist on being hanged." The learned professor did not answer his own question. Perhaps this was just as well. For the popularly held notion that every murderer jumped with delight at not being hanged was poppycock. Life is not always sweet.

"No governor has ever yet met a capital prisoner who would refuse a reprieve or did not ardently long for one," ex-prison governor Sir Basil Thomson has claimed. But as long ago as the late eighteenth century a sailor named Robert Webber was petitioning the Home Secretary against his own reprieve. Webber had been sentenced to death at Maidstone Assizes for robbery on board ship, but the judge had reprieved him and commuted the sentence to transportation. "He hopes the law won't be broken by not transporting him, death being all he requires," wrote Webber anxiously to the Minister.

As late as 1910 a murderer reprieved by Sir Winston Churchill, when Home Secretary, committed suicide soon afterwards rather than face the fifteen years he expected to spend in prison.

"The truth is," an assistant prison governor told me in the summer of 1963, "that by the time a man is in the condemned cell and the execution date comes near he just couldn't care less. He just wants to get it over with.

"That's why if it does go against a reprieve, and they're hanged, most, if not all, murderers go well. It's all so quick there is no need for the officers to support them. They walk to the scaffold. They are glad to get it over with.

"You must understand what an ordeal they have been through. Most lifers I've met have said that, at least in the early stages, they would rather have been 'topped'. And this feeling can persist for as long as two years afterwards. At the time all they

want is to be shot of life, of everything: they've had enough."
The ex-governor whom I have already quoted is an older man.
He was more guarded in his language: "I have never known a
prisoner who was not delighted to be reprieved—once he realized that it did not mean he would be in gaol for the rest of his
life. Certainly I have had cases where at the time of reprieve
the man has said he would rather the execution had gone through.
Of course, they are very overwrought at the time. But the real
reason is that they think they are going to be in gaol for the rest
of their lives. Later on they have realized just how lucky they
were. In the old days a man would serve about nine years. Now
it may have to be very much longer in some cases . . ."

Formalities still had to be complied with. The prisoner was removed at once to the prison hospital where he stayed for several
weeks under medical supervision until he calmed down and was
ready for transfer to the prison where he was to serve his sentence.

It was in the hospital, therefore, usually on the very next
day, that the governor paid his second official visit, upon receiving the formal letter from the Home Office telling him that the
Queen had approved a conditional pardon commuting the
death penalty to life imprisonment. By now the prisoner had a
pretty fair idea of what was happening, but protocol still had to
be observed. The governor formally notified him of the contents
of the letter, and countersigned it to that effect.

The early weeks in the prison hospital could be very trying for
a man. He had orientated himself to death, and now he had to re-
orientate himself to life on a completely alien basis. In the old
days most murderers had never been in prison before: now they
had to contemplate for countless years ahead a cell as their home.
"I didn't like it. I was frightened," a reprieved killer has told me.
"I didn't like the idea of going to prison with all those murderers!"
His own offence was a mere matter of striking an old man in a
drunken quarrel, robbing him, and leaving him to die in a near-by
ditch.

Religion consoled some. The chaplain kept up his visits, only
now to the prison hospital. Says an experienced prison chaplain:
"Almost as soon as he was settled in I went and saw a reprieved
prisoner. I found them extremely relieved and somewhat stunned.
They seemed not to know what had happened to them." Merely
because he was not to die did not necessarily mean that a murderer's torment had ended. The church could still help. "You
couldn't go on living", says a Roman Catholic who murdered his
sweetheart, "if you thought that the person you'd loved—and
killed—was six feet under the ground, and that was the end of it!"

So much for the capital murderers who were not hanged. What was the procedure when the Home Secretary gave the thumbs down, and a prisoner was condemned to die?

The Queen played no part. Death-warrants ceased to exist when Queen Victoria ascended the throne. The legal authority in modern times for a prisoner's execution was not a royal warrant but the sentence of death itself, pronounced by the judge at the end of the trial. If a killer was to die the Sovereign's hands were not stained: there was no official submission to the Queen from the Home Office, no conditional pardon or other document for signature. The papers were not even sent to her.

The Home Secretary's desk was cleared, and the Permanent Under-Secretary merely wrote to the Sheriff and the prison governor telling them that he was directed by the Secretary of State to inform them of his decision and that the execution would take place as planned. Much the same letter, together with the Home Secretary's 'regrets', was sent to the prisoner's solicitor and anyone else who had made representations on his behalf. The man's wife or parents were not officially informed as a matter of right, only if they had made formal representations for a reprieve to the Home Office. Official relationship to the condemned prisoner counted for more than personal relationship. The trial judge and the presiding judge who had dismissed his appeal (if any) were always informed. And at some time the Press were notified, though not necessarily at once.

Someone had to tell the prisoner. Someone had to go down to the condemned cell and tell him that he would definitely die in two days' time. This task was the prison governor's: he had expressly to tell the man that there was no reprieve and that the execution would take place, as planned, on such-and-such a date. Different men did the job in different ways, but this is one man's account of it:

"I would never read the letter in such circumstances. I'd simply say, 'Brown, I'm damned sorry but I'm afraid the Home Secretary has not been able to recommend a reprieve in your case. The execution will take place as planned next Tuesday morning!' He then might say, 'Does that mean there's no hope, sir?' and I'd reply, 'I'm afraid not. I'm awfully sorry . . .'"

It sounds terribly British and stiff upper-lip, but was there any better way of doing it?

In fact, this governor was not being 100 per cent. accurate. Occasionally the Home Secretary changed his mind and reprieved a man after he had first decided against it and both the prisoner and the Press had been told. Admittedly there is no recent instance—certainly none since the Homicide Act. But it happened several times this century before 1957. Prison governor's wife Margaret Wilson has written of one case where the change of decision did not reach her husband until 3 o'clock in the morning, on the day of the proposed execution; and Lord Tenby has told me of an instance in the mid-nineteen-fifties, when, as Home Secretary, he changed his mind because of some new fact at 5 o'clock in the evening, after having earlier that day decided against recommending a reprieve.

"It was in the last few days that one got a wonderful chance to help a man," says a prison chaplain. The prison governor would always tell the chaplain at the first opportunity of the Home Secretary's negative decision—"and one always got down fairly soon afterwards."

However, no-one could die in the condemned man's place. Only he knew the experience of contemplating imminent, certain death. Some screamed, some were terrified, a few lost their nerve at the last minute. But the amazing thing is how calmly the vast majority of condemned murderers accepted their fate. "I have always been terribly impressed by the calmness and bravery of the man in the condemned cell when he is told there is no hope and he must die. It was quite phenomenal. He seems able to find a form of strength within himself": these are not the words of some sentimental abolitionist, but of a man who has been a prison governor for many years, and is still in the prison service.

"I am quite convinced these men were given a special strength to face the ordeal," says a priest. "The calmest man at an execution was the condemned man."

Many found solace in religion: Henry Jacoby was confirmed shortly before he died, as was George J. Smith the notorious 'Brides in the Bath' murderer. Sir Roger Casement 'sobbed like a child' after submitting to his first confession, and Henry Graham, a forty-two-year-old ex-serviceman hanged in 1925 for murdering his wife, went to the scaffold chanting "O, Lamb of God, I come!"

This was particularly true of the type of murderer sentenced to death before the Homicide Act. Even so, twenty-three-year-old Russell Pascoe, a Cornish labourer hanged in December 1963 for the joint murder of an elderly hermit in the course of theft, was baptised and confirmed in the condemned cell. "It is a reminder that no-one is beyond God's reach," said the Bishop of Bristol, who officiated.

Some confessed their crime, and when this happened it used

to be Home Office practice until the start of the century to publish the news, as if to vindicate the Home Secretary's decision. Others refused to the last to admit their guilt: as did the Welsh solicitor Herbert Rowse Armstrong, who in the death cell refused an offer of £5,000 from Edgar Wallace to sell his story to a newspaper chain.

Yet all was not always sunshine and peace. After hearing on the eve of his execution that there was to be no reprieve Dr Crippen, perhaps the most famous wife-killer of all, wrote a farewell note to his young mistress, Ethel Le Neve, then broke off one of the metal side-pieces of his spectacles, and tried to slash an artery with its jagged end.

Some were fatalistic. Sex-killer Neville George Clevely Heath is alleged to have said to the hangman and his assistant as they entered his cell: "Come on, boys, let's be going!" A few were bad-tempered. Colin Wilson and Pat Pitman relate that Margaret 'Bill' Allan, the forty-three-year-old sexual misfit who was hanged in January 1949 for the murder of an elderly neighbour, kicked over her last breakfast tray and said that at any rate no-one else would enjoy it. But whatever their attitude all ended up dead. There was no modern John Lee of Babbicombe, reprieved in 1886 because three times the trap-door lever refused to function.

On his last day the prisoner would—at least until recently—for the first time since his sentence wear again his own clothes. Guardsmen died with their boots on, and murderers, until about the early nineteen-sixties, died in mufti—except for Margaret 'Bill' Allan, who had to put on a striped prison frock instead of her normal man's suit.

"It is not true that a condemned prisoner can choose what he likes for his last breakfast," Mr J. W. Holt, then Director of Prison Administration told me in 1961. "The prison medical officer has power to augment his diet at any time if he so wishes. There is no special ruling about the final meal, though a man is always offered two ounces of spirits twenty minutes before his execution —which is quite often refused. Sedatives? They are rarely given, though again it is entirely a matter for the prison medical officer's discretion."

How one describes the last scene of all is perhaps a matter of personal preference.

Albert Pierrepoint, for many years the chief executioner, gave this account in a television programme in October 1961:

"When I am inside the condemned cell I fasten the prisoner's arms behind his back with a leather strap. Then he is escorted

I

out of the condemned cell into the execution chamber. My assistant fastens the prisoner's legs while I place a white cap over his head and the noose round his neck. As soon as I see that everything is ready, I pull the lever, the prisoner falls through and it is all over in an instant."

Arthur Koestler, however, has written:

"The truth is that some prisoners struggle both in the condemned cell and under the noose, that some have to be carried tied to a chair, others dragged to the trap, limp, bowels open, arms pinioned to the back like animals; and that still other things happen which should happen only in nightmare dreams."

"No-one really liked it," says a retired prison chaplain. "I always used to say, 'Keep your eyes on me son.' There was no official form of service. The chaplain could pray silently or audibly, in cassock, or cassock and surplice, sometimes even in plain clothes. I used to say the words of the Commendation of a departing soul . . . as much for the persons present, as for the man himself."

Major Ben Grew was a tough penal administrator. For nearly thirty-five years he was in the prison service, for many of those years a prison governor. Yet he has written how he would always stand to one side of the execution chamber, where he would not be in the prisoner's direct line of vision as he entered—in case he made "a final impassioned plea for mercy which I was not in a position to give." "After witnessing my first execution I was physically sick," a former prison officer has told me, "but if you cannot face up to the job, you shouldn't take it on."

It took less than half a minute to kill a murderer. Mr Pierrepoint told the Gowers Commission that normally it took between nine and twelve seconds from the time the hangman entered the condemned cell to the pulling of the lever. Even in the few prisons where the condemned cell did not adjoin the execution chamber it took no more than twenty to twenty-five seconds. Judicial hanging may not have been pleasant to watch, but at least it was soon over.

When all was finished, and the prison medical officer certified that life was extinct, one final legal requirement remained. An inquest had to be held upon the body. Thereafter the man's prison clothes were burned, his belongings returned to his next-of-kin, and the corpse buried within the confines of the prison.

The death penalty was a terrible thing. So was, and is, murder. My primary concern is the apparatus of reprieve. I take no sides, except to mutter with Edmund Burke: "Mercy is not a thing opposed to justice. It is an essential part of it."

PART THREE

Individual Cases

So much for history and general principles. Now, our task is to investigate certain specific cases to see how the reprieve system has worked in individual instances. All types of murderers will be met in the following pages—unfaithful wives, a peeress's son, professional criminals, an ex-public schoolboy, a sex-murderer, a child-killer, an ex-Nazi, 'respectable' people driven to murder, and disreputable people murdering almost by reflex. All have ended up as names on the Home Secretary's calendar.

The cases are in chronological order, and have been selected because each one exhibits an important aspect of the reprieve system in operation. They have not been chosen at random or simply because they tell an interesting story. I have dealt only with cases where I have been able to discover new facts or publish new material. This has been the primary yardstick. This part of the book is not a hack retelling of 'famous cases', compiled from newspaper cuttings or already existing accounts.

With one exception all cases are of this century, and in each instance I have been helped by the prisoner's solicitor or someone who tried to help him or a politician who took an interest in the case; sometimes by the man who was Home Secretary, sometimes even by the defendant himself, where he was eventually reprieved and served his sentence of imprisonment. Occasionally I have been able to state certain facts only by not disclosing my source.

The one exception is the first case, that of Mrs Maybrick. She was sentenced to death in 1889, and no-one with first-hand knowledge of the affair still survives. However, I have researched into literary material not usually connected with the case, and think I can fairly claim to have something new to say.

One final matter: as with the preceding pages, I have not

*been concerned to write either a pro-hanging or anti-hanging
tract. My aim is merely to tell the truth or as much of it as
I can. At the end of each chapter the reader should be in
much the same position as the Home Secretary, and able to
decide for himself whether or not he would have granted a
reprieve. I state my own views, but there can be as many
views as there are readers.*

CHAPTER FOURTEEN

Florence Maybrick

(1889)

AN essential characteristic of the modern reprieve system was its secrecy. The Home Office never disclosed why a capital murderer was reprieved or hanged. Neither to Parliament nor the Press did the Home Secretary reveal the reasons for his decision. Even the prisoner himself did not know.

The case, more than any other, which established this principle was that of American-born Mrs Florence Maybrick. The Home Secretary made public his reasons for reprieving her, and they were such obvious nonsense that the practice, till then quite common, was discontinued.

Paradoxically, no-one has ever seriously contended that Mrs Maybrick should have been hanged. However, almost everyone has agreed that she was reprieved for the wrong reason.

The Home Secretary in question was one of the most incompetent of recent times, a fastidious Q.C. called Henry Matthews, who owed his appointment primarily to his friendship with Lord Randolph Churchill, a leading member of the Conservative Government which was formed in July 1886.

Queen Victoria did not like him from the start: "He is so mad and odd," she recorded in her journal. Three times she asked Lord Salisbury, the Prime Minister, to get rid of him. Each time Salisbury agreed, but did nothing. The Government's majority was too shaky to jettison a senior Minister. So "the French dancing master"—as a parliamentary wit dubbed this French-educated dandy—remained at Whitehall until Salisbury himself fell in 1892.

In that time he had to deal with Israel Lipski—whose case we have already seen he bungled—and Mrs Maybrick.

It was early in 1881 that Florence Elizabeth Chandler, an eighteen-year-old girl from Alabama, first met on board ship in mid-Atlantic a prosperous Liverpool cotton-broker named James Maybrick. It is difficult to understand what she saw in him. She was quite an attractive girl: he was in his early forties—a popular businessman, but hardly a Prince Charming. Perhaps she was tired of having no permanent home and being trundled across the Atlantic between her grandmother in New York and her mother and German stepfather in Cologne.

Perhaps the truth lies in the birth only eight months after their marriage of a baby boy.

Anyway, for the first three years they lived in America. Then they returned to Liverpool, where two years later a daughter was born.

Unfortunately, Maybrick had not forgotten his bachelor habits. Eventually Florence discovered that he was being unfaithful. At first there was little she could do. She was a foreigner with few friends in a somewhat dour city. Her easy-going Southern drawl was in itself enough to set her apart from the sober, bourgeois society of late-Victorian Liverpool.

Then one night Maybrick brought home a merchant friend for dinner—a young man named Alfred Brierley. Now at last Florence had consolation. She and Brierley became good friends, subsequently lovers. Both insisted that the latter development occurred only once, when they summoned up enough courage to spend two nights together at an hotel in London, in March 1889. Brierley later claimed in an affidavit that they "parted abruptly at the hotel", when it was understood that they would never do the same again.

Florence returned to Liverpool. But it is not easy for an unhappy woman to ignore her lover. A few days later she spotted Brierley at Aintree, where Maybrick had taken her for the Grand National, and, despite her husband's protests, insisted in talking to him. When they arrived home there was a quarrel, and Maybrick blacked her eye. For the first time she threatened to leave, and a family friend had to mediate.

This marked the turning-point in James Maybrick's health-chart. Up till now he had been a normally robust man of middle years. Henceforth he became nervous and apprehensive, almost a hypochondriac.

Twice during April he travelled to London to see a doctor, but apart from indigestion Dr Fuller could diagnose only a bad case of nervous anxiety.

Perhaps Maybrick had good cause, for twice during the same month Florence visited a local chemist and bought fly-papers, three dozen in all. "The flies are beginning to get troublesome in the kitchen," she explained to the assistant. Possibly not a very important purchase—except that all the fly-papers contained arsenic; two servants later saw her soaking them in water, and flies were *not* being troublesome in the kitchen.

James Maybrick's last illness started three days after Florence's first visit to the chemist. He was stricken with severe vomiting, and though sometimes showing improvement he could not throw off the malaise which gripped him. Acute dyspepsia was diagnosed, but none of the normal cures seemed to work.

Then, on May 8th, Alice Yapp, one of the servants who had seen Florence soaking the fly-papers, reported her discovery to two women friends of Maybrick. One of them immediately telegraphed his brother Michael in London in fine, melodramatic style: "COME AT ONCE. STRANGE THINGS GOING ON HERE", and went to see Maybrick's other brother, Edwin, who was living in the house. Edwin promptly ordered that in future only the nurses should give his brother food.

That same afternoon Florence, ignorant of this development, gave Alice Yapp a letter to post. It was addressed to Brierley, so the doughty Miss Yapp promptly handed it to Edwin Maybrick. Its contents were indeed suspicious: "Since my return I have been nursing Maybrick night and day. He is *sick unto death* . . . and now all depends on how long his strength will last . . . Relieve your mind of all fear of discovery now and in the future. M. has been delirious since Sunday." "Sick unto death" was heavily underlined.

Next day Florence went even farther to make people believe she was a murderess. Shortly after midnight she entered her husband's room, picked up a bottle of meat juice that was near the bed, and without a word of explanation to the mystified nurse took it into her own room. A few minutes later she returned and put it back. The nurse reported the incident to Edwin Maybrick, who sent the meat juice for analysis. The verdict: it contained half a grain of arsenic.

Nor was this all. Maybrick was overheard saying to Florence, "You have given me the wrong medicine again!" which she denied. And later: "Oh, Bunny, Bunny, how could you do it? I did not think it of you!"—to which Florence replied, "You silly old darling, don't trouble your head about things."

Twenty-four hours later Maybrick was dead. But his wife was not by his bedside. She had collapsed some hours earlier, and lay prostrate in her own room.

She lay in bed for three days. "Dazed and stricken, weak, helpless, and impotent," she afterwards described her condition. She asked to see her children, but her brother-in-law, Michael, had taken them out of the house. Finally a uniformed police superintendent walked into the room and told her she was under arrest for the murder of her husband.

No-one could blame the police. Florence might write in desperation to Brierley: "Appearances may be against me but before God I swear I am innocent," but few people could be expected to believe her. Besides the highly suspicious way in which she had acted during the last weeks of Maybrick's life, the police discovered hidden about the Maybrick house enough arsenic to kill fifty people. And three eminent pathologists after Maybrick's post-mortem delivered a joint opinion that his death was due to inflammation of the stomach and bowels set up by some irritant poison.

Most people thought it was a clear case of murder. Even Mr Justice Stephen, who was to try the case, commented in open court a few days before the trial, when arranging his list at the forthcoming assize. "Sir Charles Russell (leading for the defence) may plead guilty!" The local and national Press were full of condemnation of the friendless woman who had committed the double sin of being both a foreigner and an adulteress. When Florence was driven through the streets of Liverpool to stand her trial at St George's Hall, on the morning of July 31st, 1889, the crowds hissed as she passed by.

Yet when, exactly a week later, she was taken from court under sentence of death and driven to the condemned cell at Walton gaol the mob was silent. Their hisses and boos were reserved for the judge as he clambered into his carriage.

What brought about this remarkable change was, basically, British sense of fair play. Florence Maybrick's trial had been slipshod, rambling, and unsatisfactory. By the end the jury were convinced of her guilt. But almost no-one else.

The blame rests primarily with the judge. Mr Justice Stephen was a great lawyer, one of the most illustrious of the nineteenth century. But by the time he came to try Florence Maybrick he was a mentally sick old man. He had had a stroke four years earlier, and although he insisted on returning to the Bench it was obvious that his intellectual powers were considerably dimmed. Less than two years after *Regina* v. *Maybrick* public pressure forced his resignation, and he died fairly soon afterwards, some said in a private asylum. It would be going too far to accept the language of a local newspaperman who described him as "the great mad judge sitting down to try his last case". But the late Lord Birkett has commented that Stephen's summing up "left much to be desired", and a careful reading of the transcript leads to only one conclusion: Sir James Fitzjames Stephen was no longer capable of conducting a major criminal trial.

The summing up lasted two days, disproportionately long for

a case where the whole evidence and four speeches by counsel took only five days. It was discursive, and contained many errors. But, unfortunately for Florence, it contained clear indications to the jury that in Stephen's view she was guilty. Normally a judge of his calibre would have conquered his prejudice and not allowed it to affect his conduct of the trial. But Stephen was no longer sufficiently in command of himself to do so.

The jury of ten tradesmen and two farmers duly did what they thought the judge wanted: they convicted without wasting much time in discussion. It still happens today, and happened even more often seventy-odd years ago. It took them only thirty-eight minutes to reach their verdict and return to court—after a trial which had lasted nearly seven working days. Others did not share their notion of instant justice. Declared *The Times* next day: "It is useless to disguise the fact that the public are not thoroughly convinced of the prisoner's guilt."

The trouble was—the medical evidence.

Only about one-tenth of a grain of arsenic was found in Maybrick's body even though the post-mortem had been carried out within two days of his death. There were no traces of poison in the organs where it would have been expected nor in the dead man's bedding, where it might have been exuded while he was still alive. Of the five distinctive symptoms of arsenical poisoning only two were present—violent sickness and some abdominal pain.

Dr (afterwards Sir) Thomas Stevenson, the Government analyst, testified that he had "no doubt that Maybrick died from the effects of a poisonous dose of arsenic." Dr Charles Tidy, of the London Hospital, and Dr Macnamara, of a leading Dublin hospital, were as vehement that death had not been caused by arsenic. Both sides agreed that Maybrick had died of gastro-enteritis. The dispute was whether it had been brought about by arsenic, impure food, or a chill contracted at the races in late April.

What about the arsenic, however small in quantity, found in Maybrick's body? And the prodigious amounts found in the house? Sir Charles Russell called several highly respectable witnesses, including an ex-Mayor of Liverpool, to prove conclusively that Maybrick had been addicted to arsenic as others today are addicted to hashish or cocaine or 'purple-heart' pills. Sir James Poole, the ex-Mayor, had even warned him at their last meeting that if he did not stop, the drug would kill him.

So although the case looked black against Florence one can understand Russell's confidence when before the trial he boasted to a friend that he was sure of an acquittal. Russell was one of the greatest advocates of the nineteenth century and by nature not accustomed to modesty. To him it must have seemed that he was destined for yet another forensic triumph.

His defence was twofold: first that the Crown had not proved beyond reasonable doubt that Maybrick had died of arsenic; second that they had not proved by any direct evidence that Florence had administered sufficient quantities of the poison to prove fatal—a terribly powerful point when one remembers that she was debarred from all effective nursing three days before her husband's death.

As was shown by the furore after Florence's conviction, Russell's arguments succeeded in persuading most of the medical profession and the greater part of the public outside the courtroom. They failed inside the courtroom, because, for once, he bungled. As Lord Birkett, himself an outstanding defender, has written: "The greatest of advocates are not immune from grave errors of judgment."

In my view Russell was too single-minded in his conduct of the case. He pared everything down to his two basic points—the uncertainty as to cause of death and the lack of proof as to administration of the poison. Then, having run the whole case on these two simple issues, he committed the craven error of allowing his client to make a statement from the dock at the very end of the trial, which knocked the whole foundation of his case sideways.

In 1889 the prisoner was not permitted by law to give sworn testimony in his or her own defence. All that some indulgent judges allowed was a statement from the dock. It was unsanctified by the oath and untested by cross-examination. But at least it gave an accused person the chance to state his side of the case. It was known that Mr Justice Stephen was a judge who permitted this laxity, and Russell duly asked him to let Florence make a personal statement.

In itself this was a great mistake. It was totally unnecessary. Russell could simply have stood back and told the jury it was for the prosecution to prove their case, and they had failed to do so. No-one in a British court then or now can be convicted on suspicion alone. There was no obligation on Florence to answer a case which had been only half made out.

Three years earlier Sir Edward Clarke, Q.C., Russell's greatest rival, had adopted exactly this tactic when defending Adelaide Bartlett, another young foreign wife charged with poisoning her husband: and the gamble had paid off. She was acquitted. Lord Birkett writes that Russell should have followed Clarke's lead, and there can be little doubt he is right.

But Russell, to my mind, made a double error.

As Mr Justice Stephen commented to the jury, he must have known what his client was going to say. Yet in his questioning of the witnesses he made scant effort to substantiate in advance the allegations he knew Florence was going to make. He was so committed to his chosen line of defence that he almost ignored everything else. This passionate Ulsterman was blinded by his confidence—and his conceit.

Two things were disastrous about Florence's statement. First, her attempt to excuse the purchase of the fly-paper and second, her explanation of why she tampered with her husband's meat juice on the night before his death.

"The fly-papers were bought with the intention of using as a cosmetic," she told the court. She claimed that for many years she had used a face-wash with an arsenical base, prescribed for her by an American doctor. She lost the prescription sometime in April, and since she was suffering from a slight skin rash, she decided to try and make a substitute face-wash with the arsenic from the fly-papers. It sounds wildly improbable, but it might just conceivably have been true, and, indeed, later her mother swore an affidavit that the missing prescription had been found. This was the lynch-pin of the whole case: if there was an innocent explanation for the purchase of the fly-papers the prosecution must flounder. If there was just a chance of persuading the jury that it might be true it was Russell's duty to take that chance and hammer the point home with all the power of his vaunting personality.

He did not do so. And the omission was so glaring that even the judge commented on it.

In his final speech prosecuting counsel John Addison, Q.C., was quick to remind the jury that trouble with her skin was not the explanation that Florence had given the chemist: she had told him there were flies in the kitchen. It was an obvious observation. But Russell did not attempt to counter it either in his own final speech or in his previous questioning of the witnesses. If only he had extracted from one of the many witnesses who saw Florence during April that she appeared to have some kind of skin trouble on her face his client might have walked out of court a free woman. Yet he did not explore this avenue at all: not one question, however tentative, was directed to this issue.

As for her explanation of tampering with the meat juice, Florence claimed in her statement that Maybrick during the last days of his life "wished to have me with him. He missed me whenever I was not with him. Whenever I went out of the room he asked for me."

(Never suggested by Russell when cross-examining any of the nurses or servants!) She told the jury that on the night of May 9th, Maybrick implored her to put some powder, which he told her where to find, in his meat juice. He assured her it would not harm him, and, since he was so pressing, she gave way. She now realized that the powder must have been arsenic, but she did not know this at the time.

If Maybrick was an arsenic-addict, and the contrary was never really argued, this seems perfectly feasible. Yet again Russell had not by one mildly worded query tested this line of defence when cross-examining the nurse who gave evidence for the Crown about the incident.

Personally I believe that Russell realized he had failed his client. "I tremble to think that any want of care, or of vigilance, or of skill on the part of my able and loyal colleagues and myself should in any way imperil the interests of the client committed to our charge," he told the jury in his final speech. These were strange words for an advocate of his renown, and temperament, to use. I think they indicate a troubled conscience, as does his extraordinary behaviour after the conviction, when he personally interceded with the Home Secretary for a reprieve, and thereafter never ceased to bombard every newly appointed Home Secretary with a demand for Florence's immediate release from prison. He maintained this agitation right up to his death eleven years later, even when he was Lord Chief Justice of England. And it is perhaps revealing that some years after his death a close friend wrote to a newspaper to refute the suggestion that Russell believed his client was innocent: as he himself wrote to Florence shortly after he became Lord Chief Justice, "You ought never to have been convicted"—which is not the same thing.

No-one has seriously argued that Henry Matthews was wrong to reprieve Florence Maybrick.

Admittedly, he dithered as usual, and held innumerable conferences at the Home Office. Various witnesses were called to see the Home Secretary, including Dr Tidy, the leading defence doctor. Affidavits came in from Florence's solicitors and Alfred Brierley, her lover. Meetings were held in London and Liverpool; a petition in her favour was signed by several M.P.'s; further petitions poured in from all parts of the country, some addressed direct to the Queen or the Prince and Princess of Wales. *The Times* and most of the leading newspapers were inundated with letters from doctors, lawyers, arsenic-takers, and friends and acquaintances of the dead man.

Finally, after nearly three weeks, came the expected announcement. It was expected, because most informed persons took the same view as Mr Fletcher-Moulton, Q.C., (later a distinguished judge) who wrote to *The Times*: "The evidence for the Crown has failed to negative the explanation that Maybrick's death was due to natural causes operating upon a system in which a long course of arsenic-taking had developed a predisposition to gastro-enteritis." It was inevitable that the Home Office take a similar view: there must be an element of doubt as to Florence Maybrick's guilt.

But Matthews in the public announcement disclosed his own tortuous reasoning—and it was palpable nonsense. Instead of merely saying that the prisoner was reprieved, and leaving it at that, or saying that she was reprieved because, in view of the medical evidence, there must be an element of doubt as to her guilt, Matthews was more specific. He said:

"Although the evidence leads clearly to the conclusion that the prisoner administered and attempted to administer arsenic to her husband with intent to murder, yet it does not wholly exclude a reasonable doubt whether his death was in fact caused by the administration of arsenic."

This was poppycock. Matthews was, in effect, saying that although Florence had been convicted of murder, he thought she was guilty only of attempted murder. To this there is one obvious and immediate answer. As Lord Simon, a later Home Secretary, has observed: "She had never been tried for attempted murder and had only been defended on the charge that her murderous purpose had been fulfilled." If the charge had been different the line of her defence would have been different. And she might never have been convicted. Certainly she would have been spared the ordeal of the black cap and nearly three weeks in the condemned cell.

"It was a fatal error and quite unnecessary" for Matthews to state his reasons, Lord Simon has written. No-one could have complained if Matthews had reprieved quietly and discreetly. As it was, the official announcement caused a new furore, in which even *The Times* was critical of the Home Secretary.

In a book published in the United States after her eventual release from prison Florence has given her own overblown account of how the reprieve decision was reached. If accurate, it shows that Matthews dithered, as ever, almost until the last moment:

"I knew nothing of any public efforts for my relief. I was held fast on the wheels of a slow-moving machine, hyponotized by the striking hours and the flight of my numbered minutes, with the gallows staring me in the face. The date of my execution was not told me but I heard afterwards that it was to have taken place on August 26th. On the 22nd, while I was taking my daily exercise in the yard attached to the condemned cell, the governor, Captain Anderson, accompanied by the chief matron, entered. He called me to him, and with a voice which—all honour to him—trembled with emotion, said: 'Maybrick, no commutation of sentence has come down today, and I consider it my duty to tell you to prepare for death.' 'Thank you, governor,' I replied. 'My conscience is clear. God's will be done.'

He then walked away and I returned to my cell. The female warder was weeping silently, but I was calm and spent the early part of the night in my usual prayers. About midnight exhausted nature could bear no more, and I fainted. I had barely regained consciousness when I heard the shuffle of feet outside, the click of the key in the lock—that warning catch in the slow machinery of my doom. I sprang up, and with one supreme effort of will braced myself for what I believed was the last act of my life. The governor and a chaplain entered, followed by a warder. They read my expectation in my face, and the governor, hastening forward, exclaimed in an agitated voice: 'It is well; it is good news!' When I opened my eyes once more, I was lying in bed in the hospital."

Florence remained in custody for fifteen years, then the normal period for a reprieved murderer of good behaviour. And this creates a mystery which has remained unanswered: why was she detained for so long? If the official view was that her only proven crime was attempted murder, why did the authorities keep her in prison for the normal span of someone who had completed a murder? In 1898—six years before her final release—Russell, then Lord Chief Justice of England, wrote to Sir Matthew Ridley, Matthews's successor at the Home Office, pointing out that Florence had then served a period of imprisonment four times as long as the minimum punishment fixed by law for attempted murderers. The American Ambassador was also continually pressing for an early release for his countrywoman. Only opposition from the most powerful quarters could have helped the Home Secretary withstand such pressure.

Florence Maybrick herself suggested in her book that the explanation for her protracted imprisonment lay in the fact that although there were five different Home Secretaries during that time their decisions had "all been drawn for them by the same gentleman"—presumably, the Permanent Under-Secretary. But this cannot be right. There were three successive Permanent Under-Secretaries of State during Florence's fifteen years in gaol.

The reason for this unhappy woman's long detention has to be sought elsewhere, in a totally unexpected source—one which was both strong enough to withstand the entreaties of the senior criminal judge of the country and the protests of a friendly Government and enduring enough to survive four different changes of Home Secretary. There can be only one person who fitted this bill. And that was another woman—the Queen.

One of the few people who objected to Matthews's original decision to reprieve Florence Maybrick was Queen Victoria. Her views were naturally not made known at the time, and I believe that I am the first to give them public prominence. But her *Collected Letters*, published after her death, reveal her private secretary writing at her behest to express the Queen's anger and regret that so wicked a woman should escape "by a mere legal quibble".

Victoria had still not fully emerged from the black despair of her early widowhood. The death of her beloved Albert was still a loss that she found almost insupportable. She had nothing but loathing and condemnation for a woman who could murder her husband. "The law is not a moral profession she must say," wrote her secretary to Matthews. *"Her sentence must never be further commuted."*

The italics are mine, for I believe this sentence provides the vital clue as to why Florence dragged on for so many years in gaol. She was never released in Victoria's lifetime nor for three years afterwards.

A politician's biography reveals that the Queen maintained her interest in Florence Maybrick. Her concern was no passing whim. For when, three years later, Lord Salisbury's Government fell, and Henry Asquith succeeded Matthews at the Home Office, Asquith's official 'Life' discloses that the Queen had a long discussion with him about his attitude to his new post: his diary specifically records that she wanted to know his views about sentences, prisoners, Mrs Montague, Sir Edward Grey—and Mrs Maybrick. Why should this particular criminal be the subject of royal after-dinner conversation unless the Queen was anxious to know whether the ambitious new Minister's views coincided with her own?

Most people assume that it was masculine indifference to a woman's suffering that kept Florence Maybrick so long in prison.

The true reason may well be an aged widow's hatred of a young, adulterous wife.

In due course that young wife too became an aged widow. But Florence Maybrick did not live out her life in a palace or even in the solid Victorian splendour of a large old house on Merseyside. After her release from prison she returned to the United States, and thirty-seven years later, in 1941, a milkman kicked open the door of a squalid, tumbledown shack, outside a small Connecticut town, to see dozens of hungry wailing cats crawling around—and lying on the bed a seventy-nine-year-old woman, in rags, her hair grizzled, two of her few remaining teeth grotesquely tied together with string. She was dead. It was "Mrs Chandler", the recluse whom the locals called "The Cat Woman".

But in her youth her name was Florence Maybrick, née Chandler.

CHAPTER FIFTEEN

Ronald True and Henry Jacoby

(1922)

AFTER the 1957 Homicide Act said that diminished mental responsibility was sufficient to reduce capital murder to the non-capital
variety, the McNaughton Rules ceased to be the main escape
route from the gallows. This archaic formula for assessing the
bounds of criminal responsibility became almost forgotten. Seldom
did eminent doctors and psychiatrists contrive to testify whether
or not the accused person "Was labouring under such a defect of
reason, from disease of the mind, as not to know the nature and
quality of the act he was doing, or, if he did know it, that he did
not know he was doing what was wrong."

"Many men are still in Broadmoor today only because a jury
took a lenient view of their case under the old Rules," says Professor Desmond Curran.

Undoubtedly, in the Rules' heyday murderers tried to sham
their way into Broadmoor. They preferred to be locked up, even
in a mental institution, than die on the scaffold. Was Ronald True
such a man? In the early summer of 1922 he stood his trial for
murder: he claimed he was insane, supported that claim by overwhelming medical evidence, but the jury rejected it and held him
to be a fraud. Yet he did not hang: the Home Secretary said he
was insane, and sent him to Broadmoor.

As if that was not enough to inflame public opinion, the very
day before True's reprieve was announced the Home Secretary
allowed an eighteen-year-old boy named Henry Jacoby to be
hanged despite his jury's strong recommendation to mercy.

The reprieved man was a wealthy woman's son, some said she
was a member of the peerage: the hanged youth was an impoverished, friendless pantry boy. "Privilege!" was immediately
the cry.

All the ingredients existed for a first-class combustion, and the
tinder was not slow to ignite. The consequent explosion not
only nearly drove the Home Secretary from office, but almost
brought about the downfall of the entire Government.

K

Looking back on it now, was the Home Secretary—a burly, Northumbrian K.C. named Edward Shortt—at fault?

True was monocled, well dressed, and arrogant. Thirty-one years of age, he was not a particularly nice person, and his crime was brutal.

After spending the night with a London prostitute named Gertrude Yates in her basement flat, in Fulham, he got up early, went into the kitchen, made some tea, brought it into the bedroom, and as Gertrude stretched out sleepily for her cup struck her five times on the head with a rolling-pin. Then he rammed some thick Turkish towelling down her throat, and strangled her with the silk cord of her own dressing-gown.

There was a motive: True desperately needed money. Having lugged the half-naked body into the bathroom, he looked round for what he could steal. When he left the flat an hour and a half later he took with him £8 in cash and Gertrude's jewels, worth about £200.

He spent the £8 on replacing his bloodstained clothes and having a shave and brush-up, and pawned two of the rings to pay off a debt and give himself some more ready money. He was reckless about covering his tracks, and at about half-past nine that evening he was arrested—sitting in one of the best seats at the Hammersmith Palace of Varieties.

Sordid but straightforward: that was how it must have seemed to the police. Admittedly there were some strange features. True waited until Gertrude's maid arrived before he left the flat. He went to a tailor who knew him. He openly pawned the stolen gems.

But murderers are seldom efficient: that is often why they are caught. There was still nothing really unusual about the case until later that night, when the police heard the name of the solicitor instructed for the defence. It was Freke Palmer, a leading criminal solicitor and very expensive; not at all the calibre of lawyer usually employed by a man charged with murdering a prostitute for a few pounds in a basement flat, in Fulham. Who on earth was going to pay his bill?

The answer soon became public knowledge. It was True's mother, a lady who, after True's birth, married a very wealthy man, allegedly a member of the peerage. True may have been, both perjoratively and factually, a bastard, but he was a well-connected one. No expense was spared in preparing and conducting his defence.

True is supposed always to have maintained that he did not kill Gertrude Yates. But early on his lawyers decided that this was not the line they would run at his trial. There was only one possible answer to the charge which stood any chance of success: that True did it, but was mad at the time—a lunatic not responsible for his actions.

Freke Palmer earned his fees: his client's defence was prepared with consumate skill and industry. Highly paid doctors visited True in the hospital at Brixton Prison, where he was awaiting trial. The solicitor sent reports on True's childhood and early life to Dr (later Sir) Norwood East, the prison medical officer and Dr Young, his assistant, and they too kept True under constant observation. No fewer than fifteen witnesses were amassed from all over the country to build up a picture of True as someone who from childhood had been eccentric and grievously unbalanced. And as a final touch Palmer briefed Sir Henry Curtis Bennett, K.C., the most fashionable, if not the most able, 'silk' of the day to lead the defence.

Curtis Bennett is said never to have swerved from his belief, formed at their first meeting, that his client was homicidally insane. His biographers claim that he was also "confident and assured" of getting the verdict that he wanted—Guilty but insane. Certainly all the cards were stacked in his favour: the medical evidence was all one way—Dr East and Dr Young both gave evidence for the defence, and agreed with two 'private' specialists that True was a certifiable lunatic. And if that was not enough there was uncontested testimony that he was a morphine-addict: plus Palmer's fifteen witnesses to speak to his having tortured small animals while a child, his having abandoned his wife and family, his habit of driving about the town incessantly in hired— but unpaid for—cars, telling wildly improbable stories, and bilking people right, left, and centre with worthless cheques and lying excuses. He had even suggested to a friend that they form a 'Murderers' Club', whose members would kill "for a bob a nob" —a shilling for a victim.

Yet despite all this, Curtis Bennett lost his case. At the end of a five-day trial at the Old Bailey the jury took only an hour and a half to find True guilty and fully responsible for his crime.

Why? How could they bring in such a verdict? Dr Donald Carswell, who was both a lawyer and a doctor, has commented: "The doctors might say he was mad but the jury did not believe them." This is certainly one explanation. The jury never had a chance of hearing True give his side of the case in the witness-box: Curtis Bennett never proffered him for cross-examination. The only words the jury heard him utter before they reached their verdict were "Not guilty" at the start of the trial. Admittedly not many prisoners sit in the dock with their lucky mascots—a little toy duck and champagne cork—on the rail in front of them. But True, well-groomed and composed, looked sane enough.

Sir Richard Muir, the veteran prosecutor who conducted the Crown case against True, always said he thought True's defence was a sham and that the man was a first-class actor. When eventually True was reprieved Muir's comment was: "He fooled them to the last!"

On the other hand, Muir did not run this line of attack at the trial. He could not. With the prison doctor and his assistant giving evidence for the defence that True was a lunatic he could hardly assert that they were mistaken. The prison doctor is often an essential prop of the prosecution's case in a murder trial: Muir could not argue that this time the expert was wrong—just because, for once, he was on the other side. Besides, the prosecution could not find one specialist prepared to give an unqualified verdict that True was sane.

So Muir played the ball right down the line. He did not, in open court, challenge the evidence that True was a lunatic. He did not need to. Each one of the doctors agreed that, insane or not, True—when he killed Gertrude Yates—knew what he was doing, and knew that it was punishable by law. As Muir reckoned, these answers were enough to ensure a conviction: the McNaughton Rules clearly laid down that insanity was a defence only when it amounted to such mental disorder that an accused person did not know the nature and quality of his act or, if he did, did not know it was wrong. Medical insanity and the test of criminal responsibility were not the same thing.

And so he got his conviction.

In vain Curtis Bennett went to the Court of Criminal Appeal. "If a man is certifiably insane", he told the Court presided over by Sir Gordon Hewart, the newly appointed Lord Chief Justice, "he should not in law be held responsible for his actions. Are the jury, without other evidence, to disregard that of the doctors?"

But Hewart was not impressed. Dismissing the appeal, he not only reaffirmed the McNaughton Rules, but expressly added: "The jury were entitled to say that the facts of the case, taken as a whole, *apart from any question whether the prosecution called medical evidence upon the special point,* satisfied them that at the date of the committing of the act the prisoner was not insane." In other words Hewart was saying that—even apart from the medical evidence—what True actually did was consistent with his sanity. After all, do lunatics usually remember to steal from their victims? Or tell the police when arrested: "It is no use my

putting up a defence now, but I will do so at the proper time"?
But superficially, attractive though it may seem, this view of the
case cannot now be upheld. After True's conviction Mr Justice
McCardie, the trial judge, reported sentence of death in the normal way to the Home Secretary—and the evidence of the doctors.
Accordingly, as soon as the appeal was dismissed, Home Secretary Shortt set up a committee of three other doctors to inquire
into True's mental condition. They found that True was certifiably
insane, and on June 8th the Home Office announced that for that
reason the prisoner had been reprieved and was going to Broadmoor.

The result was a roar of public protest.

"True is not a lunatic: he is a beast and as a beast he ought to
be destroyed," said the *Pall Mall Gazette.* "There has been a gross
and dangerous miscarriage of justice," railed the *Daily Mail.*
"The Home Secretary has used the medical experts as a Second
Court of Criminal Appeal," claimed the London *Star.* Even *The
Times*—then under Lord Northcliffe's ownership—expressed its
anger: "The Home Secretary has acted in defiance of the verdict of the jury and of strongly expressed judicial sentiment,"
it declared. "He has acted, indeed, in contempt of public sentiment and of that righteous indignation which springs up on such
occasions almost unconsciously for the protection of civilized society."

Irate letters jostled in the crowded correspondence columns of
the newspapers. Lawyers complained that trial by jury had been
superseded by "trial by Harley Street". Doctors retorted that only
barbarians would want to see a lunatic hanged. Mr Justice Avory,
the Senior King's Bench Judge, saw fit to add his crackling voice
to the clamour. Addressing an assize jury four days after the reprieve, he said that he hoped their light calendar meant that
crime was abating but—"Whether it will continue to abate if the
infliction of the penalties of the law is to be left to the discretion
of experts in Harley Street, I very much doubt, for the only real
deterrent to crime is the certainty that the proper penalty will
follow upon its commission."

This was just what the newspapers were waiting for. Avory was
lauded as the custodian of our ancient principles of law. Shortt's
resignation was openly called for. Ugly, personal charges were
brought of 'class distinction' and 'improper influences'. "Why was
it that the trouble taken to secure a reprieve by hook or by
crook for Ronald True proved so successful?" demanded the
Daily Herald. Allegations were rife that True owed his life to his
mother's contacts 'in high places'. Home Secretary Shortt might

tell reporters: "I do not know who Ronald True is or who his relations are," but the outcry was too shrill, the alleged scandal too great to be ignored. Shortt was driven to make a personal explanation in the House of Commons.

The scene was tense when Shortt rose to make his statement. He was obviously nervous and spoke, said *The Times* next morning, "with no little emotion". He claimed that he had no alternative: he *had* to reprieve True. Reading from a carefully prepared statement, he maintained that once McCardie had formally informed him of the medical evidence at the trial he had been under a statutory obligation imposed by the Criminal Lunatics Act of 1884 to appoint two or more legally qualified medical practitioners to "examine the prisoner and inquire as to his sanity". Furthermore he asserted that once they reported that True was certifiable, again he had no option: he had to reprieve. "The principle that an insane man should not go to execution has been enshrined in the law of this country for at least three hundred years," he said. It was a remarkable phrase, and I can reveal that it was not of his coining: Sir John Anderson, the brilliant if dour Scot who had recently been appointed Permanent Under-Secretary at the Home Office, had suggested it.

Shortt may have been only a below-par Home Secretary—the sort of man whom even his obituarist had to admit "was somewhat indolent in the routine work of the Home Office and in detail". But he had been a highly successful junior barrister, and was well able to present a brief attractively and plausibly. By the time he sat down the House was with him, and he was loudly cheered. The uproar was over: the Minister—and the Government—were saved.

But dissentient voices persisted. Although few people challenged that Shortt was legally correct it was still felt that in some inexplicable way 'unrevealed factors' had saved True from the gallows. Nine years later the question was still sufficiently alive for an M.P. to ask Home Secretary J. R. Clynes whether there had been any change in True's condition at Broadmoor—in which case he could (theoretically) have been brought back to prison and hanged. "No, sir," was Clynes' reply; and True stayed at Broadmoor, regularly visited by his mother, until he eventually died in January 1951, after a New Year's Eve party.

Was True reprieved because he was a titled woman's son? Nowadays it may seem irresponsible for such a charge to have been made seriously. We live in an era when a Home Secretary has failed to reprieve a fellow-Cabinet Minister's son—John Amery, hanged for treason in 1946. But life was different in the nineteen-

twenties, and to a large extent Edward Shortt had only himself
to blame for the attack made upon him.

He may have had a pleasant, breezy personality, but he was
known to be the type of man who looked after his friends. During
his two and a half years at the Home Office—his only ministerial
appointment—there had already been rumblings within his own
profession at his marked partiality in naming old cronies from the
North-eastern Circuit for posts within his patronage. And it could
not be denied that True was reprieved and the hapless Jacoby
hanged.

"Why should not a panel of experts have been called in to
decide upon the state of Jacoby's mind when, in a fit of panic, he
struck an old lady with a hammer?" asked the *Daily News*. "This
is a case of one law for the rich and another for the poor," declared the London *Star*.

I have been fortunate. Although these events are now over
forty years old both Jacoby's counsel and solicitor are still alive.
They have been good enough to see me, and to allow me for the
first time to tell the full inside story of this sad young man's crime
and the way in which the Home Office dealt with the question
of his reprieve. Neither makes a pretty tale.

Although it is not popularly known and never came out at the
time, Jacoby had one thing in common with Ronald True: he
too was illegitimate. However, his mother was neither wealthy nor
an aristocrat. She was a prostitute, and when Henry was very
young used to bring men home, push the child under the bed,
and carry on her commerce over his head. "That lad had no
chance whatever," Mr Lucien Fior, his defending counsel, says.
"If ever a person were jettisoned into the world, it was he." After
his mother died he went to live with his grandmother in the
country, and when she, in turn, died he took his first job—pantry
boy at the Spencer Hotel, Portman Street, London.

Three weeks later the chambermaid brought in some early-
morning hot water for the wash-basin in Room No. 14, a large,
twin-bedded room on the first floor. Within seconds she ran out
again screaming. The place was like a charnel-house. Blood be-
spattered the walls and floor, blood was on the bedclothes, and
lying back in her bed lay the room's occupant, sixty-five-year-
old Lady (Alice) White, a gaping wound in her head, and
blood like a red veil over her face. A doctor found she was still
breathing, but some hours later she died without regaining
consciousness.

The police were baffled. Unlike the death of Gertrude Yates, this

murder seemed absolutely motiveless. Lady White, the widow of
a former chairman of the LCC (whose statue can still be seen
in Portman Place, off Oxford Circus), had no enemies: elderly
ladies living in discreet hotels with bridge as their sole passion
seldom do. She made a modest display of jewellery in the shape
of a few rings, but there was nothing to mark her out to a jewel-
thief: besides, her jewels and money were found intact. There
was no weapon, no useful fingerprints—nothing.

Guests and staff were questioned, but the only possible lead
was provided by Platt, the night porter. He told Detective Inspector Cornish, in charge of the investigations, that during the
night Jacoby, the new pantry boy, had come up from the basement where he slept and told him that he thought he had heard
voices: the two men had searched for intruders, but found nothing, and Jacoby had gone back to bed and the night porter to
his desk. Jacoby supported this story, but the policeman was not
wholly satisfied. He asked both men to visit Scotland Yard to
amplify their statements.

Wrote Cornish later:

"I was satisfied that the porter had told us everything he knew,
but Jacoby's attitude made a bad impression on us. The boy . . .
talked too much. He advanced theories of his own about the
murder and gave me the feeling that he was pretending to
act a part in a sensational film or play."

As Mr Simon Burns, his own solicitor, says: "He was a stupid little
boy. If he had not opened his mouth they would never have
caught him. Murderers always talk too much."

So it was with this pale, weedy cockney boy. For the first time
in his life he was the centre of attention. And like any child he
revelled in it. He even told the police—though it was never revealed at the trial—that the previous month he had committed a
robbery at the suggestion of a man whom he had met on the
Victoria Embankment. How on earth anyone being questioned
about a murder could say such a thing it is difficult to credit: but
young Henry did. Naturally, as soon as Cornish heard this he
decided to detain the lad.

There was still nothing—except the highest suspicion—to in-
criminate Jacoby in the Lady White murder. But the lad obligingly
soon filled the gap. On Sunday evening he asked to see Cornish
alone: "I did it. I hit her on the head with one of the workmen's
hammers!" he told the policeman. And that was that.

After being cautioned he made a full statement. "I will tell
you all about it," he said. He claimed that the earlier part of his
story was true: there *had* been voices, and Platt and he had

indeed searched the premises. But when he got back to his bed he sat brooding, and—"I made up my mind to go upstairs to the visitors' bedrooms to try to get some money . . . It occurred to me to prepare for emergency, in case I got caught up there, so I thought I would take a hammer with me and use it if I was caught." He described how he selected a suitable hammer from some workmen's tools lying about, and crept quietly upstairs in his stockinged feet.

It was pure chance that led him to Lady White's room: simply that she had not bothered to lock her door. He did not even know it was her room: "The person awoke and I saw it was a woman. She gave a slight shriek, and then I got the wind up and hit her on the head with the hammer . . . I struck her at least twice, because after I struck her the first time I heard her moaning and struck her again." He fled downstairs, washed the hammer, put it back—and went to bed.

With the help of Jacoby's drawing the police soon found the hammer, still bearing traces of blood. The boy was charged with murder, and in due course stood his trial at the Old Bailey, in front of Mr Justice McCardie, and last case in the list before that of Ronald True.

The youngster had two young men to defend him. His solicitor was Simon Burns, a softly spoken North Country man in his early twenties, who had been in practice for only two years and his counsel was Lucien Fior, also in his early twenties, and at the Bar for only eighteen months.

Mr Fior, now a highly successful solicitor, did all that counsel could for his client. But he faced an impossible task. What defence could he put forward to a jury after what Jacoby had said to the police?

The trial took only one day. In the witness-box Jacoby tried to allege that his statement to Cornish was mistaken; that having returned to his room after the abortive search with the night porter he had once more heard voices, armed himself with a hammer, and gone upstairs again. He saw the door of Lady White's room partly open, and thought he heard murmuring inside. He rushed in and, seeing a form, hit out, mistaking it for an intruder. When he turned on his torch and saw he had struck Lady White: "I was so terrified I rushed downstairs again, and got so frightened I said all sorts of things."

It was lame. Mr Fior had done his best to prepare the ground for this change of story in a strong cross-examination of Cornish, whom he alleged had "pummelled this boy with questions." But the judge was not impressed. When Mr Fior told the jury in his final speech that the prisoner had been subjected "to the third degree" McCardie interrupted sardonically: "What is the first degree, Mr Fior?"

This did not auger well for a favourable summing up, and, in fact, it was deadly. But the jury did not immediately bring in a verdict of guilty. After a while they returned, and the foreman told the judge that they all agreed Jacoby had not entered Lady White's room with intent to murder, but merely for the purpose of robbery: could they bring in a verdict of manslaughter?

In effect, McCardie ruled No. He said that even if Jacoby had gone into the room only to steal, once he had struck Lady White intending to kill her or inflict grevious bodily harm upon her he was guilty of murder.

There was no alternative: the jury had to find a verdict of guilty of the major crime. But they added a very strong recommendation to mercy on account of Jacoby's youth, and because, as the foreman said, they did not believe he entered the room with the intention of killing.

McCardie showed his own views by expressly saying that he agreed with the verdict: in his opinion the jury could not have come to any other conclusion. He would send to the Home Secretary "at once" their recommendation to mercy, but now he must sentence the prisoner to death.

The eighteen-year-old boy was taken down and placed in the condemned cell. In due course there was an appeal, Mr Fior arguing strenuously that the police evidence ought not to have been admitted, and that, in any event, the verdict should have been of manslaughter. But Lord Chief Justice Hewart did not even call on prosecuting counsel to reply. Jacoby's execution was fixed for Wednesday June 7th, at 9 o'clock.

No-one under the age of eighteen had been executed since 1887, and Jacoby was only a few weeks past his eighteenth birthday. His crime was brutal, and he had never expressed one word of remorse for what he had done. He was a strange mixture; in some ways pitiable—posing with a stupid smile on his face for Press photographers, cheerfully saying ta-ta to someone in the back row when remanded in custody at the magistrates' court—yet sufficiently astute to ask for the only woman in his jury to be replaced by a man, and sufficiently cunning to change his story in the witness-box. Still there surely must be some sympathy for a lad who could say to a policeman—as was proved at the trial—"I don't know how anyone could help not giving themselves up after doing a murder" and "If I get out of this I shall take good care not to get mixed up in anything else."

Simon Burns, at least, decided that he would do his best to see
the boy did not die.

"In those days I was young and full of vigour and vitality,"
he says. "The appeal was dismissed in the morning, and that
afternoon I went to the Home Office.

"'I want to see the Home Secretary,' I told the man at the
door—and explained why. He got very flustered, and said he
didn't think I could. I told him, 'I'm just sitting here until I
do!'—so he went off in a bit of a panic, and came back with
another official, obviously a more senior man. 'We don't take
interviews on matters of reprieve,' he told me. But I replied:
'I've got to see the Home Secretary.'

"He got quite agitated. 'It's not the normal procedure,' he
said. I told him that I wasn't interested: I was concerned for a
boy's life, and that I wanted to see the Home Secretary. 'Wait
here,' he said, and went off for about twenty minutes. Then he
returned, and said, 'Follow me, I'm taking you to see Sir Ernley
Blackwell.'

"This interview was something really marvellous! I remember it quite clearly.

"I went into Blackwell's room, where he was sitting at a desk.
Along a ledge running right the length of one wall I saw a
whole lot of tin trays, each one containing a pile of papers and
a murderer's name at the top. I saw, among others, Jacoby and
True. This man was obviously reading them. It was quite obvious
that he was the man who made the recommendation to the
Home Secretary . . . He's the fellow who really decides.

"I said, 'Good morning, sir.' He said nothing. I sat down. He
did not answer. I looked at him, and he looked at me.

"Eventually he said, 'What do you want?' I said, 'I've come
to see you about the boy Jacoby. I'm his solicitor.' He still said
nothing, so I went on, 'You realize, sir . . .' and put to him all
I had to say about the lad's unfortunate background and every
argument I could think of for not putting him to death. Blackwell said never a word from beginning to end. Finally I stopped.
There was a pause, and he said, 'Is that all Mr Burns?' and I
said, 'Yes, sir,' and he said, 'Very well, good morning.' And I
left."

It sounded a macabre interview, so I asked Mr Burns what he
thought of it. "At the time I thought it was very odd," he said.
"But looking back now I think that probably Blackwell was right.
After all, what could he say? It would have been very embarrass-
ing for him to have given me any indication one way or the
other."

Anyway, Mr Burns followed up his visit with other calls to the Home Office, and he was assured that as soon as a decision was reached he would be informed. Days went by with no news. Whitsun week-end was coming up, and Jacoby was due to die the following Wednesday morning. At 11 o'clock on Whit Saturday the young solicitor again called at the Home Office, and again was told that no information was yet available.

That afternoon he went to visit Jacoby in Pentonville. The shops were shut; a holiday atmosphere was in the streets as he went on his way. But before he saw his client the governor, Major Blake, called him into his office. "I'm very sorry to tell you," he said; "but I've received an intimation from the Home Office that the Home Secretary has been unable to recommend a reprieve for Jacoby." The governor seemed genuinely distressed: "It's a very sorry business," he said.

"Of course, I was furious," says Mr Burns. "This was the first I knew of the Home Secretary's decision, and if I hadn't by chance gone to see Jacoby that day I wouldn't have known until my office opened up again on Tuesday morning—with only twenty-four hours left to do anything about trying to stop it. I telephoned the Home Office after leaving the prison, and they confirmed that a letter was in the post addressed to my office—which didn't, in fact, arrive until the Tuesday."

Mr Burns saw his client. "How was he?" I asked.

"Oh, he seemed to take it very well," he said. "His only concern was to make a will. A bit of a joke really; he had absolutely nothing in the world. I told him not to bother!"

But Mr Burns bothered quite a bit about the reprieve. He telephoned a friend who was a reporter, and asked him to find out the Home Secretary's private address, since it was not listed in the telephone directory. The Pressman got it for him, and at about 8 o'clock that evening Mr Burns rang the front door-bell of Edward Shortt's flat. A footman opened the door. Mr Burns gave his name, and said he wanted to see the Home Secretary about a private matter. "I'm very sorry, sir," said the footman, "but I'm afraid Mr Shortt is out at the theatre. He won't be back till about 11 o'clock."

So at 8.30 the next morning Mr Burns—still in his 'lone wolf' attempt to reverse the Minister's decision—turned up again on Mr Shortt's doorstep. The footman again opened the door. Mr Burns again stated his business—but this time before the servant could reply a woman's voice called out from inside the flat: "If it's something to do with the Home Office tell him to go to the Home Office!"

"Is that Mrs Shortt?" asked Mr Burns, but the footman did not reply. He merely closed the door.

He had been told to go to the Home Office. So—later that morning, now accompanied by Lucien Fior—that is what Mr Burns did. Not that he had much success. "Anything you care to put in writing to the Home Secretary will receive attention in the ordinary way," he was told. This was now, it will be remembered, Whit Sunday morning, and Jacoby was due to hang in three days' time.

Still not rebuffed Mr Burns said: "I'm going to see the King!" And with a horde of Pressmen following him he set off in a taxi for Buckingham Palace. The cab set him down outside, and he told a policeman on duty that he wanted to see the King about a case where his client was under sentence of death on a murder charge. He was ushered into the Palace, and eventually Sir Alexander Hardinge, George V's Assistant Private Secretary, came to see him. "He was perfectly charming," Mr Burns recalls. "But he pointed out to me that I, as a lawyer, must surely appreciate that the King does not decide these matters; he only acts on the advice of his responsible Minister. How possibly could His Majesty agree to see me? I must say that this seemed obvious sense, so I left soon afterwards. But I was glad that at least I had tried to see the King!"

The drama—though at a less exalted level—continued. On Monday morning, with still no formal letter having arrived from the Home Office, Mr Burns sat down in his deserted office and wrote an angry letter to all the newspapers. Without going into intimate details or disclosing his visits to Edward Shortt's private home or Buckingham Palace he told the story of his dealings with the Home Office, and ended up: "We wonder if the jury who tried Jacoby are satisfied that their strong recommendation (to mercy) has been adequately regarded."

The letter appeared in most of the daily newspapers, including *The Times*, on Tuesday morning; and it had a prompt sequel. Before midday two men walked into Mr Burns's office. They were two of Jacoby's jurors, one of them the foreman. He told Mr Burns: "We'd never have brought in a verdict of murder if we knew he was going to hang. Is there anything we can do?"

"Indeed there is," replied Mr Burns, and he took them straight round to the Home Office.

The three men saw an official, not Blackwell this time; the two jurors made their representations, and Mr Burns handed in a petition which over the week-end a few hundred people had been persuaded to sign. He asked again to see the Home Secretary, but again was told that it was contrary to normal procedure. He was, however, assured that the jurors' representations and the petition would be considered, and that he would be informed of the Home Secretary's decision.

Later that day an official telephoned Mr Burns to say that Mr Shortt could see no reason to alter his original decision. The solicitor still did not give up: Jacoby had been confirmed in prison that morning, and that evening Mr Burns spoke over the telephone to the Archbishop of Canterbury at Lambeth Palace. But Dr Davidson, although he expressed his sympathy, declined to interfere.

At 9 o'clock the next morning Jacoby met his death. "He walked unaided to the scaffold," Major Blake told the coroner. "He stopped for a moment on the way and thanked us for our kindness to him. He said that he was satisfied with the justice of the sentence."

Two days later a prison official walked into Mr Burns's office. He said that shortly before his death Jacoby had said he wanted to leave all his possessions to his solicitor, and he had come to carry out the dead boy's wishes. He placed on Mr Burns's desk a small cardboard box. Mr Burns opened it, and saw inside a pair of socks, some underwear, a ragged tie. That was all.

Should Henry Jacoby have died? Both his lawyers are convinced that he should not. Speaking in 1964, Mr Fior said, "He had youth on his side . . . He never had a chance." Said Mr Burns, "I don't think he was absolutely responsible for what he was doing. He was a stupid little boy. Today he would not have hanged."

Many people would not then have agreed—despite the jury's strong recommendation to mercy. Said *The Times* on the day after his execution: "We are glad that Mr Shortt has been proof against the appeal of sentiment . . . this was a self-confessed and convicted murder of an elderly and inoffensive woman."

What created the uproar was not so much that Jacoby was hanged, but that True was reprieved. "There is a flagrant difference in the treatment of the two cases," claimed the *Daily News*.

If the True decision had not been announced so soon there would have been little criticism of the Home Secretary in Jacoby's case. One can argue—as does Mr Burns—that in the nineteen-sixties Jacoby probably would not have been hanged: only one eighteen-year-old murderer has since been executed—'Flossie' Forsyth, in 1960. It is also true to say—again quoting Mr Burns—that there has been "a change in the morality of the criminal law when dealing with young offenders." But this does not necessarily make Home Secretary Shortt's decision a wrong one in the context of the early nineteen-twenties.

Indeed, the responsibility for hanging Henry Jacoby is not only Shortt's. There is one man who could have saved him, but refused to do so. And that must surely be the judge. If McCardie had in private associated himself with the jury's very strong recommendation to mercy there can be no doubt that the Home Secretary would have reprieved the boy. When George Stoner, another eighteen-year-old lad, was convicted of murder, in the summer of 1935, and the jury recommended mercy the trial judge, Mr Justice Humphreys, wrote privately to his counsel, the late J. D, Casswell Q.C., to tell him that he had forwarded the jury's recommendation to the Home Secretary and that he had told the Minister he agreed with it. Stoner was reprieved.

McCardie was not the sort of judge to hide his charity under a bushel. If he wanted to be merciful to Jacoby he would not have been content with a private letter to the Home Secretary, of which the public would never have known. He would, in open court, have directed the jury as a matter of law that they could bring in a verdict of manslaughter—a device quite often adopted by humanitarian judges when they feel that justice can be satisfied by a conviction of the lesser offence. McCardie was never slow to bend the law to accommodate what he considered the merits of a case, and during his stormy seventeen years on the Bench he squabbled with more than one of his fellow-judges as a result. But he took no such course in this case. Even when the jury came back to court obviously yearning to be told that they could convict of manslaughter he gave them a textbook direction to convict of murder.

He was on good terms with Lucien Fior—"He was terribly sweet and charming . . . one of the greatest dears I have ever come across . . . I never experienced anything but the greatest of kindness, courtesy and help from him"—yet he still never wrote to this young barrister conducting his first murder defence to say that he had written to the Home Secretary agreeing with the jury's recommendation to mercy. I am convinced that he did not agree with it, and that as far as his judge was concerned Jacoby was rightly hanged.

But there was another consideration which almost certainly affected Shortt's decision—the enormity of Jacoby's crime. The Home Office have never officially admitted that so emotional a factor plays any part in the matter. But as Henry Elam, now a judge at London Sessions, told me when discussing the case of Neville Heath, whom he prosecuted: "The enormity of his crime overwhelmed considerations of mercy for their perpetrator." With this in mind a remark made by Detective Inspector Cornish to Simon Burns is particularly significant. The two men were having a cup of tea in the canteen at the Old Bailey during an intermission in the trial. Mr Burns commented that he did not think they would hang Jacoby, because he was too young, and Cornish replied: "You didn't go in that room and see the state she was in, did you?"

It is not for me to say. Perhaps a Home Secretary should not be swayed by emotion of this kind. Perhaps revulsion at what a man has done should play no part in deciding whether to be merciful. Cornish later wrote that he thought "Jacoby got what he deserved", and we know that Shortt agreed with him in that.

What is the final verdict on this case? It seems that even allowing for Henry Jacoby's youth his execution is comprehensible against the background of law and social attitudes of the time. Edward Shortt did not have to be an ogre to say that this boy should die. His decision is not in itself indefensible. But what *is* indefensible is the way in which the decision was arrived at and the inhuman insensitivity in which on this occasion the Home Secretary and the senior officials went about their job.

Mr Burns—who says, incidentally, that he is not an abolitionist —still gets angry when talking about the way he was treated by Home Secretary Shortt and his officials over forty years ago. They appear to have acted with the same detachment as if they were deciding whether to place a large stationery order for a section of the Department. A boy's life was at stake—albeit a boy who had committed a brutal murder. But they showed no consideration for either his own feelings or the mental state of the young solicitor who was battling for him.

The true criticism of Edward Shortt—and the Home Office—is not that Shortt reprieved Ronald True and did not reprieve Henry Jacoby, but that every consideration was shown to True and his advisers—when Jacoby was hanged in the same prison the Governor was even told not to toll the bell in case True heard it— whereas Jacoby's representatives were treated with scant courtesy, and the boy's solicitor shouted at by the Home Secretary's wife.

It was not social influence that saved Ronald True: whether or not he was a sham he satisfied the doctors. Once he was certified insane the Home Secretary was powerless to hang him. Nor is it true that Jacoby was hanged because he was a penniless young cockney. The pantry boy got justice in a rough sort of way. His trial was fair, his appeal rightly dismissed. One can even understand why he was not reprieved. But he did not get civility. The Home Office did their job 'hugger-mugger'.

The epilogue is ironic. For nearly half a century people have argued whether or not Jacoby should have been hanged. If reprieved he could still be alive today. Yet the boy himself did not want to be saved. "He told me before the trial that if he was convicted he did not want a reprieve," says Lucien Fior. "Unless he could get off completely he wasn't interested in anything else. He did not want to spend a long time in prison. 'If I'm reprieved, when I come out I'll be a convicted murderer,' he said. 'How could I earn a living?'"

CHAPTER SIXTEEN

Edith Thompson

(1923)

IN January 1923, some six months after Henry Jacoby was hanged, Mrs Edith Thompson met her death in Holloway gaol. Less than a mile away her lover, Frederick Bywaters, was almost running on to the scaffold at Pentonville prison. Their alleged crime was common place—the murder of a cuckolded husband. "Simple and sordid," *The Times* called it.

Yet their story remains one of the most famous *causes célèbres* of the twentieth century. And the death of the woman sparked a debate, the echoes of which still rumble in the air.

No Home Secretary's decision has caused greater controversy or been attacked with more bitterness of persistence than William Clive Bridgeman's refusal to reprieve Mrs Thompson. The week-end after it was announced, Richard Thompson, the murdered man's brother, wrote in the *Sunday Express*: "I must admit to murmuring 'Thank God!'" But on the very same page James Douglas, the newspaper's editor, was declaring: "I think the hanging of Mrs Thompson is a miscarriage of mercy and justice." In 1952, after nearly thirty years, interest was still sufficiently keen for Lewis Broad to write an impassioned book of over three hundred pages dedicated to proving "the innocence of Edith Thompson".

It is still a live issue in the nineteen-sixties. "Unquestionably, the Thompson Tragedy was a signal miscarriage of justice," wrote C. G. L. Du Cann in a book in 1960. "Let it not be thought that there was any miscarriage of justice in the case of Mrs Thompson," wrote another lawyer, J. P. Eddy, Q.C., in another book published in the same year.

Controversy even lingers over the way in which Edith Thompson died.

"MRS THOMPSON HANGED NEARLY UNCONSCIOUS AND UNABLE TO WALK" ran a newspaper headline the following day. "She was carried to the scaffold and had to be held up," wrote Ellis, her hangman, to a friend the following year. As late as March 1956

Major Gwilym Lloyd George, when Home Secretary, was telling a questioning M.P. in Parliament that because the governor thought it was "more humane", she was given sedatives and carried to the scaffold where she was supported until the trap was sprung.

Yet in February 1963 Mr Harley Cronin, then general secretary of the Prison Officers' Association, said to a *Sunday Express* reporter: "My aunt was deputy governor of Holloway Prison when Mrs Thompson was executed and was with her until the end. She told me: 'I don't believe anybody has ever died with more composure or courage than Edith Thompson. She was completely calm and rational to the end.' In fact, my aunt was talking with Mrs Thompson until seconds before she died."

The only thing on which these experts seem to agree is that she was hanged.

Why was she not reprieved? No woman had been executed in England for nearly sixteen years, not since a hot August day in 1907, when Mrs Rhoda Willis, the last of the infamous baby-farmers, was hanged at Cardiff for killing with her bare hands a one-day-old child given into her care. It had become almost accepted that without any overt change in the law women were simply not being hanged any more. Even when a man and woman were jointly tried and sentenced to death the woman was invariably reprieved. The very same month that Mrs Thompson was convicted Home Secretary Bridgeman had reprieved two women murderers. Why was not the same mercy accorded to her?

No book on the reprieve system would be complete without a study of this case and an attempt to answer these questions. But is there anything new to say? Has it not all been said already in the dozens of books and articles that have poured from typewriters of serious criminologists and hack-writers alike?

At first I thought the answer must be—No. Of the lawyers involved in the case only one still survives—Roland Oliver, junior counsel for the prosecution, later knighted, and for many years a High Court judge. But Sir Roland, now an octogenarian, would not see me on the ground that he had always refused to have anything to do with public discussion about his profession. I tried to trace any close, living relative of Mrs Thompson or Frederick Bywaters, but without success. Home Secretary Bridgeman died in 1935; his Permanent Under-Secretary, Sir John Anderson, died in 1959. Despite the Law Society's help, I could not even find anyone who had worked in the offices of either Mrs Thompson's or Bywaters's solicitors. My search seemed hopeless.

Then by a lucky chance I lit upon something in the case-cards of the late Sir Bernard Spilsbury, the pathologist who carried out the post-mortem on Mr Thompson's body. And it gave me an important clue. I was also able to talk to the three sons of Home Secretary Bridgeman, each one of whom had a clear recollection of the case and of their father's attitude to it.

As a result, and partly with the help of the present Lord Bridgeman and his brothers, I believe I am able for the first time to tell the true story of Edith Thompson.

On a night in October 1922 Edith and her husband, Percy Thompson, were walking home through the darkened streets of Ilford, an outer suburb of East London. They had been to a theatre in town, and now were returning tired and silent.

Suddenly footsteps sounded behind them. A man ran up, drew level, and turned to talk to Thompson. A knife flashed and plunged into his neck. He tried to run. But the man came after him. Again the knife plunged: this time, into his back. Still Thompson managed to keep going. Then, for the third time, the knife cut into him—deep down, penetrating the gullet and severing a vital artery. Blood gushed out. He sank down against a garden wall, his mouth frothing with blood. For nearly fifty feet the grim struggle had endured.

His wife had not screamed for help. "Oh, don't! Oh, don't!" was all a neighbour heard her cry. Only when the assailant had disappeared did she run towards some people approaching in the distance. Even then she did not disclose what had happened. "Oh, my God—will you help me—my husband is ill, he is bleeding," she sobbed. A doctor was sent for. Some minutes later he arrived. But Thompson was dead. "Why didn't you come sooner and save him?" said his wife.

When the police arrived this near-hysterical woman still did not tell the truth of what had occurred. "We were walking along. My husband said, 'Oh!' I said, 'Bear up' thinking he had one of his attacks. He then fell on me and walked a little farther. He then fell up against the wall and then on to the ground," she told a police-sergeant.

But the police were not long in the dark.

The following morning Richard Thompson told detectives of his sister-in-law's friendship with "a young fellow named Bywaters". She admitted she knew him and that he had spent yesterday evening with her family. The police noted this was only two miles away from where Percy Thompson had been killed: by six o'clock that evening they had detained Bywaters for questioning. He denied all knowledge of the murder.

Within hours two policemen searching his room found five let-

ters from Edith Thompson. They contained not only wild protes-
tations of love, but something else—something sinister:

"Yes, darlint [her spelling], you are jealous of him—but I
want you to be—he has the right by law to all that you have
the right to by nature and love—yes darlint be jealous, so so
much so that you will do something desperate . . .

"Don't forget what we talked in the Tea Room, I'll still risk and
try if you will—we only have three and three-quarter years left
darlingest . . ."

This—plus bloodstains on Bywaters's overcoat—was enough. The
young man was told he was under arrest.

As Edith Thompson was escorted along a corridor at the police
station the door of a detention room was deliberately left open.
She saw Bywaters: it was the first she knew he was in custody.
"Oh, God, Oh, God, what can I do?" she cried. "Why did he
do it? I did not want him to do it. I must tell the truth!"

She was taken into a near-by room, cautioned, and she made a
statement. Nearly forty-eight hours after, for the first time, she
admitted seeing Bywaters "scuffle with" her husband.

The youth cracked soon afterwards. When told that both he
and Edith were to be charged with murder he burst out: "Why
her? Mrs Thompson was not aware of my movements." And he
made a written statement in which he freely admitted that he had
knifed Thompson, "because he never acted like a man to his wife.
He always seemed several degrees lower than a snake. I loved
her and I could not go on seeing her leading that life."

What was this "love"? Over fifty more letters from Edith were
discovered a few days later in Bywaters's ditty-box aboard his
ship. They provided the answer. They also provided the strands
with which was woven the noose around her neck.

Edith was a highly-sexed, attractive, intelligent woman, nearing
thirty, married to a man who was sober, hardworking, and dull.
Though four years younger, she had a better job and earned more
money. She was bored and avid for what she would call romance
and adventure.

"Your love to me is new, it is something different, it is my life,"
she wrote to Bywaters.

They had known each other for years. He was twenty, a ship's
writer, and her younger sister's boy friend. He had been no more
than a friend of the family until the summer of 1921, when the
three of them and her sister spent a holiday together on the Isle
of Wight. The two men got on particularly well, and Thompson
asked the youth to spend the rest of his leave with them.

For nearly six weeks Bywaters stayed as a guest in the Thompsons' small, semi-detached, suburban house. At first Percy Thompson noticed nothing wrong. He did not know that one evening in late June Bywaters told Edith that he loved her, that they kissed. Perhaps he felt vaguely uneasy, but he was preoccupied with office worries, and, anyway, his marriage had long sunk into the trough of indifference.

It was Bywaters who caused the first clash. On August Bank Holiday the family were sitting out in the garden. Edith said she wanted a pin, and Bywaters jumped up nimbly to get it: as she later wrote to him, "that was it, darling, that counted, obeying little requests—such as getting a pin, it was a novelty—he'd never done that." Thompson bridled. There were angry words. Later, in the kitchen, he hit Edith, and threw her across the room. Bywaters ran in, and there were blows. Edith pulled them apart, and the two men stood glowering at each other. The amazing thing is that Thompson did not tell Bywaters to clear out at once.

Instead the young man stayed in the house for a further four days, and during that time it is probable that he became Edith's lover in the physical sense, if he had not already done so before.

Her emotion was deep and sincere. In the next fourteen months she only saw Bywaters on his four short home leaves in this country. For the rest she had to be content merely with writing to him. By now these letters are famous. Some commentators have described them as among the greatest love letters of all time, others have dismissed them as trash. One quality they certainly possess: they are dynamic.

On to these scraps of paper this unhappy, frustrated woman poured her very soul. She distilled into her letters the essence of her life, as it was—and as she imagined it to be. If she had read a new novel she would tell her 'darlint' about it and discuss the characters in detail. She would tell him all she did during the day, events both factual and imaginary—like "lunch at Phyllis Court at the invitation of an M.P. Mr Stanley Baldwin". If she heard an interesting piece of gossip she would pass it on; if her sister Avis had made some wistful comments about her one-time boy friend she would repeat it with triumphant glee. She would refer to her letters as 'talk', and write, "I will talk to you again next Wednesday." And that is exactly what they were—talk recorded on paper.

Yet some of the talk was dangerous. Amid the non-stop chatter and continuous declarations of love for her "darlingest boy" was mention of murder—of attempts to poison her husband: first by putting something in his porridge, then by giving him "bitter-tasting tea", then by repeated efforts to give him ground glass and fragments of smashed lamp-bulbs in his food.

Nor was this a one-way traffic. Only two of Bywaters's letters to Edith survive, but from what she wrote to him it is clear that he encouraged her in this course and, indeed, supplied her with some of the raw material.

Later both were to claim that these were mere romancings and play-acting, toying with the thought of a murder that existed only in the imagination. Edith claimed that she wrote as she did "to make him think that I was willing to do anything he might suggest, to enable me to retain his affections." Bywaters said her letters were "vapourings" and "melodrama".

Filson Young, in his introduction to the book of the trial, suggests that they were engaged in a grim game of make-believe, in which, separated by thousands of miles, they found erotic pleasure.

Whatever the truth it was vital that they give the jury at their trial a convincing explanation. For the letters were the lynch-pin of the prosecution's case against Edith: Travers Humphreys, then Senior Treasury Counsel, has written that he would never have charged her with murder if it had not been for her letters.

Unfortunately for Edith, both she and Bywaters failed dismally in the witness-box.

His defence was hopeless from the start anyway. He said that it was only after he had left Edith's parents' home on the evening of the murder that he began thinking about her and their future. On an impulse he made his way to Ilford. "I knew Mr and Mrs Thompson would be together, and I thought perhaps if I were to see them I might be able to make things a bit better." Instead Thompson told him: "I've got her. I'll keep her—and I'll shoot you!" Bywaters claimed that he used his knife only in self-defence.

No-one in court believed this for a moment. This dull shipping clerk was hardly the sort of man to threaten anyone with a gun. Besides, the medical evidence made it highly unlikely that his wounds could have been caused in the way Bywaters described.

But Bywaters gave evidence to try and help Edith, not to defend himself. Regrettably, his testimony had exactly the opposite effect from what he hoped. His grim determination not to admit anything which might conceivably implicate her only made the case against her stronger. He was possibly telling the truth when he swore that she knew nothing of his movements for the evening of the murder, that they had agreed that afternoon not to meet again till lunch-time the following day. But it was asking too much for anyone to accept that he had taken all Edith's references to poison in her letters as meaning she intended to kill *herself* and not her husband. At one point his replies were so stupid that Mr Justice Shearman, who interrupted rarely during the evidence, interposed to say: "Bywaters, do you really mean that?"

His performance, though gallant, was cretinous, and did incalculable harm to Edith. Towards the end even Bywaters realized this. As Sir Thomas Inskip, the Solicitor-General's, cross-examination grew deadlier, his face became paler, his voice weaker. He left the box obviously a brave man, but equally obviously a perjurer.

Edith fared no better. Both her counsel and solicitor had pleaded with her not to give evidence. "I could have saved her," Sir Henry Curtis Bennett, K.C., leading counsel, claimed afterwards to a journalist friend. "I had a perfect answer to everything." As long as she remained out of the witness-box he could have dared the Crown to prove its case purely on the letters alone. In English law it is always for the prosecution to prove a charge of murder, never for the accused person to establish his innocence. Few British juries would have convicted a woman on a capital charge merely because the prosecution had produced a few score scraps of paper.

But Edith was adamant. "She was a vain woman and an obstinate one. She had an idea that she could carry the jury," Sir Henry told his friend. This was to be the big scene of her life, and she was determined not to languish in the wings.

The result was disastrous. She was all right at first, when answering her junior counsel in examination-in-chief. Indeed, deftly prompted by his shrewd questions, she explained quite effectively an apparently damning letter written on the day before the murder. "Darlint", she had written, "do something tomorrow night will you? something to make you forget. I'll be hurt I know, but I want you to hurt me—I do really—the bargain now seems so one-sided—so unfair—but how can I alter it . . . Don't forget what we talked in the Tea Room, I'll still risk and try if you will . . ."

What did all this mean? Her answer was simple: far from plotting murder on the morrow, she and her lover were at last talking sensibly about their situation. At long last she was thinking seriously of freeing herself from suburban respectability and "risking all"—including probably losing her job—by setting up with Bywaters as man and wife. In the meanwhile if she had occasionally to go out with her husband on a family outing, well, at least let Bywaters console himself with taking out her sister—

"I'll be hurt I know, but I want you to hurt me . . . the bargain now seems so one-sided."

If she had maintained this cool approach during her long, somewhat bludgeoning cross-examination by Sir Thomas Inskip she might well have escaped conviction. But under the impact of this burly, heavy-going advocate her answers—like Bywaters's—soon became stupid and full of danger to herself.

Instead of agreeing with Inskip (as she had to) that Bywaters was obviously wrong when he said her various efforts with poison and ground glass were suicidal and self-administered she went recklessly to the opposite extreme, and openly admitted that he had sent her drugs to administer to her husband. But she did not mean to kill him, she said—only to make him ill so that he would have a heart attack and die!

The high-water mark of the prosecution's case, and when possibly for the first time the jurors realized they were looking at a murderess, occurred a few minutes before the court rose at the end of the third day.

"You were acting to Bywaters that you wished to destroy your husband's life?" asked Inskip.

"I was," replied Edith.

This was too much for the judge. He paused in his note-taking: "One moment," he said. "I do not want to be mistaken. Did I take you down rightly as saying 'I wanted him to think I was willing to take my husband's life'?"

"I wanted him to think I was willing to do what he suggested," replied Edith doggedly. Four questions more, and the court was adjourned—to give the jurors plenty to talk about as they broke the tension of the day with a cigarette and a chat.

Although the two main protagonists had failed so miserably in the witness-box Edith still stood some chance of an acquittal. The very last witness for the prosecution, Sir (then Dr) Bernard Spilsbury, had told the court that he had carried out a postmortem on the body of Percy Thompson one month after the murder, and had found nothing to indicate any attempt at poisoning—not a trace of poison, nor of powdered glass, nor of pieces, however small, of lamp-bulbs. At least it seemed that Edith had been telling the truth when she claimed she had never given her husband any of the noxious substances of which she had boasted to Bywaters.

A really great speech by Sir Henry Curtis Bennett might yet have saved her. He was renowned for "doing a Curtis"—winning hopeless cases by what his biographers call "a certain combination of honest bluff, cheek, opportunism and a genius in turning a

phrase." It was just possible that he might save her, and prove
that Sir Edward Marshall Hall was not the greatest advocate of
the day.

He certainly started well enough. "You have got to get into
the atmosphere of this case," he told the eleven men and one
woman on the jury. "This is no ordinary case you are trying.
These are not ordinary people that you are trying. This is not
an ordinary charge against ordinary people . . . Am I right or
wrong in saying that this woman is one of the most extraordinary
personalities that you or I have ever met? . . . Thank God, this is
not a court of morals, because if everybody immoral was brought
here I would never be out of it, nor would you. Whatever name is
given to it, it was certainly a great love that existed between
these two people!"

Curtis Bennett was carried away. For once, this portly, fashionable 'silk' was personally involved in a case. Leslie Hale, a solicitor
as well as an M.P., has commented that Curtis was one of those
advocates who can convince a jury of their eloquence without
convincing them of their client's innocence. But here, if words
coming at you from the printed page can convey anything, they
convey passion. Curtis—perhaps because at this very moment he
was himself involved in a domestic crisis which a few years later
led to divorce and the stigma of adultery—found himself in the
exuberance of his own eloquence.

And the judge did not like it.

While Curtis was still in full speech Mr Justice Shearman inti-
mated that it was time for the court to adjourn for the week-end
recess. Curtis promptly sat down, expecting the judge to rise in
the ordinary way. But he did not. Instead Shearman leaned forward and said quietly to the jury: "Before the court rises I wish
to offer you, members of the jury, this advice . . . you should not
forget that you are in a Court of Justice, trying a vulgar and
common crime. You are not listening to a play from the stalls of a
theatre. When you are thinking it over, you should think it over
in that way."

This admonition, as crucial as it was unexpected, went completely unchallenged by Curtis Bennett. He did not jump to his
feet to protest at this unwarranted intrusion into the body of his
argument. He did not raise his voice in simulated or real anger.
He said nothing. Perhaps, conscious of his own personal position,
he felt he had gone too far. Perhaps he thought that a stand-up
fight with the judge would set him back in furthering his ambi-
tion of one day himself sitting on the Bench. Perhaps this facile,
pleasure-loving man was already thinking of the Rugby Trial

Match at Twickenham that afternoon, for which the tickets were in his pocket, and which would be starting soon. Whatever the explanation nothing was said, and instead of the jury's having a defiant protest from Curtis ringing in their ears that fateful weekend, all they heard were the quietly chilling words of the judge.

On Monday morning Curtis Bennett resumed his speech. But the fire had gone. There was no more eloquence, no more passionate sincerity—merely a pedestrian narration of the facts, tailing off into one of the most tepid endings of a speech ever given by an eminent counsel for the defence.

Six and three-quarter hours later, after Inskip had replied, and the judge had summed up, the jury were returning their verdicts of guilty, Bywaters was shouting in the dock: "The jury is wrong. Mrs Thompson is not guilty!"—and an almost senseless Edith was being carried downstairs on her way to the condemned cell while the judge calmly thanked the jurors for their patient attention to "a long and difficult case".

An appeal was dismissed without counsel for the prosecution's even being called upon to reply, and the two lovers prepared to meet their death at 9 A.M. on Tuesday, January 9th, 1923.

His solicitor presented two petitions to the Home Office on Bywaters's behalf. Their signatures totalled 832,104, for the brave, good-looking young man had attracted a good deal of public sympathy. He was regarded as a mere youth ensnared by an older, more experienced woman. The paradox is that he was probably the more dominant of the two: "Darlingest, when you are rough, I go dead—try not to be please!" she wrote to him in her last letter.

There was no public petition for Edith. "It was her mind that conceived the crime," Inskip had said at the trial, and the phrase lingered in the popular memory. Society was having one of its periodic bouts of puritanism. She was an adulteress, an evil woman, who had denied her marriage vows. Why should she be shown mercy?

On Saturday, January 6th, came the official announcement that the Home Secretary had decided against reprieves.

Bywaters had shown little interest in the efforts to save himself: "I killed him, and I must pay for it," he told his mother. His concern throughout had been for Edith, and now he begged his mother to do all she could to persuade the Home Secretary to reverse his decision with regard to her. Mrs Bywaters promptly repeated his words to the reporters waiting at the prison gates: "I swear she is completely innocent. She never knew that I was going to meet them that night . . . She didn't commit the murder.

I did. She never planned it. She never knew about it. She is innocent, absolutely innocent!"

F. A. Stern, Edith's solicitor, who had the previous day laconically told a *Daily Express* reporter that he would not see his client again, as he had done all he could, now appears to have had a change of heart. "I feel it is on my conscience to make one more effort on behalf of this unfortunate woman," he now told the same reporter.

The "one more effort" took the form of high drama. It also brought considerable publicity to the late Mr Stern.

This gentleman was obviously a solicitor who did not believe in holding the Press at bay. He confided to the same zealous reporter—and his millions of readers—that armed with Bywaters's latest statement he had decided to make a last, personal appeal to the Home Secretary. The only trouble was that no-one knew for sure where he was. His town residence was deserted, and the Home Office could only hazard a guess that he was at his country home at Minsterley, near Shrewsbury, over a hundred and fifty miles from London. It was by no means certain that Mr Bridgeman was there, or that he would agree to see the solicitor—but "This is a matter of life and death," said the newly inspired Mr Stern.

With the help of the *Daily Express*, as recounted in the following Monday's editions, efforts were made to charter a plane, but no pilot could be found in time to make the flight before dark. So Mr Stern—and the reporter—made the journey by train to Shrewsbury, where a fast car waited to speed them along the narrow country lanes to Minsterley.

"Yes, I remember the front door bell ringing," says Sir Maurice Bridgeman, Home Secretary Bridgeman's son, then in his early twenties, and now Chairman of the British Petroleum Company. "Everyone else was asleep, so I got up and answered it. There were two men on the doorstep. I asked them in, and after the solicitor had told me who he was and what he wanted I woke up my elder brother Geoffrey, who got my father up. I then went back to bed, and the following morning asked my father what had happened. I cannot remember whether it was my father or my brother who answered that, in fact, they had produced no new evidence."

"Indeed they hadn't!" the Hon. Geoffrey Bridgeman, now a leading opthalmic surgeon, tells me. "My father was very much annoyed over the whole affair. He was closeted with them for one and a half hours and my impression was that the solicitor's intervention had no material effect on my father's opinion of the case.

The solicitor did not produce anything in the way of argument or fact which was not already known: Bywaters had all along maintained that the woman had nothing to do with it and did not know that he was going to waylay her husband. Not that I wish you to think that my father took the case lightly—he was more worried about that case than anything else in his life!"

On the Monday the Home Secretary consulted with his permanent advisers at the Home Office, and that evening Mr Stern received a telephone call from the Department to say that Mr Bridgeman regretted that he found no grounds for departing from his earlier decision.

Two mornings later both prisoners were dead, and their story had entered into history.

No-one has ever argued that Frederick Bywaters should not have been hanged. On the law as it then stood there was no reason for the Home Secretary to have been merciful. Admittedly, he was young, but he had an assurance and knowledge of the world far beyond his years. He was impelled by the jealousy of a full-grown man, and as a full-grown man he had to pay the consequences.

He realized this. "I did it, and I cannot complain," he told his mother. He was a good-looking boy, with a fine head and romantic, wavy hair, but he was small in stature and, like many short, vain people, he compensated for his lack of height with physical courage. According to his hangman's diary he died bravely.

With Edith there is no such straightforward epilogue. Nowadays many believe that she should never have been hanged. "Justice did less than justice to Edith Thompson," is Lewis Broad's telling phrase.

Whether or not this is fair criticism depends on two questions. First, was she rightly convicted, and second, assuming that the conviction was valid, should she have been reprieved?

Lewis Broad has no doubts. "She was innocent of the crime of which she was convicted," he writes. And the person accused of being mainly responsible for this tragedy is her judge, Sir Montague Shearman.

Shearman was a relic from the Victorian era. High principled and prudish, he was unlikely to have any sympathy for Edith Thompson. It is said that he was so appalled by her adultery that he lost all sense of fairness and gave a biased summing up. As Lewis Broad puts it: "Suspicion was allowed to take the place of proof, prejudice was allowed to turn into proof what was no more than suspicion."

This is going much too far. It is perfectly true that Mr Justice Shearman showed his moral bias: he more than once expressed his disgust at the illicit liaison between Edith and her lover, and early on told the jury that the charge was merely a "common or ordinary charge of a wife and an adulterer murdering the husband." Yet he was not exceeding the functions of his office. It has always been the law that a judge can express his personal views to a jury as long as he clearly tells them that they are the sole judges of fact and can reject any of his suggestions. As befitted a man who had already been eight years on the Bench, Shearman was scrupulous in doing this.

In fact, when he came to direct the jury as to the law of the case Shearman was distinctly favourable to Edith. He was a High Churchman and a devout Christian. He loathed sexual transgression, but he valued fairness. He defined the question of law which the jury had to decide in terms so narrow and restricted that any open-minded lawyer listening to him must have realized that he was trying to redress the balance of the case in Edith's favour, so that when the jury retired to consider their verdict the scales of justice would be evenly balanced: on the one side distaste at her story—on the other side the necessity for her guilt to be proved on the strictest possible basis. These were his vital words:

"If you find the woman guilty of murder, then you have got to consider: was this woman an active party to it; did she direct him to go; did she know he was coming, and are you satisfied that she was implicated directly in it? . . . You will not convict her unless you are satisfied that she and he agreed that this man be murdered when he could be, and she knew he was going to do it, and by arrangement between them he was doing it. If you are not satisfied of that you will acquit her; if you are satisfied of that it will be your duty to convict her."

Shearman was deliberately pitching high the hurdle which the Crown had to overcome: they had to satisfy the jury that Edith had arranged with Bywaters to kill her husband that very night and on that very occasion. This was bending the law in favour of the defence: if Edith had been acquitted, and the Crown were able to appeal, they would have stood a good chance of getting a new trial. Shearman stacked the cards too much against them.

Nevertheless, the jury convicted. On the judge's direction I think they were wrong to do so. There was no evidence that at midnight, on October 3rd, 1922, when Bywaters was sinking his knife into Thompson's body, he was doing it "by arrangement between Edith Thompson and himself". But you cannot blame the judge for the jury's verdict. If Edith Thompson's blood is on anyone's hands it is on those of her twelve anonymous jurors.

Lord Hewart, the pugnacious, newly appointed Lord Chief Justice, realized Shearman's error, and when the case came before him and two other judges in the Court of Criminal Appeal he took the opportunity of putting the matter right. The real case against Edith Thompson was that "the letters were evidence of a protracted continuous incitement to Bywaters to commit the crime which he did in the end commit," he said. It was not necessary to prove that the knifing occurred by arrangement with her. It was enough that she had continuously incited Bywaters to murder her husband, and that when he did so she was present "aiding and abetting".

The paradoxical result is that Edith Thompson was rightly convicted. But on a basis which was never put to the jury, and which was grafted on to the case only subsequently in the Court of Criminal Appeal.

Should she, therefore, have been reprieved? No—for the simple reason that the Home Secretary saw Edith's guilt in the same light as Lord Hewart. "My father took the view that Mrs Thompson incited Bywaters to commit the very crime which he did in fact commit," says the present Lord Bridgeman. "He was advised by Sir Ernley Blackwell, the Legal Assistant at the Home Office, and accepted the advice that her crime was as great as his. If she had not instigated and incited Bywaters to kill her husband he would not have been murdered." Lord Bridgeman did not discuss the case with his father at the time: he was then serving with his regiment in Turkey. Besides, Home Secretary Bridgeman did not discuss such matters with his family while he was still in office. "But he did refer to it later," says Lord Bridgeman, "and this was most definitely his attitude: the husband would still have been alive if his wife had not plotted his death."

Home Secretary Bridgeman has not been treated well by writers on the case. He has been accused of weakness in the face of the permanent officials at the Home Office, of hard-heartedness, insensitivity, and even stupidity. In his lifetime he never retorted in his own defence. He was not a professional politician, and wrote no best-selling memoirs. Nearly twenty years after his death it is perhaps time that this mild-mannered country gentleman's reputation be vindicated.

Within months of his decision Filson Young was claiming in his book of the trial that Edith was hanged because "in order to justify past weaknesses, a little show of 'firmness and determination' was indicated", and as recently as 1961 Colin Wilson and

Pat Pitman in their *Encyclopaedia of Murder* were suggesting that
Ronald True's reprieve led to the death of Edith Thompson "who
might have been reprieved but for the uproar caused by True's
escape from the hangman, and the Home Secretary's fear of
jeopardizing his position."

Such remarks are unfortunate. In December 1922 Bridgeman
had been in office for only six weeks. It was a different Home
Secretary who had reprieved Ronald True—namely, Edward
Shortt. Shortt was a Liberal serving under Lloyd George: Bridgeman was a Tory serving under Bonar Law, Lloyd George's arch-
enemy, and the man who supplanted him in circumstances of
great bitterness. Why on earth should Bridgeman care one jot for
the record of Edward Shortt? The suggestion that this genial Old
Etonian casually allowed a woman to die because he wished to
"justify past weaknesses" by a political opponent defeats common sense.

The truth, as often happens, was very different. "My father was
anxious not to hang the woman if he could possibly avoid it,"
says the Hon. Geoffrey Bridgeman. "He went into it with the judge
and with Blackwell in great detail. He would have taken any excuse to avoid hanging her. My fairly distinct impression is that
he most certainly would not have held off unless he had been
absolutely certain that the woman instigated the murder and was
responsible for it."

"I don't think anything ever gave my father greater mental
anguish than that case," says Sir Maurice Bridgeman. "And not
the least because throughout the time he was reaching his decision both my mother and he received a great number of abusive
letters. I know that the letters she received distressed him greatly."

Home Secretary Bridgeman, later the first Lord Bridgeman, was
no hard-headed ogre. He was a country gentleman in politics. Un-
pretentious and able, he was the sort of man who reacted against
all forms of excess and unnecessary drama. "That is why I know
he would have been appalled by the solicitor's arriving on his
doorstep in the middle of the night—complete with the Press,"
says the present Lord Bridgeman. "The solicitor must surely have
known that my father would do nothing until the matter had been
dealt with in the proper way and he had had an opportunity of
discussing Bywaters's new statement, such as it was, with Ernley
Blackwell at the Home Office."

Bridgeman was a man who liked things to be done in the
proper way and at the proper time. He was essentially logical.
"Though he did not at all like the idea of hanging a woman,"
says Lord Bridgeman, "he had for many years supported women's

emancipation, and now that they had acquired the vote he felt that they had to accept all the consequences of equality—both the good and the bad. He would certainly not have been prepared to reprieve a woman simply because she was a woman."

One final matter deserves to be mentioned when considering Home Secretary Bridgeman's rôle in Edith Thompson's story: he was not an out-and-out believer in capital punishment. Says Sir Maurice Bridgeman: "In today's parlance he would probably have been called an abolitionist, certainly a partial abolitionist. He would have been in favour of something like the Homicide Act, reserving the death penalty for only the worst murders." This is ironic: under the Homicide Act neither Edith nor Bywaters would have been sentenced to death.

But despite all this mildness and gentleness, Edith Thompson was hanged—the first woman to suffer this fate in nearly sixteen years. Was it just her bad luck that she struck a kindly, but sternly principled, Home Secretary? Or is the truth that, as Curtis Bennett later claimed, she was "hanged for immorality"?

I believe that neither proposition is valid. Edith Thompson's conviction was upheld in the Appeal Court because she was guilty of murder. She was hanged because she was also a poisoner. This may seem startling, but I am convinced it is so.

It has always been assumed that—in the words of Lewis Broad —"there never had been any reality in the poison plots." Look at the evidence of Bernard Spilsbury, the greatest pathologist of the day—no signs of poison in Thompson's body, no evidence of powdered glass, nor of the passage of fragments of lamp-bulbs. It seems beyond doubt.

I agree that this was Spilsbury's evidence in court. But it was *not* the sum total of his findings.

The neatly written case-card on which Spilsbury recorded the results of his post-mortem examination of Percy Thompson reveals that he *did* find indications that poison might have been administered to the dead man in his lifetime. There was fine fatty degeneration of some cells in both the liver and kidneys and, states the card, "no disease found to account for fatty degeneration of organs." What could cause such degeneration? I asked Dr Donald Teare, present Home Office pathologist, and one of the men on whom Spilsbury's mantle has fallen. His reply is remarkable:

"I think you have unearthed some very interesting information concerning the Thompson case. Personally I would find it very difficult to make a diagnosis of fine fatty degeneration in decomposed organs but we must accept that Spilsbury was able

M

to do so and that he was looking specifically for some reason
to account for such fatty degeneration . . . From knowledge of
him I think it is highly probable that he would interpret fatty
changes as being due to poisoning rather than considering less
sinister explanations. There are of course many poisons which
damage liver and kidneys including all the heavy metals."

Perhaps Edith was romancing when she wrote of feeding her
husband ground glass and pieces of smashed lamp-bulb, though
Spilsbury said in his evidence that it was possible for even large
pieces of glass to have passed through his system and left no
trace. But I think she was telling the truth when, in April 1922,
she wrote to her lover of "the Sunday morning escapade", when
Thompson complained that his tea tasted bitter and said it was
as if something had been put in it. This was shortly after Bywaters had been home on leave, and less than a month after she
had written to him at Port Said jubilant that he had "succeeded"
in something he had written to her about, and chafing that he
could not send "it" to her. What was "it?" Bywaters said in the
witness-box that this merely referred to some bitter-tasting quinine
that he had bought, and which he duly gave her on that leave.
Why quinine? She kept on writing that she wanted to commit
suicide, so he gave her this substance to placate her. "I was playing a joke on her," he said.

But this is surely nonsense.

Consider the way that Bywaters floundered when he tried to
maintain this story under the strain of cross-examination.

He had just said that he thought "the Sunday morning escapade" referred to bitter-tasting tea drunk by Edith herself, in
an attempt at suicide with the quinine he had bought her. "Look
at it again," said Inskip, holding up the April letter: "'*He puts
great stress on the fact of the tea tasting bitter "as if something
had been put in it" he says.*' To whom did it taste bitter?"

"Mrs Thompson," replied the witness.

"Do you suggest that, Bywaters?"

"I do."

"Do you suggest that is how you understood the letter when
you received it?"

"I do."

Quoting again: "'*Now I think that what ever else I try it in
again will still taste bitter—he will recognize it and be more suspicious still.*' Do you still adhere to what you say, that she is
speaking of *her* taste?"

"Yes."

To my mind Bywaters was reduced to dogged monosyllables

because he was lying. He knew full well that he had brought back poison from the Middle East, that Edith had given it to her husband—and bungled the job. "You said it was enough for an elephant," she wrote later. "Perhaps it was. But you don't allow for taste making only a small quantity to be taken . . . Darlint I tried hard—you won't know how hard—because you weren't there to see and I can't tell you all—but I did—I do want you to believe I did for both of us."

Eventually, I believe, Bywaters came to the conclusion that the risk was too great: Edith was too clumsy. When she wrote to him in July 1922, "Why aren't you sending me something . . . If I don't mind the risk why should you?" he ignored the entreaty. Their problem would have to be solved by other methods.

Even so, her ineffectual efforts as a husband-killer were enough to push into Thompson's digestive system sufficient poison for Spilsbury to find several months later "fine fatty degeneration of some cells in the liver and kidneys".

I do not think that she was the prime mover in all this. It seems clear that Bywaters was her only source for poisons. Once he refused to send her any more she was reduced to sulking and dropping hints, such as sending a quotation from a novel about the cumulative but deadly effect of the poison digitalin.

"No-one knows what kind of letters he was writing to me," she told her mother in the condemned cell. This short extract from one of the only two recovered by the police shows the swirling turbulence of this young man's passion, a passion which could very easily have persuaded this romance-starved woman to give her husband "bitter-tasting tea":

"DARLING 'PEIDI MIA,'

Tonight was impulse—natural—I couldn't resist—I had to hold you darling little sweetheart of mine—darlint I was afraid —I thought you were going to refuse to kiss me—darlint little girl I love you so much . . . Darlint Peidi Mia—I must have you—I love you darlint—logic and what others call reason do not enter into our lives . . .'"

It is small wonder that Edith was bowled over. Percy Thompson had never written her letters like that—even eight years before, when they were courting.

There is only one obstacle to my poisoning theory, why was it not brought out at the trial? Why did Spilsbury not speak of the "fine fatty degeneration" in his evidence?

The answer, I think, lies in the bumbling personality of Sir Thomas Inskip, the Solicitor-General. He was a lawyer-politician, and though he later became for a brief period Lord Chief Justice of England he was not of the highest calibre. He had seldom, if ever, had the conduct of a major criminal trial before, and he was completely out of his depth. He had been appointed Solicitor-General only six weeks earlier, and the decision for him to lead the prosecution was taken at such a late stage that he hardly had time to read the papers properly. I think that he simply did not appreciate the importance of Spilsbury's findings.

It may seem fantastic to suggest that so highly placed a lawyer was not equal to his task, but, as many a junior barrister knows who has sat behind a plodding 'leader', merely because an advocate wears a silk gown and stands in the front row of counsel does not necessarily mean that he is inspired.

The most able advocate in court was Travers Humphreys, the Senior Treasury Counsel, who would normally have led for the Crown in his own right. In 1951, nearly thirty years after the trial, the late Miss F. Tennyson Jesse claimed in a cryptic sentence in a letter to the *Daily Telegraph* that Spilsbury "considered Mrs Thompson guiltless of any attempt to poison her husband", but this cannot be right. And for this reason: Humphreys drafted the indictments in this case, and, apart from alternative charges of murder, conspiracy to murder, incitement to murder, and incitement to conspire to murder, he saw fit to allege specifically two charges—of administering poison and administering broken glass. Humphreys later became possibly the greatest criminal judge of this century. Certainly he was one of the fairest and the most lucid. It is inconceivable that he would have drafted these counts in the indictments—complete with dates—unless he had some good reason for so doing. And that good reason could only have been the results of Spilsbury's post-mortem, which had taken place a week or so earlier.

If this is right, and the Crown was in possession of evidence that Edith had administered poison to her husband, everything else falls into place. It explains for one thing why Inskip was trundled down to prosecute. It has for years been the tradition that either the Attorney-General or the Solicitor-General lead for the Crown on a charge of murder by poison: this case was only once removed from such a charge.

It also explains why Edith Thompson was not reprieved. It gives the answer to why a mild Home Secretary should condemn her to be the first woman hanged for nearly two decades, and why she alone, out of fifty-five women since Rhoda Willis, was considered so shameful as to merit death.

I believe that Spilsbury, angry with the way in which Inskip had bungled the prosecution, would have considered it his duty to make his findings known to the officials at the Home Office, and would have made strong representations as to the woman's real rôle in the affair. I cannot prove this positively, as his appointments-book no longer exists. But I have authoritative support for my belief. Dr Donald Teare confirms it. "Knowing Spilsbury as I did reasonably well," he writes to me, "I think your theory that he could have communicated with the Home Secretary is highly probable."

The point is not whether Spilsbury would have been correct in concluding that fatty degeneration of Thompson's liver and kidneys was due to poisoning, but that it is "highly probable"—to quote Dr Teare—that he would have come to that conclusion, and that he would have made it his business to say so to the Home Office.

Lord Hewart had said in the Appeal Court that it was really of comparatively little importance whether Edith was truly reporting in her letters something which she had done or falsely reporting something which she had merely pretended to do. But once Spilsbury came and told Home Secretary Bridgeman that her boastings were not false and that she *was* a poisoner one side of the scales dropped decisively. Before the passing of the 1957 Homicide Act poisoners were seldom, if ever, reprieved, and Edith Thompson was no exception.

As the law then stood she was rightly hanged.

CHAPTER SEVENTEEN

John Thomas Straffen

(1952)

THE two decades after Edith Thompson's death produced many interesting cases and quite a few highly controversial decisions by successive Home Secretaries.

In April 1925 Sir William Joynson-Hicks refused to reprieve Norman Thorne, a young poultry-farmer convicted of the murder of his girl friend Elsie Cameron, although the medical evidence as to cause of death was far from satisfactory, and the *Law Journal* attacked with unusual bitterness the way in which the trial judge was overawed by the unique prestige and acclaim of Sir Bernard Spilsbury, appearing yet again as the Crown's principal expert witness.

In 1936 Sir John Simon refused to reprieve a woman named Charlotte Bryant, convicted of poisoning her husband, a Dorset cowman, although the prosecution admitted in the Court of Criminal Appeal that their only scientific witness had made a vital error in his testimony.

In 1950 Lord Chuter-Ede refused to reprieve a young Londoner called Daniel Raven, convicted of the brutal and unexplained murder of his parents-in-law, although his solicitor Mr Sidney Rutter, presented the Home Secretary with extensive evidence as to Raven's long history of mental trouble, and the EEG tests carried out by the Home Office specialists themselves disclosed that he was suffering from idiopathic epilepsy. "It was a monstrous execution," says Mr Rutter still, "and should never have taken place. I don't dispute Raven's guilt, but he shouldn't have been hanged."

Yet perhaps the greatest public uproar was reserved for the case of John Thomas Straffen in the summer of 1952, which is ironic, and provides a fascinating insight into the British national character. For Straffen was a murderer who was reprieved. The granting of mercy to this man caused more furore than its refusal to almost any of the murderers of the preceding twenty years.

His crime was undoubtedly appalling: he was a child-killer,

who in one year strangled two little girls, and then in the following year strangled another. Admittedly after the 1957 Homicide Act
child-killers were not normally capital murderers, since they do not
normally use a gun or kill in the course or furtherance of theft or
otherwise bring themselves within its narrow scope of capital murder. But many people take the view that if there is any case for
capital punishment at all the one type of murderer who ought to
hang is the man who kills a small child. Hence the widespread
anger at Straffen's escape.

Yet the issues were not straightforward. Straffen had been found
mentally unfit to stand his trial for his first two murders, been
sent to Broadmoor, whence he escaped and committed his third
murder—after which he was promptly recaptured, tried, convicted,
and sentenced to death as a perfectly sane man.

The case is an object-lesson in how ham-fisted the law was in
dealing with the medical factors involved in homicide before the
enactment of the 'diminished responsibility' provisions of the
Homicide Act and the sweeping changes of the 1959 Mental
Health Act. It also shows that a Home Secretary will not necessarily make himself popular by being merciful to a murderer:
"What about other potential victims?" his opponents will ask.

Straffen was a certified, high-grade mental defective. In the
spring of 1951 he was released after four years in a compulsory
colony for mental defectives and allowed home to Bath under
licence to live with his mother. He already had several convictions for petty stealing and housebreaking, and there had been
one or two complaints to the police about his strangling chickens
and threatening girls. So from time to time the police visited
him and checked upon his movements.

After a few months, in early July 1951, he went to see Dr
Ashley Weston, the local medical officer of health, hoping that the
doctor would recommend cancelling his licence and give him
complete freedom to lead his own life. But Dr Weston, despite
some progress by the patient, advised that the licence should
continue for at least another six months. Straffen was bitterly
disappointed, and seems to have thought that the police, with
all their suspicions and questionings, were in some way to blame.

The same day a little girl named Christine Butcher was
strangled at Windsor, and for days afterwards the newspapers
carried stories of the tragedy and descriptions of the unsuccessful efforts by a somewhat desperate police-force to try to find
the killer. Straffen would certainly have seen these reports.

Next Sunday afternoon as he loped along a road on his usual

solitary week-end visit to the cinema he noticed five-year-old Brenda Goddard gathering flowers in a meadow, and he ambled in to commit his first murder. All his resentments and frustrations swelled up within him, and he found release in strangling this child. For him, killing Brenda Goddard was both agreeable in its own right and a foolproof way of getting his own back on the police: for it seemed to him that the strangler of Christine Butcher had shown that child-killing was an effective way of making fools of the police. "I did it to spite the police," he afterwards told a doctor.

When three weeks went by without an arrest, and he saw how easy it was to get away with murder, another little girl died. Only this time a woman saw him crossing a field with the child, and he was traced and arrested. "I bashed her head against the wall. I did not feel sorry, and I forgot about it," he told the police.

"This man is unfit to plead and stand his trial," said Dr Peter William Parkes, medical officer at Bristol prison. "One might as well try a baby in arms!" said Mr Justice Oliver. So Straffen was not tried for his first two murders. He was ordered to be detained during His Majesty's pleasure, and committed to the 'safe custody' of Broadmoor Institution.

There he stayed for seven months, until about 2.25 on the afternoon of April 29th, 1952, when he escaped. He climbed the roof of an outbuilding, jumped over the wall, and ran. Four hours and five minutes later he was recaptured. But already a third little girl lay dead.

He had not escaped with the intention of killing. He had run away because he did not like Broadmoor, because he resented authority, and this was the third institution to which in his twenty-one years of existence his mental condition had condemned him. As he later told the prison medical officer at Wandsworth gaol, he had planned his escape ever since he first entered the gates of Broadmoor. He hated it.

By the time he was picked up he had managed—with no money, and in an alien part of the land—to cross four and a half miles of Berkshire countryside. He had aimed steadily for the West Country, for home and his mother. Yet on the way he met by chance five-years-old Linda Bowyer, cycling alone along a lane. She was unknown to him. She was probably the first child he had seen since his arrest nine months previously. And compulsively he killed her.

As with his first two victims, there was no struggle, no sexual interference, no attempt to conceal the body. With the natural friendliness of the young for the simple the child went with him into a copse, and there he put his hands round her neck like a poacher round a rabbit's. Then he came back into the lane and continued on his way.

He knew what he had done. When on the following day the police came to see him at Broadmoor, and no-one had yet said a word about murder or a little girl, he said: "I did not kill her ... I did not kill the little girl on the bicycle."

No-one said he was unfit to stand his trial this time. Dr Parkes now said he was able to understand the proceedings, to remember his crime, and to instruct his counsel. For three days in July 1952 he sat sullenly in the dock at Winchester Assizes and listened to the evidence of his three crimes. Though formally charging him only with the murder of Linda the Crown received the judge's permission to tell the jury of the earlier killings as well.

Six doctors gave evidence as to his mental condition, three for the prosecution and three for the defence. Although they disagreed as to whether he came within the McNaughton Rules they all agreed that—medically speaking—he was sane. The jury of ten men and two women took only twenty-nine minutes to find him guilty. He was sentenced to death.

"Straffen did not want to die," Mr N. H. Brown, his solicitor, has told me. Nor did his lawyers think that he should. "It would have been like hanging a child," say both Mr Brown and Mr Henry Elam, his counsel (and now a judge at London Sessions). So Straffen appealed. And on August 20th the Court of Criminal Appeal dismissed his plea without even calling on counsel for the Crown to address them.

Immediately Mr Elam approached the Attorney-General for his fiat to take the case to the ultimate court of appeal, the House of Lords. The Attorney-General refused, and two days later Straffen's execution date was announced: September 4th, 1952, at Wandsworth Prison. It was now August 28th—only six days were left.

Ever since Broadmoor was opened, in 1863, no Home Secretary had ever been faced with such a decision as confronted Sir David Maxwell Fyfe (now Earl Kilmuir). Certainly there had been previous escapes from Broadmoor—six within the last two years— but no escaping inmate had ever before committed murder while at large. Surely Straffen was mad? And you cannot hang a madman. Yet the doctors at the trial said he was not insane, and the judges of the Court of Criminal Appeal had ruled that he was legally responsible for his actions: he knew, however hazily, the nature and quality of his acts and that he was doing wrong. He was therefore sane medically as well as legally. Even so, how could an

escapee from Broadmoor be normal? How could Straffen be sane
—and the law make sense?

The mere horror of his crimes would not be enough to save
him. In two recent cases Sir David Maxwell Fyfe and his immediate predecessor Lord Chuter-Ede had failed to reprieve two
appalling child-murderers.

Lord Chuter-Ede had not saved Peter Griffiths, a twenty-two-
year-old ex-guardsman, who while drunk one night broke into a
hospital, took a four-year-old child from her cot, carried her out
into a hayfield, where in the dark he raped her and beat out her
brains against a stone wall.

And in January 1952 Sir David Maxwell Fyfe had not reprieved
Horace Carter, a thirty-year-old Birmingham labourer, who raped
and strangled an eleven-year-old girl living next door. To use
his own words: "She was still breathing, so I decided to use
string. I left her then, and went for some string. I tied it round
her throat. Either I was weak or I did not like doing it. I got some
cloth and my handkerchief and put them in her mouth, turned
her face down on the bed, and there she died." Afterwards he
tied her legs and her arms behind her back and left her "in a
praying position."

One would have thought that both these men were mad. If
anything their cases seemed worse than Straffen's. They must
have been even more mentally sick. Yet they were hanged, and
on August 29th, 1952, Straffen was reprieved.

There were many, like the leader-writer in *The Times*, who
greeted the Home Office announcement with relief, yet many
people—perhaps most people—reacted with horror. The *Justice of
the Peace Journal* reported that "a large part of the unthinking
public" were opposed to the reprieve. Lord Harris wrote to *The
Times*: "In my view, it is time that insanity should no longer be
considered as an excuse for avoiding the death penalty." And
Sir Reginald Watson-Jones, Vice-President of the Royal College
of Surgeons, asked in the same newspaper: "Why is it salutary
to know that the life of a homicidal maniac has been preserved
to the peril of those he will destroy once more if he escapes
again?"

The popular theme was—Straffen was mad. But even so, he had
brutally killed three small children. He would do the same again
if ever he got the chance. Society, therefore, should put him out
of harm's way for good.

Besides, the law had been revealed as such an ass. As commented the *Justice of the Peace Journal*: "It seems to have been

decided by authority that Straffen was insane in October last (when 'unfit to plead'); sane in the middle of this year (when sentenced to death) and insane again before the end of August (when reprieved)." It was one of "the more obvious fatuities of the law", wrote a contributor to the *Medical World*, for Straffen to be found without legal guilt and confined to Broadmoor for the first two killings and guilty of murder and sentenced to the extreme penalty of the law for half the same crime six months later."

To assess whether these irate, but sincere, criticisms of Maxwell Fyfe are well grounded one must first—to use Dr Johnson's expression—"rid one's mind of cant" and clear away three great misconceptions that have arisen about this case.

The first one is that Straffen was mad. Whatever the layman may think, he was not. He had never been certified insane, and the doctors were adamant that medically speaking he was not a lunatic. It was all very well for a lawyer to fulminate in the *Solicitor's Journal*: "Ask 'Is a strangler of little girls mad?' and the answer is 'Yes'." In medical terms, at least in Straffen's case, the answer was No.

According to Letitia Fairfield, who is both a doctor and a barrister, "There is a definite distinction between mental defectives, who have never had normal intelligence, and the insane, who have once had it but lost it by mental disease. It follows that mental defectives are by definition not insane." They are "permanent children": physically quite normal, but afflicted by a sort of mental dwarfism that keeps them mentally smaller than their real age.

The second great misconception is that Straffen's being found unfit to plead at his first trial in itself means that he was mad.

It means nothing of the kind.

A finding of unfitness to plead—or 'insane on arraignment' the even more sinister-sounding jargon for the same thing—does not mean that the accused is necessarily mad, either legally or medically. In the words of the authoritative Criminal Law Revision Committee, which in 1963 considered the whole question of fitness to plead, it simply means that the accused is "unable to understand the course of proceedings at the trial so as to make a proper defence, to challenge a juror and to appreciate the details of the evidence."

In October 1951, when Straffen's first trial took place, no-one was saying that he was insane—merely that he was unable to follow the proceedings in court. That as a high-grade mental defective he simply could not understand what was going on, and therefore the best thing to do was to avoid the farce of a trial and straight away put him into safe custody. When he appeared in court at his second trial he had seen so many doctors, and been subjected to so much questioning by medical men, lawyers, and policemen alike, that he had a glimmering of appreciation of court procedure and the ways of the law. Hence he was then 'fit to plead'.

The third great misconception about the case is that only lunatics go to Broadmoor. The place is now called discreetly Broadmoor Institution, but everyone knows that up till 1948, when the Criminal Justice Act changed its formal title, it was generally known as a criminal lunatic-asylum, the only one in the country. It was difficult to accept that an escapee from Broadmoor was not a lunatic. To the popular mind it was like saying that an exhibit at Madame Tussaud's is not a wax-work.

In fact, of the three categories of patient at Broadmoor, only one comprises certified lunatics. The inmates are: (1) persons ordered to be kept in safe custody because they are unfit to plead or legally insane under the McNaughton Rules; (2) persons whom the Home Secretary orders under an Act of Parliament to be removed to a mental hospital; and only (3) persons in custody who before or after trial are certified to be insane. "There are lots of sane people in Broadmoor," said Dr Murdoch, Principal Medical Officer at Wandsworth prison at Straffen's trial. But his words were washed away in the flood of verbiage that followed Straffen's conviction.

Should Straffen have been executed? "I did not think there was a chance of his hanging," says Mr Brown, his solicitor. The day after the Attorney-General refused his fiat for the case to go to the House of Lords Mr Brown sent the Home Secretary medical reports by three eminent psychiatrists who had seen Straffen in prison, but had not given evidence at the trial. These doctors had themselves many times sat on Home Office inquiries into the mental condition of prisoners under sentence of death, and the Home Secretary seems almost to have treated their reports as an unofficial medical recommendation to mercy: the following day Straffen's reprieve was announced.

Mr Henry Elam, Straffen's leading defence counsel, had also privately urged a reprieve upon Sir David Maxwell Fyfe. He had not called his gangling client as a witness in his own defence at the trial: "I think he formed the view that it would be too unutterably cruel to Straffen to expose him to cross-examination by the Solicitor-General," comments Mr Brown. But privately he wrote to the Home Secretary and told him of a strange remark that Straffen had made to him when first they met: *"I am going to plead guilty and let the jury decide"*—which shows he hardly understood very much of what was going on.

It is obvious that although Straffen was medically and legally sane he was yet woefully sub-normal mentally. In those circumstances it was, in my view, both right for the court to treat him at his second trial as sane, and right for the Home Secretary afterwards to reprieve him because of what the doctors said as to his mental condition. Perhaps it was a paradox that a jury could find him sane, but the Home Secretary could still reprieve him for medical reasons. But it was a paradox with both logic and human compassion to commend it.

A certified mental defective has not been executed in this country since the term was first coined in the Mental Deficiency Act of 1913. We have hanged evil men, weak men, even sometimes sick men. But we have never hanged 'permanent children'.

Perhaps it was the very horror of Peter Griffiths's and Horace Carter's crimes that took them out of the Straffen class. They did not merely kill their young victims: they did appalling things to them. They were not men of dwarfed mentality. They were evil men who gave way to evil passions.

I must confess that as a layman I think they are all mad—the Straffens, the Griffithses, the Carters of this world. But I am not a psychiatrist. A Home Office medical inquiry must have been held for Griffiths and Carter, and one can only assume that the doctors advised the Home Secretary that there were no medical grounds for recommending a reprieve. To a non-psychiatrist this seems bizarre. But if I were a Home Secretary and the doctors made no objection to my hanging two brutes like Griffiths and Carter I would not have wracked either my brain or my conscience for some pretext to save them. Neither, I venture to think, would most parents administering the law as it then was.

There is an epilogue to the case of Straffen. The Home Office have remained strictly logical in their treatment of him: they have continued to deal with him as a perfectly sane prisoner.

He has therefore achieved his goal in running away from Broadmoor Institution: he has escaped permanently from a mental home. Removed to a normal prison on the day after the murder and his subsequent recapture, he has ever after remained in prison custody. Since November 1960, when Part 5 of the 1959 Mental Health Act came into effect, the Home Secretary has had power to transfer to Broadmoor any ostensibly sane prisoner whom he is satisfied to be suffering from mental disorder warranting detention in a hospital. The Home Secretary has occasionally used this power, as in the case of Edwin David Sims, who in 1961 killed and mutilated a young couple on Gravesend Marshes. He has not done so with Straffen.

Why not? It does not necessarily follow that if a man is reprieved for medical reasons he ought invariably to go to Broadmoor. But one might have thought that if Straffen's case was to make sense, in the final analysis, the Institution is the only proper place for him. Peter Baker, a publisher who was imprisoned for fraud in 1954, and has since re-established himself, has written how he saw "the long emaciated, miserable figure of Straffen" at Horfield gaol, near Bristol, and how he was told that he went on Governor's application about once a month to inquire if they had a date for his release—a date that will probably never come.

It is not a pleasant picture, and one feels that the setting of a hospital is more suitable for this man, not yet middle-aged, to live out his somewhat pathetic life. On the other hand it is perhaps not too cynical to conjecture that at least a partial reason for the Home Office's inactivity may be the anger that any transfer to Broadmoor would provoke from parents with young children living in the neighbourhood, fearful of a second escape and yet another murder. For Straffen's own solicitor admits: "It is impossible to say he would not kill again if given the chance."

And so the Home Office try to make Straffen's life at Horfield a little less prison-like. In November 1963 a television set was installed in his cell: the only private set in the whole gaol. "I don't think anyone in prison begrudges him the privilege," his mother, who visits him every month, told a *Daily Express* reporter. She is probably right.

CHAPTER EIGHTEEN

Derek Bentley

(1953)

WITHIN a year of *Regina* v. *Straffen* Sir David Maxwell Fyfe had to decide three cases in each of which his refusal of a reprieve sparked controversy and made him the object of considerable criticism.

The three cases—those of Bentley, Giffard, and Christie—remain today among the most frequently discussed of recent times.

Indeed, Maxwell Fyfe's decision that Derek Bentley should hang was so unpopular that it played a part four years later in bringing about the first step in the abolition of capital punishment in this country. Bentley was convicted of murdering a policeman, and it was alleged that the Home Secretary lost all sense of proportion, and was so overawed by the enormity of this fact that he disregarded all the many circumstances calling for a reprieve and decided willy-nilly that the prisoner should die.

"To execute Bentley was very much more like a murder than anything he did," Sydney Silverman, M.P., told me nearly a decade after his death. The language is perhaps extreme, but it reflects the anxiety and concern that many people continue to feel about the fate of this nineteen-year-old youth from a respectable, working-class home in South London.

No study of the reprieve system would be complete without considering this case and attempting to answer the question: Did Maxwell Fyfe err?

The basic facts will not take long to narrate.

At 9 o'clock on the evening of November 2nd, 1952, Bentley was seen clambering over the locked main gates of a confectioners' warehouse in Croydon. With him was a good-looking, sixteen-year-old garage-hand from Camberwell called Christopher Craig.

The police were called, and some minutes later the two youths were cornered on the flat roof of the warehouse.

There was a short scuffle, and one of the policemen managed

to grab Bentley. He was a powerful lad and struggled free. According to the police he cried, "Let him have it, Chris!" and at that moment Craig fired a gun. The policeman was hit, but courageously grabbed hold of Bentley again and pulled him down. As other policemen clambered on to the roof Craig continued firing. "He's got a .45 and plenty of bloody ammunition too," Bentley told his captors. "I told the silly bastard not to use it."

By now police reinforcements had broken into the warehouse by a ground-floor entrance, and some officers, led by P.C. Miles, were climbing an inside staircase leading to the roof. Miles kicked open a door and sprang on to the roof. As he did so Craig shot him dead between the eyes. "I am Craig. You've just given my brother twelve years. Come on, you coppers! I'm only sixteen," he cried. In fact, his brother, a dangerous gunman, had been sentenced at the Old Bailey for armed robbery only three days before.

For twenty minutes as Miles's body lay slumped beside him he continued firing sporadically. Then pistols arrived for the police. Told of this, Craig jeered: "So you're going to make a shooting match of it, are you? It's just what I like . . . Come on, brave coppers, think of your wives!" But a few seconds later he called out: "Give my love to Pam" (his girl friend), and took a head dive off the roof. Surprisingly, he was not killed, his fall being broken by hitting the corner of a greenhouse. Still conscious, but with an injured spine and breast-bone, he told the first policeman who reached him: "I wish I was f—— dead. I hope I killed the f——lot."

Bentley was more muted. On his way to the police-station, he said, "I knew he had a gun, but I did not think the silly bugger would use it."

They were both charged with murder, and after a trial lasting several days at the Old Bailey before Lord Goddard, then Lord Chief Justice, they were both found guilty. Although he was already under arrest when Craig shot P.C. Miles the crucial evidence against Bentley was that, despite subsequent denials, he had admitted knowing that Craig had a gun when they set out on their warehouse-breaking and the vital words—albeit denied by both prisoners in the witness-box—"Let him have it, Chris!" The jury, however, recommended mercy in Bentley's case.

He needed it. For although Craig was merely ordered to be detained during the Queen's pleasure, as being two years too young to hang, Bentley was sentenced to death.

The case had already attracted a great deal of public attention. "GUNMAN KILLS LONDON P.C." had run the banner headlines on the morning following the murder, and the Press had maintained a

Above: The murdered parents of Miles Giffard.

Photos: Press Association Photos, Ltd.

Below: The cliff-top at Porthpean off which the bodies were bundled.

Photo by courtesy of the Chief Constable, Cornwall County Constabulary

192   *Inset:* Miles Giffard.   *Photo: P.A.—Reuter*

Guenther Fritz Podola between two police officers on his way from Brixton Prison to make his second appearance at West London Magistrates' Court.

Photo: Mirrorpic

Ruth Ellis and David Blakely, the man she shot, at the races.

Photo: Mirrorpic

high-powered interest in the proceedings. The parents of both young men were courted by reporters and Press photographers, and when Craig's mother and father arrived at the Old Bailey to attend the trial they drove up in a chauffeur-driven Rolls Royce, provided by a national newspaper, with the inevitable reporter beside them.

Public concern, fanned by the Press, continued during the following weeks, when Bentley's appeal was dismissed, and the date was announced for his execution. It is fair to say that most people expected a reprieve: the boy's youth, the fact that the murder was committed when he was already in custody, the jury's recommendation of mercy, the fact that Craig was not to die, all these —and other considerations—seemed to indicate that Bentley would not be hanged. When it was announced that Sir David Maxwell Fyfe had refused a reprieve it undoubtedly came both as a surprise and a shock to very many people, and it evoked a wave of indignation. As level-headed a journalist as Kenneth Allsop wrote that the nation was plunged into an emotional upset comparable to only two other recent events—Dunkirk and the death of King George VI.

In a desperate effort to force the Home Secretary's hand and make him disclose in public his reasons for disregarding what R. T. Paget, Q.C., M.P., has called "the assembly in the highest degree of every ground upon which the Prerogative of Mercy has formerly been exercised," Sydney Silverman, M.P., put down on the Order Paper of the House of Commons a Motion "respectfully" dissenting from Sir David Maxwell Fyfe's decision and urging him to reconsider the matter. The Motion was signed by two hundred Members, including ten ex-Ministers, but the Speaker, feeling himself bound by the rulings of previous Speakers in earlier cases, ordered the Motion to be removed from the Order Paper.

The following day Mr Silverman forced a debate on the propriety or otherwise of the Speaker's decision. The late Aneurin Bevan cried: "A three-quarter-witted boy of nineteen is to be hung for a murder he did not commit and which was committed fifteen minutes after he was arrested. Can we be made to keep silent when a thing as horrible and shocking as that is happening?" Other Members took part in the discussion, but it all turned on the question of whether the Speaker was right in ruling that the Home Secretary's decision in a capital case could not be debated in Parliament until after the sentence had been carried out. A great deal of oratory was thundered, but the Home Secretary was not flushed into making a single public statement as to his reasons for deciding that Bentley must be hanged.

N

The Speaker maintained his ruling, and it was supported by a majority vote in the House of Commons.

Public protests continued. Various M.P.'s went to see the Home Secretary. Crowds congregated outside Wandsworth prison, where Bentley was in the condemned cell. But on January 28th, 1953, he was hanged.

There is no doubt that in law Bentley was guilty of murder.

"It is quite unnecessary (Lord Goddard told the jury) where two or more persons are engaged together in an unlawful criminal act, to show that the hand of both of them committed the act . . . What you have to consider is: Is there evidence from which you can properly infer that these two youths went out with a common purpose, not merely to warehouse-break but to resist apprehension, even by violence, if necessary. That is all. It is, as I repeat, no answer if you come to that conclusion, for one to say: 'Yes, but I didn't think he would go as far as he did.' "

With respect, this is an impeccable statement of the law, and it was, indeed, upheld in the Court of Criminal Appeal.

The only question that therefore arises in Bentley's case is purely one of mercy. It has nothing to do with the law as such. Granted that Bentley was guilty, ought he—in human compassion—to have paid the ultimate penalty for his offence?

There has been a Bentley Industry: almost everyone who possibly could has written about the case. R. T. Paget claims that probably never in history has there been so much public feeling against an execution, and he may well be right. Books, tracts, numerous articles, and countless chapters about the case have appeared in general works on murder and crime. It is one of the most famous murder cases of the twentieth century. From all these outpourings it seems that basically there are five main grounds on which Sir David Maxwell Fyfe's decision is criticized. Sometimes the issues have been blurred by overwriting, exaggeration, and mawkish sentimentality. I propose that we now study these five grounds in some detail and see what merit, if any, they each contain.

First—Bentley was, to quote again Aneurin Bevan in the House of Commons, "a three-quarter-witted boy of nineteen". It is indisputable that he was nineteen, but it is inaccurate to call him "three-quarter-witted". He was a strong, muscular lad, who worked for the local Council as a dustman. However, he was undoubtedly of low intelligence: he suffered from epilepsy as a child, and had been rejected for National Service six months before the murder as being, to quote an official letter to his father, "mentally sub-standard".

R. T. Paget has gone so far in his chapter on the case in *Hanged—and Innocent?*—an abolitionist book published some years afterwards—to claim that Bentley was "Grade 4 Mentally Deficient"; and Arthur Koestler and C. H. Rolph, also well-known abolitionists, refer to him in their study *Hanged by the Neck* as "a grade 4 mental defective". These terms are misleading. Bentley was no Straffen. He was never certified as mentally defective, and had never been confined in a compulsory colony for mental defectives or treated for this mental condition. He was simply of very low intelligence, like many other people pursuing humble callings who yet do not get involved in armed murder.

Bentley was a fool. So have been a great many people sentenced to death. It is not a reason for granting a reprieve.

And we have already seen, his mere youth alone would not have saved him. As the Home Office told the Gowers Commission, youth is merely one of the factors to be considered in any individual case.

Second—again to quote Mr Paget: "Bentley had been recommended to mercy and the judge had used words which appeared to add the imprimatur of his approval to the recommendation. Nobody could recollect a case in which mercy had been withheld where both judge and jury concurred."

This line, taken by other commentators as well, assumes that Lord Goddard agreed with the jury's recommendation of mercy. In the light of this agreement the subsequent refusal of a reprieve is demonstrated as being even more regrettable.

But what did Lord Goddard say which could give rise to such a supposition? After sentencing Bentley to death and ordering Craig to be detained during the Queen's pleasure Lord Goddard went on: "I shall tell the Secretary of State when forwarding the recommendations of the jury in Bentley's case that in my opinion you are one of the most dangerous young criminals who has ever stood in that dock." That was all. Nothing more was said about Bentley after the jury's verdict. And on this slender basis has been built the theory that Lord Goddard thought that Bentley should not die.

Whether or not one used to agree with what he said no-one would have called Lord Goddard reluctant to express his views on any matter at all while on the Bench. In truth, he was one of the most outspoken—and powerful—judges of this century. If he really meant to express his agreement with the jury's recommendation of mercy there is no doubt whatever, to my mind, that he would bluntly and characteristically have said so when mentioning sending the recommendation to the Home Secretary.

I have discussed this case with Lord Goddard who, however, does not wish himself to be quoted at this stage. Even so, his words at the actual trial seem to speak for themselves.

Once the jury's recommendation is thus stripped of the presiding judge's concurrence it is clear that it would not have had much of an effect on the Home Secretary's mind. We have already seen how the yardstick of a recommendation's effectiveness is whether or not the judge agrees with it.

So this ground of criticizing Sir David Maxwell Fyfe's decision is also invalid.

Third—it was said that Parliament was deprived of its ancient and essential right to call the Home Secretary to account for the discharge of his duties.

"Bentley's was a particularly atrocious execution," says Sydney Silverman, M.P. "I would remove all inhibitions which prevent the Home Secretary being influenced by Parliament. It is not his mercy or that of the Crown, it is the mercy of the people of England. And in our country their voice is that of Parliament."

It is a bold claim and sincerely advanced. However, with respect, it does not seem well made out. It is now nearly eighty years ago since Henry Matthews, Q.C., when Home Secretary, refused to answer a question in Parliament about whether he intended to reprieve Israel Lipski. Since that case in 1887 there have been several instances where Home Secretaries have refused to dismiss the exercise of the Royal Prerogative of Mercy while the condemned prisoner was still alive; and in 1920 this ministerial opposition was supported for the first time by a ruling of the Speaker in the case of Cyril Saunders, in which Mr Speaker Lowther refused to accept a Motion for the Adjournment in much the same way as Mr Speaker Morrison refused to accept Mr Silverman's motion in Bentley's case. Mr Speaker Lowther's ruling was followed in subsequent cases by at least three different Speakers prior to 1953. Whatever may have been the practice before 1887 and Henry Matthews's stand in Lipski's case it is now a well-established rule of the House of Commons that any case involving a capital sentence in which the exercise of the Prerogative of Mercy is concerned shall not be the subject of question or discussion in the House while the sentence is pending. Afterwards—admittedly, when it is too late to do anything about a *negative* decision—the Home Secretary can be criticized on the relevant Vote in Supply or on a Motion for the Adjournment.

Lord Gardiner is one of many prominent abolitionists, unlike Mr Silverman, who does not regret this situation. "Within the existing framework of the law the present system of reprieve is the best one," he has told me. "The Home Secretary coming to a conclusion in calmness after a study of all the facts and documents seems to be about the best way to do it."

When occasionally some astute parliamentarian manages to force a debate in the House on a capital case—as Mr Silverman did again in the case of George Riley, in 1961, by putting down a question asking the Home Secretary to order an inquiry into whether a miscarriage of justice had occurred, and them moving a Motion of Censure on the Speaker for ruling the question as out of order—the standard of debate is revealed as not very high. False points are made, allegations are advanced on an inadequate command of all the facts, sometimes politics creep in, often parliamentary verbosity has its head. It is not always an edifying spectacle.

Mr Speaker Morrison was acting sensibly, as well as in accord with precedent, when refusing to let Sir David Maxwell Fyfe be subjected to the pressure of a parliamentary debate on his refusal of a reprieve.

Fourth—it was said that Sir David Maxwell Fyfe gave far too much consideration to the fact that the man killed by Craig and Bentley was a policeman. It was argued that a law existed whereby police-killers, once sentenced to death, were never reprieved.

If so, it was a new doctrine. Nearly a century ago a young man named Habron, aged eighteen and a half, was convicted upon what appeared to be the clearest possible evidence of the murder of a policeman in Manchester. He was reprieved primarily because of his age. Later the notorious Charles Peace confessed to the murder, and the boy was released and compensated for his imprisonment.

In fact, this so-called law did not exist. Obviously, and one would have thought rightly, when an unarmed police-officer was murdered while carrying out his public duty of protecting society a Home Secretary considered most carefully before deciding that the criminal should not suffer the full penalty of the law for his crime. But within the precious fifteen years there had been two cases in which murderers of policemen had been reprieved.

There was Donald George Thomas, who shot dead P.C. Nathaniel Edgar in the course of his duty, and was reprieved by Lord Chuter-Ede in April 1949, during the period of automatic reprieves while Parliament was debating the clause of the Criminal Justice Bill (later deleted) proposing a five-year suspension of the death penalty.

And, more to the point, there was Stanley Clarence, convicted in 1938 of the murder of P.C. John Potter of the Devonshire County Constabulary, whom Sir Samuel Hoare (later Lord Templewood) reprieved. Indeed, there were several similarities between Clarence's case and that of Bentley.

Clarence and an accomplice, like Bentley and Craig, were caught red-handed by the police while breaking into a factory, this time a cider factory in Exeter. There was a fight, and P.C. Potter died. Both intruders, like Bentley and Craig, were jointly charged with murder. But there the similarity ends: the jury acquitted the other man, and Clarence alone was sentenced to death. However, the jury recommended mercy, and after Clarence's appeal was dismissed Sir Samuel Hoare acceded to the recommendation.

Admittedly, Hoare was a known abolitionist, and the percentage of reprieves increased during his period of office. But at least the case of Clarence is there in the books, and it stands as a precedent against the argument that, to use Aneurin Bevan's indignant words, "where a policeman is killed somebody must be hung."

This ground of criticism of Sir David Maxwell Fyfe is therefore also shown to be unfounded.

Fifth—finally it was said that Bentley had not fired the fatal shot, that he was already in police custody when the murder occurred, and that it was unfair and unjust that he should hang, while his companion who fired the gun was saved solely because of the accident that he was three years younger and, therefore, under the minimum age for execution—eighteen.

To my mind this is the one argument which is valid and which in itself makes the execution of Derek Bentley a miscarriage of justice. Craig, the young man shouting threats of violence at the unarmed policemen on the warehouse roof, who put a bullet through P.C. Miles's head, and said he hoped he had killed the f—— lot, is now free. After over ten years in prison he was released in May 1963: a changed person. His years in prison were not wasted. The one-time youth is now a decent, honourable citizen; a thoroughly worth-while member of society. Craig's successful rehabilitation makes it all the sadder that his weaker-willed, far less intelligent companion of that November night in 1952 was not given the same opportunity. It is surely a denial of justice that merely by the fluke of the ages Bentley—who did not fire the gun—was hanged, while Craig—who carried and fired the gun—is now free.

Sir David Maxwell Fyfe could have saved Bentley. There was, as we have seen, no 'unwritten law' saying that all police-killers must be hanged. Of course, it is right that to most Englishmen the killing of a policeman is perhaps the most serious of all crimes. When criminals take advantage of our unarmed police they are committing a crime against all of us: they are undermining one of the stoutest pillars of our freedom. Indeed, if Craig— as he then was—had been over eighteen and both he and Bentley had been hanged I, for one, would not have said that the Home Secretary had failed in his duty. But Craig did not hang. And, in those circumstances, for Sir David Maxwell Fyfe to say that Bentley should forfeit his life is, to me at any rate, a monstrous decision.

CHAPTER NINETEEN

Miles Giffard

(1953)

IF one seeks to delve deeper and attempt to find some psychological reason why Sir David Maxwell Fyfe failed to recommend a reprieve for Bentley, a dustman from South London convicted of murdering a policeman, it can perhaps be said that class prejudice was, however unconsciously, a factor. But such a thought cannot even arise in the case of Miles Giffard, whose name next appeared on the Home Secretary's calendar of impending executions.

Giffard was that rare phenomenon—a murderer with an upper-class background. "Murder is in most cases an incident in miserable lives in which disputes, quarrels, angry words and blows are common," Sir John Macdonell wrote at the turn of the century. This could not be said of Giffard.

An ex-public-school boy and amateur cricket-player for his county, his family traced their descent back to an Osborn de Giffard who came over from Normandy with William the Conqueror. His father was a solicitor and Under-sheriff of Cornwall, his uncle was a distinguished general, and when the time came to plead for mercy a bishop, his ex-headmaster, attempted to intercede for him.

When Maxwell Fyfe sat down with the Giffard papers in front of him he was not a sophisticated politician considering the plight of someone remote from his own experience. This was like deciding on like—the Establishment passing judgment on a member of the Establishment.

It used to be said that law in England is a class-conscious affair. It certainly was not in the Giffard case. Maxwell Fyfe decided Miles Giffard's fate as coldly and clinically as he would that of a barrow-boy from Stepney. Perhaps—who knows?—even more coldly.

For Giffard had 'let the side down'. Despite the advantages of his birth, he was in conventional terms "an idle little waster". That was how prosecuting counsel the late John Scott Henderson, Q.C., and the Giffard family doctor described him in court. And that is how he must have seemed to most members of his class and, indeed, it is fair to say, to most right-thinking people.

At the age of twenty-six he was a remittance man, living in London on his wits and £15 a month remitted by his father from his cliff-top home at Porthpean, near St Austell. Periods of training, first in a solicitor's and then an estate agent's office, had proved disastrous. In fact, while at the estate agent's he had put his hand in the till and been saved from prosecution only by his father's making up the deficiency. He had also stolen from his parents.

He showed no sense of responsibility. Inheriting a legacy of £750 in November 1951, he had spent it all by March. Then, to use his own words to the police, he "scrounged about a bit", and eventually ended up selling ice-cream.

After some time back at home with his parents he returned to London in the middle of August 1953, and—again to use his own words—"I was living from hand to mouth. I had odd bits of money from various people, and there were some cheques which were R.D. I was drinking very heavily."

Nowadays we might call him a beatnik, except that he had no pretensions to art or artiness. Short but good-looking, with a square face and romantically unruly hair, he had a certain unshaven charm. A failure in everything else, he was a success with women. The money that he did not spend on drink he spent on them.

Then, in the early autumn of 1952, he met someone with whom he felt he could truly find happiness. He was besotted with Gabrielle Vallance, a nineteen-year-old girl he met in a public house in Chelsea. This was no promiscuous affair, this was a deep and more meaningful relationship. His whole life centred on the girl: he was jealous of her, begrudged every moment when he was not with her. But although she was quite happy to go around with him and drink with him Miss Vallance after a while began to complain about his untidy appearance. Bohemianism is one thing; scruffiness is another. Finally Giffard said he would go back home, collect some decent clothes, and come back to town. On Friday, October 31st, 1952, he set off by hitch-hike. On the following Sunday he arrived home.

The result was a row with his father. "You've got to stop here and continue with your studies," said Charles Giffard. It was time his Peter Pan of a son grew up.

But no sooner was Giffard in Cornwall than he wanted to return to London—and Gabrielle Vallance.

"I have had the hell of a row with the old man, [he wrote to her] made far worse by the fact that as usual he is right. The upshot of the whole thing is that he has forbidden me to return to London at any rate for the time being. He says he will cut me off without even the proverbial shilling, so there does not seem to be any alternative until I get a job . . . I am dreadfully fed up as I was looking forward to seeing you tomorrow and now God and the old man know when I shall. *Short of doing him in, I see no future in the world at all.*"

I have italicized the last sentence, since at Giffard's trial Mr Scott Henderson was to say it helped prove the premeditation of the murder that he was shortly to commit. And Mr Philip Stephens, of the firm of Stephens and Scown, Giffard's solicitors, has admitted to me that it was one of the high-water marks of the case against his client.

For about mid-week, two days after the letter was written, Miles Giffard decided—despite his father's edict—to return to London. And on the Friday evening he telephoned Gabrielle at 5.30 to say he was coming up to do some business for his father: and at 8.15 that evening he telephoned again to confirm that he was definitely coming and with his father's car. Between the two telephone calls he committed one of the most horrible crimes of recent years: he battered both his parents to death and threw their bodies over the near-by cliff-top.

Here is his laconic account, as told two days later to a detective superintendent of the Cornish Police:

"At the time of my first phone call my father and mother were both out. They came back almost together in separate cars at about 7.30 P.M.

"My father was doing something to mother's car. Both cars were in the garage. God knows for what reason I hit them over the head with a piece of iron pipe. I hit him once then. He slumped to the ground unconscious. Mother had gone into the house. I went into the house after her. I found her in the kitchen. I hit her from behind.

"Everything went peculiar. I got into a panic. Shortly after this I made a second phone call to Gabrielle in London about 8.15 P.M. and told her I was definitely coming to London with my father's car. I asked her if I could come round to her house in the morning for a wash and shave.

"I went with the intention of getting the car and found my father coming around. I hit him again several times, then I got the car out and went in to get some clothes and my mother was coming around then. So I hit her again. She was bleeding very heavily. They both were by this time. I did not know what to do. There was blood everywhere. I got out the wheelbarrow, put my mother in it, took her out to the point and pushed her over. I then went back and did the same with my father's body. I pushed the wheelbarrow over that time.

"I went back to the house and washed the place out. I went to my mother's room and took some pieces of jewellery . . . I took some money from father's coat pocket. I packed a change of clothing. My own clothes were very blood-stained. Then I drove the car out and drove to London.

". . . I can only say I have had a brain storm."

To the minds of the police and prosecuting counsel this was no brainstorm. It was, said John Scott Henderson, Q.C., "a premeditated murder . . . a murder planned and planned over some days." Its sole object—to steal something worth selling and get to London so that he could be with Gabrielle Vallance.

When Giffard's trial started at Bodmin Assizes, in February 1953, few could be blamed for not accepting this uncomplicated view of the case. Giffard had indeed driven straight to London after the murder, right to Tite Street, Chelsea, where Miss Vallance lived. He had slept in the car, and then, at about 8 o'clock, rung her bell. He had spent nearly the whole day with her—a visit to the cinema (to see a Charlie Chaplin film, of all things!), followed by a trip round the public houses. Then, towards the end of the day, he told her he had "done something dreadful": he had killed his parents. She was "very upset". They drank some more, then returned to Tite Street—where the police were waiting for him. All day his father's car, with its distinctive number-plate ERL 1, parked openly in the street was a silent testimonial of his presence in London—even to Giffard's bloodstained clothing lying on the rear seat.

An observer hearing the facts unfolded at St Austell magistrates court after his arrest may perhaps have thought it a little odd that Giffard should have been so casual about bloodstains, or been so foolhardy as to give two hitch-hikers a lift on his way to London on the Friday evening, or given his truthful name to the jeweller to whom he sold his mother's stolen jewellery for £50 on the Saturday morning, or been so foolish as not to wipe his father's blood off his old Rugby School tie before he rang Gabrielle Vallance's front-door bell. But even if such thoughts had occured they could have been dismissed by the further thought: "Well, murderers are sometimes careless. That's how they're caught."

Besides, not many people in Cornwall were feeling very sympathetic towards Miles Giffard. His parents had both been highly

respected and popular. Charles Giffard had at least been dead
before his sixteen-stone body was heaved over the cliff-edge, but
the pathologist's evidence was that Mrs Giffard was still alive
when her son trundled her over the top. "This in particular, gave
rise to much local feeling," Mr Philip Stephens has told me.

There was very little in the prosecution case that could help
Mr Scown and Mr Stephens. Their client had even given the
police a detailed account (which I have quoted) of how he committed the murder. What possible defence could there be?

Giffard himself was of no help. He showed no remorse for his
crime and was completely indifferent to what he had done. His
only concern when arrested had been not for the parents he had
slaughtered, but for the girl for whom he had done it: "Will
Gabrielle be brought into this? . . . I want to be frank. I did it.
I don't want Gabrielle brought into it," he told the police.

But the young man had friends, almost despite himself. His
eldest uncle, General Sir George Giffard, made himself responsible for his nephew's defence. "Why?" I asked him before his
death in late 1964. "Why pay for the defence of the man who
killed your brother?" His answer merits, I think, to be quoted:
"He was my nephew. I did not think it was a proper affair that
any relative of mine who was in trouble should be defended on
legal aid. I did not know at the first whether he was guilty or not.
But that did not come into it."

And so when John Scott Henderson, Q.C., told Mr Justice Oliver
at Bodmin Assizes, on the second day of the trial, "That is the case
for the prosecution, my Lord," John Maude, Q.C., then perhaps
the most fashionable defender on the Western Circuit, rose to
his feet to open the case for the defence. It was simple: Miles
Giffard was insane.

Mr Stephens, the solicitor, puts the situation forcibly:
"In these acts of apparent horrible brutality lay the clearest
indication of insanity. Could a jury believe that a sane man
would kill his mother—whom, so far as was known, he loved—
without rhyme or reason? Would any man kill his parents
merely to steal a car, a few pounds, and some jewellery? Does
not the fact that he returned and, as it seems, so brutally beat
his father and mother again and again indicate that at that time
he was—as indeed he says—having a brainstorm."

The lawyers were fortunate. They had what Mr Stephens calls
"a trump card—perhaps the only one—in a hand not notable for
its strength." They did not have to cast about after the murders
to try and build up a defence as to the mental and psychol-

ogical state of the accused. They did not have to rely on purely post-crime examinations or on what some psychiatrist said about a man who had never exhibited any form of mental instability before the crime was committed. No less than twelve years earlier Dr Roy Neville Craig, one of the leading psychiatrists in the West of England, had written to the Giffards' family doctor on the question of the accused's sanity: "The door which was slowly closing—if indeed it had not very nearly closed entirely—is slowly opening again towards the outside world." At that time Miles Giffard was only fourteen years of age!

Nor did the "slowly opening door" continue to open. After a temporary improvement in his later years at school and while he was on the lower deck in the Royal Navy Giffard's mental condition deteriorated again. Two years before the murders Dr Craig warned the young man's father: "Something ought to be done about Miles before it is too late."

The truth was that Miles Giffard was mentally abnormal from early childhood.

His first nurse was a martinet. She used to beat him and shut him in a dark cupboard, and if he went for help to his parents he was at once remitted to the care of this dangerous disciplinarian.

Finally, when he was four, his original nurse was replaced by a kindly girl of sixteen. But by then much of the damage had been done. She found him a very nervous little boy, who suffered terribly from nightmares. Several times a week she would have to leave her evening supper and go to soothe the child, because he was screaming in his sleep. If she came into the room unexpectedly he would throw himself on the floor shrieking, "No, no, don't do it!"

He loved his mother dearly in those early days, and nothing gave him greater pleasure than for her to come and have tea with him and his younger brother in their nursery. But almost throughout his life he was wary of his father.

Charles Giffard was a Victorian father: he did not beat his children, but he believed in keeping them firmly in their place. Neither son was allowed to speak at table unless spoken to. If the father rejected a piece of cake as being fly-blown it was given to Miles. In the early years he could easily reduce the impressionable child to tears with his taunting remarks, "Don't be such a little baby. You really are a baby!" And he continued in this vein throughout the boy's adolescence. Miles once commented to Mr Stephens during one of their prison interviews: "The only time I ever saw my father demonstratively affectionate was with his dog—but never with his son."

"All through his life Miles was sat upon," General Giffard has told me of his nephew. "I thought Charles was far too severe with him. It was most distressing," says Lady Giffard, his wife.

Eventually came the time for Miles to go away to a boarding preparatory school. He was heartbroken. Completely devoted to his mother, fond of the new nanny, whom he had grown to love, he was terrified of the idea of leaving home. And with good cause: at the new school he received an abnormal amount of punishment and beating. He seemed to the staff idle, solitary, and unco-operative. He was unusually untidy and grubby, even for a small boy. His intellectual inhibitions made it difficult for him to concentrate, and he seemed impervious to either praise or blame. The result at such a school was perhaps inevitable—more and more beatings.

Then came the public school, and Miles was packed off to Rugby, where his father and uncle had distinguished themselves before him. The result was almost equally disastrous. At home the father, Charles Giffard, was suffering from a mental breakdown. At school Miles was screwing up his sheets at night and tearing large holes in them with his teeth. He was untidy, dirty, irresponsible, and an almost pathological liar. He was unpopular and solitary. Only in one respect did he seem to show any promise, and that was on the cricket field. Unfortunately, it was not enough: after four terms Charles Giffard was asked to take his son away.

It was then that the Giffards took Miles for the first time to see Dr Roy Neville Craig, to whom it was at once clear that the boy was on the verge of a serious breakdown. He was transferred to Blundell's school, much nearer home, and for over a year he was subjected to a sustained course of psycho-analysis. It seemed to do some good, and although Miles never particularly shone at Blundell's, and a schoolmate was later to say in court that he was always rather odd and backward and did not get on with people, he managed to last out his school career without any other major incident.

Then came four years in the Royal Navy, where the discipline of the lower deck appears, oddly enough, to have agreed with him. He still was backward, and never became an officer. But at least he seems to have enjoyed life: for most of the time he was in destroyers in the North Sea and the Far East.

Then followed the return to civilian life, a continuous, downhill deterioration in his mental condition—and the murder of his parents.

Dr Roy Neville Craig, by then retired in Eire, came to court to speak for Miles, whom he had seen again in prison after his crime. In his view the accused was certifiably insane, suffering from a constitutional psychopathic personality with, probably, an underlying psychosis as well. There was no room for doubt in his diagnosis:

"At the time he did this thing he was in a schizophrenic episode [he said]. He would know what he was doing, but in schizophrenia there is a split in the mind—a split between the unconscious or primitive part of the mind and the more superficial, conventional part. When the split takes place the primitive mind takes charge, uncontrolled any longer by the conventional part . . . Schizophrenic patients will develop a kind of fixed idea which dominates the whole of their thinking processes for the time being. It just takes charge over everything. In this case I think the fixed idea was to go and see this girl in London. In my view he did not know at the time of killing that what he was doing was wrong in law or morally, owing to his disease of mind."

It was a logical diagnosis, supported by a mental history going back twelve years. Why did the jury not then accept it?

For a number of reasons.

First, at least in my view, the defence overplayed their hand. Not content with Dr Craig's clear and authoritative testimony, John Maude, Q.C., also called another eminent doctor, A. P. Rossiter Lewis, a Harley Street psychiatrist, who had seen Giffard only after his arrest, and who put forward a somewhat different view as to his mental condition. According to Dr Rossiter Lewis, Miles was indeed insane (within the meaning of the McNaughton Rules) at the time he committed the murders, but this was occasioned not by his long-standing schizophrenic condition, but because of spontaneous hypoglycaemia. This was a somewhat new medical term to describe the condition in which the blood sugar suddenly drops abnormally low, causing clouding of consciousness. It had never before been suggested that Giffard suffered from such a thing, and Dr John Matheson, principal medical officer at Brixton prison, called in rebuttal by the Crown, pointed out that on the day of the murders Giffard had enjoyed a good lunch and half a bottle of whisky in the afternoon, which would surely have sent his blood sugar zooming.

With respect, it is difficult to understand why so able a defender as John Maude (now Judge Maude) called Dr Rossiter Lewis. This distinguished doctor may well have been perfectly right in his diagnosis, but it was rather at variance with Dr Craig's. Whenever a defence is run in double harness, a jury finds it difficult to know which horse to back.

Second Dr Craig's evidence was itself challenged by Dr Hood, the Giffards' family doctor. He was no psychiatrist, but he had known the family for years, and when he said in the witness-box, with all the sincerity of someone who had been Charles and Betty Giffards' friend as well as their doctor, "The picture was more of just an idle little waster," it was a phrase that ran truer in a West Country jury's ears than "schizophrenia" or "spontaneous hypoglycaemia".

Dr Hood is now dead, but it is not perhaps unfair to comment that it ill became him to sneer at psychiatrists and pooh-pooh the evidence of Dr Craig: it was on his own recommendation that the Giffards sent Miles to Dr Craig in the first place! Comments Mr Stephens: "Dr Hood had never made the slightest secret of his willingness, and indeed anxiety, to assist the prosecution. He seemed to consider he had a mission in life, which was to ensure the execution of the idle little waster who had murdered his personal friends, Mr and Mrs Giffard." Nevertheless, he was palpably sincere, and his sincerity impressed the jury.

Third, the attitude of the judge affected the outcome of the case. Mr Justice Oliver was of the generation that did not listen easily to the evidence of psychiatrists. Though not for one moment stepping beyond the bounds of propriety in his conduct of the trial he yet clearly indicated where his own sympathies lay. "The judge was dead against us," says General Giffard. When in his summing up Mr Justice Oliver leaned towards the jury and said of the accused: "Is that the act of a madman or is that the act of an utterly wicked man?" few people in court could have doubted which way he would himself have answered the question.

And perhaps fourth the fact that Miles Giffard did not give evidence in his own defence. The judge commented on this failure: "He could have gone into the box perfectly well and been asked some of the questions that are unanswerable . . . But we have not been given the chance. His memory is perfect; he knows everything he did, and all the order in which he did it. Why should he not come and tell us?"

The jury may indeed have wondered why. It is always a gamble when the accused on a capital charge does not go into the witness-box to tell his own story, and seldom does the gamble come off. Here, however, I think it was justified. For if Miles Giffard had given evidence he could only but have harmed his case. His testimony would only have made the jury even more unsympathetic towards him. For he would not have pronounced one word of remorse for the ghastly things he had done. Even to his uncle, whose brother he had killed and who continued to visit

Victor John Terry arriving at London Airport from Glasgow with a police escort on his way to Worthing to be charged with the capital murder of Henry Pull, a bank guard.

Photo: Associated Press, Ltd.

A drawing by Terry of Mr William Scales, his solicitors' managing-clerk, drawn at Brixton Prison while Terry was awaiting trial.

Reproduced by courtesy of Mr. Scales

Right:

Timothy John Evans arriving under police escort at Paddington Station from Wales in December 1949.

Photo: Associated Newspapers Ltd.

Below:

John Reginald Halliday Christie.

Photo: Mirrorpic

209

Below:

Christie's tobacco-tin containing clumps of female pubic hair found in his Flat.

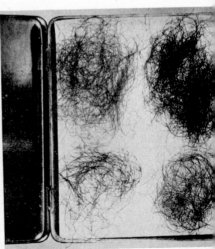

him until the eve of his execution, he said nothing: "He never even mentioned it to me ever," said General Giffard.

How could the defence possibly have called such a man to be cross-examined by so effective a prosecutor as John Scott Henderson, Q.C.?

In the result, the jury at the end of a four-day hearing took only thirty-two minutes to find Miles Giffard guilty. In the classic phrase, he displayed no emotion on receiving sentence of death.

There was no appeal, as counsel advised there was nothing on which an appeal could be launched. All efforts to save Giffard centred solely on Home Secretary Maxwell Fyfe. General Giffard wrote to him, the General came up to town and saw a senior official at the Home Office; the Bishop of Coventry, who had been Miles's headmaster at Blundell's, also intervened. Various other letters were written, and reasonably high-powered steps taken to try and persuade Maxwell Fyfe to spare this young man's life. In the press appeared letters that Miles wrote to Gabrielle Vallance from the condemned cell.

One letter in particular reached the Home Secretary which General Giffard told me he thought Maxwell Fyfe might have acted on. It was from a Mrs Angele Clemence Godfrey, one of the jurors at Miles's trial. She wrote that she had disagreed with the verdict of guilty, because she was convinced that Miles was insane at the time of the murders, but owing to a misunderstanding the disagreement was not made known to the judge; being of French origin she did not understand English court procedure.

When, on the Saturday before Miles Giffard's execution was due to take place, it was announced that there was to be no reprieve Mr Stephens (who knew of the juror's letter) made public its contents. Reporters hastened to the Home Office, where an official blandly told them that the matter had been considered, but it made no difference to the Home Secretary's decision. "It goes to the secrecy of the jury room," he explained cryptically.

To a psychiatrist who came to see him in prison Miles said he wanted to live: which was nothing unusual. But when asked why his reply was perhaps just a little odd: "Well, quite frankly, I want to live to see if England can beat the Australians at cricket this year."

When taken to the Burden Neurological Institute, at Bristol, for his EEG readings prior to trial the prisoner was so unconcerned he fell asleep. Dr Ralph Sessions Hodge, the distinguished psychiatrist who took the readings and interviewed Miles over a total of ten hours, told Messrs Stephens and Scown in his re-

o

port: "While his intellectual development has been adequate and proceeded by normal stages, his emotional development remains at the level of a child of the nursery age."

Taking up his nursery theme, the solicitors concluded their brief to defence counsel with this trenchant paragraph:

"It may not be without symbolical significance that on the night of November 7th when the Accused at the age of twenty-six battered to death his father . . . and his mother for whom he felt so great a love that his nanny remembers his love for her twenty years later—there in the garage where his father fell battered to death stood a silent witness to the tragedy, the wooden rocking horse which had been one of his pet toys in his nursery days. If that rocking horse could have spoken, many mysteries might be solved in this case!"

And so Miles Giffard was hanged. Lady Giffard has given me permission to quote a short extract from the last letter that he wrote to her. It shows that at the end Peter Pan had at last grown up: "As of course you know by now, the Home Secretary has not found any excuses for me."

In one sense Sir David Maxwell Fyfe cannot be faulted for hanging Giffard. As I have said more than once before, in matters of mental responsibility the Home Secretary takes the advice of the doctors who see the man in prison after sentence, and if they certify that there is no medical reason for recommending a reprieve the blood is on their hands in a doubtful case, not his. However, General Giffard said that his nephew should not have been hanged: he was not fully responsible for his actions. And, personally, as a layman I take the same view: the man must have been mad to do what he did. Nor can it be argued that it was simply a sordid crime to get some money: the next-door neighbours were away, and Miles had their key so he could feed their cat. Nothing could have been easier than for him to slip next door and steal something worth selling: he did not have to wait till his parents returned in the evening and then bludgeon them to death.

But, the Home Office doctors obviously considered Giffard perfectly sane, and it is only fair to say that Dr Lindesay Neustatter, one of the country's most eminent psychiatrists, has preferred in a technical study of the case not to give a firm diagnosis of his condition, and to add: "The Home Secretary was clearly in a very difficult position in making a special case and it was understandable that he felt it difficult to grant a reprieve."

Even so, medical considerations were not the only factors. There was also Mrs Godfrey's letter. As long ago as 1922 the Lord Chief Justice, Lord Hewart, had said in the case of Herbert Rowse Armstrong, the Welsh poisoner: "The inestimable value of a jury's verdict is created only by its unanimity." If there was half a chance that Giffard had not, in fact, been convicted by the unanimous decision of his twelve jurors, he ought to have been reprieved.

Maxwell Fyfe was a lawyer, a distinguished Q.C. (later Lord Chancellor), who had built up an extensive practice in Liverpool and on the Northern Circuit before turning to politics. Like all barristers, he was, no doubt, brought up on the principle ingrained in the fabric of English law that you cannot go behind a jury's verdict: that no-one, not even the House of Lords—as was demonstrated in the case of *Thompson* v. *Director of Public Prosecutions* in 1962—can inquire into the secrets of the jury-room. This may be good law, but it is not good justice.

And it becomes even worse justice when one discovers that Mrs Godfrey, who died as recently as December 1963, retained to her death the firm conviction that Miles Giffard was insane. Mr Stephens knew her personally, and he tells me: "It haunted her for the rest of her days."

Here was a man accused of a crime so terrible that most people would consider it capable of being committed only by someone suffering from some kind of diminished mental responsibility. His defence of insanity, supported by two doctors and a mental history going back twelve years, was rejected by a jury, one member of which afterwards said to her dying day that she had not agreed with the verdict. In law, the carrying out of the sentence was beyond challenge. In morality it seems to have been a disgrace.

One cannot help having the feeling that this particular Home Secretary allowed his legal training and frame of mind to outweigh every other consideration. In Miles Giffard's death the law triumphed over justice.

One question remains: why *did* Giffard kill his parents? What sparked off those terrible moments of violence?

At the trial it never became apparent. The only person who could say—Giffard himself—did not, for good reasons, go into the witness-box. And his prior statement to the police, detailed though it was, also did not give the answer: "God knows for what reason I hit them," it reads.

It is the one loose end of the case that has never been tied up: once, that is, one does not accept the prosecution's theory of a premeditated murder for gain "planned and planned over some days." General Giffard though he never gave evidence, because he knew nothing of the facts at first-hand, yet knew the character of his brother and nephew very well, and had his own theory of the killing. It was neither planned, as the prosecution maintained, nor a sudden impulse for "God knows what reason", as Miles told the police. It was almost certainly sparked off by something that the brusque Charles Giffard said when he returned to the house at the end of a gruelling day's work.

"I rather suspect," the General told me, "that Miles asked his father if he could have the use of the car to drive up to London. Charles probably realized why he wanted it—to see this girl. And knowing Charles, he probably would not have been content with merely saying No. He probably added one or two well-chosen, obectionable remarks about the girl as well. And that did it! Miles thereupon laid him low."

It is an interesting reconstruction, and, to my mind at least, makes sense of the case. Miles, half a bottle of whisky inside him and driven into a frenzy by these remarks of the father whom he hated, then had his "brainstorm". That was how he came to kill his mother, whom he adored. "Why he attacked her, God alone knows!" said the General. But the explanation is perhaps painfully simple: for a space of probably not more than half an hour Miles Giffard ran amok in that large house, perched on top of a cliff, in Cornwall. For that half an hour he was a homicidal maniac.

CHAPTER TWENTY

John Reginald Halliday Christie

(1953)

FIVE months after Miles Giffard died Sir David Maxwell Fyfe was faced with a similar problem all over again. On the one side doctors told him that there was no medical reason to recommend a reprieve. On the other side most intelligent laymen agreed with the prisoner's counsel: "he is as mad as a March hare."

There was a further complication: it would have been in the Home Office's best interests for the prisoner—John Reginald Halliday Christie—to die. As long as he lived he was a potential star witness in a case against the Department. The charge—the wrongful hanging three years earlier of an innocent man.

Everyone knows the basic facts of the case: how in 1949 a near-illiterate lorry-driver named Timothy John Evans was charged with strangling his wife and baby daughter, convicted of the child's murder, and hanged—despite his protests that the real killer was Christie, the prosecution's main witness. 10 Rillington Place, the dilapidated tenement house in North Kensington, where they both lived, has become the most notorious address in English criminal history. It was here that in 1953 the remains of six women were found hidden about the place. Christie admitted he had strangled them: and also claimed he had killed Mrs Evans.

To many people it was inconceivable that two stranglers could have lived at the same time in the same small, six-roomed house. The Home Secretary asked John Scott Henderson, Q.C., (who had prosecuted Miles Giffard) to conduct a private inquiry to see if a miscarriage of justice had occurred. Mr Henderson reported: "I am satisfied that there can be no doubt that Evans was responsible for both murders." On the same day it was announced that Christie was not to be reprieved. Two days later he was hanged.

His voice may have been silenced, but the clamour to 'vindicate' Evans has seldom since been still for long. Debates have taken place in Parliament, a free pardon has been requested and refused, books, articles, and tracts written, countless speeches spoken. The case still continues today as a live subject of controversy.

At first I thought there was nothing new that I could contribute. In 1961 appeared Mr Ludovic Kennedy's exhaustive analysis *Ten Rillington Place*: he seemed to have explored every possibility for research. His conclusion was firm and impassioned: Evans was innocent, Christie did all the killings. Yet as one studied Mr Kennedy's book with care and referred back to his sources it became clear that perhaps all was not as he alleged.

But where else to look for new information?

I realized that there was one vital person whose 'evidence' had not yet been made public—Mr Ambrose Appelbe, Christie's solicitor. Surprisingly he was not even asked by Mr Scott Henderson to attend his official inquiry, and no previous writer had been to see him. Surely he could contribute something of importance?

I decided that if I could get to see Mr Appelbe it might be worth while writing about the case. He agreed to see me. With fascination I listened to what he had to tell me, and I followed up some leads he gave me. The result is, I think, more of the truth about Evans and Christie than has ever before been published.

To start at the beginning: on the afternoon of November 30th, 1949, Evans walked into a small Welsh police-station and gave himself up.

"I have disposed of my wife. I put her down the drain," he told an incredulous detective-constable.

"You realize what you are saying? Just think before you say any more," said the policeman.

"Yes, I know what I am saying," replied Evans. "I can't sleep, and want to get it off my chest. I will tell you all about it and you can write it down."

The near-illiterate had chosen his words with care. He did not thereupon admit to murder—only to 'disposing' of his wife's body.

He told the policeman how she had not wanted to have another baby, how a man in a café had given him something for her to take, and the next thing he knew was he came back from work to find her dead. That night he dragged her body downstairs, and pushed it into the drain outside their front door. He then got his baby looked after, handed in his cards at work, sold his furniture, and came down to his aunt in Merthyr Tydfil. He told her that his wife and baby had gone to Brighton for a holiday.

It did not take long for the police to discover there was no body in the drain. "No, I said that to protect a man called Christie."

said Evans. "It is not true about the man in the café either. I'll tell you the truth now."

And he made his second statement to the Welsh police. Now he said that his wife had arranged with Christie for him to give her an abortion. "When I came home in the evening he was waiting for me. He said, 'It's bad news. It didn't work.' I asked him where she was . . . I looked at my wife . . . She was dead." Christie said he would dispose of the body and that he knew "a young couple over in East Acton" who would look after the baby. Evans helped him carry the body downstairs: "Leave the rest to me," said Christie.

He never saw his wife's body again, and Christie told him he had put it down a drain.

A few days later he returned from work to find his baby had gone. Christie told him that the couple had called and taken her away. "Now the best thing you can do is sell your furniture and get out of London somewhere," he advised. And that is what Evans did.

What happened to the baby? "I went back on the Wednesday or Thursday after I came down. I wanted to see about my child. I called at Christie's and asked him where my child was. He said, 'She's all right. You can't see her yet. It would be too early . . .' I then came back to Merthyr Tydfil."

Two days later the bodies of Mrs Evans and her daughter were found neatly parcelled in a wash-house, at the back of 10 Rillington Place. Both had been strangled: a man's tie was still knotted round the child's neck. Mrs Evans was pregnant, but there was no evidence of any attempt at abortion.

That evening Evans, accompanied by two policemen, arrived at Paddington Station from Wales. He knew nothing of the discovery of the bodies. Taken straight to the police-station, he was at once told and shown the corpses' clothing. He was cautioned, and according to Chief Inspector George Jennings "then made a statement which I took down in my notebook and which he later signed."

This is the statement:

"She was incurring one debt after another and I could not stand it any longer so I strangled her with a piece of rope and took her down to the flat below the same night whilst the old man was in hospital. I waited till the Christies downstairs had gone to bed, then I took her to the wash-house after midnight. This was on Tuesday, November 8th. On Thursday evening after I came home from work I strangled my baby in our bedroom with my tie and later that night I took her down into the wash-house after the Christies had gone to bed."

This was followed by a much longer, detailed account of the killings. Its language is sometimes more like that of a police report than a lorry-driver's confession. Nevertheless, Evans signed it.

Five weeks later, at his trial, he went back on both signed confessions, and said the truth was what he had told the Welsh police in his second statement. In effect he said he felt involved in his wife's murder, because he knew beforehand of the abortion. That was why he had helped Christie dispose of the body. But he had played no part in murdering his child.

Why then did he sign two confessions to *both* murders? asked Mr Malcolm Morris, his counsel, at the Old Bailey.

"I was upset, and I do not think I knew what I was saying. I was upset pretty bad, sir, I had been believing my daughter was still alive."

Christie gave evidence, and denied all knowledge of any abortion or any complicity whatsoever in either death. Indeed, he said that on the night of November 8th he was startled by "a very loud thud" overhead, followed by a noise as if furniture was being moved around. His wife, Mrs Ethel Christie, corroborated this evidence, and seems to have believed it, for when, after Evans had been sentenced to death, his mother shouted at Christie, "Murderer! Murderer!" she shouted back: "Don't you dare call my husband a murderer. He is a good man."

Three years later she stirred in the night, and her "good man", to use his own words, "got a stocking and tied it round her neck to put her to sleep." Then he stuffed her ample body under the floorboards.

It sparked off a minor orgy of murder. During the next few weeks he brought back three prostitutes to his flat: each one of them he murdered. His method was always the same: he got them partly drunk, then persuaded them to sit in a rickety deckchair in the kitchen. A piece of rubber tubing hung down from a gas-pipe near the floor. He turned on the gas and within minutes the women lost consciousness. Then he raped them and strangled them.

Eventually, almost penniless, he left the house and wandered the streets as a near-derelict. Arrested gazing mournfully at the river on Putney Embankment, he soon confessed to murdering these women. Later he also admitted killing Mrs Evans and raping and strangling two other women, whom he had brought back on different occasions to the house during the Second World War, and whose bones were dug up in the garden.

Why strangle these women? As a youth in his native Yorkshire his lack of sexual prowess had earned him the nickname "Reggie-no-dick". Professor Francis Camps, the pathologist's, theory is that he was such a bad performer he needed a woman to be un-conscious before he could possess her. This is understandable. But why kill them as well?

Ludovic Kennedy has no doubt as to the reason: Christie was a necrophile, he says. In his reconstruction of the case he conjec-tures Christie strangling his victims *before* intercourse. The late F. Tennyson Jesse agrees: "a necrophilic strangler", she describes Christie in the *Notable British Trials* series. And this is the gener-ally accepted view among many commentators on the case—for example, Arthur Koestler and C. H. Rolph, who state in their book *Hanged by the Neck,* "Christie murdered at least six women and practised necrophilia after their death."

Certainly if this were true it would be difficult to argue that he was not "as mad as a March hare". Dr Clifford Allen, a psychia-trist of great experience, has written that necrophiles are very rare, and that he had never seen it in a sane person. Sir Norwood East, perhaps the most eminent prison doctor of the century, has commented: "Necrophilia is very uncommon and my own exper-ience is limited to four cases . . . It is difficult to believe that anyone could commit this act unless gross mental abnormality was present." If Christie was, indeed, a necrophile the decision not to reprieve him is deplorable. "The wickedest man in the world", the *Sunday Pictorial* called him, "The Monster of Rillington Place", was another popular nickname. Even so, if he had sexual intercourse with dead bodies he was mad and should not have been hanged.

But the truth is that he was not a necrophile.

Mr Kennedy, the late Miss Tennyson Jesse, *et alii* are stretch-ing the scientific evidence much too far. "It is not possible for a pathologist to diagnose that intercourse has taken place after death," Dr Donald Teare (who carried out the post-mortem on Mrs Evans) has told me; and Professor Camps (who carried out the post-mortems on the other bodies) also confirms there was no evi-dence of post-fatal intercourse. In his *Medical and Scientific In-vestigations in the Christie Case* he writes, "An opinion was formed that intercourse had taken place at or about the time of death." Nothing is said about intercourse after death.

Christie though he made three long statements to the police and had several interviews with psychiatrists never himself ad-mitted to having intercouse with dead women. Even in the account of his crimes that he wrote in the *Sunday Pictorial* when awaiting the reprieve decision after conviction—when it would have paid him to make himself as crazy as possible—he maintained that the sex-act came first, then the strangling.

What seems nearer the mark, and more consistent with his evidence in court, is that as, with difficulty, he reached his sexual climax he strangled the woman, as if to express his complete victory over them—and himself. What greater triumph in the battle of the sexes than to kill at the moment of conquest? What better retort to the young Halifax slut who had once taunted him "Reggie-no-dick"?

Once passion was spent and, bathed in perspiration, he saw the body lying there dead he made no further attempt to penetrate. A necrophile will defile a body when it is cold, even partly decomposed: sometimes corpses are taken from graves for this purpose. But this was not for Christie. A dead body, as such, was not a sexual object. He did not kill to possess: he killed as the climax of possession. His own words testify to this:

"While I was having intercourse with her, I strangled her with a piece of rope . . . I believe I had intercourse with her at the time I strangled her . . . There was a piece of rope hanging from the chair. I don't remember what happened but I must have gone haywire. The next thing I remember she was lying still in the chair with the rope round her neck."

Yet Christie killed for a definite purpose as well as by reflex. He *did* use the bodies of his victims after death. But not for sexual intercourse. The truth is even more bizarre.

We start off with known facts. Christie was a hair-fetishist, one of those people who derive sexual satisfaction from contemplating or touching human hair. We know this, because a tobacco-tin containing clumps of female pubic hair was found in his flat, and Christie never denied they were taken from his victims. We also know from chemical analysis of his clothing that he used to practise masturbation fully clothed—conceivably while handling these hairs.

We also know from already published material that he had an unhappy childhood. "I always lived in dread of my father. He was stern, strict and proud," he wrote in the *Sunday Pictorial*. But he loved his mother: "She was a wonderful woman." He was also fond of his maternal grandfather, who lived with them, and it was a shock for the little boy when the old man died.

Christie was aged eight, and at that young age he saw his first corpse. Colin Wilson and Pat Pitman have commented: "It has not been established what effect the sight of his grandfather's body had on the development of a morbid attitude towards death and sex." These words are percipient. For the secret of the murders at 10 Rillington Place is to be found in the scene, over forty years earlier, when a nervous little boy tiptoed into the front parlour of a lonely house on the Yorkshire moors to gaze at the body of an old man he had loved.

This is where I am indebted to Mr Appelbe, Christie's solicitor. He is not only a lawyer, but has had some training in psychology, and was intrigued by the case.

"As a matter of public interest [he says] I tried to get out of him why he did it. On two or three occasions he nearly told me —then just at the point he veered off again.

"Finally I was talking to him about his childhood in the condemned cell, at Pentonville, three or four days before he was due to be hanged. I was delving into the past and trying to get at the truth. He told me about his grandfather, as, indeed, he had done before, but now for the first time the full story came out.

"The old man was laid out in the front parlour, and he went in there to touch him for the last time; to make his last farewell, you might say. But his mother was there, combing the old man's hair. And she pushed him away: perhaps understandably she would not let him touch the body. And that had a tremendous effect upon the boy.

"As he grew older the memory lived with him, and he began to have a compulsive desire to comb the hair of a dead and dear object—a corpse. *The one thing he did with his victims' bodies was to comb their hair.* He admitted to me that he combed their head and pubic hair every morning until the smell got too bad. It was the one interesting thing about their bodies.

"He made them dear and near to him by having intercourse —admittedly while they were stupefied, because that was the only way he could perform the sex-act—and then he killed them and combed their hair."

There was no gap between the two war-time murders and Mrs Evans's death. Christie told Mr Appelbe that he vaguely remembered killing about twenty-one or twenty-two women, most of them during the war, when he had easily been able to dump the bodies on bomb-sites—after the ritual hair-combing.

As sometimes happens when a psychiatrist extracts something deep from a person's sub-conscious, Christie reacted violently against his prober.

"If the warders had not been there he would have attacked me [says Mr Appelbe]. At the moment of truth his trust and affection for me turned to violent hatred. I had to leave: he was in a 'highly emotional state.' "

But not before he had promised Christie that he would not reveal to the authorities what he had just told him.

"I've often wondered if I had brought it out, it might have made a difference. But in any event Christie did not want a reprieve, and would have been disappointed if he got one. Now it seems only fair to his memory that the story should be told: for the hair-combing was the overriding passion of his life. He was compelled to do it. He lived for nothing else in the end. He was as batty as a coot on this respect, and he was very annoyed when he realized—as I did—the root of his trouble. It was like someone cutting out a part of him."

This is what the newspapers call "a sensational disclosure". It certainly is macabre, and it is only fair to say that all three doctors who gave evidence at Christie's trial agreed that he was a pathological liar, whose word was to be accepted only when it could be corroborated by some undoubted, objective fact. But Mr Appelbe is convinced that Christie a few days before his imminent execution was speaking the truth, and it is difficult to see why he should then have lied. Admittedly Professor Camps has looked again at the photographs for me, and writes: "I do not think there is really any evidence of combing in spite of what he said." But it does fit in with the pubic hairs, carefully kept in the tobacco tin, and it relates back to the known encounter with the grandfather's body. Furthermore if—as seems clear—Christie was not a necrophile it provides a reason for the murders.

Should he have been reprieved? All three doctors at his trial agreed that he was not insane though psychiatrist Dr Jack Hobson, called by the defence, said that he thought Christie was a gross hysteric. Mere fetishism, as distinct from necrophilia, would not necessarily stamp him a madman. Once not insane it fully accords with Home Office practice that he was not reprieved.

For Christie is only one of a long line of sane sexual killers who have been hanged. In 1942 Gordon Frederick Cummins, a young airman who murdered four women in four days, was executed. In 1949 Neville George Cleveley Heath, who murdered two women and mutilated their bodies, was executed. And again in 1959, even after the Homicide Act, Bernard Hugh Walden, a college lecturer who shot dead a young couple in a fit of jealous temper, claiming that he meant to paralyse the boy from the waist down, was executed.

The Home Office doctors have never been inclined to find medical reasons for recommending mercy for non-insane sexual offenders. Home Secretary Maxwell Fyfe was merely following precedent when he decreed no reprieve for Christie.

Certainly I think there was no cynical sending of a man to his death in order to silence his tongue. Many people in authority still believe that Evans murdered his wife. High passions have been engaged on the topic. An angry speaker has even gone so far in a moment of heat, during a parliamentary debate, as to accuse Mr Scott Henderson of dishonesty in saying there was "no doubt" that Evans was the killer. Personally I am convinced he was innocent, and that Christie was telling the truth when he claimed that he killed her. But a further question remains: Evans was hanged for his baby's murder—not his wife's. Was he guilty of *this* murder?

Again Mr Appelbe helps to fill in the picture. What persuaded Mr Scott Henderson almost above all else that Christie was lying was evidence before him that in the condemned cell Christie told the prison chaplain that he confessed to Mrs Evans's murder only after obtaining the impression, in the course of interviews with his solicitor, that it was necessary for him to confess to murders, and that it was a case of "the more the merrier". Reported Mr Scott Henderson:

"I am satisfied that Christie gradually came to the conclusion that it would be helpful in his defence if he confessed to the murder of Mrs Evans. In saying this I wish to make it clear that I do not think that his solicitor or his doctor did anything improper to induce him to make his statements about Mrs Evans."

It was consistent with this viewpoint that in answering his questions at Pentonville prison pending execution Christie should veer from the clarity of his previous confessions and say, "I cannot say one way or the other."

But this view of Christie's evidence is based on a false premiss. Despite what he later said to the chaplain, before his trial Christie was not in the position of being forced to wrack his memory to conjure up an impressive roster of victims. The truth was quite the opposite: "At first he admitted to twenty-one or twenty-two murders," says Mr Appelbe; "and that would admittedly have much improved his chances of a guilty but insane verdict at the trial. But as the hearing approached he began to feel a slight sense of guilt at so many murders. He got more and more cagey, and more and more 'respectable'. In the end it was quite an effort to make him divulge the murders that had to be admitted because of the bodies."

In turn, this ties in with Christie's known pretensions to 'respectability': his feeling of being a middle-class gentleman, living in lower working-class squalor because of his (largely imagined) physical ill-health. It ties in with his affectation of medical knowledge, his pride in being a War Reserve policeman (despite some previous convictions in his younger days for minor dishonesty), his affected dislike of public houses, his use of such pidgin-French expressions as *San fairy ann* (*Ca ne fait rien*), learned in the trenches in the First World War, and what psychiatrist Professor Desmond Curran called at his trial his "obsequious servility".

If, in fact, by the time he came to give evidence at the Old Bailey Christie was at the stage of minimizing the number of his victims rather than exaggerating them, why still maintain in the witness-box—as he did—that he murdered Mrs Evans? There can be only one answer: because it was true. Timothy John Evans had told the truth in his second statement to the police at Methyr Tydfil police-station: his wife was already dead when he returned home from work, and Christie told him, "I have bad news. It didn't work."

Admittedly, Christie never confessed to killing Mrs Evans in the way that Timothy John Evans alleged—under cover of an attempt at abortion. He was too 'genteel', too concerned with his spurious respectability to admit publicly that he dabbled in back-street abortions. But he was known in the area as the local abortionist, and there is even a theory that Mrs Christie used to help him. Christie claimed that he killed Mrs Evans while atempting to help her commit suicide: it would have been impossible for him to have revealed the abortion aspect. But its absence does not, however, to my mind, invalidate the confession.

Yet this still does not necessarily make Evans's execution a miscarriage of justice. Though originally charging him with the murder of both his wife and his child the prosecution elected to proceed only on the charge of killing the child, and it was of that offence that he was convicted.

Throughout Christie rigidly maintained that he was innocent of this crime. And though Mr Appelbe believes he killed Mrs Evans, he thinks that he did not kill the child. "In my personal view, I don't think he'd kill a baby. I still feel he was a very nice person. He loved children and adored chocolates—I used to bring him chocolates."

There is nothing in Christie's record to indicate a tendency to violence against the young. In fact, according to Mr Appelbe, he was—apart from his sexual fixations—a sensitive, gentle man, who would not harm anyone.

On the other hand, Evans was of low intelligence, callous, and a bully. Some months before her death his wife had had enough of his violence, and had tried unsuccessfully to leave him. On the night before he knew she was going to submit herself to Christie's attempts at an abortion he admitted to the police he went out drinking, leaving her alone, without comfort or support. He claimed to be fond of his small daughter, but he was quite capable in the anxious days that followed his wife's murder—a murder in which he felt himself implicated, and which on his own word he had helped to keep from the authorities—of tying a tie round the squalling infant's neck and pulling it tight.

There are, however, two possible objections to this theory.

First, if Evans killed his child, why did he come back to London the week after the murder and visit Christie at Rillington Place? We know such a visit occurred because it was confirmed in evidence at his trial by both Christies. Evans explained that he came because he was anxious about the child and wanted to know from Christie what had happened to her. But it could also be that he was getting jittery—that staying with his aunt several hundreds of miles away, he wanted to have a chance to talk to his accomplice Christie and find out at first-hand how things were shaping.

After all, this is a man who some days later walked into the local police-station and gave himself up.

Second, if Evans killed his child, how can one explain that in his two signed confessions to the London police he admitted responsibility for both murders? If one accepts that his confession to his wife's killing is false it is perhaps difficult to argue that his confession to his child's killing is genuine.

I think that the answer is to be found in the strange mentality of the man. As Miss Tennyson Jesse has written, he was "a most phenomenal liar". He would say—and swear—whatever suited him best at the time. Even his champion, Ludovic Kennedy, has confirmed, "His most outstanding characteristic was his ability to lie." He lied to his aunt and to his mother, he lied to his employer and to the detective-constable at the Welsh police-station. He was congenitally incapable of telling the truth. The fact that his confession to murdering his wife is false does not mean his confession to murdering his child is equally false.

Evans was no figure of shining integrity. He had knocked his wife about, he was a heavy drinker, he was—to use Chief Inspector Jennings' words—"quite worldly", despite his near-illiteracy. He has been variously described as "a tiny little fellow", "a funny little chap", "primitive and shrewd", and "a little runt of a man". I believe that he was also the murderer of his own child.

Mr Kennedy makes much of the fact that right up to the end Evans maintained to his family that Christie had committed both murders. But how could he admit to his mother that he had killed his own baby, her grandchild?

Lord Chuter-Ede, the Home Secretary who failed to reprieve Evans, now thinks that his decision was wrong. "I did not make a mistake," he has told me. "The mistake was that the whole of the facts were not before the court." Nevertheless, with respect, I do not believe that a mistake was made.

Everyone, including the Home Office, now concedes that if Evans's jury had known all the facts about Christie and his crimes they would not have convicted Evans. Mr R. A. Butler, when Home Secretary, expressly admitted this in the House of Commons in 1961. But that does not prevent the evidence pointing, overwhelmingly, to my mind, to there being, indeed, two stranglers living at 10 Rillington Place at the same time. Only their victims were different: one murdered the mother, the other the child.

However, it would be stupid to contend that the guilt of each strangler is equally established. There can be little doubt now that Christie killed Mrs Evans, but basically it is only supposition that Evans killed the child. The tie found knotted round the baby's neck carries the case no farther: it was not positively proved as belonging to either Evans or Christie. It was the sort of cheap neckware that either could have purchased though both, in fact, disowned it.

Both Christie and Evans died, and neither death reflects credit on our system of justice.

Despite all that one can say about Christie's not being a necrophile and, therefore, not being necessarily insane in strictly medical terms, so that technically one can endorse Sir David Maxwell Fyfe's decision to hang him, it still seems inhuman. The man was obviously grievously unbalanced mentally. Whether his mental condition reached that specific state of chaos which the doctors call insanity is, from the humanitarian point of view, irrelevant. Christie may have got his just deserts according to law, but he was cheated of mercy.

As for Evans, no-one can criticize Lord Chuter-Ede for failing to reprieve him on the facts as they were known in 1950. Indeed, as I have said, I believe that he was guilty. But it is still appalling that years afterwards one cannot be sure.

CHAPTER TWENTY-ONE

Michael John Davies

(1953)

WHEN they are finally released from prison all that most reprieved men want to do is slink away and lick their wounds—retire into obscurity and hope that no-one will remember them. I have managed to speak to three reprieved men: two would only do so on the basis that I did not divulge their names. The third was defiant: "Use my name, quote me if you like," he said. "But don't call me a reprieved murderer. I'm not. I'm a man who has been sentenced to death for murder, and reprieved. That is all."

This man's name is Michael John Davies.

On October 22nd, 1953, at the age of twenty he was convicted at the Old Bailey of the murder on London's Clapham Common of John Ernest Beckley, a seventeen-year-old youth. After over three months in the condemned cell Davies was reprieved, and his sentence commuted to life imprisonment. He served seven years of that sentence, and in October 1960 was released. His first words to a waiting newspaperman were: "I was wrongfully convicted."

Ten days later he was declaring in the pages of the *Sunday Pictorial*, "I am no murderer". A few months later he was petitioning—albeit unsuccessfully—Home Secretary R. A. Butler for a free pardon.

Still today he hopes that eventually the authorities may relent and accept his innocence. "It's not right that I should be called a murderer for the rest of my life for something I did not do," he told me.

There can be no dispute that Sir David Maxwell Fyfe was right in January 1954 to reprieve Michael Davies. Even at that time there was too much uncertainty about the case to justify the exaction of the irrevocable penalty of death. But the more interesting question is: "Was Davies guilty?" Did his hand hold the knife that caused young Beckley's death?

I think I know the answer.

P

The evening of July 2nd, 1953, was warm and pleasant. Clapham Common, that arid stretch of parkland amid the rows of Victorian suburbia, seemed almost beautiful in the balmy twilight. A band was playing on the bandstand, while couples danced around it, and others sauntered on the grass. Davies was there, like many another young man, to try to pick up a girl, have a dance, or simply chat with his cronies.

Best clothes were worn. Davies and his friends sported the latest in youthful fashion—the tight, stovepipe trousers and tightly buttoned jacket of the Teddy boy. It was Thursday night, the night before pay night. Not much money could be spent: one's excitement had to come free of charge.

And just before half-past nine it did.

The evening's dancing was due to stop at any minute, and Ron Coleman, a fifteen-year-old shop-assistant, and Davies's friend, turned to go. But his path was blocked by four youths—Johnny Beckley, Fred Chandler, John Ryan, and Brian Carter—who sat sprawling on one seat, with their feet right across the pathway on another. Coleman, who had a girl with him, asked to go through. "Walk round the other side, you flash ——!" said one of the lads.

Coleman was not going to be treated like this, especially with a girl on his arm. He went back to his friends at the bandstand and told them what had happened: "I'm going to get some of the boys," he said. Later two young men named Leaver and Wood, and Wood's girl friend, a Miss Sylvia Pilkington, were to say that Davies was in the group and immediately produced a small knife from his pocket, saying "It will be all right with this!"

In the witness-box, Davies denied having been a member of this group or having said anything about a knife. But whether this is so or not it was obvious to the four lads on the benches that trouble was afoot, and they had better make off while there was still time.

They got up and walked away. But as they reached a drinking-fountain they were set upon by Coleman and seven or eight of his Edwardian-clad friends. Someone shouted, "Get the knives out!"

On his own admission Davies was a party to this fight. "When I got as far as the water-fountain I heard a scuffle behind me. I saw a big, blond-headed fellow knock Ronnie Coleman down. There were several others scuffling at the same time . . . I went for the big blond fellow because he was fighting Coleman," he later told the police.

The big blond fellow was John Ryan, and at least three others

attacked him as well as Davies. There was a short, vicious fight
in which Ryan tried to defend himself, but when he saw there were
so many he turned and ran for it. He managed to beat Davies and
his friends to the edge of the Common, and hared off homeward.
Only when he was nearing home did he realize he was bleeding
from a stab-wound in the shoulder. At least one of "the knives"
had, indeed, been out.

Meanwhile Davies and his comrades turned back to the fountain. A general scrimmage was still going on. Two youths were
punching and kicking Fred Chandler, Brian Carter was on the
ground, and three youths were piling into young Johnny Beckley.
As Davies and the others arrived the attacked threesome managed
to struggle free and ran off towards North Side, a road that skirted
the common.

Brian Carter made a complete get-away, and disappeared
from the night's story. Johnny Beckley and Fred Chandler had
no such luck. They jumped on a bus that was stationary at traffic
lights in North Side, and stood panting for breath on the platform
as it trundled slowly off. They thought they were safe: but hood-
lum violence had come to Clapham Common that evening. The
Teddy boys came whooping out of the Common, spotted the bus,
and sprinted towards a request stop a little farther down the road.
They stopped the bus, jumped on it, and dragged the struggling
—and by now terrified—Beckley and Chandler off on to the pavement. And there at the bus stop, while the passengers looked
bewilderedly on, they piled into the two young boys again.

No-one saw a knife, but amid the kicks and punches it was
doing its work. When Chandler got back on to the bus he was
bleeding from a stab-wound in the stomach. By then Beckley had
broken away and run off down the road. The gang surged after
him. The bus moved slowly forward, and its passengers saw the
attackers catch up with Beckley and close around him again. Then
they saw him half sink to the ground, and the Teddy boys ran
off. Two of the passengers ran to Beckley's assistance, and one of
the departing Teddy boys—*not* Davies—threatened them: "If
you don't keep your nose out you'll get the same!"

Beckley was dying: blood was pouring from his face, and he
had been stabbed no less than six times. The last person to touch
him was a youth whom a Miss Frayling, sitting in front, on top
of the bus, saw shake him by the shoulders and then run across
the road with another boy. On the other side of the road he made
a shutting motion with what looked like a knife, and put it in
his inside jacket-pocket. As he ran he peeled off his brightly
coloured tie and put that too in a pocket. At the Old Bailey Miss

Frayling was to say that she had "not a single doubt" that this youth was Michael John Davies.

There was other evidence against Davies. George Bernard Wood—known to his friends as "Splinter" Wood—told the police that he had seen the fight, at least at the fountain, and that after the whole incident was over, and Beckley had been left by the roadside, he heard Davies say, "No claret on it." He did not know what "it" was, but "claret" was a slang term well known to him: it meant blood. Another friend of Davies's, an eighteen-year-old carpenter named Allan Albert Lawson, told the police that afterwards, when the Teddy boys were discussing their night's work at a near-by coffee-stall, Davies said—about Beckley—"All I tried to do was run a knife up and down". And two girls told the police that on the Friday and Saturday after the murder Davies said to one: "It will be bad for the ones who told," and to the other: "If the police get hold of me, when I come out I'll get somebody to hurt you, and I'll make sure I'll be in prison for some small offence like drunk and disorderly."

Not surprisingly the police visited Davies's home on the Sunday morning and told his mother that they would like to see the boy for questioning. At 4.30 that afternoon he walked into Clapham Common police-station and said: "You wanted to see me?" Told by Detective Superintendent James Davies that he had reason to believe he was one of the youths who had caused Beckley's death, his reply was characteristic: "I was there, but I did not use any knife." He then made a written statement, in which he fully admitted taking part in the various fights that evening, but—"I did not have a knife in my hand, and I only used my fists."

I say that Davies's reply to the detective superintendent was characteristic, because it seems remarkably candid. Throughout his evidence at the two murder hearings that followed he never substantially varied his story and never tried to mitigate his rôle as one of the assailants in a cowardly attack by a band of youths on four boys, about half their number.

"You have told a story, Davies, which shows you behaved disgracefully in a fight; you agree that, do not you?" David Weitzman Q.C., his leading counsel, asked him at the Old Bailey.

And he agreed, "Yes, sir."

It is, to my mind, consistent with this attitude that when first he went to the local police-station of his own accord to answer questions, from the very start he did not deny that he took part in the attack, but merely said, "I did not use any knife."

This is in contrast with the five other youths whom the police arrested and charged in connection with this murder. Without exception their first reaction was to deny they had been in any fight at all: only later did they change their stories and admit they were there, but did not use a knife.

The knife—or knives—that were used were never found. No witness came forward to say he had seen Davies use a knife, nor even to say that they had seen him strike the dead boy. Allan Albert Lawson, the young carpenter, went back partially on his story, and told the police in a second statement that Davies said to him at the coffee-stall after the fight, "All I've done with the knife was up and down, *and I didn't stab him*". The police searched Davies's home, but could find no weapon consistent with Beckley's injuries. A first-class witness from the bus, a retired policeman named Mellows, told them he had seen the whole incident at the bus stop and the subsequent scrimmage round Beckley farther up the road, but although he identified some of the other attackers he could not recognize Davies. Miss Margaret McCarthy, another witness on the bus, told the local magistrates that she too, like her friend Miss Frayling, saw some youths run across the road and one of them pocket a knife, but she was sure he was wearing a brown suit—whereas Davies wore a blue suit that night, which bore only minute traces of human blood, such as could have been caused in a fist fight.

How could the prosecution make their case stick? So far as four of the six youths charged with murder were concerned, they did not even try. When the trial opened at the Old Bailey on September 14th, 1953, before Mr Justice Pearson. Mr Christmas Humphreys, leading for the Crown, told the judge that no evidence would be offered against four of the young men in the dock: this left only Coleman and Davies to face a charge of murder.

Two of the youths freed from the dock by the Crown's action gave evidence against their former mates. Terence David Woodman, a sixteen-year-old street-trader, told the jury that after the fight he heard Davies say at the coffee-stall, "I only tried to run the knife up and down the fellow's face," though he became confused under cross-examination and agreed that Davies might have said "*Someone* had tried to run the knife . . ." Allan Albert Lawson, who too had originally been charged with murder, also agreed under pressure from Mr Weitzman that Davies could have said, "Someone must have run the knife up and down . . ." fifteen-year-old Ronald Coleman also put in a bad word for his one-time friend beside him in the dock: he said that after the fighting he saw Davies with what he thought was a knife in his hand, and Davies asked him, "What shall I do with this?"

Mr Justice Pearson warned the jury in his summing up that they must treat this evidence with caution: these three youths were Davies's accomplices in the attack on Beckley and his comrades. Of course, they could accept their testimony if they wanted to, but it would be dangerous to rely on it without corroboration. At the end of a seven-day hearing the jury deliberated for three hours and forty minutes, but could not reach agreement. Mr Humphreys at once rose to say that the Crown would not proceed farther against Ronnie Coleman: the murder was now at Davies's door alone.

The following morning Coleman and the four other young men from the dock pleaded guilty to charges of common assault. "The gravity of this offence was the persistence with which the assaults were carried out, the concerted action, and the fact that even a bus was not safe from its hooliganism," Mr Humphreys told the judge. In the circumstances the sentences were remarkably light —nine months for each of the offenders, except Lawson, the only one without a previous conviction, who got six months. Why only the comparatively minor offence of common assault when clearly, on the evidence, both Ryan and Chandler were stabbed in addition to the murdered boy? Their injuries alone would have justified a charge of grievous bodily harm.

The Crown chose not to pursue this course. They did not have the ammunition. Eye-witnesses had picked out all five common assaulters' at identification parades. But there was no evidence against any of them bringing in the use of a knife: that lonely privilege belonged to Davies.

Said Mr Humphreys to a new jury when Davies's second trial opened at the Old Bailey on October 19th, 1953: "The case for the Crown against Davies is that a knife was seen in his hand just before the fight, when he was boasting of the fact that he was prepared to use it, and that a knife was seen in his hand immediately after the fight, when he was talking in a way as if he had just used it.

"There is no evidence of any other knife being used, and that is why the Crown say that all these three boys, who were stabbed by somebody, were stabbed with the same knife held in the same hand."

All turned on this vital question. As in the previous trial, Dr Donald Teare, the pathologist, said that Johnny Beckley's wounds could have been caused by a green-handled semi-flick knife, Exhibit 6, which was identified by witnesses as similar or identical to the weapon they had seen in Davies's hand. The deepest wounds in Beckley's body were three and one-eighth inches deep:

how could a knife like Exhibit 6, which had a blade only two inches long, inflict such injuries? asked Mr Weitzman. Dr Teare replied that he had experimented on a dead body with this knife and found it possible.

"But does not Dr Keith Simpson state in his book on *Forensic Medicine*: "The deepest wound will always provide a measurement of the minimum length of the blade?" countered Mr Weitzman.

"Yes," replied Dr Teare, "but I have pointed out this sentence to Dr Keith Simpson, who proposes to amend it in the next edition." Point—counter-point.

In fact, Dr Simpson has carried out Dr Teare's suggestion, and the current edition states: "The deepest wound is a guide to the minimum length of the blade."

The evidence given at the first hearing was repeated. Again Mr. Weitzman cross-examined Leaver, Wood, and Miss Pilkington to try and shake their story of Davies's producing a small knife before the fight and saying, "It will be all right with this!" This was a concoction to try and protect Wood, who was arrested by the police, but subsequently not charged, alleged Mr Weitzman. But none of the three witnesses would give way.

Davies went into the witness-box and gave again his non-knife version of the evening's fighting. He admitted that he had four previous convictions for minor offences of larceny and receiving, but none of them was for a crime of violence. He had not even struck Beckley: he had fought only Ryan and Chandler, and on both occasions only with his fists. At the end, as he ran past Beckley, half-collapsed against a garden wall, he saw blood on his face, and realized the boy had been cut: that was all. He denied threatening the two girls, he denied saying about a knife or anything, "There's no claret on it," he denied telling Lawson afterwards that he had only tried to run a knife up and down Beckley's face: he said that it could not possibly have been he whom Miss Frayling saw run across the road and pocket a knife.

Of course, such a defence—even if it were true—left him wide open to cross-examination.

"In effect does it come to this," said Mr Humphreys "—that all the evidence given against you is untrue and untrue to the knowledge of the people who have given it?"

"Yes, sir," replied Davies.

"Leaver, Wood and Miss Pilkington are telling lies about you with a knife in your hand before the fight?"

"Yes."

"Lawson, Brenda Wood, Sylvia Chubb, and again Wood are all wrong in what you were saying after the fight?"

"Lawson is mistaken; the others are wrong."

"Lawson mistaken and the others untrue?"

"Yes."

"So that makes five who are deliberately lying, and one who is mistaken, and they are all your friends or acquaintances?"

"Acquaintances."

"Miss Frayling and Miss McCarthy are entirely wrong about you, at any rate, having a knife in your pocket after that fight?"

"Yes, sir, they are."

Soon it was time for final speeches and the summing-up. Then, after just over two hours' deliberation, including a brief return to court to ask the judge a question on the evidence, the jury found Michael John Davies guilty of murder. Mr Justice Hilbery passed sentence of death. The prisoner was taken below, all his possessions removed, including his cigarettes, and he was left alone to brood until the car came to take him to the condemned cell at Pentonville.

Here is Davies's own account of what it feels like to be sentenced to death. He was talking to me in my living-room:

"I really think you're in a kind of mental state. I mean, you must, I think, have a shock, although you don't feel it as a shock. I mean, it must numb your mind. I mean, for example, someone says to you, 'Fenton Bresler, you're going to be hung' —I mean you're perfectly healthy, and it's just coldly told to you that you're going to be hung at nine o'clock. You can't imagine what it's like, because, I mean, you can't imagine someone saying it to you seriously, so you haven't had the feeling . . .

"It was about half an hour, I should say, a good half-hour later when it hit me what they'd done. And I realized, you know. And it was then that I broke down. Because it really did hit me. I couldn't make out what I'd done to be hung. I realized he'd sentenced me to death—I couldn't figure it out.

"I quite expected to go to prison—I thought, well, the boy's died, you can't just walk out of court. But then when I realized they'd only got nine months, the rest of the boys, and one had got six, I could only have got nine months. I mean, if he'd given me five years I'd have probably had the needle, although it would have been warranted up to a point that we all should have got five years, I suppose, for being in the fight.

"And the chap that done it, that really killed Beckley—well, what he should have got is anyone's opinion."

But in the eyes of the law Davies was "the chap that done it", and his execution date was fixed.

The youth appealed, and for three days David Weitzman, Q.C., argued his case before the Court of Criminal Appeal. It was not inconsiderable. For Mr Justice Hilbery had failed to do what Mr Justice Pearson had done at the first—abortive—trial, he had not issued one word of warning to the jury to treat the evidence of Allan Albert Lawson with discretion, because Lawson was an accomplice. Mr Weitzman demanded that, in the absence of any such warning, the conviction should be quashed. But Lawson was only an accomplice to the common assault, to which he pleaded guilty, and not an accomplice to the murder charge, of which he was acquitted, ruled the appeal court. Davies was told in prison that a new execution date had been fixed.

He appealed still farther. On December 10th, 1953, the Attorney General took the rare step, in a murder case, of granting his fiat to enable the case to go to the House of Lords: Mr Weitzman's argument on the judge's failure to treat Lawson as an accomplice was so important, legally, that it justified the senior appeal judges, the law lords, pronouncing on it.

At this stage an incident occurred which to my knowledge has never been made public before, and which typifies all that is best in the traditions of public prosecution in this country. Davies was being defended under legal aid, which in those days meant that very little money was available. The cost of appealing to the House of Lords would be prodigious: each law lord would have to be supplied with a complete transcript of the trial and the judgment of the Court of Criminal Appeal, the grounds of appeal would have to be printed, counsel's arguments would have to be formulated beforehand and submitted in printing to their lordships: both Mr T. V. Edwards, Davies's indefatigable solicitor, and the three counsel who represented him would have to do a great deal of their work for no reward.

Against this background the office of Sir Theobald Mathew, then Director of Public Prosecutions, wrote to Mr Edwards that they would supply him with all the requisite transcripts—and would contribute 100 guineas towards the cost of the appeal. Only in Britain would the State Prosecutor offer to help defray the cost of a convicted man's last effort to reverse the conviction! "And within days of the appeal being heard came their cheque", says Mr Edwards.

The appeal was argued over three days in mid-January, 1954. Cases were cited going back as far as 1787, the air was thick with the courteous, measured voices of law Lords and lawyers: "I was well lost!" comments Davies.

And indeed he was, in more ways than one. At the conclusion

of the hearing Lord Simonds, the Lord Chancellor, said: "My Lords, the House has heard full and careful argument from both sides and I understand that your Lordships agree with me in entertaining no doubt that this appeal should be dismissed." Davies was taken back to the condemned cell, and that evening Mr Edwards wrote a seven-point letter to the Home Secretary urging a reprieve.

"I wouldn't have left it with just a letter," he has told me. "I would have followed it up with further representations." But Mr Edwards was pushing on a partly opened door. Sir Lionel Heald, Q.C., the Attorney-General, who led for the Crown in the House of Lords, had given him what he describes as "a broad hint" that Davies would be reprieved, and quickly. And so it turned out: five days later Mr Edwards received a letter from Sir Frank Newsam, then Permanent Under-Secretary at the Home Office, to say that Sir David Maxwell Fyfe had advised the Queen to respite the capital sentence, and that Davies's sentence had been commuted to imprisonment for life.

Four days earlier, and after the law lords had thrown out his appeal, Davies had written to Mr Edwards from the condemned cell thanking him for all he had done. "I was moved," says Mr Edwards. "He's a very likeable fellow in many ways."

Did this "likeable fellow" commit murder? Throughout his time in prison he continued to deny it. Almost every month some representation went in to the Home Office urging a reconsideration of the case: either from Davies himself or his family or Lord Longford, who had early on taken an interest in his welfare and satisfied himself of his innocence. Finally, in June 1958, came an interview with Mr Gilbert Hair, then Governor of Wormwood Scrubs, when, according to Davies, Mr Hair told him that he had received a letter from the Home Secretary stating that he had reviewed all the evidence in the case and all the further statements submitted since his trial and could find no reason why he should interfere with the finding of the Court. But in view of all the submissions made on his behalf the Home Secretary, then R. A. Butler, had decided that he would be released as soon as he had done seven years.

"Now, how would you interpret that statement?" Davies has asked me. "How would you interpret that statement which was made?"

"It's obvious, isn't it?" I replied. "They're not sure that you did it."

But this explanation does not satisfy Davies: "I'd bombarded the Home Office with petitions and appeals, sort of thing . . . I'd been having an argument for years. From my family, Lord Longford—someone always had a go at the Home Office all the time. They were sick to death of me, I can assure you of that."

According to a parliamentary answer once given by Mr Butler, the average life sentence for a reprieved murderer sentenced to death under the old law before the 1957 Homicide Act was nine years. Yet Davies was freed two years earlier for a murder, which if he did commit it was a particularly cowardly crime. Why? He himself puts it down to his successful harrowing of the authorities over the years, so that they were "sick to death of me", and to the fact that "things were coming to light" about the case which might cause embarrassment. I cannot repeat Davies's allegations, becuse they are certainly libellous if untrue, and I have no means of knowing whether they are true or not: the important point is that he is not terribly grateful for his early release. He still feels bitter about serving any time at all in prison for a murder which he did not commit.

After his release Davies co-operated with the *Sunday Pictorial* in a reinvestigation of the case. Together with Harry Ashbrook, an experienced journalist, he went on a tour of South London public houses, cafés, and back-street clubs, trying to gather evidence. They met silence, even hostility, but some information was forthcoming. One man who recognized Davies told him: "I was in that fight on Clapham Common. You didn't carry a knife, and you couldn't have killed young Beckley. I should have spoken up before, but I was only a kid at the time, and I didn't know my way about." Others declared they knew the truth, but were afraid to tell it. One stated: "You were at least thirty-five yards away from Beckley when he was attacked for the last time."

Ashbrook managed to uncover the fact that on that night after the murder one of the youths from Clapham Common appeared at a near-by coffee-stall in a bloodstained brown suit, and a friend took him home and changed his suit for him. One of the six youths originally charged with Beckley's murder told Ashbrook: "I am convinced that Davies is innocent." Another said: "Who killed Beckley? Everyone knows it. But it wasn't Davies." A witness who had said that Davies had a knife that night said: "I was confused."

At about the same time an anonymous letter appeared in the *Sunday Graphic*, now defunct, but then a rival of the *Sunday Pictorial*. "I admit I was there," it ran. "I have always doubted that Davies was the actual killer and I do know that two men stabbed young Beckley."

All this published information, and other unpublished material besides, was forwarded to the Home Office. But it did not alter the official position. On July 11th, 1961, Home Secretary Butler stated in a parliamentary reply that he could find no grounds on which he would be justified in recommending the grant of a free pardon. In respect to the statements submitted, the police had investigated the allegation that a bloodstained suit had been exchanged for a clean one, and they were satisfied that it was without substance. Davies was back to square one.

Mr Butler's reference to the suit-changing allegation is perhaps a little odd. In fact, the *Sunday Pictorial* was not the first to uncover this story. Davies's sister, working with Mr Edwards, his solicitor, had hit upon it seven years earlier, while he was still in the condemned cell. They had duly reported it to the police, and no-one had then indicated it was without substance. It may well even have been one of the factors that contributed towards the reprieve.

To be fair to the prosecution, we know that at least one major Crown witness has refused to change his story: James Leaver—the young man who said that before the fight Davies took out a knife and said, "It will be all right with this!"—told journalist Ashbrook: "You don't expect me to change my story after all these years. What I said in the court was true."

Even so, the questions still remain: Did Mick Davies have a knife that night? And, if he had, did he use it on Beckley?

His evidence at the Old Bailey was unequivocal. At his second trial he was asked by Mr Weitzman:

"Now, Davies, at the fight at the fountain, did you use a knife?"

"No, sir."

"Did you have a knife?"

"No, sir."

"Did you know that a knife had been used?"

"No, sir."

And later:

"Did you fight with Beckley or attack Beckley at the bus stop in any way?"

"No, sir."

He admitted fighting—albeit with his fists—with Ryan and Chandler, and we know that both boys were stabbed. But in the mêlée any one of the attackers could have used a small knife and no one would have noticed. Neither youth knew he was being stabbed at the time: realization came only afterwards.

Even as to the murderous attack on Beckley himself, both Woodman and Lawson who originally said Davies had told them:

"I only tried to run the knife up and down the fellow's face" and "All I tried to do was to run a knife up and down" agreed with Mr Weitzman, in cross-examination, that Davies might have said "*Someone* had tried to run the knife . . ." and "*Someone* must have run the knife up and down . . ."

Personally, I believe that Davies was telling the truth: he had no knife and he did not murder Beckley. I realize that his second jury at the Old Bailey came to a different conclusion. And, admittedly, accepting his evidence leaves some loose ends unresolved—such as, why should the two girls whom he admitted in court bore him no previous animosity, come forward and give apparently untrue testimony about his alleged threats. So be it. But in few court cases are *all* loose ends satisfactorily tied up. This is the great fallacy of too many literary commentators on criminal trials basing their judgments solely on the cold, printed words of trial transcripts and other documents. Justice is still a pragmatic affair. Computers with their so-called 100 per cent. efficiency have not yet found a place in our courtrooms.

Nor am I forgetting the vital evidence of Miss Frayling, the witness on top of the bus. I know she identified Davies as one of the two youths who ran across in front of her, and pocketed what looked like a knife when he reached the opposite pavement. One would not question this lady's integrity for a moment, but it is notorious how unreliable even the most honest evidence of identification can be. The bus driver described the road ahead as "dark", Miss Frayling had never seen Davies before, and she did not see him again for nearly a month; not until August 1st, when she was giving evidence in the magistrate's court and identified Davies as the youth she had seen. Davies never was invited to attend an identification parade, and this lady had an opportunity of checking her identification only when she saw him a month later, standing in the dock of a criminal court. Is it any surprise that she may have made a mistake?

In truth, there is no doubt that two youths did run across the road together in front of the oncoming bus. One of them said so in the witness-box at the Old Bailey. And he also said that immediately prior to running across the road he and his companion ran up to Beckley, and he told them: "I've been stabbed, don't touch me!" Could not these have been the two youths who Miss Frayling saw?

Her evidence as to the object she saw in one of the youth's hands could support this supposition. In the magistrates' court when first telling her story Miss Frayling said: "No-one suggested to me the green object I saw was a knife. At the time I thought it was a razor or a knife. I thought it was one of the two. It was the action that made me think it was either a razor or a knife. He seemed to shut something and put it in his pocket." By the time that Miss Frayling got to the Old Bailey for the second trial, and was relating this incident for the third time in court, she had thought about it more and was then clear that the shutting action would have been applicable for a semi-flick knife, such as Exhibit 6. But perhaps her initial impression was the more accurate? If the "shutting action" that she saw made her first think the object was either a razor or a knife it means that it could not possibly have been a knife like Exhibit 6. Such a weapon closes in a completely different way from a razor or knife—such as a penknife—that closes like a razor. If you wanted to put away the blade of Exhibit 6 you simply pressed a button and gently slid the blade up into the handle with your thumb—a totally dissimilar action.

I believe that Miss Frayling did see two youths run across the road and that one of them closed a razor or a penknife and put it in his pocket. But it was not Davies whom she saw. Neither was it the knife, Exhibit 6.

This theory is perhaps confirmed by the fact that Miss McCarthy, her friend sitting beside her, could not identify either of the youths, but was positive that the boy who "had a knife in his hand" was wearing a brown suit. This ties up with the story of the boy in the bloodstained brown suit who after the murder made a dramatic quick change. Davies was wearing a blue suit that night.

"Davies was definitely not guilty of the murder of which he was convicted," says Mr Edwards. "I don't know who did it, but it definitely was not Michael Davies. Those boys were like soldiers with guns. They had knives and just had to use them."

Perhaps too many tears should not be shed for Michael Davies, likeable character though he is. I believe he was innocent of murder, but he was a tough lad. He had already been half-way round the world in the Merchant Navy, and had served with credit in the R.A.F. Even if one accepts his story in its entirety, on the evening of July 2nd his conduct—as he admitted himself in court—was disgraceful.

However, his ninety-two days in the condemned cell and his seven long years in prison for a crime of which he was innocent have left their mark on him. His experiences show in the lines of his face. It would have been an affront to justice to have hanged him, and Sir David Maxwell Fyfe was courageous in refusing to give way to clamour from certain sections of the public to hang this twenty-one-year-old Teddy boy, and make an example of him for the youth of the nation.

And who knows? If Mr Justice Hilbery had not made new law and refused to warn the jury to treat Lawson as an accomplice—as Mr Justice Pearson had done—Davies might not even have been convicted. After all, when Mr Justice Pearson *did* warn a jury to treat Lawson's evidence with suspicion they refused to convict. If Mr Justice Hilbery had summed up differently Davies might never have seen the inside of a condemned cell.

CHAPTER TWENTY-TWO

Ruth Ellis

(1955)

"THERE is a natural reluctance to hang a woman." Sir Frank Newsam, speaking for the Home Office, told the Gowers Commission in the early nineteen-fifties. And most Home Secretaries have agreed with this view.

Since Edith Thompson's death in 1923 only eight women have been hanged.

The last was Ruth Ellis, a name that will live in the history of capital punishment. There was little to commend her. An ex-call-girl and drinking-club manageress, she shot dead in the street her lover, an even more unpleasant young man called David Blakely. He was trying to break off the affair, and doing it brutally and hurtfully. So two weeks after miscarrying his child Ruth Ellis took a gun, waited for him outside a Hampstead public house, and shot him down. Her aim was so wild that one bullet ricocheted off a wall and injured a passer-by.

"I do not want to live," she wrote to a friend a week before her execution date. She was not disappointed. Lord Tenby, then Home Secretary, did not recommend a reprieve.

Life plays tricks on politicians. In November 1954 Lord Tenby reprieved a man who pleaded guilty to murdering his former fiancée, although the killer did not want to live and had tried to commit suicide by throwing himself under a train. Many people would have said it was a brutal murder and that the man was lucky to be spared simply because he lost his legs in the suicide attempt and therefore could not be "expeditiously" hanged, to use the Home Office phrase. Yet Lord Tenby thought humanity and decency demanded that a legless man should not be carried on to the drop, and refused to permit his execution. The case was unsensational and not extensively reported. Lord Tenby received no thanks from the Press, and few members of the public even knew what had occurred.

Yet in July 1955 he stood adamant against a nationwide campaign to save Ruth Ellis. And in so doing subjected himself to a

tirade of personal abuse and set off a train of events which culminated in the near-abolition of the death penalty in this country.

Nor is this hyperbole. Ruth Ellis died on July 13th, 1955, as a
crowd of about a thousand men, women, and children jostled outside the prison gates. "The hangman has been reprieved, and
medievalism has won the day," said the late Sir Beverley Baxter.
Within a month the National Campaign for the Abolition of Capital Punishment was founded. Within seven months the House of
Commons passed a Motion calling for the abolition or suspension
of the death penalty. In just over a year the Government were
forced to bring in the Homicide Bill restricting capital punishment to only six kinds of murder.

Ruth Ellis's death, on top of the hanging of Timothy John
Evans and Derek Bentley, caused a revulsion in the nation's
attitude to capital punishment. Or at least in a majority of the
nation's representatives assembled in Parliament. "By their decision to execute Ruth Ellis, the Home Office have abolished the
death penalty," wrote Rupert Furneaux shortly afterwards.

Why was this woman hanged when at her trial even prosecuting
counsel agreed that she had been "disgracefully treated" by David
Blakely and that any ordinary, reasonable human being would
have been in "an intensely emotional condition"? Did Lord Tenby
err?

It has not been easy to find the answer to either of these
questions. A full-scale book by Robert Hancock called simply
Ruth Ellis was published in 1963, and many commentators have
written on the case. Mr Hancock's book contains much useful information and is readable and well researched; but no writer has
yet succeeded in telling the full story: everyone so far has been
writing more or less in the dark. Luckily I have been able to
interview the three men who know most about the truth—John
Bickford and Victor Mishcon, the two solicitors who acted for
Ruth Ellis, and, perhaps most important of all, Lord Tenby.

It is with their help—from both sides of the fence—that this
chapter is written.

Mrs Ruth Ellis, whose marriage ended in divorce (there was a
young son), first met David Blakely in the summer of 1953. It
was in a night club called Carroll's Club, where she was a 'hostess'.
He was an ex-public-school boy, with a wealthy stepfather and pretensions to the playboy status. He had a rapidly dwindling in-
heritance from his father, and was financing the building of a
racing car.

They were together for just over a year. It was neither a con-

Q

tinuous nor a uniformly happy relationship. Blakely was away every week-end at his mother's and stepfather's home in Penn, Buckinghamshire, and for many other nights besides. And for much of the time he was officially engaged to another girl.

As long as this engagement lasted Ruth Ellis did not take her affair with Blakely too seriously. Admittedly, she had to have an abortion because of Blakely, but this was nothing new to her. Her first abortion had been four years earlier, when she was twenty-two.

In July 1954 Blakely broke off his engagement. And that completely altered the casual nature of his affair with Ruth Ellis. As she afterwards told a friend: "From then on David paid even more attention to me, he literally adored me, my hands, my eyes, everything except my peroxided hair, which he always wanted to be brunette.

"At the time I thought the world of him. I put him on the highest of high pedestals. He could do nothing wrong . . . I was entirely faithful to him."

But Blakely was not faithful to Ruth Ellis. She discovered another affair of his. He struck her. She hit him back. Their quarrels became frequent and vicious. Both were possessive and jealous. There were more quarrels and alcoholic, sensual reconciliations.

On February 9th, 1955, Ruth Ellis moved to a one-room flatlet at 44 Egerton Gardens, Kensington. Blakely also moved in: "Mr and Mrs Ellis" the housekeeper called them.

"I won't knock you about any more," Blakely promised. But there were more blows. And the affair continued in its unstable pattern: a tiff one minute, lovemaking the next, drinking much of the time, and always overshadowed by a brooding unhappiness.

In late March 1955 Ruth Ellis had her third miscarriage. Again it was Blakely's child.

The following week-end they went to Oulton Park motor-races to watch Blakely's car perform. But it broke down on a practice run, and another row flared. "It's your fault. You jinxed me!" fumed Blakely at the woman who had just miscarried his child. He wormed £5 out of her by a trick, and spent it on drinking with his motor-racing cronies.

Blakely was smooth. On Wednesday Ruth Ellis, still weak from the miscarriage and a chill caught at the races, opened an envelope he brought home, to find inside a new photograph of himself. It bore the legend: "To Ruth with all my love, David." The following night at the pictures he was "very sweet" to her. It looked as if they might yet be happy.

In fact, Blakely was anxious to bring the whole affair to an end.

The following day was Good Friday, and at 10 A.M. he left Egerton Gardens to meet a friend. "I'll be back at about eight o'clock this evening to take you out," he told Ruth Ellis. But he never returned.

At lunch-time that day Blakely had a drink with two friends, Anthony and Carole Findlater. And afterwards he went back with them to their flat—to stay the week-end.

Ruth Ellis soon realized that Blakely had sought refuge in the Findlaters' second-floor flat, in Tanza Road, Hampstead. But her every effort to contact him was foiled.

She telephoned, she waited for hours in the street outside, she rang the doorbell, she damaged Blakely's car. But she could not get through to Blakely.

The Findlaters had a new nanny, a nineteen-year-old girl, and Ruth Ellis was torn with sexual jealousy. Waiting outside the flat on the Saturday evening, she saw Blakely and Mr Findlater come out with the girl to get some drinks for a party, and afterwards said she heard Blakely say to the girl: "Let me put my arm around you for support." When later she saw the light go out in the room that she (erroneously) thought was the nanny's she was convinced—quite wrongly, as it turned out—that he was in there with her and that the whole episode was a plot by Carole Findlater to get Blakely away from her. In fact, there was no such 'plot': it was utter nonsense. But the important thing is that Ruth Ellis believed it to be true.

After three days without hearing from Blakely, not a call, not a word—nothing, she killed him as he came out of a public house with some drinks to take back to the Findlaters. As he lay face downwards on the pavement she continued to pull the trigger, until all the movement caused was the dull click of an empty pistol. One of her shots injured a woman passing by, a fact of which little notice was taken in the great controversy over the case, but which was to prove finally of the utmost significance.

She had intended to shoot herself, but there were no more bullets left. "I am guilty. I am rather confused," she said at Hampstead police-station.

She considered she was justified in killing Blakely. He had treated her abominably and deserved to die. She was content to die with him. Life no longer had any attraction. "All I want", she said before her trial, "is that the jury should hear my full story."

Her leading counsel was Mr Melford Stevenson, Q.C. (now Mr

Justice Stevenson). He was a master of cross-examination, but his questioning of the prosecution witnesses could not be extensive because the basic facts were not in dispute.

If Ruth Ellis had anticipated some vicious or sensational attack on the people who gave evidence about the killing or about her affair with Blakely, the lover who betrayed her, she was bound to be disappointed. No counsel could risk antagonizing a jury in that manner.

When she herself gave evidence Mr Stevenson carefully took her through the story of the poignant events which preceded the shooting. No doubt the defence had hoped that she would be a good witness, that at the very last her story might draw a recommendation to mercy from the jury. But her replies and explanations were often cold, mechanical, and listless.

Perhaps—blinded by her unreasoning and unjust resentment of those who had been Blakely's friends—she was disappointed that in the interests of her own case no malicious attack had been mounted on them.

For the Crown Mr Christmas Humphreys asked her only one short, damning question in cross-examination: "Mrs Ellis, when you fired that revolver at close range into the body of David Blakely, what did you intend to do?"

"It was obvious that when I shot him I intended to kill him."

The sole legal basis of the case which Mr Stevenson hoped to present was that a woman so provoked by jealousy and ill-treatment should have the charge reduced to manslaughter. After a psychiatrist had been called to state that women are more prone to hysterical reactions than men and that Blakely's treatment of Ruth Ellis would probably have had a greater effect on her than equivalent behaviour in a woman would have had upon a man, the jury were dismissed, and Mr Stevenson sought the judge's permission to put his basic proposition to them in his final speech.

"But that is new law!" said Mr Justice Havers.

Nevertheless, Mr Stevenson continued to press the vital submission on which his client's life depended, and eventually the judge said he would give his decision the following day. But it was only a temporary respite. Soon after the court sat the following morning the judge ruled: "There is not sufficient material, even on a view of the evidence most favourable to the accused, for a reasonable jury to form the view that a reasonable person, so provoked, could be driven, through transport of passion and loss of self-control, to the degree and method and continuance of violence which produces the death." The battle was lost.

Mr Stevenson did not make a final speech. "I cannot now with propriety address the jury at all," he told the judge. "Because it would be impossible for me to do so without inviting them to disregard your Lordship's ruling."

So Ruth Ellis sat in the dock to hear the judge sum up without anything further being said on her behalf or by the prosecution to the ten men and two women who were her jurors.

It took the jury exactly fourteen minutes to convict her—without a recommendation to mercy.

Stoically Ruth Ellis received sentence of death. There were no screams, no moans, no protest: and next day John Bickford, her solicitor, announced that there would be no appeal. The execution date was fixed three weeks ahead.

Ruth Ellis took no part in the campaign for a reprieve. She told her mother that she did not want a petition organized, and spent her time making dolls, doing jigsaw puzzles, and reading the Bible. She appeared completely unconcerned about her fate.

Not so her family nor her solicitor. Without his client's instructions, but encouraged by her relatives, Mr Bickford wrote a seven-page foolscap letter to the Home Secretary setting out the grounds for a reprieve. "I could not believe that they would hang her," he says. In his anxiety he even asked Mr Leon Simmons, managing clerk with Victor Mishcon and Co., the solicitors who had acted for Ruth Ellis in her divorce proceedings, to write to the Home Office and tell the Home Secretary what he knew of the condemned woman—which Mr Simmons did.

Mr Bickford followed up his original letter with others. Newspapers ran highly charged articles about her plight; even Raymond Chandler, the American thriller writer on a visit to London joined in. "It will be brutal and uncivilized to hang Ruth Ellis," he wrote in the *Evening Standard.*

The least touched by all the commotion was Ruth Ellis. "She was as tough as an old boot," declares Mr Bickford. "And she had a wonderful sense of humour. She referred to the execution chamber as 'the doings' and once said, 'I gave David a lot of rope—come to think of it, he's giving me quite a bit now!'" She was quite happy to die. Her one complaint was that her full story did not come out at the trial.

Inevitably, an M.P. came to see her. Said George Rogers, M.P., to a reporter: "I was approached by her friends who begged me to see her. And I never turn down a request for help if it is in my power to give it." At the end of a forty-five minute interview he got her authority to appeal to the Home Secretary for clemency.

She also asked Leon Simmons, the managing clerk she had met years earlier when dealing with her divorce, to come and see her. Having obtained Mr Bickford's consent he visited her in the condemned cell, and she asked his advice about a possible change in her will. Mr Simmons gave that advice.

At this time another woman was in a condemned cell, though her case attracted little public attention. In Leeds prison, forty-year-old Mrs Sarah Lloyd was awaiting execution for the brutal murder of Mrs Edith Emsley, an eighty-six-year-old neighbour, whose head she had battered in with a spade. The case was almost completely ignored by the national Press, and there were no widely canvassed petitions for her reprieve. Yet on July 6th it was announced that Lord Tenby had decided she would not die: her sentence was commuted to life imprisonment.

That week-end Lord Tenby went down to his sister Lady Megan Lloyd George's home in Wales with Ruth Ellis's papers in his bag. On the Monday morning he returned, and at 3.14 that afternoon a Home Office messenger took a taxi from Whitehall to Holloway prison carrying with him the official rejection of a reprieve.

How did Ruth Ellis receive that news?

Undoubtedly, she turned angrily on John Bickford. This greatly experienced solicitor, who had not stinted himself for his client, found only bitterness and abuse when he went to see her later that afternoon. Ruth Ellis wanted no more to do with him: she insisted on seeing again Leon Simmons.

Newspapers at the time and later writers have said that Ruth Ellis called in Mr Simmons because she wanted to make a desperate, last-minute change of story to try to avert the execution that was now only thirty-six hours away.

My inquiries reveal that this is nonsense. Ruth Ellis did not call for Leon Simmons because she was frightened of dying. There was no final panic, no frenzied attempt to stay the hangman's coming. She merely said that she wanted to see Mr Simmons: he then spoke to John Bickford over the telephone, and said that he would call and see him before seeing Ruth Ellis. *It was no part of any message from Ruth Ellis that she wanted to see Mr Simmons to ask him to try to get Lord Tenby to alter his decision.* That idea was entirely Mr Simmons's and that of his principal, Victor Mishcon. Mr Simmons spoke to his principal, who, apart from being a solicitor, had recently completed a highly successful year of office as Chairman of the London County Council, and was a prominent member of the Labour Party, and Mr Mishcon said that he would go to see Ruth Ellis with Mr Simmons.

The following morning—the day before the proposed execution —Mr Mishcon and Mr Simmons visited John Bickford in his office before proceeding to Holloway prison.

"Have you any lead that might help us to save her, even now?" asked Mr Mishcon.

"Ask her where she got the gun!" replied Mr Bickford—still faithful to his client—and the two lawyers hurried off to prison.

"I must say I was quite amazed at the calm of Ruth Ellis," Mr Mishcon has told me. "There was a little of the actress about her. She wore a dressing-gown over prison clothes, yet completely acted the charming hostess. 'How kind of you to come,' she greeted us. 'I wanted Mr Simmons to know certain facts which I think may have some bearing on my will.' "

But Mr Mishcon implored her to tell him all the facts as well, and not only for the purposes of the will. There was still time for a reprieve, he urged upon her. It was just after 11.15 A.M., she still had nearly twenty-one hours to go. But she was not interested: "I am now completely composed," she told Mr Mishcon. "I know that I am going to die, and I'm ready to do so. You won't hear anything from me which says that I didn't kill David. I did kill him. And whatever the circumstances you as a lawyer will appreciate that it's a life for a life; isn't that just?" The words were so memorable, and Ruth Ellis's demeanour so calm, that Mr Mishcon still remembers them exactly.

He tried to argue with her, and said that surely it was right that her son, when he grew up, should know the true facts from her own lips and not simply what he read in the newspapers.

It was this shaft that got home. Reluctantly Ruth Ellis agreed to tell the two men what had really happened on the evening of Easter Sunday.

But she had one last reservation: "I'll tell you," she said, "if you promise not to use it to try and save me."

Mr Mishcon, fighting against this woman's own desire not to save herself, refused to be bound. "Let's make no promises. You tell us the story, and we can then decide what to do. Don't worry, we won't do anything without your consent."

Up till now neither Mr Mishcon nor Mr Simmons has disclosed what happened between them and Ruth Ellis or what her story was. But she is now long dead, and her memory demands that her wish should be granted and the truth told.

The story that emerged was that Ruth Ellis claimed she did not commit her crime alone.

As Mr Mishcon wrote down her words he learned how Ruth Ellis and a man, whose name was given, had been drinking for most of the final week-end. Subsequent versions of the statement that have appeared from some source [*not*, Mr Mishcon assures me, from him] have already shown that by the morning of Easter Sunday Ruth Ellis and this man were in a maudlin state: "If I was near David now I'd shoot him!" she said. "Well, I've got a gun," he replied. And he took down an old revolver, oiled it, and loaded it. Then he drove her and her young son out to Epping Forest and gave her firing practice.

That evening, when there was still no word from Blakely and her son was asleep in bed, the man drove her to the end of the road where the Findlaters lived, handed her the gun and said: "Go and shoot him!" and as she turned to walk down the street with his gun in her hand he drove off. Minutes later Blakely was dead.

In the newspaper *The People* in early 1956 a crime reporter named Duncan Webb claimed that Ruth Ellis kept quiet about her accomplice until the last moment because of a deal they made after her arrest that in return for her silence he would safeguard her son's future, and that she told the truth only at the last moment, because she then realized he would never honour his word. But this is not so. Ruth Ellis told the police on the evening of the murder a false story about having had the gun in her possession for three years as a pledge for a debt, and this was within hours of the killing, before she could possibly have had time to make such a deal. Besides, it runs contrary to what she told Victor Mishcon and Leon Simmons. She bore no hatred for the man who had given her the gun, such as one would expect if he had, in fact, welshed on her: indeed, a major concern was that he should not suffer through her statement. "I don't want to bring anyone else into this," she said. "One life's enough!"

After two hours her visitors had gone. Some time after 1 o'clock the lawyers left the condemned cell: with them they had the signed and witnessed change in Ruth Ellis's will and also her fresh statement hand-written and signed by her. Grudgingly at the end she had agreed to let the lawyers show it to the authorities. Mr Mishcon telephoned the authorities from the prison and asked that he and Mr Simmons should be seen immediately.

They hurried to the Home Office. "Even without the facts contained in her last statement, I think there was more than enough to justify a reprieve," Mr Mishcon has told me.

At the Home Office Mr Mishcon asked to see Sir Frank Newsam, but Sir Frank, it appears, was away for the afternoon at the races. A telephone call was put through to Ascot, and Sir Frank agreed to return at once to London. In the meanwhile Mr Mishcon spoke to a senior Home Office official. He was most courteous. Mr Mishcon handed him the statement; he read it, and said, "You can rely on this, every inquiry will be made to verify these facts." Could it be done in the few hours left? He would not say. But he assured the solicitor that immediate steps would be taken—"though I cannot say that the facts, even if verified, will necessarily justify a reprieve."

After fifty minutes Mr Mishcon left the building, having told the Home Office official that he was completely at their disposal if anything further was required from him. He asked if it was not possible to see the Home Secretary, and was told that the Home Secretary made it a practice not to see any lawyer involved in a reprieve case. As he left the Home Office Mr Mishcon told waiting reporters who asked for a statement, "It is far better that I say nothing at this stage, a life is at stake."

At 5.15 that afternoon Ruth Ellis's parents and her brother Granville Neilson left the death cell after making their last farewells to the condemned woman. "She appeared to be absolutely calm and unafraid of what was going to happen to her," Mr Neilson told a reporter.

She now had little more than twelve hours scheduled to live. Lord Tenby refused to see a deputation of M.P.'s anxious to discuss the case. But Sir Frank Newsam instructed Mr (now Sir) Richard Jackson, head of the CID, to check her new story.

By now the last-minute moves for a reprieve were blazoned all over the evening newspapers. Victor Mishcon's telephone was beleaguered with calls: a peer's son phoned to ask if it would help if his father exercised his constitutional privilege to demand an audience of the Queen and ask her personally for mercy. But at 9.30 Ruth Ellis sat down quietly to write to Leon Simmons: "I did not defend myself. I say, a life for a life . . . I have spoken the truth, and I want you to make the truth known for my family and son's sake . . . I am quite well, and not worrying about anything."

Even on the morning of the execution her attitude had not altered, for in a postscript to her letter to Mr Simmons she wrote at 7 A.M.: "This is . . . to console my family with the thought that I did not change my way of thinking at the last moment."

Says Mr Mishcon: "I think I would have disappointed her if I had gone back and told her I had obtained a reprieve." The need did not arise: in the early hours of the morning, the Home Office telephoned Mr Mishcon, who was waiting up at his home, that the Home Secretary had decided finally that the execution was to take place as planned.

A very few hours later Ruth Ellis walked steadily from the

condemned cell to the execution room. As she entered the room she glanced towards the crucifix that a humane prison-officer had placed on the wall at her request. She stood on the trapdoor. Hangman Albert Pierrepoint placed a hand on her shoulder, and with the other he pulled the lever. "She was the calmest woman who ever went to the gallows," a prison officer told a *Daily Mirror* reporter.

"The Home Secretary did not give Scotland Yard enough time to check Ruth Ellis's last statement," accused Duncan Webb in *The People*. "It was a tragic error of judgment." Mr Mishcon agreed: "I don't know how the most efficient police officers could have done the job in the time," he says. "I had hoped that the very least the Home Secretary would have done would be to postpone the execution so that proper inquiries could be made."

What does Lord Tenby say?

His answer is simple and presents a completely new light on the case: "The police were, in fact, able to make considerable inquiries. But anyway it made no difference. If anything, if Mrs Ellis's final story was true it made her offence all the greater. Instead of a woman merely acting suddenly on impulse here you had an actual plot to commit murder, deliberately thought out and conceived with some little care. Even if a man were also guilty he would only have been an accessory before the fact: she would still have been the principal."

I asked Lord Tenby why he had not reprieved Ruth Ellis on the facts as brought out at the trial, in Mr Bickford's letters, and the articles in the Press. "For a start," he replied. "I do not think that a Press campaign should affect the Home Secretary one way or the other. I'd rather have reprieved everyone if I could, but as Home Secretary I had to administer the law of England.

"And according to that law the plea of provocation—even without the later developments—just did not stand up. This was no inflamed murder in the heat of the moment. She travelled all the way up to Hampstead from her home in Kensington, looked in the window of the public house, waited for him to come out, and then shot him six times. It was a deliberate killing!"

In the years following the 1957 Homicide Act, people who shot their faithless wives or their lovers were in a stronger position. Ernest Fantle, the Polish ex-airman who shot his wife's lover in 1958, and Harvey Leo Holford, the Brighton club-owner who in September 1962 killed his wife Christine, were both given three years' imprisonment.

Both their crimes were reduced to manslaughter because of their diminished responsibility. Certainly the provocation in those cases was immediate. They were very different from the case of Ruth Ellis. Nevertheless, it seems that now the doctrine of *crime passionel* has almost entered into English law.

But no such considerations affected Lord Tenby's mind in 1955. That was one of the reasons why Continental commentators bitterly attacked his decision: in Corsica, two days after Ruth Ellis was sentenced to death a woman who had premeditatedly killed her lover was given a suspended prison sentence and put on probation. The contrast with Ruth Ellis's fate was taken as an instance of typical Anglo-Saxon barbarism.

Many Anglo-Saxons thought so too. The hanging was "degrading and retrograde", said Dr Donald (now Lord) Soper, the Methodist preacher. Even eight years afterwards Robert Hancock could write with scorn of Lord Tenby as "this not very successful son of a famous father." But why did it happen? Why did Lord Tenby, who on July 6th saved Mrs Sarah Lloyd, not save on July 11th, Mrs Ruth Ellis?

His explanation, is forceful and discloses a point of view which writers on the case have chosen to disregard.

He was concerned not merely with the fate of Ruth Ellis, but with the safety of the 'forgotten woman' in the case—the innocent woman who had been injured when Ruth Ellis fired shot after shot at her lover.

"We cannot have people shooting off firearms in the street!" Lord Tenby told me. "This was a public thoroughfare where Ruth Ellis stalked and shot her quarry.

"And remember that she did not only kill David Blakely: she also injured a passer-by. As long as I was Home Secretary I was determined to ensure that people could use the streets without fear of a bullet."

Whether one agrees with Lord Tenby or not his viewpoint puts the case into proper perspective. It is all very well to dilate on the undoubted horror of hanging a woman, and particularly hanging a woman as overwrought and badly treated as Ruth Ellis. But the Home Secretary owes a duty to the public at large.

He owed as high a duty to Mrs Gladys Yule, walking up the road to have a drink at the Magdala public house with her husband, as he did to Mrs Ruth Ellis shooting her lover. Mrs Yule, who referred throughout her evidence to Ruth Ellis as "the young lady", was shot in the thumb. As she herself wrote in a letter to the *Evening Standard*: "She might easily have killed me as an innocent passer-by, a complete stranger. As it is, I have a partly crippled right hand for life, for which there is no compensation."

Lord Tenby thought of both women, weighed up his duty to each on the scales of his conscience, and came down on the side of Mrs Yule. Is it really possible to say that he was so wrong? The public are entitled to expect that they can use the streets without risk of being shot at.

Indeed, by an odd paradox, if Ruth Ellis had been a more accurate shot she probably would not have been hanged. If a stray bullet had not caught Mrs Yule I am almost certain that Lord Tenby would have reprieved her. This amiable politician would have been only too relieved to show Ruth the same mercy as a few days earlier he had shown Sarah Lloyd. Everyone misses this point: they write of Lord Tenby as if he were an insensitive dullard.

But is it so reprehensible to want to protect innocent passers-by from erratic marksmen settling private scores in public places?

CHAPTER TWENTY-THREE

Guenther Fritz Podola

(1959)

CAN you hang someone for a murder he says he does not remember committing? That was the problem facing Mr R. A. Butler when, as Home Secretary, in the autumn of 1959, he had to consider whether Guenther Fritz Erwin Podola should die.

Podola was a thirty-year-old German, an ex-member of the Hitler Youth. He was a thief and a burglar, a professional, gun-carrying, criminal.

And on Monday, July 13th, 1959, he drew his black automatic and shot dead Detective-Sergeant Raymond Purdy. His guilt was beyond doubt. Another policeman stood no more than thirty feet away and saw the gun fire and the man fall to the ground.

Yet Podola's trial was one of the most outstanding in recent years, and his judge said his name was assured of a secure place in the legal history of this country.

For Podola's defence was unique. There was no precedent for it in the books. For the first time in our criminal law a man was saying: "I am sane but . . . I cannot stand my trial—let alone be hanged—because I cannot remember what happened!" It was not only a legal but a religious issue as well. As Mr F. Morris Williams, Podola's solicitor, wrote to Mr Butler after the trial:

"The law may be putting to death a man who cannot, to use the words of the Order for Morning Prayer in the *Book of Common Prayer*, acknowledge and confess [his] manifold sins and wickedness . . . and confess them with an humble, lowly, penitent and obedient heart to the end that [he] may obtain forgiveness for the same."

Appeals to religious scruple are not usually an effective approach to a politician. But Mr Butler was a known church-goer and practising Christian. Would he be moved? Would Podola receive at his hands what C. P. Snow has called "Justice for the enemy"?

On May 21st, 1959 Podola took a plane at Düsseldorf and flew to London. It was his first visit to this country. But he was no idle tourist. Soon after he arrived he bought himself an automatic pistol, a shoulder holster, and some ammunition. He had work to do.

For nearly six weeks he plied his normal trade: burgling and petty larceny. Then, on the first week-end in July, he decided to upgrade himself in the roster of crime. He made his first attempt at blackmail.

It arose out of a chance discovery in one of his routine house-breakings. When breaking into the flat of an American model, on a visit to this country, he spotted—and took—not only her jewellery and a mink stole, but three passports. They belonged to the lady, her daughter, and an American friend. And they appear to have given him the idea that she might be amenable to some discreet extortion.

With the passports in front of him he sat down and wrote a two-page letter. It is rather a fatuous document, and one wonders why on earth he ever thought she might comply with his request. He announced himself as a private detective, R. M. Levine, of New York, U.S.A., and wrote that "certain parties" had hired him for the purpose of looking into her conduct during the past years. He had been paid a retainer of $500, and if Mrs Schiffman—for that was the American lady's name—were willing to meet his price he would be "most happy" to hand over his complete file.

In fact, Mrs Schiffman was a perfectly respectable woman and all she did was go straight to the police. Thereafter she acted under their instructions.

Podola followed up his letter with two telephone calls, which merely served to alert the police. They told the telephone authorities, and post-office engineers waited for the next call, when, with luck, they might be able to trace the caller.

Soon after 3.30 on the afternoon of Monday, July 13th, Mrs Schiffman's telephone rang again. At once she recognized the slightly German voice with the transatlantic accent. She kept the man talking, haggling over details, spinning out time while the engineers worked furiously to trace the call. Within minutes two detective-sergeants, Raymond Purdy and John Sandford, left Chelsea police-station for South Kensington underground station, and as they arrived they saw Podola in a call-box by the barrier—still talking.

There was a scuffle. Mrs Schiffman heard her caller cry out, "Hey, what do you want?" Then another voice said, "O.K., lad, we are police-officers." And after a pause it came on the line: "Mrs

Schiffman? This is Detective-Sergeant Purdy. Remember my name?"

It seemed the routine arrest of a routine blackmailer.

But the happenings of the next fifteen minutes were of a different order.

Podola accompanied the officers to their waiting car. And as they came into the street he twisted himself free, broke away, and ran off. There was a chase, Podola sprinting through the half-empty streets on this warm summer's afternoon, the two policemen gaining on him in a commandeered taxi.

In desperation Podola streaked up the steps of a block of flats, at 105 Onslow Square. He must have thought he could get through and out by the back. The two detectives were bounding after him. They burst into the spacious entrance-hall, and there was their man, trying to hide behind a pillar—trapped.

There was only one way out for Podola; and he took it. As his gun fired and Sergeant Purdy slumped to the ground Podola ran past his falling body, through the door, and out again into the street. Sergeant Sandford tried to catch him, but it was hopeless. An Olympic runner would have found it difficult to overhaul him.

The police did not get their man until three days later. And this time there was no chase, nor hope of escape.

At about 3.45 on the afternoon of Thursday, July 16th, eight police officers and Flame, an Alsatian police-dog, stood on a hotel landing outside Room No. 15. The scene was the Claremont House Hotel, 95 Queen's Gate, not more than a few hundred yards from 105 Onslow Square. Inside the room was Podola— frightened, exhausted, and tense. After shooting Sergeant Purdy he had sprinted straight back to this room, hidden the pistol in an attic overhead, and not ventured out of doors. For three whole days he had remained in his room, without food, except for some cigarettes and bread that his landlady had brought, and without news of the outside world, except for what his radio told him.

Then, suddenly, he heard the thud of a policeman's body hurled at the door of his room. "Police! Open this door!" was the cry. The door remained closed. There was a pause of about fifteen seconds. Then the waiting policemen heard from inside the room a slight metallic click: it could have been the cocking of a gun. Contrary to usual practice four of the policemen carried revolvers. But they did not use them. Instead a burly, brave detective-sergeant named Chambers threw himself at the door. At that moment it opened: Podola was standing right behind it. The door burst back into the room. Chambers caught a glimpse of Podola as it struck him full in the face. The impact made

Podola stagger back and topple backwards over the arm of a chair, finishing up with his head in the fireplace. Chambers was taking no chances. His momentum was so great he probably could not help himself anyway: the full weight of his seventeen stone spreadeagled the slightly built Podola.

Podola struggled. He tried to push Chambers off, but the detective grabbed his flailing hands and tried to pull them into his body. A police inspector threw himself on Podola's right arm, and a detective-constable on his left, while a fourth policeman seized his feet, which were threshing about, and removed his shoes. Chambers, whose face was right against Podola's, noticed the man was bleeding from a small cut above his left eye. "All right, we are police," he said. "Keep still so we can talk to you!"

But Podola continued to struggle.

Then suddenly he went limp. He lay there, on the floor, silent—his face uppermost, his eyes closed. The policemen dragged him on to the bed, bathed his head and eye, sprinkled water over him, and put a cold compress at the back of his neck. Slowly he regained consciousness. He managed to sit up on the edge of the bed and gulp down some water; his nose and the cut over his eye were bleeding, and the eye itself was rapidly closing. While the detectives searched the room he sat there without a word, following their movements intently. "He was watching us not as a normal person would look around," Sergeant Chambers was later to say at his trial.

And there was something else unusual. "He had a peculiar trembling which was most noticeable in the hands," reported Sergeant Chambers. "It was a sort of trembling and shaking which we could not understand. We thought perhaps he was suffering from cold. We took some bedding off the bed and put it round his shoulders, and we put pillows at his back to keep him warm." But he continued to tremble and twitch.

Eventually, his head covered with his own jacket, he was led, barefoot, downstairs and out to a waiting police-car. On his arrival at Chelsea police-station—the same station at which Sergeant Purdy had served—a doctor was called. And while they waited for police surgeon Dr John Shanahan to arrive detectives fanned their prisoner as he lay inert on a couch.

Later a Labour M.P. was to ask the Home Secretary in the House of Commons: "What happened to Guenther Podola during his six hours at Chelsea police-station?" Rumours were rife that the police had used the time to revenge themselves upon the man who had killed their comrade. Charges of vicious police beatings were made and, by some, believed.

In fact, as F. H. Lawton, Q.C. (now Mr Justice Lawton), Podola's counsel, was later to say at the Old Bailey: "There is no evidence of any kind that any violence was done to Podola at Chelsea police-station. Indeed, such evidence as exists points the other way."

Dr Shanahan, who examined Podola twenty minutes after his arrival at the station, found it already impossible to make contact with him. He could not get Podola to say anything, though he would obey simple commands such as "Open your mouth!" The doctor concluded that he was recovering from possible concussion, and that he was 'withdrawn' from reality: he appeared frightened, dazed, and exhausted. He probably could not, rather than would not, talk.

Dr Shanahan returned to the station at about midnight, and on trying—again without success—to make contact with Podola, said he must be admitted to hospital right away. And so, in the early hours of the morning, Podola was carried from the police-station on a stretcher and taken by ambulance to St Stephen's Hospital, Chelsea.

Handcuffed to his bed and screened from other patients and their curious visitors, Podola was in a ward at St Stephen's for three and a half days. During this time he was under constant observation by police-officers by his bedside, and was seen frequently by Dr Philip Harvey, the hospital's consultant physician, and Dr Latham, the house physician. At the end of this time Dr Harvey told the police: "Mr Podola is now fit to be interviewed." But he added: "He is fit to understand the nature of a charge, but is not able at this moment, in my opinion, to act in a testamentary capacity regarding events leading up to his admission, because of the presence of retrograde amnesia." In simple English this meant that the first medical specialist to examine Podola, and one who could not possibly have any axe to grind, thought that the man could not give evidence about events before his admission to hospital, because he was suffering from a genuine loss of memory about everything prior to his head injury on the afternoon of July 16th.

What was that injury?

"Concussion and cerebral contusion," ran Dr Harvey's first report to the Commissioner of Police. And although later laboratory tests indicated that there was, in fact, no damage to the brain and therefore no cerebral contusion or bruising all the doctors who afterwards gave evidence in the case agreed that undoubtedly Podola had been concussed in the skirmish in Room No. 15.

R

But was that concussion—and the circumstances in which it was sustained—adequate to cause "retrograde amnesia"?

"Yes," said the five doctors who subsequently gave evidence for the prisoner, and no-one put it more graphically than consultant neurologist Dr Michael Ashby some time later:

"Podola had been hiding from the police for three days, virtually without food. Prolonged fear by raising the tempo of many bodily functions is very exhausting to the nervous system. The sudden and unexpected blow on the door and the shout of 'Police!' must have been like the crack of doom.

"Podola received a terrific blow on the head from the Yale knob of the door. The police officers threw themselves upon him as they well knew that his gun might again do its deadly work. As Podola struggled desperately with Chambers and another officer lying over his abdomen, he lost consciousness during this last battle for freedom.

"It was probably at this moment, in pain from the blow, with strength and consciousness fast ebbing from him, as his enemies were upon him in the most literal sense, that his brain as it were snapped; when he came round a few minutes later he was already in his new and abnormal state of mind. The horror of it all had been obliterated completely, just as in similar cases on the battlefield so well known to doctors during the war."

Though at first slow to make progress, from his third day in hospital Podola's condition improved almost hourly. He played pontoon with his guards and chess with Dr Latham. "When did you learn to play?" asked the doctor. "I've been playing it since I was young," said Podola.

At two o'clock on the fourth afternoon Podola was sitting up in bed playing chess when Dr Harvey, three senior police-officers, and a solicitor entered the ward. The solicitor, Mr F. Morris Williams, had—unknown to Podola—been retained by a group of anonymous business men a couple of days earlier to defend him. He had tried to see his prospective client on the Saturday, but for seventy-two hours had been kept from Podola's bedside by a doctor's certificate saying that Podola could not be interviewed. Now, in the presence of the others, Mr Williams asked him if he wanted his services. The reply was unexpected: "What has that got to do with my eye?"

Eventually Mr Williams made himself understood, and Podola accepted him as his lawyer. A police superintendent then stood forward and told the pyjamaed patient: "I am a police-officer. On July 16th you were arrested for the murder of Detective-Sergeant

Raymond Purdy. I am going to take you to Chelsea police-station, where you will be charged with that murder."

Shortly afterwards Podola was taken to West London Magistrates' Court. Frozen faced, with dull, unseeing eyes, he stood dazedly in the dock while Mr Morris Williams told the magistrate that he had "definite instructions for his defence." The prisoner was remanded in custody until July 28th, and was driven off to Brixton prison. Press photographs of Podola seated in the back of the police car clearly showed a bluish stain round his bruised left eye.

The black eye fed public concern about the case, and when, some days later, Mr Morris Williams told the magistrate that his client had "lost his memory", and that he could not obtain adequate instructions for the defence, everyone knew that legal history was about to be made.

Dr Francis Brisby, then Principal Medical Officer at Brixton prison, and one of the most experienced members of the prison medical service, had perhaps the best opportunity of studying Podola. He examined him soon after his arrival at Brixton, and had six long interviews with him before his trial. He also saw him at intervals during the trial, and studied the day-to-day reports of his medical staff. It is perhaps significant that this experienced medical man came to no quick diagnosis. From the start he suspected he was malingering, but he admitted in court: "I don't think I was ever clinically more in the dark than I was in this case." He did not come to a firm decision that Podola was 'swinging the lead' until some seven weeks after he had entered prison, when he was writing his report to the Prison Comissioners on September 7th. Even then, he said that he found his decision "difficult."

There seems little doubt that if Podola was indeed a malingerer he was either extremely clever or phenomenally lucky. Whether or not he was genuine, all five doctors who gave evidence for the defence were agreed that his symptoms were the right ones. Hysterical amnesia taking effect over all the patient's past life is a rarity: it would be difficult, if not impossible, for a faker to 'read it all up' in a textbook and then simulate the condition. Yet Podola throughout the period prior to his trial appears to have acted—with one major possible exception—either as if he had learned the symptoms out of a book or else as if he really was genuine.

It was in keeping with genuine hysterical amnesia blotting out memory that there should be as time went on patchy returns of memory. These patchy openings in the blackness were described at the trial by Dr Michael Ashby as "windows of memory"—visual, almost photographic. For a moment one looks out from the darkness of one's amnesia and through the window of recollection 'sees' a picture from one's past.

It is almost inconceivable that Podola would have known this. Yet Dr Brisby told the court that on the very first occasion that he interviewed Podola the prisoner volunteered the information that he had "a mental picture" of a girl and child, "Ruth and Micky". In fact, the girl was Ruth Qandt, a past mistress from Germany and the boy "Micky" was their son.

Another "window of memory" was a picture of himself lying between two rails on the railway track and a train passing over him. Dr Ashby, who first saw Podola in prison nearly four weeks after his admission, considered this particularly important. The alleged memory was purely photographic, like an old silent film—exactly what he would have expected.

In all, seven doctors examined Podola in his seven weeks at Brixton, three for the Crown and four for the defence. Of the three Crown doctors only one was a consultant psychiatrist—Dr Denis Leigh, a medical man of the highest distinction, called in by the Prison Commissioners. Podola manifested to him the same symptoms as to the other doctors, but he took a different view of them from his colleagues of the defence. The train incident he regarded as either a definite prevarication or a fantasy.

Among the reasons why Dr Leigh thought that Podola was not genuine was his general knowledge—he knew who Dr Adenauer and the Queen were, for instance—and his ability to play chess, tie his own shoe laces and shave himself. According to Dr Leigh a true hysterical amnesiac would not be able to tie his laces or shave himself, would not know that a banana is a banana, and could not recognize an elephant as an elephant.

In September 1959 the doctors argued between themselves in public for nine days as they followed one another into the witness-box at the Old Bailey. The crucial question was: Was Podola "fit to plead"? The jury had to decide if his amnesia was genuine. If it was, Mr Justice Edmund Davies would then have to rule whether that genuine loss of memory made him unfit to plead. Even if the jury believed him Podola would still have that legal hurdle to surmount.

In truth, a Scottish judge had decided fourteen years earlier that a man who does not remember the facts can still be made to stand his trial—provided he is sane. And it was odds on anyway that Mr Justice Edmund Davies would follow this decision and rule that even a genuine Podola's trial must continue.

As it was he did not have to make a decision. After three and a half hours the jury returned to court and said that Podola was a sham, that he remembered perfectly well what had happened on that afternoon when Sergeant Purdy died.

Podola's solicitor, Mr Morris Williams, still believes today that was a wrong verdict. "I have no doubt in my mind at all that his claim was genuine," he has told me. "I am convinced that not only at the time of his trial did Podola have no recollection of the events of that afternoon, but it is probable that he went to his death with no recollection of it."

Why then did the jury reject his plea?

For a number of reasons. Firstly because of the doctors. Sometimes even those called for the defence could not agree between themselves. There is no branch of medicine more prone to mumbo-jumbo and abtruse reasoning than psychiatry. There was a gaggle of doctors in Podola's case, and at the end of nine days of it the jury, cooped up in their box, after interminable hours in that hot, stuffy courtroom, must not have known whether they were coming or going.

For instance, *was it—or not—a feature of genuine hysterical amnesia that acquired skills are retained?* If Podola was genuine could he possibly have known how to play chess or clean his teeth or have a game of pontoon with his guards? Eminent psychiatrist Dr Denis Leigh, called for the Crown, said No. Eminent psychiatrist Dr David Stafford-Clark, called at his own request by the defence, said Yes. Who was right? How could the jury possibly tell?

Was it—or not—a feature of genuine hysterical amnesia that the patient exhibited "la belle indifférence," a French phrase meaning a state of blissful indifference to reality? Consultant neurologist Dr Colin Edwards, called by the defence, said that in a certain sense "they go hand in hand". Consultant psychiatrist Dr Edward Larkin, also called for the defence, said that he wished to avoid "the unfortunate term *la belle indifférence,* which no-one in the court so far has understood, I am afraid."

Did Podola manifest—or not—this state of "beautiful indifference"? "Yes," said Dr Colin Edwards: as Podola had left him to be taken into court he had calmly unwrapped a sweet and popped it in his mouth—he showed "surprising unconcern". "Podola is concerned about being hanged," said Dr Edward Larkin. "He showed remarkable, but not continuous, *la belle indifférence,*" said Dr Michael Ashby. "I have found no exaggerated responses or sensory changes in Podola and no sign of *la belle indifférence,*" said Dr Denis Leigh for the Crown.

After over a week of this sort of cross-fire the only piece of
medical evidence that the jury probably felt they could fully
accept was Dr Leigh's remark in cross-examination: "I think so
many things in psychiatry can be interpreted differently."

To my mind, in the secrecy of their room the jury probably
ignored the medical evidence completely and came to their conclusion on the other evidence available to them. And if one looks
at that evidence one can hardly blame them for their verdict.

That other evidence consisted of two things—a letter written
to Podola while he was at Brixton awaiting trial and his reply, and
his own testimony in the witness-box.

As for the letter, Mr Justice Edmund Davies told the jury:
"If there was ever a point fitted for a jury's determination it is
this." He would not let the doctors be asked their view on it. He
was adamant that it was entirely a matter for the jury, untram-
melled by the contending experts.

What had happened was that at Brixton prison—while still
vehemently maintaining his total loss of memory—Podola received a postcard from a man called Ronald Starkey. Later Starkey was to give evidence that he knew Podola and had last seen
him three days before Sergeant Purdy's death. "Dear Mike," ran
the card (Starkey knew Podola as 'Mike'), "Is there anything I
can get you in the way of tobacco or eats, if so drop me a visiting
card and I will come to see you. Best of luck. Ron." Two days after
receiving this card Podola wrote a cordial reply suggesting that
Starkey come to see him, and asking for some cigarettes and
magazines. The letter began: "Dear Ron, Thank you for your card. I
was very pleasantly surprised to hear from you," and ended: "It sure
was nice to hear from you, Ronny . . . Cordially yours, Mike."

The Crown put forward the obvious contention that this was
a fantastic blunder on the part of Podola: he clearly remembered Starkey, and was so anxious for cigarettes and something
to read that he threw aside discretion. To this the defence retorted that Podola must have known that the letter would be
intercepted by the prison authorities, since when given the paper
to write it on he was told not to seal the envelope, and that in
truth, Podola deliberately made out that he knew Starkey so that
he would be permitted as a visitor, and he could 'touch' him for
some tobacco. Furthermore, the defence called as a witness a
fellow-prisoner of Podola's, who said that Podola showed him the
card and said it was probably from a crackpot, and that he did
not know the sender.

"I sedulously abstain from expressing my view of this letter,"
Mr Justice Edmund Davies told the jury in his summing up. "But

this I say to you: if I had the privilege of exercising the functions you are called upon to discharge I think I would begin my deliberations by coming to a conclusion—which side does the truth lie in regard to that letter?" There is more than one way of killing a cat and the jury may well have felt from this passage that, despite the judge's careful and deliberate refusal to express his own opinion, they yet could discern which way Sir Edmund's mind was working. And, after all, when so much in the case was supposition and hyperbole, was it not comforting to have something concrete, something in black and white to latch on to? Certainly if one approached Podola's letter with a mind anxious for some sheet-anchor amid the swirling sands of the doctors' debate one could be forgiven for thinking that the words meant exactly what they said.

As for Podola's testimony itself, he was in the witness-box for three-and-a-half hours. The jury had ample time to make up their own minds, by looking at the man and studying his demeanour, whether or not he was "beautifully indifferent", whether or not he really remembered what had happened.

Again, if one tries to picture oneself sitting in that jury-box during those warm September days one can perhaps understand why the jury reacted to Podola in the way they did.

At the magistrates' court in early August observers had noticed his frozen face, his apathy, his air of almost total unreality. But this was not so now. J. P. Eddy, Q.C., a former judge in India and a retired metropolitan stipendiary magistrate, has commented on the difference that had come over the man:

"He was transformed. The frozen face, had become a normal face, the pitiable figure an active figure, the dull eyes which I had seen in the court below were lighted up with interest. He followed the proceedings not as an outside spectator but as one who was personally involved."

The doctors argued that *la belle indifférence* meant that a man could be "beautifully indifferent" to the reality of the original event which caused his amnesia, but still very worried as to what was to happen to him *now* as a result. One can be "indifferent" to the fact that one has apparently murdered a policeman, yet very concerned indeed as to whether one will be hanged for it: such at least was the contention put forward by some of the doctors who gave evidence. But was a jury likely to believe it? When they saw a man so clearly and intelligently giving his evidence, and observed him frequently scribbling notes to his lawyers while he sat in the dock, could they be blamed for thinking that this man was "fit to plead"? That the smartly

dressed young man in the dock was very much 'on the ball', and
knew perfectly well what was happening to him now and what had
happened to Sergeant Purdy back in July?

Lord Devlin has described juries as predominantly middle-class,
middle-aged, and middle-minded. It would have required a high
degree of subtlety and imagination to conceive that a man who
looked and sounded as normal as Podola could yet be suffering
from a mental illness so bizarre and strange-sounding as hysterical
amnesia. British juries are not renowned for their sublety or powers
of imagination: rude common sense is their forte. And rude common
sense must surely have indicated that Podola was malingering.

Indeed, if there was any slight doubt lingering in a juror's mind
it was probably resolved by something that the judge had done
on the first morning of the trial. For Mr Justice Edmund Davies
then ruled that the burden of proving his unfitness to plead
rested on the accused: it was not for the Crown to prove that he
was fit, but for Podola to prove that he was not. Admittedly,
Podola only had to prove it on the balance of probabilities
whereas if the burden had been on the Crown they would have
had to satisfy the jury beyond all reasonable doubt. But it can
be questioned to what extent, if at all, this academic sophistry
affected the jury's decision. As far as they were concerned, Podola
had to prove that he had lost his memory.

Incidentally, the judge could have decided the other way. In a
case two years earlier at Birmingham Assizes, Mr Justice Salmon
had ruled that the burden of proof was on the Crown.

As it was, once the jury had rejected Podola's plea the rest of
the Old Bailey proceedings became a rather drawn-out anti-climax
before another jury, taking a day and a half. The prisoner formally
said that he was "not guilty" of capital murder, and the Crown
set about the almost too easy task of showing that he was.

In the witness-box Detective-Sergeant John Sandford was courteous, precise, and deadly. He described in quiet, unemotional
tones how after Podola had been arrested and was sitting on a
window-ledge in the entrance-hall of 105 Onslow Court he had
tried to find the housekeeper, and had called back to Sergeant
Purdy that he could not get a reply to the housekeeper's bell.
Purdy turned his head towards him. And as he did so Sandford
saw Podola slide off the ledge and put his right hand inside his
jacket. "Watch out, he may have a gun!" he shouted. But it was
too late. Podola drew a black automatic pistol and shot Purdy pointblank through the body. "It was all over in a matter of seconds."

F. H. Lawton, Q.C., Podola's leading counsel, was without instructions from his client. Yet properly, in the exercise of his

duties as defence counsel, he questioned Sergeant Sandford as to whether in some way the shooting might have been accidental. But the Sergeant was firm: there was no extenuation for a cold-blooded act of murder.

Even so, the last word remained with Podola. Branded before the court as a liar and a fake, would he now admit his deceit and try to advance some argument that could mitigate his guilt? He did not. He refused to go into the witness-box and give evidence on oath as to the events of that July afternoon. Instead he rose to his feet in the dock and made a personal statement of his own, explaining why he was unable to challenge what Sergeant Sandford had said.

Standing between two warders and reading a sheet of paper this is what he said:

"Your Honour, ladies and gentlemen of the jury. I stand before you accused of the murder of a man. Throughout the course of this trial I have listened to the various witnesses, and I understand the accusations. The time has now come to defend myself against these accusations, but I cannot put forward any defence. The reason for this is that I have lost my memory for all these events. All I can say in my defence is that I do not remember the circumstances leading up to the events in connection with this shooting. I do not know if it was me, or whether it was an accident, or an act of self-defence. I do not know whether at that time I did realize that the man was in fact a detective. I do not know whether I was provoked in any way. For these reasons I am unable either to admit or deny the charge against me.

"Thank you."

It was a simple, perhaps moving, moment in the trial. But it did not deter the jury from their inevitable verdict of guilty or the judge from pronouncing the inevitable sentence. "How did Podola take it?" I asked Mr Morris Williams. "He was a trained Nazi," was the reply. "He accepted his fate in the same way as a guardsman would accept a military catastrophe."

If Podola accepted it Mr Williams did not. Like many a solicitor, his first thought after his client's conviction was to appeal. But F. H. Lawton, Q.C., advised that this was impossible: there was no legal provision for an appeal from a jury's findings of fitness to stand trial. Podola's defence had been unique, and the legal apparatus simply did not exist to test it further in the courts.

The only barrier between Podola and the hangman was the Home Secretary.

So on October 5th, 1959, eleven days after the sentence of death, Mr Williams wrote to Mr Butler. It was a closely-reasoned, four-page letter, setting out all the arguments in favour of mercy that Mr Williams could think of. "We submit that the law, the facts and the principles of Christian religion, all give grounds for a reprieve," he wrote.

But Mr Butler did not consider the letter immediately. On the very day he received it, he announced that he was referring the case to the Court of Criminal Appeal for them to deal with as if Podola had appealed. Technically a Home Secretary has had this power ever since the Court was created, in 1907, but it was the first time he had exercised it in a capital case. Podola was making legal history again.

For two days in mid-October 1959 the Podola reference was argued before five judges of the Criminal Appeal Court. The number of judges itself showed the importance of the event: normally only three sit.

The court ruled that, in fact, Podola did have a right of appeal. But it availed him nothing. Mr Justice Edmund Davies's summing up was upheld, and the Lord Chief Justice said that, even if Podola's loss of memory had been genuine it still would not have made him unfit to stand trial. Loss of memory meant that a jury must be specially careful before convicting. It did not mean that an accused cannot be put on trial.

Mr Williams tried to appeal still further, to the House of Lords. But the Attorney-General refused his fiat, then still necessary. The courts had done with the case. Once again Podola's only chance of staying alive rested with Mr Butler.

Stories began to appear in the newspapers that Podola's memory was 'flooding back'; that he was now saying he had an alibi; that he was nowhere near 105 Onslow Square when Sergeant Purdy was killed. In fact, a letter exists in which Podola wrote again to Ronald Starkey asking him to help with information—"Because I know now that it wasn't I who did it." Rumours were even current that Podola was a spy in the service of the West German Government—hence the presence of the two German Embassy observers at his appeal—and that the murder had some mysterious James Bond-type connotation, with the suggestion of intrigue and international villainy.

So much was speculation from the outside. In truth, in the guarded solitude of the condemned cell Podola's memory *was* coming back. Consultant neurologist Dr Colin Edwards had said at the Old Bailey that once the trial was over he would expect memory to return "if it didn't matter any longer." And this was happening.

Podola drew a diagram of a block of flats, and handed it to Mr Williams saying he had "done a job" there on the afternoon of the murder: could the solicitor trace it? Mr Williams believed in his client. With only Podola's rough diagram to help him, and no idea of where in London the block of flats might be, he set out to try and check his man's story. By sheer hard work he was able to locate a block in Chelsea corresponding to the diagram, and to ascertain that a flat there had indeed been broken into on July 13th.

But what of it? Mr Williams must have asked himself. Podola could well have broken into this flat during the earlier part of that day and yet been the man who was telephoning Mrs Schiffman from South Kensington underground station at 3.30. How did this 'other job' help establish his possible innocence?

Podola supplied the answer a few days before his impending execution. It was a remarkable story. He claimed that he returned to his hotel room on July 13th to find an old friend and associate named Bob Levine sitting on his bed, waiting for him— and holding a gun. "I've shot a policeman," said Levine, and appealed to Podola for help. "Give me the gun. I'll hide it for you," said Podola, and took it upstairs to the attic, where three days later the police were to find it wrapped in a newspaper. "You've got to trace Levine!" Podola told Mr Williams. He saw it was his only chance of avoiding the gallows.

But there was no "Bob Levine" to trace. Podola's backmailing letter to Mrs Schiffman had been signed "R. M. Levine". "Bob Levine" was himself: it was a name he used as an alias for some of his own criminal endeavours. Consultant neurologist Dr Michael Ashby later told a meeting of doctors and lawyers in London discussing the case that the story suggested to him that, like so many subjects of hysteria, Podola had a dream-world. And this is Mr Williams's own view: "I am satisfied in my own mind that he was a pschizoid," he says. "In a very long letter that Podola wrote me from prison he claimed that he bore a striking resemblance to 'Bob Levine': 'We were as like as two pins,' was his phrase. I am sure the man had a split personality."

Indeed, this seems likely, for there was no rational purpose served in putting forward the "Bob Levine" defence. The evidence that Podola was the man who telephoned from the underground station and shot Sergeant Purdy was overwhelming: even apart from the incontrovertible evidence of Sergeant Sandford there was Podola's palm-print on the window-ledge where he had been sitting in the entrance to the block of flats and his notebook

in his own handwriting left behind in the telephone kiosk. For
Podola to deny the shooting was rank stupidity or else the working of a mind that, despite all that the trial doctors had said
about his sanity, was *not* perfectly normal.

Obviously the three doctors who went to see Podola after the
verdict, at the request of the Home Secretary, did not agree
with this supposition. There was clearly in this case no medical
recommendation for a reprieve. But—"It was a very brief, casual
encounter," says Mr Williams. "I was not present, of course, but
I had told Podola beforehand that the doctors would be coming
to see him, and he told me about it afterwards. He was a very intelligent man, and he realized what it was all about. Apparently, he was called into a room without being told why; a warder
simply saying, 'These gentlemen want to interview you.' For about
fifteen minutes three men asked him questions, he answering as
best he could, and then they said, 'Thank you, Mr Podola. We'll
make our report.' It was only then that he realized for the first
time these men were the doctors of whom I had warned him."

No-one had asked Mr Morris Williams to come to the Home
Office or had done anything about his first letter except formally
to acknowledge its receipt. So he wrote again to the Home Secretary, referring to the rumours in the Press about Podola's condition, and saying, "We think we should explain the position to
you to remove any possible misunderstanding."

He confirmed that Podola's memory was returning in patches,
and attributed it to the arrival in this country of Ruth Quandt,
his one-time mistress. An enterprising newspaper had brought her
over from Germany, and she had written to Podola asking him
to see her. He had refused, and Mr Williams had interviewed
her instead. In the solicitor's view her letter and his own report
of the interview "had certainly shocked Podola emotionally", and
caused the onset of the return of memory, though Mr Williams
maintained it was still patchy. He disclosed to the Home Secretary
what he had been able to discover of Podola's visit to the Chelsea
flat on July 13th, and invited him to make inquiries for himself.

For the rest, he quoted Dr Edward Larkin, the consultant psychiatrist who had given evidence for Podola at the Old Bailey, as
confirming that Podola's returning patches of memory were entirely consistent with genuine hysterical amnesia, and repeated his
plea for a reprieve.

His reply came five days later—an official letter from Sir Charles
Cunningham saying that after carefully considering all the circumstances of the case Mr Butler had been unable to recommend
any interference with the due course of the law.

"How did Podola take the news?" I asked Mr Williams. "Better than my husband did!" interposed his wife. For Mr Williams, who had never met his client until a week after the killing, had become emotionally involved in the case. He had seen Podola fourteen times at Brixton prison, interviewed him at the magistrates' court five times, and seen him every day during the eleven days' proceedings at the Old Bailey, plus several emotionally charged visits to the condemned cell. "He was one of the best clients I have ever had," says Mr Williams. "He accepted my advice throughout, never once complaining, and had a pleasantly dry sense of humour."

At 9 o'clock on the morning of November 5th this model client was hanged. There were no protesting crowds outside the prison.

Should Podola have died? "I am convinced his memory never came back so far as the events of the murder are concerned," says Mr Williams. "I saw him for the last time on the day before he was hanged, and at that time he still had no recollection of the crime—though his memory had pretty well returned so far as his private life was concerned." As against this Dr Francis Brisby told a meeting of the Medico-Legal Society some months after the execution: "I never had a case where I had less doubt that a man was lying."

Although this issue will remain the main fascination of the case it is not really the basis on which one can consider the question, Was a reprieve rightly refused? The man had been convicted by a jury of his peers, and the Court of Criminal Appeal, sitting in full strength, had upheld that conviction and the legal reasoning on which it was based. By referring the case to the appeal court Mr Butler had shown that he was leaving the legal issues to the courts. The effect of Podola's loss of memory, if genuine, on his legal responsibility was for the judges to assess. Once Lord Parker, the Lord Chief Justice, declared that his loss of memory, even if genuine, was no bar to his trial the logic of expecting amnesia to form the basis of a reprieve went. We have seen this characteristic several times since the Court of Criminal Appeal was created: the Home Office leave legal issues for the courts to decide. They will generally intervene only for some outside, non-legal reason.

Was there some such extra-legal reason for a reprieve in Podola's case? I think there may have been, but it has nothing to do directly with his loss of memory. I believe that if Podola had been able adequately to instruct his legal advisers at the time of the trial he might have been able to put forward successfully to the jury a defence that in the circumstances was never raised. He might have run the line of "diminished responsibility" so as to reduce his crime to manslaughter.

This too is the view of Mr Morris Williams. "I'm perfectly satisfied of his guilt in the sense that he did the deed," he says. "But all sorts of defences might have been open to him if only we had been able to obtain positive instructions—for example, diminished responsibility."

As it was, no-one could adduce any evidence at all as to Podola's state of mind when he pulled the trigger. We simply do not know what his mental condition was at that time. His later references to "Bob Levine" seem to indicate pschizoid tendencies. This ex-Hitler Youth had long boasted to his cronies that he would use his gun to get himself out of trouble. There is little doubt that sooner or later he would have killed a policeman: he did not carry that automatic in its snug-fitting holster under his shoulder just for the fun of it. He was a man whose whole life had conditioned him to violence and bloodshed: he was a Nazi who had outlived Nazism.

And so when he shot Sergeant Purdy he perhaps was not fully responsible for his actions. Perhaps it was not a deliberate act, but an almost instinctive reflex. Perhaps he was not a cold-blooded, intentional killer, but a violence-indoctrinated thug, responding automatically to an emergency.

Undoubtedly Podola was our enemy: just as any gun-toting criminal must be the enemy of organized, decent society. But did we give him justice?

Personally I think we did. It is all very well to argue in terms of 'maybe' and 'perhaps', But Podola had been convicted on overwhelming evidence of a cowardly and brutal murder. That conviction had been upheld by the courts. Three doctors had then inquired into Podola's mental condition and found no cause, whether or not the amnesia was genuine, to recommend a reprieve. What reason could there be for the Home Secretary to take this step?

Mr Morris Williams still argues that it was un-Christian to hang a man who even at the moment of execution still may not have remembered the offence for which his life was being taken. But that is irrelevant. Many people contend that judicial hanging is in itself un-Christian anyway.

In law the decision not to reprieve Podola is unassailable, given the law as it stood at the time. For my part, I can see no valid reason why Home Secretary Butler should have stayed its hand.

CHAPTER TWENTY-FOUR

George Riley

(1961)

WESTLANDS ROAD is a quiet suburban road on the outskirts of Shrewsbury. On one side the neat, semi-detached houses back on to fields. It is a modern road, where people with moderate incomes live in well-designed houses with clean, bright kitchens, a television set in the lounge, and a garage for the car.

In October 1960 twenty-four hours in the lives of two people in this ordinary road ensured it an extraordinary place in the history of the reprieve system. Their names are Mrs Adeline Mary Smith, a frail sixty-two-year-old widow living alone at No. 47 and George Riley, a husky, good-looking lad of twenty-one living with his family at No. 38, almost exactly opposite.

The inquiry as to what really happened in those twenty-four hours eventually exploded into the House of Commons, despite the heavy restrictions on parliamentary discussion of capital cases. Seven years earlier, in the Bentley Case, Sydney Silverman had unsuccessfully tried to move the Adjournment of the House to discuss Sir David Maxwell Fyfe's refusal of a reprieve. Now he tried another tack, and put down a question asking for an inquiry to see whether there had been a miscarriage of justice. There was no reference to the refusal of a reprieve. But the question was still disallowed, and the debate siphoned off until after the lad had been hanged, when Mr Silverman moved a formal dissent from the Speaker's ruling.

During the course of this historic debate, bitter allegations of police irregularity and suppression of evidence were made, and a full-scale attack mounted on Mr R. A. Butler for having sent Riley to his death. "He was convicted of capital crime and hanged without there being one scrap of objective evidence against him," thundered Mr Silverman.

Is this so?

I have visited Shrewsbury. I have seen and spoken to Riley's solicitor, his parents, his brother, his M.P., and others connected with the story. I have read the 337 foolscap pages of the tran-

script of his six-day trial. I think I have discovered the truth as
to his guilt or innocence. I believe I know whether or not his plea
for mercy was rightly rejected.

A good starting-point is to set down what is uncontested fact
about the vital twenty-four hours.

At about 7 o'clock on the evening of Friday, October 7th, 1960,
a young man called in his car for his friend and workmate George
Riley.

They worked in the same butcher's shop. It was pay night, and
they went on a drinking expedition. George was wearing his best
clothes—a dark blue suit, cut in the Italian style, black suede
shoes and a smart white shirt.

They visited various public houses, met various friends. By
closing time George had had ten pints of beer.

But their night was not yet over. There was a dance at the
local Rolls-Royce canteen, with the bar open to 12.30 A.M. So
the party went on there. By the time the barman put the shut-
ters up George, on his own reckoning, had drunk seven to nine
whiskies—on top of the beer.

"I have never been so drunk in my life," he said later.

He became involved in several fights, and the police had to
be called. When they arrived he was struggling with another youth
on the red canteen-floor.

Finally, at 1.30, the little car drove back to Westlands Road,
and George was deposited at his garden gate.

At two o'clock Mrs Smith's next-door neighbour heard a pierc-
ing scream.

At half-past four that morning George's brother Terrance, whose
work required an exceptionally early start, was having breakfast
in the dining-room at No. 38. He heard a knocking on the
window. A dishevelled George was standing outside. He explained
that he had forgotten his key and slept on a settee in the garage.

Terrance noticed the state of his clothes and a slight graze on
his forehead. "Have you been in a fight?" he asked.

"Yes," said George.

"Who won?"

"He did a bit, and I did a bit," replied George, and went up to
bed. The time was about five o'clock.

He was up again at 6.45, and was at work by eight. His employer thought he looked ill, and made him drink a glass of fruit-
salts.

Meanwhile, at ten o'clock that morning, Mrs Smith's body was
discovered, following inquiries when she had not answered the

telephone. She was lying on the floor of her bedroom. Her night-dress was torn. Her head was unsightly.

Two senior police-officers were soon at the house.

One, Detective Inspector William Brumpton, head of Shrews-bury C.I.D., from the start appeared to have had a pretty good idea of the culprit. Even on the basis of his cursory examination of Mrs Smith's house he said at once that he thought the man responsible "could be" George Riley.

He lost no time in putting his theory to the test. At half-past eleven he left No. 47 and walked straight across the rainswept road to No. 38.

The only person at home was David, George Riley's sixteen-year-old brother. The inspector went upstairs, opened George's wardrobe, and what he saw appeared to confirm his hunch. The jacket of George's best suit was badly stained red, and the trou-sers, socks, and shoes were saturated with mud, as if the wearer had recently walked across a sodden field.

Inspector Brumpton went directly to the shop where George worked. He arrived at twelve o'clock. Ten minutes later George was with him at the police-station, and at 6.55 that evening he signed a full confession of his guilt, which he had written out him-self, and which no-one had dictated to him. The words were in-disputably his own. They were not couched in policeman's Eng-lish and written in George's own spelling.

After relating the earlier events of the evening and how he went to the garage to sleep on the old settee the statement con-tinued:

"I don't know how long I stayed there but the next thing I recollect I was in Mrs Smith's house, and I was after some money. I had spent more than I meant too that night. I knew she had lots of money and knew she kept her handbag up-stairs, because I have been to her for change and always saw her run upstairs for it. I got into the bedroom next to her bed and all of a sudden she jumped up and started shouting at me. I then grabbed hold of her by the nightdress and pulled her off the bed it then tore down the front. I hit her in the face a couple of times to stop her from shouting because I was very frightened. She still continued shouting and grabbing hold of me to stop me running away. I then hit her once more and she let go of me and I run out, she was still shouting as I run down the stairs. I got out the same way as I got in. I didn't take anything at all from the house. I was frightened. I ran over the fields, I don't know in which direction and I didn't care as long as I got away. After I had been running for about

S

10 minutes I stopped and found myself nere the Grapes Inn. I then cut across the fields to my house, and went into the garage. I did not mean to hurt Mrs Smith because I know her very well, and I only hit her because she jumped up and shouted and frightened me. I am very sorry things have ended like this, I didnt want to harm her. I only wanted some money. Signed. G. RILEY."

Later Mr Tony Hayes, George's solicitor, arrived at the police-station. He came as quickly as he could from a court some miles away. "No panic. It's all right. He's croaked!" Brumpton greeted him.

It must have seemed a watertight case.

Popular feeling was against George. His solicitor gave a great deal of thought to the question of an adjournment of the case to Stafford, then the next assize town on the circuit. "It was more or less obvious," he has told me, "that if he were tried in Shrewsbury he wouldn't stand a chance. His guilt would have been pre-judged. One lady told me that she thought I ought to be hanged along with him!" Fortunately, the late Ryder Richardson, Q.C., who was going to lead for the defence, could not appear if the case was to be heard at Shrewsbury Assize; a successful application was therefore made for the matter to be heard at Stafford, and the difficulties were solved.

His confession was not made public until half-way through his trial, yet local prejudice was strong. Why? "Because of the enormity of the crime and the fact that he was not unknown," says Mr Hayes. In fact, though it was not disclosed at his trial George had a bad record. At the age of fourteen he had twice been convicted of larceny, and less than two years previously he had been sentenced to nine months' imprisonment for wounding with intent to cause grievous bodily harm. The case had received wide coverage in the local Press, and had not made a pretty story: then too, George had been drunk, and while in that condition had stabbed two fellow-teenagers with a flick-knife. One of them was in danger of his life, and the original charge was attempted murder. Luckily for George it was, in Mr Hayes's words, "sand-papered down to g.b.h. [grievous bodily harm], and the prosecution accepted a plea of guilty."

Detective Inspector Brumpton was the officer in charge of that case. Indeed, this probably explains why on sight of Mrs Smith's body, and almost certainly knowing of George's condition at the canteen the night before, his path went straight to George's door.

Nevertheless, by the time George's trial for the capital murder of Mrs Smith started at Stafford on December 5th, 1960, some of Brumpton's original confidence must have dissipated.

The 'blood' on George's jacket had turned out to be red staining from the floor of the Rolls-Royce canteen. There *were* some specks of human blood on George's trousers and jacket, but they were too small to be grouped for comparison with Mrs Smith's, and could well have resulted from the fight at the canteen. Even more damaging, although Dr E. G. Evans, the Crown pathologist, was to say in court that it was likely that blood would have splashed up on to the assailant's front and stained his shirt and tie George's shirt and tie had borne not the slightest trace of blood.

Dr Evans thought that Mrs Smith had been killed by six or seven heavy blows to the face by a powerful fist wearing a ring such as George's. He also thought that the murderer's face and hands must have been covered with blood. But although Inspector Brumpton had promptly taken possession of George's ring before lunch-time, on the day of his arrest, it was found to bear only one minute speck of human blood, too small to be grouped for identification purposes.

Smears of what looked like blood on the jamb of a broken window and on wallpaper at Mrs Smith's house had, indeed, been established as human blood. But again they were insufficient for grouping.

The inspector later admitted that he had been hoping that scrapings from under Mrs Smith's fingernails would reveal minute particles of skin which might tie up with the scratch on George's forehead. But the forensic science laboratory found nothing.

Fingerprint experts had been all over Mrs Smith's house checking for fingerprints. But none had come to light. A footprint found in the garden had not coincided with George's shoes. And as for proving that the murder was committed 'in the course of furtherance of theft,' which was essential if the crime was to be capital, on the morning after George's arrest Brumpton himself found Mrs Smith's red purse in her dressing-table drawer—intact and containing 3*s*. 7½*d*.

If George Riley was to be found guilty it was to be entirely on his own word: the independent evidence was nowhere near strong enough. Kenneth Mynett, Q.C., leading for the Crown, conceded this at the trial. And Mr Justice Barry directed the jury accordingly: "If you disregard the statement, if you don't think this is a confession, then the prosecution do not invite you to say that all the remaining evidence is sufficient to convict this man of this very serious offence."

The success of the prosecution hung by a very slender thread. But, on the other hand, if the "confession" was not true, what possible explanation could George offer for making it?

"His first proof was his last proof," says Mr Hayes. "He never changed his story." From the start he told his solicitor that he had no real recollection of what he did that night after his return from the canteen. The binge had been too much even for hard-drinking George: "He didn't know what he had done and what he hadn't done." He alleged that Brumpton and his assistant, Detective-Sergeant Phillips, wore him down with their questions and their bluff, until finally he cracked and told them what they wanted to hear: that he was guilty.

"They had been over it so many times that I was convinced I had done it, they seemed to have all the evidence," George told Mr Hayes.

In the witness-box George swore that from the start Inspector Brumpton put on the pressure. He alleged he said: "You're a bloody fool, George. You are in it this time," as they walked to the station. And that once they arrived at the police-station there was no let-up.

This is George Riley's account of his dealings with the police, reconstructed from his replies in the witness-box.

Brumpton told him he was investigating a breaking in at "the old lady's," Mrs Smith's—that he thought George had something to do with it. George said he knew nothing about it. "Of course you do!" replied the police-officer.

The inspector [alleged George] told him his shoe-print was in the garden, and he had tracked his route back to his house. He told him that he had broken into No. 47 and made his way upstairs: "What were you going for anyway—money or something like that?"

George claimed he said he still knew nothing. Men came into the office and handed the inspector slips of paper, from which he would announce the finding of some new piece of damning evidence: "The Yard have been in and they've checked on your fingerprints in the house." Then the ultimate slip of paper: "Prepare yourself for a shock—the woman is dead!"

The inspector [according to George] described how he visualized the killing: The woman had jumped up and shouted; George had grabbed her and punched her a few times—"I have already been to your house and got your suit and clothing from there. They are heavily bloodstained with Mrs Smith's blood!"

And so [according to George's evidence] it went on. Even when Inspector Brumpton once left the room Sergeant Phillips did not let the tension relax: "The inspector is only trying to help you. Make a statement, and it'll be all right!"

Just before lunch the inspector asked for the ring off George's finger. He took it and examined it: "This is the final evidence. This clinches it. This is the ring which made the marks on the woman's body." Would he make a statement?

Again George said No.

After lunch Sergeant Phillips returned first. "Feeling better now you've had dinner?"

"No, not much better."

"Well, you would feel a bit bad—a boy on a charge like you." He told George that the inspector was trying to help him.

Then Inspector Brumpton returned and asked George to strip to the waist. George felt him pointing out 'scratches' on his back to a superior officer.

Later George was again left alone with the sergeant. "He was talking to me all the time," he said in court. It was general chat: "People around town, people I knew, and cars . . . Every time he talked about somebody he always seemed to twist back to the case and all the evidence and what was the most important— and to making a statement."

George doodled on a piece of paper. He said he couldn't recall much of what happened the night before. He went on doodling.

"Come on, you did it, didn't you? Didn't you?" said Phillips. Finally from George: "Yes."

"Why did you say Yes?" Ryder Richardson, Q.C., George's leading defence counsel asked him at the trial. Each person must form their own view of the adequacy of the reply: "Well, I was getting a bit—I was getting fed up really, and I did not feel very well, and he told me—he kept telling me—of all the evidence he had against me, and I believed him."

The sergeant, according to George, followed up his successful thrust: "How did you do it?"

"I did it like the D.I. said."

"Good, you can make a statement now."

George asked why, and was told it would go much easier for him.

Asked at the trial what he thought as he wrote the confession, George replied: "I thought it would help me . . . I knew I would

remain a prisoner, but I thought they would, you know, stop—
leave me alone."

After he started to write Inspector Brumpton came back into
the office, looked at what he had written, and said: "Keep it up."
Later he asked: "Were you going up for money?"

"Yes," replied George.

"Well, go on then, put that down!"—and George wrote: "I knew
she had lots of money and knew she kept her handbag upstairs
. . ."

Later again, "It's no use putting a sorry on this one, is it?"
said George.

"You put what you like," was the reply.

All this, it must be stressed, is George Riley's account of how
he came to make the confession. It gives rise to two questions:
first did it happen? and second, if it did, would it have been sufficient to make a twenty-one-year-old ex-Army Cadet, with previous experience of dealing with the police, 'crack', and write in
his own hand a detailed, false story?

The two police-officers' versions of events were, of course, different from George's in vital respects. They said there was no
impropriety in the questioning in Detective Inspector Brumpton's
office, no talk of bloodstains or fingerprints, or any prompting to
make a statement.

The inspector insisted that he did not tell George in the
morning that Mrs Smith was dead, for the very reason that he
wanted to tell him as little as possible about the details of the
crime. It was not, he said, until 2.30, when he saw George again
after lunch, that he told him that Mrs Smith was dead.

Sergeant Phillips swore that for an hour and a half—from 4.10
to 5.40—he was alone with George in Brumpton's office. But
according to him there was not in all that time one word spoken
between them: George sat at the desk, and he went about his
routine duties.

Ryder Richardson cross-examined him strongly about this aspect of his testimony:

"Not a word passed between you?"

"No."

"He never asked when he was going to be let go?"

"No."

"Or what you were holding him there for?"

"No."

"Or whether he was charged?"

"No."

"He never at any time asked for his solicitor?"

"He did not."

"Or his father?"

"No, sir."

Suddenly, according to the sergeant, the spell was broken at 5.40. George, he said, asked him: "They top you for capital murder, don't they?" There was discussion about the meaning of capital murder. Then, according to Phillips, George said: "She was alive when I left her. I wanted some money. I can't remember everything. I was drunk."

"Why did you say 'She was alive when you left her'?" Ryder Richardson asked George at the trial.

"I just did not like the thought of killing anybody and leaving anybody dead on the floor," was the reply.

This is the fulcrum of the whole case. Bearing in mind the determined attack that was later to be raised in the House of Commons upon the integrity of Detective Inspector Brumpton, it is important to observe that George's remark was made when the inspector was not even at the station.

Statement forms were brought, and George wrote out his confession. Brumpton returned. "Is this what you mean to say?" he asked. "Yes," George replied. Was he prepared to sign it? Yes. And George signed the fourth, final sheet and initialled the three earlier ones.

In comparing the accounts of how the confession was obtained, and in assessing its value, three factors must be borne in mind.

First, it is no unknown thing for an accused person to regret statements he has made soon after arrest and to seek to vary them in court. In those circumstances a claim that the original statement was made under pressure is almost inevitable.

Second, a genuine confession is admissible evidence. It is the proper duty of police-officers to try to obtain that evidence, particularly when—as in this case—other evidence is likely to be insufficient to secure a conviction.

And one of the heaviest burdens laid on police-officers is that they are subjected in court to the most rigorous questioning about the manner in which statements are taken from people in custody.

Third, the judge allowed the jury to hear the evidence of George's confession. If he had not been satisfied that it was obtained by proper means Mr Justice Barry would have ruled it inadmissible—though, of course, the jury could still have rejected it if they wished.

While the jury were out considering their verdict Ryder Richardson spoke to Mr Riley, George's father. "He's a bit of a lad, your George, isn't he?" said the Q.C.

"Ah well, it's in the hands of God!"

Subsequently Mr Riley was to tell me ruefully: "I didn't realize till later that it was in Mr Butler's hands!"

And so it proved to be. It took the ten men and two women on the jury just under two hours to reach their verdict—guilty.

As they trooped back into their box George showed no emotion, except to glance towards his father. He answered with a firm No when asked if he had anything to say before sentence of death.

Three days later he signed an Application for Leave to Appeal, But on January 23rd, 1961, the Court of Criminal Appeal took only ten minutes to dismiss the application. Peter Northcote, his junior counsel, told the Lord Chief Justice: "No summing up can be completely impeccable, but we feel there is nothing of sufficient substance that would justify us in urging the court to take any course open to you on the grounds set out in the notice of appeal or on any other grounds."

"We only appealed because we were told that the Home Office wouldn't touch the question of reprieve until after the judges of the Court of Criminal Appeal had reviewed the case," Mr Hayes, the solicitor, has told me.

"We have studied the papers with considerable care," said Lord Parker, the Lord Chief Justice. But there was no flaw that he and his two fellow-appeal judges could find.

At this stage the case had aroused little or no interest on a national scale: the odd down-page paragraph in the daily Press, but that was about all.

Two days after the appeal Mr Hayes posted a five-page letter to the Home Secretary asking for a reprieve. He set out all the arguments in favour of his client—the absence of bloodstains, the evidence by Professor Webster, the defence pathologist, that some of the murdered woman's blows were probably inflicted with a weapon, the lack of corroboration, the fact that basically George had been convicted on his own statement. He also enclosed a report from a psychiatrist that George displayed "a degree of abnormality which may well justify the view that it would be inappropriate for him to pay the ultimate penalty". "I thought then, and I think now, that George should not have been hanged on the evidence," Mr Hayes has told me.

The following day he received an acknowledgment from the Home Office, and then heard nothing more until the official refusal of a reprieve arrived on Tuesday, February 7th—two days before the day of execution.

Mr Riley had also been fighting to save his son's life. Within hours of the appeal court's decision he told a local reporter: "We have not given up hope. We shall never give up hope." He—and the members of his family—began gathering signatures for a petitition, and he wrote himself to Mr Butler pleading for mercy.

But it was still a small-scale effort. Until the Friday before the date of execution, when a well-known abolitionist received a letter about the case from an anonymous Shrewsbury citizen. He immediately got in touch with Louis Blom Cooper, then legal correspondent of *The Observer*, who with his editor's permission caught the 5 o'clock train to Shrewsbury. He sat up until the early hours of the morning talking to Mr Hayes, wrote his article overnight, and then telephoned it through to London in time to appear as an anonymous, powerful front-page piece in that Sunday's newspaper. "ANOTHER EVANS CASE?" ran the headline. It asked whether or not a grave miscarriage of justice was about to be committed —the hanging of a man on his own retracted statement, with no corroborative evidence.

The following afternoon, Monday, Sydney Silverman put down a question on the Order Paper of the House of Commons, asking for an inquiry into whether justice had miscarried. That evening, together with two other Labour M.P.'s, Victor Yates and Eric (now Sir Eric) Fletcher, he went to see Mr Butler.

There is little doubt that the three politicians produced evidence to Mr Butler that Detective Inspector Brumpton, the principal prosecution witness, had within the past twelve months been suspended from duty on an accusation by three women in Birmingham that he had tried to tamper with their evidence during a Ministry of Health inquiry concerning fees charged by a National Health doctor. The inspector was suspended from duty, and a disciplinary inquiry held by the Chief Constable. The three women gave evidence; Brumpton also gave evidence, and was exonerated.

This was, after all, a complete acquittal, and neither the prosecution nor the defence had mentioned this matter to George Riley's jury. Nor was there any legal need to do so. Yet the three callers pressed upon Mr Butler that no-one knew how it might have affected the jury's view. The Home Secretary promised that he would consider fully all the facts they had put before him.

But by the first post the following morning arrived in Mr Hayes's post-box the letter saying "no reprieve". Mr Victor Yates later said in the House of Commons: "I regard that Monday evening as a black Monday evening, for I had the feeling that, even though Mr Butler told me that the information which I had given him was in his brief-case, and that he was taking it home to study with all the other relevant information, he had then made up his mind in the matter." When Mr Yates learned the following morning that two people had received a letter by first post declining a reprieve he "felt even more strongly".

Mrs Elizabeth Howard, then Acting Secretary of the Howard League for Penal Reform, has made the same complaint to me. Breaking the usual Howard League policy of non-involvement in particular cases, she discussed the case with Blom Cooper over the week-end, and at 9 o'clock on the Monday morning handed in a letter to Mr Butler "putting quite briefly the points which I felt to be unsatisfactory". She too received her reply by first post on Tuesday.

With respect, these attacks are not quite on target. The letters declining a reprieve would have gone out bearing Sir Charles Cunningham's signature as a matter of office routine late on Monday afternoon to be received the usual forty-eight hours before execution. But this would not have prevented a strong-willed Home Secretary going back on the decision and personally reversing it. It had happened before.

Yet Mr Butler has only himself to blame for this bad feeling. If only he had said to Mr Yates and his colleagues: "Well, this matter has already been decided, but I'll only be too happy to see if your new information affects my decision," no-one would have felt misled.

As it was, Sydney Silverman raised that afternoon in the House of Commons the Speaker's refusal of the previous day to let his question asking for an inquiry remain on the Order Paper, and threatened to raise the issue again on a formal Motion of Censure. Mrs Howard made a statement to the Press regretting the Home Secretary's decision. Sir John Langford-Holt, Conservative M.P. for Shrewsbury, did not publicize his efforts, but he too was privately attempting to persuade Mr Butler to change his mind. And, back in Shrewsbury, Mr Hayes went to see George to tell him that Peter Northcote and he were going to work on a petition to the Queen that night. "My God, she'll have to be bloody quick!" said George.

The Palace officials were indeed expeditious. Before noon on Wednesday Mr Hayes received the telegram saying the petition had been passed to the Home Office. By the time he left the office that evening he had received a telephone call from Whitehall to say that the original decision still stood.

Mr Hayes went to report the result of his petition to his client. "It took a year or two off my life to go and see him on that last night," he says. "It's an awful thing to go and tell a man who has put his trust in you that you have failed. He said quietly, 'I'd like to thank you for everything you've done.' It upset me considerably."

That same afternoon Mr Riley went alone to pay his last visit to his son: his wife was too ill to accompany him. George seemed cheerful. He did not cringe. "Don't worry, I'll be all right. Never forget me!" he said as his father left.

Later that evening George's three brothers went to see him. They talked embarrassedly, then finally said their farewells. The two living at home—Terrance and David—left the condemned cell first: Edward, the oldest, away from home and serving in the Army, hung back. "George, did you do it or not?" he asked. "No, I didn't," said George.

That night people living in Albert and Victoria Streets, adjoining Shrewsbury prison, heard cries and chantings from the prisoners: "Don't hang Riley!" "Don't let George hang!" "It was terrible," one woman told a reporter. "I have never heard anything like it. The horror of all it meant was sickening." People came out and stood in their gardens to listen to the cries and shouts, rattling of windows, and rhythmic banging of doors from behind the walls of the prison.

At 8 o'clock the next morning George Riley was hanged. Death was instantaneous, the prison medical officer told the coroner.

Sixty M.P.'s voted in favour of Sydney Silverman's formal Motion of Censure on the Speaker for disallowing his question demanding to know whether an inquiry would be set up into the case. The debate took place a week after George's death amid scenes of some heat and bad-temper. It proved, if anything, that Parliament was not the most appropriate place for such discussions. Mr Silverman admitted that he had not read the transcript of the trial, and it seemed that other critics of the Home Secretary's decision must have been labouring under the same difficulty. Despite their obvious sincerity they made no less than five serious errors of fact in the course of their speeches.

Sir John Langford Holt, who had written to Mr Butler privately on George's behalf, took no part in the debate, and abstained from voting. "Bearing in mind your views on the failure to reprieve, why didn't you speak out publicly against the Home Secretary?" I have asked him. "Because I do not think that Parliament is the place for such matters, nor do I think that the Home Secretary should be harassed by public pressure while he is endeavouring to reach a decision," he replied.

"I have satisfied myself of the prisoner's guilt," said Mr Butler; "and after close and prolonged scrutiny of the evidence before the court, as well as other evidence available to me, I could find no ground for recommending a reprieve."

Certainly if George Riley was guilty there would appear to be no grounds for exercising mercy. His previous record was against him, as was the horror of the crime: the photographs were dreadful, and Mr Justice Barry perhaps let his own attitude slip into view when—rather unnecessarily—directing the jury to take them with them when considering their verdict. It seems unlikely that he, for one, would have given a favourable report on the prisoner.

Despite the psychiatrist's letter that Mr Hayes sent with his application for a reprieve, there can be no real doubt that George's responsibility for his actions was not impaired. For one thing his EEG examination before trial revealed no abnormality.

The only basis for mercy could have been a doubt as to his guilt—the old, familiar 'scintilla of doubt'.

Mr Hayes says: "He shouldn't have been hanged on the evidence. I don't think so. On the evidence, no." The lad's father says: "I firmly believe he didn't do it! He was a fine lad, a fine-looking lad." His mother says: "I can't possibly see him going over and doing that to that poor old dear!" Sir John Langford Holt, his M.P., says: "For a man to be condemned by his own words later withdrawn raises, at least to my mind, a sufficient doubt that justice is not certain."

What is the truth? Should Mr Butler have reprieved?

The starting-point of the inquiry is, as Mr Butler himself told the House of Commons: "Neither I as Home Secretary nor Parliament can retry the case."

Perhaps the jury might have taken a different view of Inspector Brumpton if they had known of his suspension and exoneration by a disciplinary inquiry, which M.P.'s hinted was possibly a whitewash. But it must be remembered that the inspector was out of the police-station for a considerable time that afternoon, and George was alone with Sergeant Phillips—not Brumpton—when he 'cracked' and admitted the killing. Furthermore, if the defence had sought to bring out Brumpton's suspension the prosecution would have been entitled to disclose George's past record, and what chance of an acquittal would he have had after *that*?

The answer to the problem of his guilt or innocence is to be found in his statement itself. The whole basis of his defence was that the police told him how he committed the crime, and over-awed by their seeming knowledge he accepted what they said. It must surely follow that if one can find passages of the statement which are true—and which either he did not say the police suggested or the police could not then anyway have known—his guilt stands exposed.

Regrettably—and I say regrettably, because I have enjoyed the hospitality of Mr and Mrs Riley's home, and know them still to be badly scarred by their son's tragedy—this sort of test does indicate George Riley's guilt.

One starts with what he admittedly said to Detective-Sergeant Phillips just before beginning his statement: *She was alive when I left her.*" Is it not significant that both Crown and defence pathologists agreed that Mrs Smith would have been still alive when the murderer left her?

Then to the statement itself: *"I knew she had lots of money and knew she kept her handbag upstairs because I have been to her for change and always saw her run upstairs for it,"* he wrote. How could the police possibly have known that he had been to her for change? Mr Riley tells me that this is true: George had been across to her for change on two occasions. And it was never alleged in court that this particular part of his statement was suggested to him by either Brumpton or Phillips.

"She was still shouting as I ran down the stairs." It was not alleged that the police had suggested that: but how could they have known it anyway? How could George have known it—unless he was there?

"I didn't take anything at all from the house." Again, there is no allegation that the police had suggested this particular item: and would they have done so on the Saturday when they were still searching for Mrs Smith's purse—not found until the following morning? And if the police did not suggest it, why did George write it down—taking his own time, and choosing his own words?

The biggest hurdle to believing in George's guilt is the question of motive: why did he do it? He had just started in a good job, he was popular there and trusted. His employer told Mr Riley that if George had wanted to rob anyone he could always have robbed him: every week he had between £100 and £200 in his safe, and George had the key to the shop. Why go over the road, break into a house, and batter to death a helpless, frail old woman?

The explanation given in George's statement is, it must be admitted, rather inadequate, at least to rational minds: "I was after some money. I had spent more than I meant too that night."

Had he spent more than he meant to that night? This is the key; for if he had we have a motive for murder. A stupid, besotted, irrational motive—but still a motive. And one that might appeal to a young man with George's proven record.

On this crucial question, his 'proof of evidence' given to his solicitor before the hearing varies from what he actually said in court.

The statement to Mr Hayes was quite specific: he took £3 out with him. In court he was equally definite: he took only £1 out of his wages plus what was left of a 25*s.* sweepstake win—at the most, £2 5*s.*

Why did he change his story? Could not the motive be that he realized he had taken out more money that night than usual, that during the course of his biggest binge ever he had spent more than his customary pound to thirty shillings—and that, in the words of his statement, "I was after some money. I had spent more than I meant to that night?"

I think that George Riley was guilty. I think he was guilty of capital murder in the course of furtherance of theft, and I must agree that no improper pressure was put on him by the police, who emerged creditably from the legal ordeal they had to face. But in Scotland he would not even have been convicted, let alone hanged: under Scots law, in the words of Sir J. H. A. MacDonald, Lord Justice Clerk in the mid-nineteenth century, and one of the greatest Scots criminal lawyers of all time: "No extra-judicial confession is, by itself, sufficient for conviction . . . What additional evidence shall suffice is a question of circumstances. A merely suspicious circumstance will rarely be enough."

Should, therefore, George Riley have been hanged?

"I still feel very bitter," says his mother. Such feelings are natural, and one respects Mr and Mrs Riley for their grief. But George had a fair trial, he was defended by one of the most able circuit lawyers of the day, the summing up was, in the view of the Court of Criminal Appeal and his own lawyers, unassailable. What more did the Home Secretary need to justify a hanging within the existing law?

There were no other extenuating circumstances. This was not a first conviction. It was a dastardly crime. What else could Mr Butler do?

Personally, I would have reprieved; despite all the arguments and all the dictates of logic, my pen still would have wavered before condemning a man to death by reason of his own confession in a police-station. Perhaps I am soft, perhaps I am a sentimentalist. Certainly I would have made a very bad Home Secretary. But this sort of question, especially in a case such as George Riley's, can find its answer only in each individual's conscience.

CHAPTER TWENTY-FIVE

Victor John Terry

(1961)

HENRY WALLACE used to describe the twentieth century as "the Century of the Common Man". So far as the first fifty years are concerned he is probably right. But it would be more accurate to describe the second half of the century, at least so far, as "the Age of the Youngster".

Youth now has its head. Pop-singers, the bloom of puberty still on their cheeks, earn more than Cabinet Ministers and University professors. Black-jacketed louts speed through the night on high-powered motor-cycles "getting a ton-up". Every year an increasing number of schoolgirls know the pleasures of sexual intercourse. Huge sums of money are spent—and even larger sums earned—pandering to the tastes and delights of the young—pop-records, ten-pin bowling alleys, smart clothes, fancy hair-styles. "The Affluent Society" is breeding the children it deserves.

And they do not stop at murder.

In June 1960 four young thugs lay in wait in a quiet, darkened alley in Hounslow, a suburb of London. They were Francis "Flossie" Forsyth (18), Norman James Harris (23), Christopher Louis Darby (23), and Terence Lutt (17). They did not know who their victim would be: "Let's jump somebody!" had been the suggestion. It was purely a matter of chance who might in the last half-hour before midnight walk down the narrow footpath.

In fact, a twenty-three-year-old engineer named Alan Jee turned into the alleyway. Lutt punched him hard. He fell down covering his face with his hands and shouting, "What do you want me for?"

The answer was petty theft. As Harris later told the police, "The lads held him down, and I put my hand in his inside pocket to get his wallet, but there was nothing in there at all. Me, Darby, and Lutt were holding him down, and Forsyth was standing above us . . . I saw some blood on my hand . . . I realized 'Flossie' had put the boot in."

Indeed "Flossie" had. As he also told the police "The fellow was struggling, so I kicked him in the head to shut him up."

He succeeded only too well. Alan Jee died two days later, and when the police arrested "Flossie" Forsyth his blood was still on Forsyth's sharp-pointed, winkle-picker shoes.

Chris Darby, who denied taking part in the attack, though he admitted being present, was convicted of non-capital murder and sentenced to life imprisonment; the three others were convicted of capital murder in the course or furtherance of theft. Lutt, because he was under eighteen, was ordered to be detained during Her Majesty's pleasure. Forsyth and Harris were sentenced to death.

On November 10th, 1960 they were hanged. There was something of an outcry at "Flossie" Forsyth's death: he was the first eighteen-year-old youth to be hanged since Henry Jacoby in 1922. But young men of eighteen now consider themselves adults: why should they not bear the responsibilities of adulthood? As one lawyer interested in the case has told me, "I did not do anything about a reprieve for Forsyth. On the law as it stood I could see no reason for a reprieve. His youth was not a factor."

Norman Harris, five years older than Forsyth, was hanged without almost any public protest, though according to some people —including Mrs Elizabeth Howard, former Acting Secretary of the Howard League for Penal Reform—his death was more to be regretted than Forsyth's. After all, Harris himself had not kicked Jee, and there was no evidence that he knew beforehand that Forsyth was going to do so. "I believe that Harris was not legally convicted," Mrs Howard told me. "His offence was not capital."

No-one would question Mrs Howard's sincerity, but, with respect, she is wrong in law. Section 5, subsection (2) of the 1957 Homicide Act was quite explicit:

"If, in the case of [capital murder] two or more persons are guilty of the murder, it shall be capital murder in the case of any of them who by his own act caused the death of, or inflicted or attempted to inflict grievous bodily harm on the person murdered, *or who himself used force on that person in the course or furtherance of an attack on him.*"

The words I have italicized are vital, for they exactly describe what Norman Harris did—to quote again from his statement to the police: "Me, Darby, and Lutt were holding him down . . ." This statement was not evidence against Darby or Lutt, but it was enough to hang Harris; holding down the victim of an attack is certainly 'using force.'

There is no mystery about Home Secretary Butler's refusal to reprieve either of these two young men. As long as capital punishment remained, the Forsythes and the Harrises of this world were hanged. In such cases "youth was not a factor."

The Hounslow Footpath Murder is a suitable introduction to the far more complex case of Victor John Terry. For the two cases are linked by a bizarre coincidence: "Flossie" Forsyth and Terry knew each other. They came from the same drab, western suburbs of London. They had been friends. And on the day that Forsyth was hanged Terry also killed.

One hour and three minutes after Forsyth's execution Terry, with a gun hidden under his overcoat and accompanied by seventeen-year-old Philip Tucker, walked into the sub-branch of Lloyds Bank at Durrington, near Worthing.

Twenty-one-year-old cashier Andrew Barker was alone behind the counter. "What's this?" he asked. At that moment Henry Pull, the bank's grey-haired guard, came out of the cloakroom, where he had been boiling up a kettle for tea. The kettle was in his hand. He started as he saw the intruders, and jerked up his hand, something he used to do when about to speak. His hand touched Terry's arm. Terry stepped back, took out his gun, and at pointblank range fired.

The full shot entered Mr Pull's left eye, and he fell to the ground, dying.

"Where's the money?" asked Tucker.

Mr Barker said it was in a case behind the counter. Tucker came round and grabbed hold of a small leather Gladstone bag. He started towards the door. "No, not that one!" called out Mr Barker. Tucker returned, threw down the bag, and took hold of a large attache-case containing £1000 in cash. Then he and Terry left the bank.

It was all over in minutes. "It was a concerted plan to rob a bank embarked upon and thought out carefully and coolly," Geoffrey Lawrence, Q.C., was later to say at Terry's trial.

Waiting outside in a stolen car were Alan Hosier and eighteen-year-old Valerie Salter, Terry's current girl friend. While the bank's alarm bell clanged the car roared away.

Later that morning it was found abandoned in Worthing. In it was the single-barrelled shot gun that Terry had fired, but no sign of the occupants or the money. Tucker and Hosier were soon picked up: a taxi-driver did not think they were the type of customer to give him a 10s. note for a 2s. 6d. fare and say "keep the change!" With remarkable quick thinking he immediately told the police.

Terry and Valerie Salter saw Hosier and Tucker being questioned by detectives on the Worthing front, and knew they must get away. Collecting the money at Valerie's home, where they had hidden it, they took a bus to Littlehampton, and hired a taxi to

T

take them on to Portsmouth. Three times the taxi was stopped at road blocks, but the police were looking for two young men— not a man and a woman.

On the Chichester By-pass a sergeant stopped them and asked their names. "I am Valerie Brown, and I live at Wiston Road, Worthing, No. 28," said Miss Salter. "Not 'Brown' much longer, dear, is it?" said Terry, holding her hand and cuddling her. He explained that they were on a shopping spree for her trousseau: they were going to be married in a few days' time.

The marriage was not the kind solemnized in church. On the following Sunday they were arrested at a Glasgow hotel, where they had booked in as "Mr and Mrs Diamond", a honeymoon couple from south of the border.

They were flown to London and driven to Worthing, where Terry was charged with capital murder, Tucker and Hosier with non-capital murder, and Valerie Salter with harbouring and assisting Terry, knowing him to have committed capital murder.

It was a dastardly crime, and coming so soon after the Hounslow Murder there was very little public sympathy for any of the young people in the dock. To the police Terry had claimed that the murder was an accident: that Pull had tried to wrench the gun away, and as his finger was on the trigger it went off. But the preliminary evidence at the magistrates' hearing disclosed that Pull's fingerprints were not on the gun.

Yet he always maintained to Mr William Scales, the solicitor's managing clerk, who not only fought for him as a lawyer, but became his friend, that Pull's death was an accident. "I asked him didn't he think about "Flossie" Forsyth when he set out on the job," Mr Scales has told me. "But he insisted that Forsyth's case was totally different. It was nothing to do with it. 'If the old man hadn't grabbed the gun it wouldn't have gone off,' he said. 'Why then was it loaded?' I asked. 'I might have fired it to frighten someone,' said Terry. 'But you couldn't kill a cat with it at ten yards. It's a garden gun for scaring cats!' "

So far as the judge and jury were concerned, this then was Terry's defence—his only defence—throughout the early stages of his trial. It did not get very far. Mr Lewis Nicholls, director of Scotland Yard's Forensic Laboratory, said that the gun, though only a cheap 9 mm. shotgun, would be lethal at close range against exposed portions of the body. He agreed it had no safety catch, but maintained that it could not go off accidentally.

Alan King Hamilton, Q.C., Terry's leading counsel (now an Old Bailey judge), tried to persuade Andrew Barker to admit that there was a struggle for the gun between Terry and Henry Pull. But the

young cashier was adamant: there was no fight between the two
men, they did not even touch, except for a slight brush on Terry's
arm by Pull's involuntary gesture with his hand.

When the prosecution case ended, on the third day of the trial
at Lewes Assizes in March 1961, no-one would have laid decent
odds on Terry's acquittal. He had been positively identified by
Barker. The gun had been traced to him. His prints were on it.
He had been in Worthing on the day of the murder, he had fled
with money stolen from the bank, and his plea of accident seemed
a non-starter. What more could the jury want?

At this stage Mr King Hamilton rose to his feet, and in his
opening speech for the defence transformed this run-of-the-mill
bank shooting trial into something extraordinary. For the first
time the jury heard of a new defence—a defence that, if true,
would inevitably reduce Terry's crime to manslaughter.

Mr King Hamilton pleaded that his client was suffering from
"diminished responsibility", that, to use the words of the Homicide Act, Terry "was suffering from such abnormality of mind . . .
as substantially impaired his mental responsibility for his acts
and omissions in doing or being a party to the killing".

What form did his abnormality take? Mr King Hamilton explained: "Terry believes that the spirits of dead people invade
the bodies of living persons, and at times he believes he behaves
as the spirits tell him. He has been under the impression that
his body and mind have been invaded by the spirit and mind
of the American gangster who achieved some notoriety under
the name 'Legs' Diamond . . . It was not Terry and the girl who
were making their get-away from the crime. It was 'Legs' Diamond
and his gangster moll."

It was a tall story to expect the jury to believe. Joan of Arc
and General de Gaulle hear their voices, and we all know of people
who think they are Jesus Christ or the Duke of Wellington. But
Jack 'Legs' Diamond? Was he a feasible candidate for reincarnation?

Mr King Hamilton told the jury that Terry, who was born during
an air raid, was brought up by an uncle and aunt while his father
was in the Army, and had twice lost pet dogs destroyed for
attacking chickens. His childhood was unhappy, and when finally
his uncle of whom he was genuinely fond, died, "he lost every
object of his affection." He developed a grudge against the world,
and exhibited symptoms of schizophrenia. Then, to top it all, since
the summer of 1960 he had taken to drugs and become an amphe-
tamine-addict.

Terry did not himself go into the witness-box to testify as to

T*

one word of this—or be cross-examined by Geoffrey Lawrence, Q.C., for the Crown. Instead witnesses were called to support the story. Mr and Mrs Terry told the jury of their son's strange moods, of how—for instance—he was once seen standing for six minutes with his arms rigid and flexed at the elbows looking into a mirror. Mrs Terry told how he used to talk about visitors from outer space and once said he wanted to wear a space suit. And his father spoke of his eleven jobs in two years, and said the lad was getting so difficult he told him he ought to go and see a psychiatrist.

The drug-addiction was confirmed by a number of witnesses, including a Worthing detective inspector, who while inquiring into the circulation of drugs among young people in that town learned that Terry—who was working there—took 'purple hearts', the so-called pep pills which contained amphetamine in a potentially dangerous proportion and should only have been available on a doctor's prescription.

His employer also came to tell the jury of an incident when he saw Terry sitting at a table surrounded by girls, in true gangster fashion. The youth was leaning back, throwing 'purple hearts' in the air and catching them in his mouth. "You nut case, what are you doing?" asked the man. "That's nothing!" replied Terry. "I've already taken seven today!" According to P. H. Connell, an expert on amphetamine addiction, such a dosage would be enough in itself, if maintained, to cause symptoms of insanity. The employer soon dismissed him.

'Purple hearts' were not the only form in which Terry took amphetamine. If he could not get it any other way Terry would buy a benzedrine inhaler at a chemist's, break open the holder, and eat the amphetamine-soaked strips inside, a young Worthing friend named Peter Russon told the jury. He admitted he had done so himself as well, but his intake was much less than Terry's.

"When a man takes as much amphetamine as would be found in one benzedrine inhaler he is expected to be out of touch with reality and unable to appreciate the consequences of his acts. He is not, however, confused," a psychiatrist has told me. Terry not only took the drug: he washed it down afterwards with beer or rum—maintained Russon—which would only have made its effect all the worse.

Certainly Terry's behaviour in the weeks preceding the murder seems to have been erratic. Russon told the jury of an incident when he tried to throw himself from the top of the ballroom where he worked, and a girl came forward to describe an occasion when he ran down to the beach and stood staring out to sea with a gun in his hand.

But the most impressive witnesses were two psychiatrists—Dr A. Spencer Paterson, Physician in Charge of the Department of Psychiatry at the West London Hospital, and Dr Felix Brown, Consultant Psychiatrist at Hampstead General Hospital. Their evidence was clear cut: in their view Terry was not shamming. According to Dr Paterson he was living in a dream-world induced by incipient schizophrenia aggravated by drugs. Dr Brown too said, "Terry is an extremely psycopathic personality who has had episodes of a schizophrenic type of psychosis, especially under the influence of drugs."

Both experts agreed that Terry was not insane within the meaning of the McNaughton Rules: he knew what he was doing and that he was doing wrong. But both were adamant that he was suffering from diminished responsibility. If he had not taken the drugs he would not have committed the murder, said Dr Brown.

In answer the prosecution called two expert witnesses: Dr John Dalziel Wyndham Pearce, in charge of the psychiatric department at St Mary's Hospital, Paddington, and Dr Francis Brisby, then principal medical officer at Brixton prison, where Terry had been held awaiting trial.

Their evidence was totally opposed to that of the two psychiatrists for the defence. Both said that they had found in their interviews with Terry no evidence of mental deficiency, psychosis, psycho-neurosis, or psychopathic state. His mental responsibility for his acts was in no way diminished. As to Jack 'Legs' Diamond, Dr Pearce called Terry a sham. In his low Scots tones he told the jury: "In my view, Terry is trying to pass himself off as a person who is strange and abnormal—not too mad, but mad enough."

One did not have to be telepathic to discern which set of experts the judge preferred. At one point Mr Justice Stable interrupted Mr (now Sir) Geoffrey Lawrence's cross-examination of Dr Paterson to say: "Mr Lawrence, I imagine the jury would agree with the proposition that if Terry's story was true and the whole of this operation was carried out by him while he really thought he was 'Legs' Diamond, a distinguished Chicago gangster, obviously they would not be able to hold him responsible for what he is doing, if that story is true." The "*distinguished* Chicago gangster" is rather choice.

In his summing up at the end of the eight-day trial the judge did not spend much time on the doctors. He had in front of him three volumes, totalling 103 pages, of the transcript of the medical evidence: it was his copy, scored with red pencil marks, and with some pages turned down. "I am not going to attempt to analyse these three volumes of medical evidence," he told the jury. "I am going to hand you the transcript, and you can study them at your leisure." He read them the words of the "diminished responsibility" section of the Homicide Act, told them that basically the dispute between the doctors was whether Terry was shamming or not, and if they thought he was his defence of abnormality of mind fell to the ground—and that was all. The jury received no further direction as to the law or facts of the medical issue, until some time later they came back into court and asked the judge for his further assistance—when Mr Justice Stable went into the matter a little more fully.

The judge was also concerned that the jury should not be under any misapprehension as to Terry's now half-forgotten plea of accident. During his summing up he got up, asked for the gun, walked over to the jury-box, pulled the trigger, and showed the jury that it could not be fired without being cocked. It was an effective demonstration.

The jury took two and a half hours to consider their verdict. And while they were out Mr Scales went downstairs to see his client. He appears to have been more worried than Terry was: he found the three young men sitting in a cell singing.

The verdicts, when they came, were—guilty on all counts. Terry was sentenced to death, Hosier and Tucker to life imprisonment. The only possible surprise was in Valerie Salter's fate: after a speech by the judge, in which he told her that she did what she believed to be right and spoke of her "very young heart", he put her on a year's probation. "Go, go back to your friends and family, and start life afresh," said the judge.

Beneath the court, Terry was adjusting himself to his new life— the few weeks that remained of it. "Well, I suppose that's it!" he said to Mr Scales.

"No, there are plenty of things yet!" replied the solicitor's clerk.

And, indeed, Mr King Hamilton argued Terry's appeal in front of the Lord Chief Justice, Lord Parker, and Justices Ashworth and Lawton with considerable persistence and power. "The jury were told, in effect, to sum up and analyse the medical evidence for themselves," he maintained.

Terry was in court throughout the hearing. The courtroom was crowded, as is usual when the Lord Chief Justice's court hears a major appeal. I was there myself: one could sense the tension beneath the soft voices of the lawyers.

When finally Lord Parker came to give judgment, for a while

it seemed as if the appellant had won. "The court would like to say emphatically that they disapprove of the judge's merely reading the words of the 'diminished responsibility' section to the jury," said Lord Parker. "A proper explanation of the terms of the section ought to be put before the jury." Later the Lord Chief's language was even stronger: "So far as the handling of the two transcripts of medical evidence to this jury is concerned, the court feels that that is a bad practice and in an ordinary case would not be an adequate direction to the jury in regard to the medical evidence . . . It is an objectionable practice."

But the appeal was still dismissed. Explained Lord Parker: "It is perfectly clear that at the end of the eight days, and when the jury retired, the real and only question was: Was Terry fooling his psychiatrists or was his story a genuine story? . . . In the light of what clearly, therefore, was the question in the end, it seems to this court that the summing up is quite unexceptionable."

He refused Mr King Hamilton's application for a certificate that a point of law of general public importance arose so as to carry the appeal farther, to the House of Lords. The courts had pronounced their last word.

Once again Mr Scales trudged downstairs to see his client in the cells beneath a court. "What now?" asked Terry.

"This still isn't the end!" said Mr Scales.

A conference was held between Mr King Hamilton, John Bolland, his junior, and Mr Scales. A petition was prepared by the two barristers; Mr Scales went through it with them, made certain suggestions, and then a final draft was typed out and sent to the Home Office. Terry was not asked to sign it.

In due course came a letter from Sir Charles Cunningham saying that the petition had been considered but rejected. Terry must die, as planned. The execution date—Thursday, May 26th.

"Time was running out," Mr Scales recalls. "I made an appointment to see someone at the Home Office on the Wednesday. At about 10.30 A.M. I presented myself there and saw Mr Graham-Harrison. He explained that Mr Butler, the Home Secretary, was in Spain, but that he had a telephone call booked to him at 3 o'clock that afternoon. He said he would be only too happy to hear what I had to say and pass it on to the Secretary of State."

"What did you tell him?" I asked Mr Scales.

"Well, I told him what I knew of the boy personally," he said. "He was a very likeable fellow—not the sort of man I would want to bring home, but apart from his criminal exploits a very likeable boy, with a good sense of humour."

Throughout the many hours they spent together Mr Scales had

continually tried to trip up Terry in his 'Legs' Diamond story, and every time he failed. "I told Mr Graham-Harrison this," he said. "And I also told him something that Terry said to me the very first time I saw him at Worthing, on the morning before he appeared in front of the magistrates for the first time. The boy said, 'If I go inside for some time, they'll have to give me treatment, you know, because if they don't I'll probably do the same thing again when I come out. If I go inside and they don't give me treatment I may as well swing now.' It was a remarkable thing to say, and I told Mr Graham-Harrison that.

"I was there for about two hours, and I said all I could." The while Mr Graham-Harrison took notes.

Mr Scales did not again see his client. The men had become close, and called each other by their first names. Terry had drawn a sketch of Mr Scales while he was at Brixton awaiting trial. "If he was shamming he must have been a very good actor," comments Mr Scales. "At the end I think I knew him better than anyone else. Quite honestly I think he was a psychopathic case."

The two men said their farewells two days before the execution, on the Tuesday, when Mr Scales went to tell him of his forthcoming visit to the Home Office on the next day. "He seemed pretty normal and to a certain extent resigned," says Mr Scales.

Whether resigned or, as a fellow-prisoner has claimed in the now extinct magazine *Today*, screaming "Let me go! Please, God, help me!" Victor John Terry was taken to the execution room and hanged.

There was nothing in Terry's police record to justify a reprieve. He had been convicted of crime four times before; first at the age of nine, lastly, in December 1958, when he was sent to Borstal for robbing with violence an old man, whom he had bludgeoned with a sand-filled sock.

He came out of Borstal for this offence only four months before he killed Mr Pull, and in that time he did little honest work, apart from his stint at the Worthing dance-hall. He was a boastful, vain young criminal.

Nor were there any extenuating circumstances about the crime itself. Dr Spencer Paterson has admitted to me, "It can be said that one could not have a more cold-blooded case of killing a man whose job it was to defend society."

Nevertheless, Dr Paterson and Dr Felix Brown still maintain today that Terry should not have been convicted of capital murder, and that he certainly should not have been hanged. To quote Dr Paterson: "I am most unhappy about this case. I cannot under any circumstances imagine myself as a psychiatrist of thirty years' experience having written a report to the Home Secretary which would have led to this man's execution."

The fact remains that five other doctors took a contrary view: Doctors Pearce and Brisby at the trial, and the three other doctors who saw Terry at the medical inquiry that I know the Home Office held after the trial and before the execution. I have spoken to one of these other doctors, and I can surely be revealing no official secret when I say that the medical inquiry found no medical reason to recommend a reprieve. Indeed, it is obvious: if they had Terry would never have been hanged.

"He is absolutely sane," Dr Pearce has said at his trial. "This man's defence was a desperate defence, inspired by a ruthless, callous, cunning young man," his prosecutor had told the jury.

Are they right? Or does the truth lie with the still-obstinate Doctors Paterson and Brown? Or does it rest, as so often in life, shimmering uncertainly in the mist between two diametrically opposed points of view?

To try to answer these questions one must go back to Terry's arrest and see how thereafter his defence evolved.

With the co-operation of Mr Scales and Doctors Paterson and Brown I have been able to peel off the onion-skins of how his case was prepared for trial.

"I saw him in the cells at Worthing on Monday, the day after his arrest," says Mr Scales. "I only knew of the case from what I had read in the newspapers, and I told him I would be going into the whole matter later. But in the meanwhile I asked him if, merely as background, he would let me have his life as he remembered it up to embarking on the raid. I asked him to write it all down. 'How many pages do you want?' he asked. 'As many as you like,' I replied. And next week when I saw him again he handed me five hand-written pages of foolscap."

On reading the statement, Mr Scales thought it was a matter for a psychiatrist. He consulted with Mr John Bolland, Terry's junior counsel, and he agreed. This is how Doctors Paterson and Brown came into the picture: Mr Scales asked them to visit Terry at Brixton.

I have read this statement, and it is, indeed, a very full account of Terry's life—from the opening sentence describing the night of an air raid, when he was two years old, to the last: "All I have said is true I only hope something or somebody can change me before it's too late."

It tells the story of an unhappy early life, much the same as that outlined by his counsel at the trial. But it is also a tale of delinquency, of thieving and drinking and fighting, mixed up with references to "this feeling that processed me",—a feeling of hate that would not let "the real me" speak. He worshipped gangsters like Al Capone, 'Baby Face' Nelson, and John Dillinger, and knew that one day he would model himself on them. He says that he knew that one day he would kill.

However, it is perhaps significant that the statement contains no allusion to drugs or to Jack 'Legs' Diamond—or to the theory that his mind was taken possession of by the mind and spirit of a dead American gangster.

This arose only when Dr Paterson went to see Terry at Brixton. The doctor had been reluctant to go: "This has been a terrible murder, and I don't think I'll find anything at all," he told Mr Scales. But on January 5th, 1961, he saw the prisoner: it was the first of two long interviews before the trial.

Terry had already been in custody for nearly two months, and had frequently been seen by Dr Brisby. To this experienced prison doctor he appears to have said nothing about his having been 'possessed' by the spirit of the dead Diamond. But to Dr Paterson it was different: as Mr King Hamilton said, he was being questioned by a psychiatrist of experience, who had lived for years in a mental hospital, and was therefore familiar with how the mind of a schizophrenic worked. He unburdened himself, and described the onset and development of his early psychosis, and described the symptoms of amphetamine psychosis with its aggressions, its intense morbid elation, and its suicidal depression. States Dr Paterson: "I treated the prisoner entirely as if he were a patient. No prison doctor had attempted to gain his confidence and try to see the world through his eyes."

Dr Paterson has kept a verbatim record of his two interviews. It makes fascinating reading.

Terry seems to have spoken freely. He talks about having felt doomed from the age of thirteen, that at one time he believed he was not his parents' real child, that he thought he was an 'ally' from another planet—and then, almost in the same breath, he is talking about his hallucinations of grandeur: "I have even gone to the extent of thinking I could take over the rest of the world."

For the past two or three years he was convinced that there would be a war in 1960 or 1966—and that he would be hanged the same year.

He speaks of his addiction to drugs and, particularly, amphetamine.

And—most important of all—he describes how over the years he has felt himself increasingly subject to spells of being taken over by the mind and spirit of Jack 'Legs' Diamond. He was sure that it was this specific gangster, because—bow-legged like himself—Diamond's life was "more or less based on mine".

On the Tuesday before the murder he chewed up and swallowed five folds of amphetamine-soaked material—the entire contents of a benzedrine inhaler—and washed it down with beer and more beer on the Wednesday. From the Tuesday until the following Sunday, when he was arrested in Glasgow—apart from one lucid interval of five minutes in a Portsmouth cinema on the Friday—he claimed that he was possessed by the dead American gangster and powerless to modify his actions.

"Do you ever think of the man you killed or his family?" asked Dr Paterson.

"When I am in a mood and have these feelings I couldn't care less", said Terry. "But as I feel now—well, there is no feelings I could express—I feel such sympathy for them."

"And you say that this is the real you?"

"Yes."

"Does the real you ever talk to the 'Legs' Diamond you?"

"Often."

"Does he talk to you?"

"When I feel like this it drives me mad."

"What?"

"Trying to figure out what is inside me."

Later comes the even more bald passage:

"Was it you or 'Legs' Diamond who killed the bank guard?"

" 'Legs' Diamond."

Dr Paterson is still convinced that at the end of their first interview 'Legs' Diamond came back—at least in Terry's mind—to possess him. "He suddenly gave me a funny look," he has told me—and the transcript reads: "But doctor I have got that feeling now. I do want to be the greatest criminal in the world."

"Do you think that you are 'Legs' Diamond?"

"Yes."

The conclusion of the second interview was on a quieter note: "Do you think there is any chance of my getting rid of this thing?"

"What do you mean by 'this thing'?"

"These feelings I get. I just can't stand it much longer."

Dr Paterson saw Terry's parents, and a social worker also interviewed them. In early February 1961 the psychiatrist wrote to Mr Scales that in his view Terry was a borderline case of insanity caused by incipient schizophrenia aggravated by the effects of amphetamine. A copy of his findings was sent to Dr Brisby,

and as a result Dr Pearce was called in by the Director of Public
Prosecutions to visit the prisoner. He also had two interviews with
Terry, and in due course copies of his report and Dr Brisby's
were submitted to the Director, and further copies sent to Dr
Paterson.

This was not the only medical preparation for the trial. In late
February Terry was taken to Dr Dennis Hill's laboratory at the
Maudsley Hospital for an EEG investigation. But all the doc-
tors agreed that in this case the EEG was of no diagnostic value.

The stage was thus set for the battle of the experts at Lewes
Assizes in late March 1961.

And it had to be a battle of experts only, for the defence did
not produce one single relative, friend, or acquaintance to go into
the witness-box and tell the jury: "Vic Terry has said to me, 'I
am Jack "Legs" Diamond!'"

Dr Paterson is adamant that the importance of Terry's drug-
taking was not fully appreciated by the Crown's experts. Nowadays, everybody knows about 'purple hearts', but in 1961 this
was not so. Dr Pearce in the witness-box admitted that he had not
read Connell's *Amphetamine Psychosis*, a new and revolutionary
study of the effects of the drug. Furthermore, the judge wrongly,
in Dr Paterson's view, withdrew from the jury any consideration of
its influence upon Terry. "Drug-addiction is a disease," Mr King
Hamilton had argued. "It's a bad habit," retorted the judge—and
refused to let the jury consider the effect of the drug upon the
prisoner's mental condition.

Both Doctors Peterson and Brown are still unrepentant. "If
Terry had not committed a murder there is not the slightest doubt
that he would have been diagnosed as a schizophrenic and had
appropriate treatment," says Dr Paterson. "I think that after five
years of treatment he would have been a perfectly normal chap,"
says Dr Brown. "When he raided the bank at Worthing he was
acting a part in a fantasy of his own making."

These are two gentlemen of considerable repute, and held in
high esteem in their profession. It is difficult to believe that they
could have been fooled by a young villain aged twenty.

On the other hand, Doctors Pearce and Brisby—and the doctors
of the medical inquiry—are also of high repute.

Why did Home Secretary Butler prefer one set of medical men
to the other? What tipped the balance?

The obvious answer is that Terry's jury—albeit without seeing
and hearing him tell his own story—rejected him as a sham. And
clearly this is a view with which agreed the experienced and human
lawyer who sat as his judge.

At the trial all was concentrated on the simple issue: was Terry lying when he said he was possessed by Jack 'Legs' Diamond? Even Dr Paterson at one stage was impelled in cross-examination by Geoffrey Lawrence to concede this the central issue:

"What is the abnormality of mind which you say this man was suffering from at the time when he committed these acts?"

"That he had a delusion that he was possessed by another person—by a spirit."

"Anything else?"

"No, that is the main thing."

"That is the abnormality?"

"Yes."

On this stark point the defence of Victor John Terry was based —and ultimately came to ruin.

It seemed a wildly improbable story. And we know that it took Terry some time to present it even to those endeavouring to assist him. Dr Paterson explained: "It is very common for a schizophrenic to be extremely shy about his symptoms, even when his life is at stake; he is ashamed. I know of many men who would rather go to the gallows than admit to insanity.' But the fact remains that only to Dr Paterson—and only two months after the murder—did Terry first say to anyone: "I am Jack 'Legs' Diamond!"

Dr Paterson thinks that Terry was not reprieved because of public opinion—"the man had committed a dastardly crime, and must expect to undergo the extreme penalty"—and because "there did not seem to be any practical alternative. The psychiatrists could not say that the man was certainly curable; although I do not believe he would ever have committed such a crime again."

Possibly this is right. Possibly, however, the reason for the hanging is altogether different: I have reason to believe that in the condemned cell Terry may have admitted to a visitor that the Jack 'Legs' Diamond story was not true.

Personally, I think that Terry died because he pitched his case too high. Like the Home Secretary, I have no psychiatric qualifications. But, to my mind, his story was just too pat, just too perfect an answer. Even Dr Brown will not commit himself unreservedly to a statement that Terry genuinely believed himself to be Diamond. "I do not know, and no-one can know", he has told me at his London club, "whether he genuinely believed that he was taken possession of by the spirit of Jack 'Legs' Diamond. I only know that he told me he was, and that such forms of possession are a known medical fact—especially with schizo-

phrenics. Terry was not a constitutional schizophrenic, in my
view, but he would, under the influence of amphetamine, undoubtedly have displayed symptoms not easily distinguishable
from those of schizophrenia.

"He was an immature, emotionally unstable young man, who
had hysterical fantasies—which, I quite agree, he may well have
exaggerated."

And the exaggerations did him down.

Perhaps there is a case to be made for Terry as a psychopathic case, as a young man in whom incipient schizophrenia
merged with amphetamine-addiction to produce a killer on the
borderline of sanity. But nuances were lost in the vivid black-and-
white world created by his own defence.

I believe the truth is that Terry from time to time in adoles-
cent day-dreams played make-believe with himself, picturing himself as a gangster. In his handwritten, potted biography to Mr
Scales at the very start of the case he wrote that he worshipped
people like Capone, Nelson, and Dillinger, and it is quite con-
ceivable that on occasions he weaved fantasies in his mind about
his being a 'tough', remorseless gangster—whether it be Capone,
Dillinger, or 'Legs' Diamond. He read only trash, mostly dealing
with gangsters and horror: his favourite films were 'tough-guy'
gangster stories. He was star-struck with violence and gangsterism.
He was 'Billy Liar' with a gun.

It may well be that this attitude of mind—coupled with his
other symptoms and addiction to a dangerous drug—is in itself
a mental illness. That such a person is, in psychiatric terms, a
psychopath, and not wholly answerable for his actions.

He did not want to die. He was not some world-weary killer,
anxious only to escape into the relief of death. Neither was he a
fool. A psychiatrist—a friendly, competent psychiatrist (Dr Paterson)—comes to see him. He talks more freely about himself than
perhaps he has ever done before. He talks about being 'possessed'
by 'Legs' Diamond. Obviously, this is important, because then
comes another able psychiatrist (Dr Pearce), who also asks him
about his 'possession'. Perhaps this is something that will save
him? Perhaps there is something in all this psychiatrist stuff after
all.

He is a bright lad. He exaggerates a bit. Yes, of course, he was
'Legs' Diamond at the time he committed the murder: no doubt
about it. It was not Victor Terry who killed the old man in the
bank, it was Diamond. You cannot hang Vic Terry for something
Diamond did, can you?

Dr Pearce listens, studies the boy—and thinks he is lying. Dr

Paterson listens, knows more of amphetamine addiction (because of his knowledge of the work of P. H. Connell), and believes he is telling the truth. Neither expert is a fool; neither is insincere. And what is my conclusion? That they were both right.

There is too much in Terry's early history, corroborated at a very early stage in his defence, to be ignored. The fantasy that he was not his father's child, that he was different from other people, that he wanted to kill, that he came from outer space, the catatonic stances with arms rigid and flexed at the elbows: they cannot all be gainsaid. Neither can the effects of the amphetamine drug in the 'purple-heart' pills and the benzedrine inhalers. A standard textbook on Clinical Psychiatry states unreservedly; "Amphetamine addicts not infrequently present a paranoid picture which leads to their being diagnosed as suffering from schizoprenia."

It is too facile to discount all this merely because it only came to light as part of the defence of a young thug charged with capital murder. To quote Dr Paterson again: "If Terry had not committed a murder there is not the slightest doubt that he would have been diagnosed as a schizophrenic and had appropriate treatment."

Even so, I think he exaggerated to Doctors Pearce and Brisby. He 'laid it on', and these two able doctors saw through it. At the same time I believe that possibly they did not fully appreciate the effect of amphetamine addiction. 'Purple hearts' had been on sale to the general public until about a year before: so little did the authorities know of their dangerous side-effects. Only when the Council of the Pharmaceutical Society of Great Britain protested did the Government put the pills on the Poisons List, available on prescription only. Yet still the authorities remained laggard in their treatment of this menace: three years after Terry was executed, in February 1964, the Council was again complaining to the Government and calling for executive action—this time to make unlawful possession of the drug a criminal offence.

Against this background, the evidence of Doctors Pearce and Brisby—and the failure to recommend mercy by the Home Office medical inquiry—becomes comprehensible.

The only reason for a reprieve would have been medical. Yet the Home Secretary's advisers in perfect good faith told him that no such reason existed. At the time, I am not saying that they were wrong. But one cannot quell the disturbing thought that it was not the law, but medicine that failed in Terry's case.

If more had then been known in official circles of the vicious

effects of amphetamine, might not the doctors have advised Mr
Butler differently? A young man, not wanting to die, played up
his (I believe) genuine mental plight and the result, in the state
of current medical knowledge, was an execution over which one
can still feel uneasy.

PART FOUR
Epilogue

CHAPTER TWENTY-SIX

Some Personal Conclusions

THE reprieve system was typically English, evolved over the centuries, as much a creature of chance as of planning.

Other countries have decided the fate of capital offenders differently. In India and some of the American states the trial judge has a discretion, in parts of the Commonwealth the whole Cabinet takes the decision, in France (the only European country where capital punishment is still effective for civil crimes) judge and jury together decide. In no other country in modern times has it been the responsibility of a single Cabinet Minister, as in Britain.

Abolitionists tended to disapprove of the system more than those who favoured capital punishment. If the decision had not been taken privately by one man they believed that more people might have been reprieved. It was done hugger-mugger, and was, therefore, suspect.

Admittedly, some abolitionists thought the whole question unimportant. The Earl of Harewood wrote to me:

"I am afraid I cannot help you. If there is a field kitchen supplying food to starving people, an inquiry into the quality of the cooking is of a very specialised interest. I do not believe this country, or any other, should operate the death penalty, so I suppose that I believe that, while we retain barbaric laws, the Royal Prerogative should be exercised on every single occasion—but this point of view is not particularly interesting in your historical survey."

Yet as long as capital punishment continued the decision had to be taken somehow. Someone had to decide whether the sentence of the court should be carried out. Up to now I have refrained from expressing my own views on the overall merits of the system: they would have been out of place in the historical narrative of Parts I and II. But at the end of the book, and after several years' research, this is perhaps the time to attempt a personal evaluation.

There were four main criticisms of the system. To my mind, two were not valid, one was, and one was partially valid.

First, it was contended that a committee should have decided, and not one man alone. There should have been "a standing advisory committee composed of experts selected for their exceptional ability," Edward Gardner, Q.C., M.P. told me. Sydney Silverman, M.P., went even further and said that the accused man should have been entitled to be present, both sides should have been represented by counsel, and the tribunal should have given a reasoned judgment—as if it were a court.

At least one Home Secretary—the late J. R. Clynes—also advocated a committee, in his *Memoirs* published in the mid-thirties. But this view was not shared by any of the three Home Secretaries to whom I have talked: Lords Chuter-Ede, Tenby, and Morrison of Lambeth were all against the idea. Said Lord Chuter-Ede: "In the end, you get to one man—even in a committee of three."

Personally I agree. Committees are to be distrusted. As Maurice Wiggin once wrote in the *Sunday Times*: "Put three easy-going Englishmen round a table and call them a committee, and they instantly put on the committee face and start behaving like different people." Committees do not act boldly, and the decision for a reprieve sometimes had to be a bold one.

Besides, the Home Secretary always had facilities for expert advice—from the senior officials of his department.

Second, it was argued that it was contrary to justice for the Home Secretary not to reveal the reasons for his decisions. Even the prisoner himself never knew what factors affected his fate. "I still don't know why they did it!" a reprieved man has said to me.

Some saw this as a deliberate smokescreen, behind which the Home Office played blind man's buff with men's lives.

But Lord Gardiner—speaking with the immense prestige of a Lord Chancellor—spoke for most reasonable people when he told me in his office at the House of Lords in the early spring of 1965: "I think it is just as well that the Home Secretary does not give his reasons for refusing a reprieve. It would make his task even more difficult than it is already."

In fact, in Lord Gardiner's view the Home Secretary's task was not merely difficult: "It is, in truth, impossible. The reprieve system operates on the basis, as put forward in the Home Office memorandum to the Gowers Commission, that there are some cases of murder for which the penalty should be death and others —considered less terrible—where mercy can be exercised: that there is an unbroken chain of murders from the most heinous at one end to the least heinous at the other.

"The trouble is that wherever the Home Secretary draws the line at any particular point, the two cases on either side—up as

well as down—will be much the same. It is impossible for the
Home Secretary to do full justice in such circumstances—even
if one were to accept that capital punishment was in itself com-
patible with justice."

Third, it was alleged that it was flouting the wishes of the jury
not to accede to a recommendation for mercy unless the judge
concurred. Why have a system of jury recommendation if they
are not adhered to?

I must confess that this criticism appears to be sound. It is
impossible to estimate the number of people who were found guilty
of murder or sentenced to death only because a jury, in doubt as
to guilt, compromised on a mercy recommendation. It is also impossible to estimate how many prisoners convicted in this way were
yet hanged—which means that we hanged capital offenders whose
guilt was not necessarily accepted by every member of their jury.
We hanged people whose guilt was only half, or three-quarters,
proved.

The recommendation to mercy in capital cases was a nonsense, and should have been abolished many years ago. It was
effective only if the judge also recommended mercy. It was, as
Sir John Anderson once openly admitted, "merely a frill".

Fourth main criticism of the reprieve system was that it was
unfair. That it was arbitrary, illogical, and devoid of consistency.

"It's a thoroughly bad thing," Sydney Silverman told me, "that
I cannot tell whether or not at the time of his conviction, a man
will be reprieved." This may well have been true. But it did not
necessarily mean that reprieves were arbitrary or that there were
no rules.

To my mind, it simply meant that the infinite variety of human
life could not be caught upon the hooks of precise formulae,
that inevitably justice must be pragmatic. Certainty is an illusion
outside the world of mathematics.

In the end it was essentially a matter of confidence: whether or
not one trusted the strength of mind and basic, human compassion of
the civil servants and politicians who administered this aspect of the
nation's government.

They did not lack for critics to assail either their compassion or
their integrity. Some people whose views I canvassed regarded the
Home Office with cool cynicism, sometimes even with disgust.
Yet the fairest assessment of the Department came from a man
who was a dedicated abolitionist, Hugh J. Klare, Secretary of the
Howard League for Penal Reform: "I know the Home Office officials
and I know that they take these matters extremely seriously. They
conscientiously, carefully and seriously consider these things."

Even so, there is one aspect of the Home Office record which calls for adverse comment: the way they handled cases where the mental condition of the prisoner was in issue.

The Home Office paid lip-service, and rightly so, to the doctrine that if a capital offender's responsibility for his crime was substantially diminished by reason of his mental condition he should not be hanged—even though not certifiably insane. No doubt some would regard a bestial murderer's mental capacities as irrelevant. But to most people—and indeed to myself—it was the hallmark of any civilized system of criminal justice that you did not hang the mentally sick.

This was the Home Office's attitude. But if this was so, how can one explain—or accept—the hangings of Miles Giffard, Christie, and Victor John Terry? These three all committed appalling crimes, yet to the layman there was abundant evidence of mental impairment: a fourth man—Daniel Raven—was hanged in 1950 for the inexplicable murder of his parents-in-law, though he was an undoubted epileptic.

It seems that the Home Office did not always know where to draw the line between illness and evil. Perhaps modern science itself was to blame: as Hugh J. Klare wrote to *The Times* in March 1964, "We need to establish more sensitive machinery for obtaining all the medical, psychological and social facts that are necessary to assess the full implications of homicidal and suicidal behaviour." Nor is it any answer to say that, as happened in Terry's case, the jury considered the defence of diminished responsibility at the trial and rejected it: a jury was not a suitable tribunal for deciding conclusively where truth lay between two contending sets of courtroom psychiatrists.

The plain truth is—and this has nothing to do with whether one was for or against hanging—that in the mid-twentieth century we hanged murderers who were more sick than sinful. The psychiatrists may have learned a good deal about the human mind, but despite their pretensions, there were still many gaps in their knowledge. Freud was born not much more than a hundred years ago: how can one say that the psychiatrists who advised the Home Secretary that there were no medical reasons for saving Giffard, Christie, or Terry had any monopoly on truth or accuracy?

There remains the future. In years to come the Home Secretary's decision will not be: "Shall this murderer live or die?" but "How long shall he remain in prison?" Section 27 of the Prison Act of 1952 puts the responsibility for releasing prisoners from gaol under licence solely upon his shoulders. There are no legal

v

rules, no statutory limitations: it is entirely a matter for the Home Secretary's discretion.

In the early part of this century the average period of imprisonment served by a reprieved murderer was fifteen years. By the time the Homicide Act was enacted, in 1957, it had come down to nine years. And this was an enlightened policy, for reprieved murderers were—as was indicated by their being reprieved —people for whom there was something to be said. They were the kind of murderer whose moral guilt was the least.

But now all murderers are lumped together. The sentence of the court is the same for all—imprisonment for life. How long will life be in future? For how long should deliberate killers remain in prison, either by way of punishment or by way of protecting society from their havoc?

No-one knows. This is a new problem which the centuries of our history cannot help us to solve. It is a twentieth-century dilemma.

Lord Parker of Waddington, the Lord Chief Justice, once said: "If imprisonment is the proper way to deal with these people . . . then it must be a life sentence which approximates more to life." And Home Secretary Sir Frank Soskice said in the House of Commons debate on the Second Reading of Sydney Silverman's final Abolition Bill: "It might be a sex murderer, a murderer who had obvious inherent vicious propensities; a man whom one would say to oneself reluctantly was a man who would always be a danger and a menace to society. A man like that had to be kept in confinement for very long periods of time, it might be almost for the whole of his life."

On the other hand, Sir Alexander Paterson, one of the most respected prison administrators of the century, said in the early nineteen-thirties that to imprison a man for more than ten years was to "institutionalize" him: "It requires a superman to survive twenty years of imprisonment with character and soul intact . . . I gravely doubt whether an average man can serve more than ten continuous years in prison without deterioration."

"So what?" many people may counter. Exactly what "character and soul" does a brutal murderer possess that is worth preserving —at the risk of possible danger to innocent human beings? If John George Haigh, the acid-bath murderer of the late nineteen-forties, had not been hanged he might well now be released, padding across the carpeted lounge of yet another South Kensington hotel, seeking out a fresh victim.

In 1958 Donald George Hume was released after serving eight years of a twelve-year term for being accessory to the murder of Warren Street car-dealer Stanley Setty, in 1950. He promptly wrote in the *Sunday Pictorial*: "I did murder Setty." Within months he had shot and wounded a bank-manager in Brentford, and the following year he was convicted of a second murder in Switzerland. Should not such a man be incarcerated for the rest of his life?

Besides, experience in the United States has shown that Paterson was not necessarily correct in his gloomy views about the effect of long prison sentences.

Nathan Leopold, who served thirty-four years in gaol for his part in the notorious "Compulsion" murder of a young schoolboy in Chicago in 1924, and Robert Stroud, the famous 'Bird Man' of Alcatraz, are just two well-known instances of men who have survived apparently crippling terms of imprisonment without substantial impairment of their mental or physical faculties. In fact, they improved as human beings over their long years in prison.

But even were this not so, even if to imprison a man for more than twenty years was to make him rot; then let him rot—if his crime was sufficiently heinous, and his release constituted too great a danger to the public. In an age which condemns double-agents like George Blake to a sentence of forty-two years' imprisonment or Great Mail Train Robbers to thirty years' imprisonment, why alone should murderers be granted special leniency? Is not their crime at least as great?

Appendix

NOTES OF MAIN PRINTED SOURCES
PART I

Chapter 1

LAURENCE, JOHN: *A History of Capital Punishment with special Reference to Capital Punishment in Great Britain* (Sampson Low, 1932).

WHITELOCK, D.: *English Historical Documents*, vol. I, c. 500–1042 (Eyre and Spottiswoode, 1955).

POLLOCK, F., AND MAITLAND, F. W.: *History of English Law before Edward I*, vol. II (C.U.P., second edition, 1898).

POTTER, H.: *Historical Introduction to English Law and its Institutions* (Sweet and Maxwell, 1958).

PLUCKNETT, T.F.T.: *Concise History of the Common Law* (Butterworth, fifth edition, 1956).

HOLDSWORTH, W. S.: *A History of English Law*, vol. II (Methuen, third edition).

AUGUSTINE, ST.: *Epistles* (No. cxxxiii).

Chapter 2

STUBBS, W.: *Select Charters of English Constitutional History* (O.U.P., ninth edition, 1913. [The translation of the Latin text of William I's decree is the Author's.]

POLLOCK, F., AND MAITLAND, F. W.: *History of English Law before Edward I*, vol. II (C.U.P., second edition, 1898).

LANDMEAD, T. P. T-.: *English Constitutional History* [ed. T. F. T. Plucknett] (Sweet and Maxwell, tenth edition, 1947).

PLUCKNETT, T. F. T.: *Concise History of the Common Law* (Butterworth, fifth edition, 1956).

WELLS, C. E.: "Early Opposition to the Petty Jury" (in *Law Quarterly Review*, Vol. 30, Sweet and Maxwell).

KOESTLER, A., AND ROLPH, C. H.: *Hanged by the Neck* (Penguin, 1961).

STEPHEN, SIR JAMES FITZJAMES: *History of the Criminal Law of England*, vol. I (Macmillan, 1883).

Thompson v. *Director of Public Prosecutions*, reported in *The Times*, February 14th, 1962.

Bushell's Case, reported in 6 *State Trials* (1670) at p. 999.

ANDREWS, WILLIAM: *Bygone Punishments* (Philip Allan, second edition, 1931).

POTTER, H.: *Historical Introduction to English Law and its Institutions* (Sweet and Maxwell, 1958).

PLUCKNETT, T. F. T.: *Edward I and the Criminal Law* (C.U.P., 1960).

Chapter 3

CHITTY, JOSEPH, THE YOUNGER: *A Treatise on the Law of the Prerogatives of the Crown* (Butterworth, 1820).

Jurisdiction in Liberties Act, 1535 (27 Henry VIII, c. 24).

PICKTHORN, KENNETH: *Early Tudor Government: Henry VIII* (C.U.P., 1934).

CALVERT, E. ROY: *Capital Punishment in the Twentieth Century* (Putnam, 1927).

LAURENCE, JOHN: *A History of Capital Punishment with Special Reference to Capital Punishment in Great Britain* (Sampson Low, 1932).

BLACKSTONE, SIR WILLIAM: *Commentaries on the Laws of England*, vol. IV (O.U.P., 1769).

RADZINOWICZ, L.: *A History of English Criminal Law*, vol. I: "The Movement for Reform" (Stevens, 1948).
KOESTLER A., AND ROLPH, C. H.: *Hanged by the Neck* (Penguin, 1961).
An Act for better preventing the Horrid Crime of Murder, 1752 (25 Geo. III, c. 37)
CHITTY, JOSEPH, THE YOUNGER: *The Criminal Law* (1826).
Foster's "Crown Cases", 1762 [for the Case of William York].
RAYNER, J. L. AND CROOK, G. T. (ed): *Newgate Calendar*, vol. II (Navarre Society, 1926) [for The Case of 'Half-Hanged Smith'].

Chapter 4
TROUP, SIR EDWARD: *The Home Office* (Putnam, 1925).
NEWSAM, SIR FRANK: *The Home Office* ("New Whitehall" series; Allen and Unwin, 1954).
The First Report of the Commissioners (inquiring into the Home Office) appointed by Act 25 Geo. III, c. 19 (Command Paper 309-1806).
THOMSON, M. A.: *The Secretaries of State 1681–1782* (O.U.P., 1932).
TEMPLEWOOD, VISCOUNT: *The Shadow of the Gallows* (Gollancz, 1951).
CHITTY, JOSEPH, THE YOUNGER: *A Treatise on the Law of the Prerogatives of the Crown* (Butterworth, 1820).
PARKER, CHARLES STUART (ed.): *Sir Robert Peel, Early Life from Papers*, vol. I, (John Murray, 1891).
GARDINER, GERALD: *Capital Punishment as a Deterrent: and the Alternative* (National Campaign for the Abolition of Capital Punishment, 1961).
GASH, NORMAN: *Mr Secretary Peel* (Longmans, 1961).
WAKEFIELD, EDWARD GIBBON: *Facts relating to the Punishment of Death in the Metropolis* (London, second edition, 1832).
DYMOND, ALFRED W.: *The Law on its Trial; or Personal Recollections* (Bennett, 1865).

Chapter 5
Morning Herald: A Selection of Papers upon Punishment of Death, vol. II (Hatchard, 1836).
The Judgment of Death Act, 1823 (4 Geo. IV, c. 48).
Report and Evidence of the Royal Commission on Capital Punishment 1866.
HALE, LESLIE: *Hanged in Error* (Penguin, 1961).

Chapter 6
STEPHEN, SIR JAMES FITZJAMES: *History of the Criminal Law of England*, vol. I (Macmillan, 1883).
TEMPLEWOOD, VISCOUNT: *The Shadow of the Gallows* (Gollancz, 1932).
BUCKLE, G. E. (ed.): *Letters of Queen Victoria*, second series, vol. II (Murray, 1925).
DYMOND, ALFRED W.: *The Law on its Trial; or Personal Recollections* (Bennett, 1865).
Report and Minutes of Evidence of the Royal Commission on Capital Punishment, 1953 (Cmd 8953, H.M.S.O.).
LEE, SIR SIDNEY: *King Edward VII: A Biography* (Macmillan, 1927).
Report of the Royal Commission on Capital Punishment, 1866.

Chapter 7
Report and Minutes of Evidence of the Royal Commission on Capital Punishment, 1953 (Cmd. 8953, H.M.S.O.).
TROUP, SIR EDWARD: *The Home Office* (Putnam, 1925).
Regina v. Lipski was reported extensively in *The Times*. Home Secretary Mathews's pronouncement in the House of Commons is reported in Hansard for August 12th, 1887 (col. 753).
GARDINER, A. G.: *The Life of Sir William Harcourt*, Vol. I (Constable, 1923).
Home Secretary Gladstone's dictum to the House of Commons is reported in Hansard for April 11th, 1907 (Col. 366).

Appendix

Appendix 315

Chapter 8

SAMPSON, ANTHONY: *Anatomy of Britain Today* (Hodder and Stoughton, 1965).

CAMPBELL, GEORGE A.: *The Civil Service in Britain* (Penguin, 1955).

NEWSAM, SIR FRANK: *The Home Office* ("New Whitehall" series; Allen and Unwin, 1954).

Rules regulating the execution of capital sentences (S.R. and O. No. 444, H.M.S.O., 1902).

THOMPSON, SIR BASIL: *The Criminal* (Hodder and Stoughton, 1925).

Report and Minutes of Evidence of the Royal Commission on Capital Punishment, 1953 (Cmd. 8953, H.M.S.O.).

Hansard (House of Lords) Vol. 20, cols. 1191/1202 [for Homicide Bill debate in House of Lords].

GIBSON, E., AND KLEIN, S.: *Study in Causes of Delinquency and the Treatment of Offenders*, No. 4: "Murder", Home Office Research Unit Report (H.M.S.O., 1961).

Observer March 18th, 1962 [for assessment of post-Homicide Act reprieves].

Hansard (House of Commons) Vol. 632, col. 74 [for written answer by Home Secretary on pre-trial medical reports).

Chapter 9

Prison Rules, S.I. No. 1073 (H.M.S.O. 1949).

SMITH, L. W. MERROW, AND HARRIS, J.: *Prison Screw* (Herbert Jenkins, 1962).

BOWKER, A. E.: *A Lifetime with the Law* (W. H. Allen, 1961) [for letter of Judge informing Home Secretary of capital sentence].

Regina v. *Xinaris*, reported in (1955) 43 Criminal Appeal Reports at page 29 *n*.

Regina v. *Porritt*, reported in (1961) 45 Criminal Appeal Reports at page 348.

Regina v. *McMenemy*, reported in *Daily Express*, November 7th, 1961, and *The Times*, November 25th, 1961.

LAURENCE, JOHN: *A History of Capital Punishment with special Reference to Capital Punishment in Great Britain* (Sampson Low, 1932).

GREW, B. D.: *Prison Governor* (Herbert Jenkins, 1958).

BENNETT, JOHN WHEELER: *John Anderson, Viscount Waverley* (Macmillan, 1962).

TAYLOR, H. A.: *Jix; Viscount Brentford* (Stanley Paul, 1933).

Hansard (House of Lords) [for Lord Stonham's speech, November 9th, 1961].

Regina v. *Thatcher*, reported in *Daily Express*, March 13th, 1963.

WOODLAND, W. LLOYD: *The Trial of Thomas Henry Allway* (Geoffrey Bles, 1929).

PART II

Chapter 10

Hansard (House of Commons) Vol. 634, col. 1795 [for Mr Butler's speech].

Regina v. *Thatcher* reported in *Daily Express* March 13th 1963.

Report and Minutes of Evidence of the Royal Commission on Capital Punishment, 1949–1953 (Cmd 8953, H.M.S.O.).

Prison Rules, S.I. No. 1073 (H.M.S.O., 1949).

SMITH, L. W. MERROW AND HARRIS, J.: *Prison Screw* (Herbert Jenkins, 1962).

BOWKER, A. E.: *A Lifetime with the Law* (W. H. Allen, 1961).

Regina v. *Oswald Augustus Grey*, reported in *The Times*, October and November 1962.

Regina v. *Xinaris*, reported in (1955) 43 Criminal Appeal Reports at p. 29 *n*.

Regina v. *Porritt*, reported in (1961) 45 Criminal Appeal Reports at p. 348.

WOODLAND, W. LLOYD: *The Trial of Thomas Henry Allaway* (Geoffrey Bles, 1929).

Daily Mirror, October 3rd, 1958 [for condemned prisoner marrying in prison].

GREW, B. D.: *Prison Governor* (Herbert Jenkins, 1958).

GOWERS, SIR ERNEST: *A Life for a Life* (Chatto and Windus, 1956).

NEWSAM, SIR FRANK: *The Home Office* ("New Whitehall" series; Allen and Unwin, 1954).

TAYLOR, H. A.: *Jix; Viscount Brentford* (Stanley Paul, 1933).

Chapter 11
Report and Minutes of Evidence of the Select Committee on Capital Punishment, 1929–1930.
CLYNES, J. R.: *Memoirs*, vol. II (Hutchinson, 1937).
BENNETT, JOHN WHEELER: *John Anderson, Viscount Waverley* (Macmillan, 1962).
TEMPLEWOOD, VISCOUNT: *The Shadow of the Gallows* (Gollancz, 1951).
Hansard (House of Commons) Vol. 634, February 16th, 1961, col. 1798 [for quotation from R. A. Butler].
Regina v. *Dunford*, reported in *Sunday Times*, January 3rd, 1965.
KOESTLER, A., AND ROLPH, C. H.: *Hanged by the Neck* (Penguin, 1961).
Regina v. *Edgar Valentine Black*, reported in *Daily Telegraph*, November 7th, 1963.
Rex. v. *William John Gray*, reported in *Daily Express*, April 5th, 1948.
Regina v. *Christopher Simcox*, reported in *Sunday Times*, March 15th, 1964, and *Daily Express*, March 16th, 1964.
KOESTLER, A.: *Reflections on Hanging* (Gollancz, 1956).

Chapter 12
SAMPSON, ANTHONY: *Anatomy of Britain Today* (Hodder and Stoughton, 1965).
BENNETT, JOHN WHEELER: *John Anderson, Viscount Waverley* (Macmillan, 1962).
HYDE, H. MONTGOMERY: *Roger Casement* ("Famous Trials", ninth series; Penguin, 1964).
MORRISON OF LAMBETH, LORD: *Herbert Morrison: an Autobiography* (Odhams, 1960).

Chapter 13
MAITLAND, F. W.: *Constitutional History* (C.U.P., 1908).
THOMSON, SIR BASIL: *The Criminal* (Hodder and Stoughton, 1925).
RADZINOWICZ, L.: *A History of English Criminal Law*, vol. 1: "The Movement for Reform" (Stevens, 1948) [for story of Robert Webber].
Sunday Express, May 14th, 1939 [for story of Henry Graham].
Regina v. *Pascoe*, reported in *Daily Mail*, December 18th, 1963.
WILSON, COLIN AND PITMAN, PATRICIA: *Encyclopaedia of Murder* (Arthur Barker, 1961).
KOESTLER, A.: *Reflections on Hanging* (Gollancz, 1956).
GREW, B. D.: *Prison Governor* (Herbert Jenkins, 1958).
The Works of the Right Hon. Edmund Burke, vol. III, 1854–89 (Bohn's British Classics).

PART III

Chapter 14
IRVING, H. B. (ed.): *Trial of Mrs Maybrick* ("Notable British Trials" series; William Hodge, 1922).
SIMON, VISCOUNT: *Retrospect: The Memoirs of the Right Hon. Viscount Simon* (Hutchinson, 1952).
BIRKETT, LORD: *Six Great Advocates* (Penguin, 1961).
MAYBRICK, FLORENCE: *Mrs Maybrick's own Story: My Fifteen Last Years* (Funk and Wagnalls, 1905).
BUCKLE, G. E. (ed.): *Letters of Queen Victoria*, third series, vol. I (John Murray, 1930).
SPENDER, J. A., AND ASQUITH, CYRIL: *Life of Herbert Henry Asquith; Lord Oxford and Asquith*, vol. I (Hutchinson, 1932).

Chapter 15
CARSWELL, DONALD (ed.): *Trial of Ronald True* ("Notable British Trials" series; William Hodge, 1925).
CORNISH, GEORGE W.: *Cornish of the "Yard"* (John Lane, 1935).

Appendix 317

Pollock, George: *Mr Justice McCardie* (John Lane, 1934).
The Times for March–June 1922.

Chapter 16
Young, Filson (ed.): *Trial of Frederick Bywaters and Edith Thompson* ("Notable British Trials" series; William Hodge, 1923).
Broad, Lewis, C.: *The Innocence of Edith Thompson: a Study in Old Bailey Justice* (Hutchinson, 1952).
Browne, Douglas G., and Tullett, E. V.: *Bernard Spilsbury, his Life and Cases* (Harrap, 1951).
Wild, Roland, and Curtis-Bennett, Derek: *"Curtis"; the Life of Sir Henry Curtis-Bennett, K.C.* (Cassell, 1937).
Hale, Leslie: *Hanged in Error* (Penguin, 1961).
Wensley, Frederick Porter: *Detective Days; the Record of Forty-two Years' Service in the Criminal Investigation Department* (Cassell, 1931).
Daily Express, Sunday Express, and *The Times,* miscellaneous articles.

Chapter 17
Fairfield, Letitia, and Fullbrook, Eric P. (ed.): *The Trial of John Thomas Straffen* ("Notable British Trials" series; William Hodge, 1954).
Eddy, J. P.: *Scarlet and Ermine: Famous Trials as I saw them from Crippen to Podola* [chapter on Straffen] (William Kimber, 1960).

Chapter 18
Hyde, H. Montgomery (ed.): *Trial of Craig and Bentley* ("Notable British Trials" series; William Hodge, 1954).
Furneaux, Rupert: *Famous Criminal Cases; No. 1* (Allan Wingate, 1954).
Paget, R. T., and Silverman, S. S.: *Hanged—and Innocent?* (Gollancz, 1953).
Bentley, William George: *My Son's Execution* (W. H. Allen, 1957).

Chapter 19
Furneaux, Rupert: *Famous Criminal Cases; No. 1* (Allan Wingate, 1954).
Neustatter, W. Lindesay: *The Mind of the Murderer* (Christopher Johnson, 1957).
The Times, February 1953.

Chapter 20
Jesse, F. Tennyson (ed.): *The Trials of John Evans and John Reginald Halliday Christie* ("Notable British Trials" series; William Hodge, 1957).
Kennedy, Ludovic: *Ten Rillington Place* (Pan, 1963).
Eddowes, Michael: *The Man on Your Conscience: an Investigation of the Evans Murder Trial* (Cassell, 1955).
Camps, Francis Edward: *Medical and Scientific Investigations in the Christie Case* (Medical Publications, 1953).
Sunday Times, March 3rd, 12th, and 19th, 1961 [for correspondence between Ludovic Kennedy and Dr Donald Teare].
The Times, June 16th, 1961 [for House of Commons debate on Evans].

Chapter 21
Furneaux, Rupert: *Michael John Davies* (Stevens, 1962).
Sunday Pictorial, October 23rd and 30th, 1960.

Chapter 22
Hancock, Robert: *Ruth Ellis* (Arthur Barker, 1963).
Furneaux, Rupert: *Famous Criminal Cases; No. 3* (Allan Wingate, 1956).

Chapter 23
Furneaux, Rupert: *Guenther Podola* ("Crime Documentaries" series; Stevens, 1960).

EDDY, J. P.: *Scarlet and Ermine* [chapter on Podola] (William Kimber, 1960).
ASHBY, MICHAEL: paper on the case read to Medico-Legal Society and published in the *Medico-Legal Journal*.

Chapter 24
Shrewsbury Chronicle.
The Observer, February 5th, 1961.
Hansard (House of Commons) vol. 634, cols. 214–222, February 7th, 1961, and cols. 1773–1841, February 16th, 1961.

Chapter 25
The Times, March 1961.
Regina v. *Terry*, reported in (1961) 45 Criminal Appeal Reports at p. 180.

INDEX OF NAMES

Bywaters, Frederick, 162 *et seq.*
Bywaters, Mrs (mother of Frederick), 171

CAESAR, JULIUS, 16
Campbell, G. A., 65
Camps, Professor Francis, 217, 220
Canterbury, Archbishop of—*see* Davidson
Canute, King, 20, 21
Capone, Al, 298, 302
Caroline, queen of George IV, 42
Carswell, Dr Donald, 147
Carter, Brian, 226–7
Carter, Horace, 186, 189
Casement, Sir Roger, 119, 128
Casswell, J. D., 93, 99–100, 159
Catherine of Aragon, 29
Chalker, Edward Poole, 50
Chambers, Detective-Sergeant, 255–6
Chandler, Fred, 226–7, 230–1, 237, 239
Charles I, 30
Charles II, 30–1
Chitty, Joseph, junior, 41
Christie, Ethel, 216, 222
Christie, John Reginald Halliday, 78, 191,
  213, 214, 215, 309; gives evidence at trial
  of Timothy John Evans, 216; murders
  committed by, 216; theories on murders
  committed by, 216–24
Christophi, Stylou, 112
Churchill, Lord Randolph, 133
Churchill, Right Hon. Sir Winston, 120, 125
Chuter-Ede, Right Hon. James, Baron
  Chuter-Ede of Epsom, 63, 71 *et seq.*, 106,
  110 *et seq.*, 119, 120, 184, 186, 197, 224,
  307
Clarence, Stanley, 198
Clarke, Sir Edward, 138
Clynes, Right Hon. J. R., 71 *et seq.*, 104–5,
  150, 307
Coke, Sir Edward, 29–30
Coleman, Ron, 226 *et seq.*
Comyn, Peter, 45–7
Connell, P. H., 292, 303
Conyngham, Elizabeth Lady, 43, 46
Conyngham, Henry, first Marquess of, 46
Cooper, Louis Blom, 281, 282
Cornish, Detective Inspector, 152–3, 160
Coventry, Right Rev. Neville Vincent
  Gorton, Bishop of, 209
Coward, Fleming, 49
Craig, Christopher, 191 *et seq.*
Craig, Dr Roy Neville, 205 *et seq.*
Crippen, Hawley Harvey, 129
Cromwell, Thomas, first Earl of Essex, 39
Conin, Harley, 163
Cummins, George Frederick, 220
Cunningham, Sir Charles, 64, 65, 72, 87, 93,
  94, 100, 108, 123–4, 268, 282, 295
Curran, Professor Desmond, 74, 95, 101,
  145, 222

DANBY, THOMAS OSBORNE, FIRST EARL OF,
  30–1
Darby, Christopher Louis, 287–8
Davidson, The Most Rev. Randall Thomas,
  Baron Davidson of Lambeth, Archbishop
  of Canterbury, 158
Davies, Detective Superintendent James,
  228
Davies, Michael John, 109, 118, 225; in-
  volved in fight, 226–7; evidence against,
  227–8; trial, 229–30; second trial, 230–2;
  his feelings on death sentence and im-
  prisonment, 225, 234–5; appeals, 233–4;
  investigations and opinions on case of,
  234–9
Davies, Mr Justice Edmund, 260, 262 *et seq.*
Devlin, Right Hon. Lord Patrick Arthur,
  264
Diamond, Jack "Legs", 83, 291 *et seq.*
Dillinger, John, 298, 302
Donovan, Right Hon. Baron, 121
Douglas, James, 162
Du Cann, C. G. L., 162
Dunford, Peter Anthony, 108
Dymond, Alfred H., 44, 54, 57 *et seq.*

EAST, SIR NORWOOD, 113, 147, 217
Edmund, King of Wessex, 18, 19
Eddy, J. P., 162, 263
Edward I, 27
Edward II, 27
Edward III, 27
Edward VII, 70–1, 73, 116
Edward the Confessor, King, 21
Edwards, Dr Colin, 261, 266–7
Edwards, T. V., 233 *et seq.*
Eichmann, Adolf, 31
Elam, Henry, 110, 159, 185, 188
Eldon, John Scott, first Earl of, 35–6, 40–1
Ellis, —, (hangman), 162
Ellis, Ruth, 74, 78, 111, 240, 241; friendship
  with David Blakely, 241–3; murders
  David Blakely, 243; trial, 243–5; cam-
  paign for reprieve of, 245–9; execution of,
  249–50; opinions on case of, 250–2
Eliot, T. S., 56
Elizabeth I, 25, 29
Elizabeth II, H.M. Queen, 29, 72, 115–16,
  123, 126, 234, 249, 260, 282
Emsley, Edith, 246
Ethelbert, King of Kent, 18
Evans, D. E. G., 275
Evans, Gwynne Owen, 85
Evans, Mrs (wife of Timothy John), 213
  et seq., 219 *et seq.*
Evans, Timothy John, 72, 78, 213 *et seq.*,
  221 *et seq.*, 241

FAIRFIELD, LETITIA, 187
Fantle, Ernest, 250